DEAD MAN'S HAND

**ALSO AVAILABLE FROM
JOHN JOSEPH ADAMS AND TITAN BOOKS**

Wastelands: Stories of the Apocalypse (January 2015)
Wastelands 2: More Stories of the Apocalypse (February 2015)

DEAD MAN'S HAND

AN ANTHOLOGY OF THE WEIRD WEST

EDITED BY
JOHN JOSEPH ADAMS

TITAN BOOKS

Dead Man's Hand
Print edition ISBN: 9781781164501
E-book edition ISBN: 9781781164518

Published by Titan Books
A division of Titan Publishing Group Ltd
144 Southwark Street, London SE1 0UP

First edition: May 2014
10 9 8 7 6 5 4 3 2 1

"Introduction" by John Joseph Adams. © 2014 by John Joseph Adams. Original to this volume.
"The Red-Headed Dead" by Joe R. Lansdale. © 2014 by Joe R. Lansdale. Original to this volume.
"The Old Slow Man and His Gold Gun From Space" by Ben H. Winters. © 2014 by Ben H. Winters. Original to this volume.
"Hellfire on the High Frontier" by David Farland. © 2014 by David Farland. Original to this volume.
"The Hell-Bound Stagecoach" by Mike Resnick. © 2014 by Mike Resnick. Original to this volume.
"Stingers and Strangers" by Seanan McGuire. © 2014 by Seanan McGuire. Original to this volume.
"Bookkeeper, Narrator, Gunslinger" by Charles Yu. © 2014 by Charles Yu. Original to this volume.
"Holy Jingle" by Alan Dean Foster. © 2014 by Alan Dean Foster. Original to this volume.
"The Man With No Heart" by Beth Revis. © 2014 by Beth Revis. Original to this volume.
"Wrecking Party" by Alastair Reynolds. © 2014 by Alastair Reynolds. Original to this volume.
"Hell from the East" by Hugh Howey. © 2014 by Hugh Howey. Original to this volume.
"Second Hand" by Rajan Khanna. © 2014 by Rajan Khanna. Original to this volume.
"Alvin and the Apple Tree" by Orson Scott Card. © 2014 by Orson Scott Card. Original to this volume.
"Madam Damnable's Sewing Circle" by Elizabeth Bear. © 2014 by Elizabeth Bear. Original to this volume.
"Strong Medicine" by Tad Williams. © 2014 by Tad Williams. Original to this volume.
"Red Dreams" by Jonathan Maberry. © 2014 by Jonathan Maberry. Original to this volume.
"Bamboozled" by Kelley Armstrong. © 2014 by Kelley Armstrong. Original to this volume.
"Sundown" by Tobias S. Buckell. © 2014 by Tobias S. Buckell. Original to this volume.
"La Madre Del Oro" by Jeffrey Ford. © 2014 by Jeffrey Ford. Original to this volume.
"What I Assume You Shall Assume" by Ken Liu. © 2014 by Ken Liu. Original to this volume.
"The Devil's Jack" by Laura Anne Gilman. © 2014 by Laura Anne Gilman. Original to this volume.
"The Golden Age" by Walter Jon Williams. © 2014 by Walter Jon Williams. Original to this volume.
"Neversleeps" by Fred Van Lente. © 2014 by Fred Van Lente. Original to this volume.
"Dead Man's Hand" by Christie Yant. © 2014 by Christie Yant. Original to this volume.

A CIP catalogue record for this title is available from the British Library.

Printed and bound in the United States.

Did you enjoy this book? We love to hear from our readers. Please email us at readerfeedback@titanemail.com or write to us at Reader Feedback at the above address.

To receive advance information, news, competitions, and exclusive offers online, please sign up for the Titan newsletter on our website: www.titanbooks.com

For
WILD BILL HICKOK

CONTENTS

INTRODUCTION

JOHN JOSEPH ADAMS

The phrase "dead man's hand" refers to the poker hand held by the gunfighter Wild Bill Hickok when, in 1876, he was shot and killed by the coward Jack McCall. There's little doubt that Hickok was playing cards at the time of his death, but what Wild Bill was actually holding seems to be open to some debate. Legend has it that Hickok's hand was comprised of black aces and eights (with the fifth card a mystery), but in some accounts it's jacks and tens, or other variations. I suppose the only way we could ever know for sure would be to ask the man himself by reanimating his corpse or traveling back in time… both of which are the stuff of the "weird western" tale.

Not to be confused with "space westerns" like Joss Whedon's beloved, cancelled-too-soon TV show *Firefly*, weird westerns generally take place right here on Earth, only the world we all know and love is just a little bit different. Like worlds where vampires are real. Or clockwork cowboys roam the frontier. Or 49ers head to California to mine for mana. Or airships patrol the skies. In other words: weird westerns are stories of the Old West infused with elements of science fiction, fantasy, or horror, and often with a little counterfactual twist thrown into the mix.

You might be thinking: that kind of sounds like steampunk. And it's true that steampunk and weird westerns are similar in a lot of ways, and you'll find some stories—like Cherie Priest's Clockwork Century novels—that could certainly be considered both. But where steampunk can take place anywhere (and often is set in Victorian-era Britain), the weird western almost always takes place in the American Old West; where steampunk is often focused on urban settings and the accouterments of its period, the weird western is typically a darker, grittier take on a similar notion, with strong elements of the traditional Western genre—the wild frontier, the gunslinger/cowboy, gold fever. And while in both you often see anachronistic uses of technology, steampunk tends to be more focused on counterfactual scientific advancements; whereas the weird western welcomes that but also equally embraces magic and other elements of the supernatural. So while both may have clockwork automatons, it's in the weird western where you are most likely to have a dead man reanimated by a necromancer only to be subsequently gunned down in a duel by the aforementioned automaton.

The origins of the genre can be clearly traced as far back as the '60s with television shows like *The Wild, Wild West*, and the '70s with Stephen King's *The Dark Tower* series—and perhaps all the way back to the 1930s with the works of Robert E. Howard and the strange Gene Autry serial *The Phantom Empire*—but it was Joe R. Lansdale's acclaimed novel *Dead in the West* (1986) that truly blazed a trail; the book, which features the gunslinging Reverend Jebediah Mercer, is considered by many to be the definitive example of weird western literature, and consequently helped define the genre.

As such, this book would be incomplete without a contribution from Mr. Lansdale; happily, I did not have to contemplate such a notion, for the good Reverend Mercer has a new unholy monster to battle in the very first story in the anthology, "The Red-Headed Dead."

Unlike the abovementioned story, many of the tales in the anthology have no literary antecedents—such as "Neversleeps," *Cowboys & Aliens* writer Fred Van Lente's wildly inventive tale of magic, alternate history, and clockwork chrysalises, and Walter Jon Williams's "The Golden Age," a rip-roaring adventure story of superheroes in the Old West—but several of the other writers herein, like Lansdale, have already staked their weird west claims and, at my request, have returned to mine them once again:

Alan Dean Foster, who over the last thirty years or so has written more than a dozen tales about Mad Amos Malone and his magical steed Worthless, brings the mountain man back to battle the occult once again in "Holy Jingle."

Orson Scott Card's Alvin Maker, the seventh son of a seventh son who is locked in an epic battle against the Unmaker, returns in "Alvin and the Apple Tree"—the first new Alvin tale in more than a decade.

In "Stingers and Strangers," Seanan McGuire brings us a new InCryptid story in which cryptozoologists Frances Brown and Jonathan

Healy encounter some very weird wasps (plus some other unpleasant surprises).

And in "Second Hand," Rajan Khanna returns to the world of his story "Card Sharp," in which decks of playing cards are imbued with a magic that makes any deck of cards a deadly one.

That's just a little taste of what this anthology has in store for you, and that last example brings us right back around to playing cards and our eponymous dead man's hand. To sum up, in the weird western, we take the historical hand we're dealt, but we bluff reality and make what you would think is an impossible play.

So that's the game, pard. Pull up a chair, ante up, and I'll deal you in. The game's "Weird West," no limit, and *everything's* wild.

THE RED-HEADED DEAD
A REVEREND JEBEDIAH MERCER TALE

JOE R. LANSDALE

East Texas, 1880

Reverend Mercer knew it was coming because the clouds were being plucked down into a black funnel, making the midday sky go dark. It was the last of many omens, and he knew from experience it smacked of more than a prediction of bad weather. There had been the shooting star last night, bleeding across the sky in a looping red wound. He had never seen one like it. And there had been the angry face he had seen in the morning clouds, ever so briefly, but long enough to know that God was sending him another task in his endless list.

He paused his horse on a high hill and pushed his hat up slightly, determining the direction of the storm. When the funnels were yanked earthward and touched, he saw, as he expected, that the twister was tearing up earth and heading swiftly in his direction. He cursed the god he served unwillingly and plunged his mount down the hill as the sky spat rain and the wind began to howl and blow at his back like the damp breath of a pursuing giant. Down the hill and into the depths of the forest his horse went, thundering along the pine-needle trail, dashing for any cover he might find.

As he rode, to his left, mixed in with the pines and a great oak that dipped its boughs almost to the ground, was a graveyard. He saw at a glance the gravestones had slipped and cracked, been torn up by tree roots, erosion, and time. One grave had a long, metal rod poking up from it, nearly six feet out of the ground; the rod was leaning from the ground at a precarious due west. It appeared as if it were about to fall loose of the earth.

The pine-needle trail wound around the trees and dipped down into a clay path that was becoming wet and slick and blood red. When he turned yet another curve, he saw tucked into the side of a hill a crude cabin made of logs and the dirt that surrounded it. The roof was covered in dried mud, probably packed down over some kind of pine slab roofing.

The Reverend rode his horse right up to the door and called out. No one answered. He dismounted. The door was held in place by a flip up switch of wood. The Reverend pressed it and opened it, led his horse inside. There was a bar of crudely split wood against the wall. He lifted it and clunked it into position between two rusted metal hooks on either side of the doorway. There was a window with fragments of parchment paper in place of glass; there was more open space than parchment, and the pieces that remained fluttered in the wind like peeling, dead skin. Rain splattered through.

Down through the trees swirled the black meanness from Heaven, gnawing trees out of the ground and turning them upside down, throwing their roots to the sky like desperate fingers, the fingers shedding wads of red clay as if it were clotted blood.

The Reverend's horse did a strange thing: it went to its knees and ducked its head, as if in prayer. The storm tumbled down the mountain in a rumbling wave of blackness, gave off a locomotive sound. This was followed by trees and the hill sliding down toward the cabin at tremendous speed, like mash potatoes slipping along a leaning plate.

Gravestones flew through the air. The Reverend saw that great iron bar, sailing his way like a javelin. He threw himself to the floor.

All the world screamed. The Reverend did not pray, having decided long ago his boss had already made up his mind about things.

The cabin groaned and the roof peeled at the center and a gap was torn open in the ceiling. The rain came through it in a deluge, splattering heavily on the Reverend's back as he lay face down, expecting at any moment to be lifted up by the wind and drawn and quartered by the Four Horsemen of the Apocalypse.

Then it was over. There was no light at the window because mud and trees had plugged it. There was a bit of daylight coming from the hole in the roof. It filled the room with a kind of hazy shade of gold.

When the Reverend rose up, he discovered the steel bar had come through the window and gone straight through his horse's head; the animal still rested forward on its front legs, its butt up, the bar having gone into one ear and out the other. The horse had gone dead before it knew it was struck.

The only advantage to his dead mount, the Reverend thought, was that now he would have fresh meat. He had been surviving on corn dodgers for a week, going where God sent him by directions nestled inside his head. In that moment, the Reverend realized that God had brought him here for a reason. It was never a pleasant reason. There would be some horror, as always, and he would be pitted against it—less, he thought, for need of destroying evil, but more out of heavenly entertainment, like burning ants to a crisp with the magnified heat of the sun shining through the lens of a pair of spectacles.

The Reverend studied the iron bar that had killed his horse. There was writing on it. He knelt down and looked at it. It was Latin, and the words trailed off into the horse's ear. The Reverend grabbed the bar and twisted the horse's head toward the floor, put his boot against the horse's skull, and pulled. The bar came out with a pop and a slurp, covered in blood and brain matter. The Reverend took a rag from the saddlebag and wiped the rod clean.

Knowing Latin, he read the words. They simply said: *And this shall hold him down.*

"Ah, hell," the Reverend said, and tossed the bar to the floor.

This would be where God had sent him, and what was coming he could only guess, but a bar like that one, made of pure iron, was often used to pin something in its grave. Iron was a nemesis of evil, and Latin, besides being a nemesis to a student of language, often contained more powerful spells than any other tongue, alive or dead. And if what was out there was in need of pinning, then the fact the twister had pulled the bar free by means of the literal wet and windy hand of God, meant something that should not be free was loose.

For the first time in a long time, Reverend Mercer thought he might defy God and find his way out of here if he could. But he knew it was useless. Whatever had been freed was coming, and it was his job to stop it. If he didn't stop it, then it would stop him, and not only would his life end, but his soul would be flung from him to who knows where. Heaven as a possibility would not be on the list. If there was in fact a Heaven.

There was a clatter on the roof and the Reverend looked up, caught sight of something leering through the gap. When he did, it pulled back and out of sight. The Reverend lifted his guns out of their holsters, a .44 converted Colt at his hip and a .36 Navy Colt in the shoulder holster under his arm. He had the .44 in his right fist, the Navy in his left. His bullets were touched with drops of silver, blessed by himself with readings from the Bible. Against Hell's minions it was better than nothing, which was a little like saying it was better than a poke in the eye with a sharp stick.

The face had sent a chill up his back like a wet-leg scorpion scuttling along his spine. It was hardly a face at all. Mostly bone with rags of flesh where cheeks once were, dark pads of rotting meat above its eyes. The top of its head had been curiously full of fire-red hair, all of it wild and wadded and touched with clay. The mouth had been drawn back in the grin of a ghoul, long fangs showing. The eyes had been the worst: red as blood spots, hot as fire.

Reverend Mercer knew immediately what it was: the progeny of Judas. A vampire, those that had descended from he who had given death to Christ for a handful of silver. Christ, that ineffectual demigod that had fooled many into thinking the heart of God had changed. It had not; that delusion was all part of the great bastard's game.

There was movement on the roof, heavy as an elephant one moment, and then light and skittering like an excited squirrel.

The Reverend backed across the room and found a corner just as the thing stuck its head through the gap in the roof again. It stretched its neck, which was long and barely covered in skin, showing little, greasy disks of bone that creaked when its long neck swayed.

Like a serpent, it stretched through the roof, dropping its hands forward, the fingers long and multiple jointed, clicking together like bug legs. It was hanging from the gap by its feet. It was naked, but whatever its sex, that had long dissolved to dust—and there was only a parchment of skin over its ribs, and its pelvis was nothing more than bone, its legs being little more than withered gray muscle tight against the bone. It twisted its head and looked at the Reverend. The Reverend cocked his revolvers.

The monster snapped its feet together, disengaging from the roof, allowing it to fall. It dropped lightly, landed on the damp horse, lifted its head, and sniffed the air. It spotted the Reverend, but the dead animal was too inviting. It swung its head and snapped its teeth into the side of the dead horse's neck, made a sucking noise that brought blood out of the beast in a spray that decorated the vampire's face and mouth. Spots of blood fell on the sun-lit floor like rose petals.

It roved one red eye toward the Reverend as it ate; it had the kind of look that said: "You're next."

The Reverend fired his pistols. The bullets tore into the creature, blue hell-fire blasting out of the wounds they made. The thing sprang like a cricket, came across the floor toward the Reverend, who fired both revolvers rapidly, emptying them, knocking wounds in the thing that spurted sanctified flames, but still it came.

The Reverend let loose with a grunt and a groan, racked the monster upside the head with the heavy .44. It was like striking a tree. Then he was flung backwards by two strong arms, against the window packed with limbs and leaves and mud. The impact knocked the revolvers from his hands.

It came at him like a shot, hissing as if it were a snake. The Reverend's boot caught the skin-and-bone brute in the chest and drove it back until it hit the floor. It bounced up immediately, charged again. The Reverend snapped out a left jab and hooked with a right, caught the thing with both punches, rocked its rotten head. But still it came. The Reverend jabbed again, crossed with a right, uppercut with a left, and slammed a right hook to the ribs; one of them popped loose and poked through the skin like a barrel stave that had come undone.

It sprang forward and clutched the Reverend's throat with both hands, would have plunged its teeth into his face had the Reverend not grabbed it under the chin and shoved it back and kicked it hard in the chest, sending it tumbling over the horse's body.

The Reverend sprang toward the iron bar, grabbed it, swung it, and hit the fiend a brisk blow across the neck, driving it to the ground. His next move was to plunge the bar into it, pinning it once again to the ground in the manner it had been pinned in its grave. But he was too slow.

The creature scrambled across the floor on all fours, avoiding the stab, which clunked into the hard dirt floor. It sprang up and through the hole in the roof before the Reverend could react. As the last of it disappeared, the Reverend fell back, exhausted, watching the gap for its reemergence.

Nothing.

The Reverend found his pistols and reloaded. They hadn't done much to kill the thing, but he liked to believe his blessed loads had at least hampered it some. He worked the saddlebag off his horse, flung it over his shoulder. He tried the door and couldn't open it. Too much debris had rammed up against it. He stood on his dead mount and poked the bar through the hole in the ceiling, pushed it through the gap far enough that he could use both ends of it to rest on the roof and chin himself up. On the roof, he looked about for it, saw it scuttling over a mass of mud and broken trees like a spider, toward a darkening horizon;

night was coming, dripping in on wet, dark feet.

The Reverend thought that if his reading on the subject was right, this descendant of Judas would gain strength as the night came. Not a good thing for a man that had almost been whipped and eaten by it during the time when it was supposed to be at its weakest.

Once again, the Reverend considered defying that which God had given him to do, but he knew it was pointless. Terror would come to him if he did not go to it. And any reward he might have had in Heaven would instead be a punishment in Hell. As it was, even doing God's bidding, he was uncertain of reward, or of Heaven's existence. All he knew was there was a God, and it didn't like much of anything besides its sport.

The Reverend climbed down from the roof with the rod, stepping on the mass of debris covering the door and window, wiggled his way through broken trees, went in the direction the vampire had gone. He went fast, like a deranged mouse eager to throw itself into the jaws of a lion.

As he wound his way up the hill, it started to rain again. This was followed by hail the size of .44 slugs. He noticed off to his left a bit of the graveyard that remained: a few stones and a great, shadowy hole where the rod had been. With the night coming, he was sure the vampire would be close by, and though he didn't think it would return to the grave where it had been pinned for who knew how long, he went there to check. The grave was dark and empty except for rising rainwater. It was a deep hole, that grave, maybe ten feet deep. Someone had known what that thing was and how to stop it, at least until time released it.

The light of the day was completely gone now, and there was no moon. With the way the weather had turned, he would be better off fleeing back to the house and waiting until morning to pursue. He knew where it would be going if it didn't come back for him: the first available town and a free lunch. He was about to fulfill that plan of *hole up and wait and see* when the dark became darker, and in that instant he knew it was coming up behind him. It was said these things did not cast a reflection, but they certainly cast a shadow, even when it was too dark for there to be one.

The Reverend wheeled with the iron bar in hand, and the thing hit him with a flying leap and knocked him backwards into the grave, splashing down into the water. The bar ended up lying across the grave above them. The Reverend pulled his .44 as he kicked the beast back. It was on him as he fired, clamping its teeth over the barrel of the revolver. The Reverend's shot took out a huge chunk at the back of the thing's head, but still it stood, growling and gnawing and shaking the barrel of the gun like a dog worrying a bone.

The barrel snapped like a rotten twig. The vampire spat it out. The Reverend hit him with what remained of the gun. It had about as much effect as swatting a bull with a feather. The Reverend dropped the weapon and grasped the thing at its biceps, trying to hold it back. They went down together, splashing in the cold, muddy water of the grave, the vampire trying to bring its teeth close to the Reverend's face. The Reverend slugged the thing repeatedly.

Kicking the thing off of him, the Reverend came to his feet, leaped and grabbed the bar, swung up on it, and out of the grave. Still clutching the bar, he stumbled backwards. The vampire hopped out of the hole effortlessly, as if the grave had been no deeper than the depth of a cup.

As it sprang, the Reverend, weary, fell back and brought the rod up. The sky grew darker as the thing came down in a blind lunge of shape and shadow. Its body caught the tip of the rod, and the point of it tore through the monster with a sound like someone bending too-quick in tight pants and tearing the ass out of them. The vampire screamed so loud and oddly the Reverend thought the sound might knock him out with the sureness of a blow. But he held fast, the world wavering, the thing struggling on the end of the rod, slowly sliding down, its body swirling around the metal spear like a snake on a spit, then bunching up like a doodle bug to make a knot at the end of the makeshift spear. Then it was still.

The Reverend dropped the bar and came up on one knee and looked at the thing pinned on it. It was nothing more now than a ball of bone and tattered flesh. The Reverend lifted the rod and vampire into the wet grave, shoved the iron shaft into the ground, hard. Rain and hail pounded the Reverend's back, but still he pushed at the bar until it was deep and the thing was beneath the rising water in the grave.

Weakly, the Reverend staggered down the hill, climbed over the debris in the cabin, and dropped through the roof. He found a place in the corner where he could sit upright, rest his back against the wall. He pulled out his .36 Navy and sat there with it on his thigh, not quite sleeping, but dozing off and on like a cat.

As he slept, he dreamed the thing came loose of the grave several times during the night. Each time he awoke, snapping his eyes open in fright; the fiend he expected was nothing more than dream. He breathed a sigh of relief. He was fine. He was in the cabin. There was no vampire, only the pounding of rain and hail through the hole in the roof, splashing and smacking against the corpse of his horse.

The next morning, the Reverend climbed out of the cabin by means of his horse footstool, and went out through the hole in the roof. He walked back to the grave. He found his saddlebags on the edge of it, where they had fallen during the attack. He had forgotten all about them.

Pistol drawn, he looked into the grave. It was near filled with muddy water. He put the revolver away, grabbed hold of the rod, and worked it loose, lifted it out to see if the thing was still pinned.

It was, knotted up on the rod like a horrid ball of messy twine.

The Reverend worked it back into the grave, pushing the bar as deep as he could, then dropped to his knees and set about pushing mud and debris into the hole.

It took him all of the morning and past high noon to finish up.

When he was done, he took a Bible from his saddlebags and read some verses. Then he poked the book into the mud on top of the grave. It and the rod would help to hold the thing down. With luck, the red-headed dead would stay truly dead for a long time.

When he was done, the Reverend opened his saddlebags and found that his matches wrapped in wax paper had stayed dry. He sighed with relief. With the saddlebags flung over his shoulder, he went back to the cabin to cut off a slab of horsemeat. He had hopes he could find enough dry wood to cook it before starting his long walk out, going to where he was led by the godly fire that burned in his head.

—In memory of and tribute to Robert E. Howard

THE OLD SLOW MAN AND HIS GOLD GUN FROM SPACE

BEN H. WINTERS

Sacramento, California, 1851

Whether Caleb and Crane came out to California separate and partnered up later on—or whether they knew each other from some eastern clime and made their way westward as a pair—well, who the devil can tell and what the devil does it matter? Suffice it to say that whether they came to their claim as partners or came to it alone, Crane and Caleb came the same as all the rest of 'em: maybe overland on some slow-rolling desperation caravan from Oxford, Mississippi or Albany, New York, jouncing on rutted wheels through Salt Lake, Deadwood, Barstow; maybe aboard a leaky old cutter, or rounding down around Cape Horn, dipping and rolling on the seasick waves.

Some way or other, the point is, they came. Drawn like iron shavings to a magnet, drawn to the golden promises of Sutter's Mill. Drawn by hope, fool's hope, by that same mania that had lit up the eyes of poor men and rich men and credulous men and wise, that had seized 'em up and drawn 'em down from all across the continent and all around the world.

Caleb and Crane weren't nothing special and never would they have been, if it weren't for the spaceman.

"Tomorrow," Caleb would assure his partner, every night, before stretching out weary on his thin rucksack, emptying out his day's sad pocketful of flakes and powder. "We'll strike it rich tomorrow."

"Tomorrow," Crane would answer, and then they'd close their eyes, the both of 'em closed their weary eyes and dreamed their dead dreams of gold.

Tomorrow never seemed to come though, not for most of 'em out there, and certainly not for Caleb and Crane. April through May, May to June. Heavy work, long days. Flakes and dust, a teensy nugget now and again; now and again a tiny little half of a half of a half ounce of gold. Nothing to speak of. Nothing to hold. Just enough to keep you scratching at it.

This was the summer of 1851. Long ago the easy pickins had been picked. Long ago them few big winners that was ever gonna be had filled their pockets, filled their buckets, filled their wagonbeds up with gold and rolled away.

And yet they said it, Caleb and Crane, and felt it, too, in aching bones—needed to know that it was true:

"Tomorrow."

"Tomorrow."

Caleb—so you know—was big. Legs like ox-legs, neck like a bull neck, torso like the petrified trunk of an old-growth tree, sturdy and unbending. He looked not like a man-of-woman-born, but like a figure of a man someone carved in a barn door and animated by some manner of charm. A sturdy muscled golem, fit to hoe a row, work a shovel, dig a mine.

Crane was little. Taut and thin and steely as a loop of wire, with a long nose, and little delicate glasses perched on the end of it.

You'd have seen the two of them—Caleb with his ropy neck and ship's-anchor fists, Crane with his spectacles—and you'd have figured Crane was the brains of the operation. But you'd've been wrong: there weren't no brains to this operation. Just sweat and hope and tired exhausted dreams of the mother lode.

June to July, August to September, camped out there on the lip of their rutted square acre on the Sacramento banks, their dope's claim. Giant Caleb and wiry Crane with their ramshackle cabin and rickety apparatuses, digging and muttering about tomorrow; six months their drumbeat was the flat thud of shovel on clay, the rat-a-tat of new handfuls of gravel—the daylong rush of water sluicing through the Long Tom, the rusty scrick of the cradle as it rocked, separating, separating, seeking.

If you'd'a said to big Caleb, at some point, that long summer, "You're madmen, you and your friend," he'd'a laughed, a snorting bull's laughter. Pointed you away with the long barrel of his rifle.

If you'd'a said to Crane, "You're madmen, you're dunces—you'll die out here before you strike it rich," he'd've chuckled bitterly, told you to go do something dirty with a donkey, twisted his small bent body back to the work of his shovel.

It would'a been as crazy as to say that a man from Neptune will come, and make you a strange proposition, and then die of violence on the banks of your claim.

That's what happened though. One night—late September—that is indeed what did occur.

"Wake up, there, you boys. I got a proposition for you."

This's what the old man said by way of greeting, but too quiet to rouse Caleb and Crane from their respective golden-castle dreams.

"Wake up, there," he repeated, a little louder—loud enough, now.

"Who's that?" said Crane, blinking awake.

"It's a goddamn tramp," answered Caleb, "is who it is," and hefted himself into a sitting position and landed his big bear feet on the dirt floor of the cabin. It was so late it was almost early, almost the next day; the old man, ancient and tiny and slow, was surrounded by dawn's first glow, so that with his wild uncombed white hair and his lined face, he looked a little like a saint, a little like a ghost.

"Oh, good," muttered the man. "You're stirrin'."

The old man's voice was harsh and gravelly. He was bent with age, and his right arm was shriveled and deformed. His mustache was bushy, yellow, and unkempt. He wheezed heavily. Over his shoulder was a black sack.

Caleb was on his feet by now, holding the old man steady with the creaky long-barreled hunting rifle he'd fetched out from under his pillow. "The heck you want?"

"I already said." The old man cleared his throat laboriously, tottered unsteadily into the cabin, cast a quick glance at big Caleb's long rifle like it was a children's finger-puller. "I got a proposition for ya."

"Now wait a minute, wait just one minute," sputtered Crane, snatching his spectacles from beside his bedroll and sliding them into place. "Just who the devil are you?"

"Well I reckon that I could tell you m'name, but it won't do much good," said the old slow man. His white hair was a wiry tangle atop his thin head. "It's in a language you won't understand."

"If you mean Spanish, you're wrong about that," said Crane, who prided himself on his ¿como estas? and his uno-dos-tres, which he'd picked up off a Mexican whore.

The old man snorted. "Not Español, son. I'm from Neptune. The dark side of the planet Neptune."

There was a long silence in that moment, after the old slow man said he had come from the dark side of the planet Neptune. In the dawn outside the cabin you could hear the pleasant morning babbling of the creek, hear the gentle morning calling of the California birds roosting in their California trees. If someone in the proper frame of mind were there, they might have felt that the surroundings were downright peaceful. It might have occurred, to such a tranquil observer, that whatever precious metals were or were not to be found beneath the surface, there was a copious bounty of a different kind—the squirrels at play, the sun glimmering off the green—right here out in the open.

No one in the present company, however, was in such a frame of mind.

"Did you say you're from Neptune?" said Caleb.

"Yep," said the old man, and coughed. "The dark side."

Caleb drew back the hammer of the rifle.

"What? Where is Neptune?" said Crane, looking from the old slow man to Caleb and back to the man. "What is that?"

"It's a planet," said Caleb, gesturing heavenward with the barrel of the gun. "But this man ain't from there. He's from a drunk tank or an alleyway. He's a tramp and a thief."

"No, sir," said the old man. "I'm from Neptune, like I said. And I got a proposition for ya."

"Nuh-uh," said Caleb, and spat on the ground, and leveled his rifle at the old man's face. "See, I got a proposition for you. You get the hell out of our cabin, and get good and clear of our claim, or I'm going to put a bullet inside your head. Right, Crane?"

Crane didn't say nothin'. He had taken off his spectacles and was staring at the old slow man, squinting, as if merely by looking at him hard enough he could puzzle out the truth or falseness of the man's wild declaration.

"Crane?" said Caleb.

Still, Crane didn't say nothin'. The old man, meanwhile, stared steadily back at Caleb while the smallest curl of a smile turned up beneath his droopy mustache. "Go ahead then," he said. "Shoot me."

It was almost comical, the bravado with which the old man faced Caleb's rifle, given how small he was—how frail—especially compared to the massive claim digger—how decrepit with age.

"You're crazy, old-timer," was all Caleb could think of to say, while the old man still stood there on his pipe-cleaner legs, and Crane stood there staring, scratching his head. Caleb lowered the gun so it pointed at the floor, murmured it again: "Crazy."

The old man looked around the cabin with rheumy eyes, wheezing slightly. Crane, in the meantime, still staring at the old man, had brought out his pouch of tobacco. "Oh, hell, Caleb," he said, rolling himself a cigarette, "let's hear what he's got to say."

And that was that. Caleb shrugged, Crane pinched his cigarette closed at the ends, and the old man was permitted to make his slow way into the cabin, and to take a seat on one of the upturned packing crates that served for seats. And what he did next, instead of talking, was he slowly drew open the drawstring of the bulging satchel, and took out an antique flintlock pistol, dust-caked and rusted.

Caleb looked at Crane. Crane shrugged. Caleb looked back at the old man.

"You on your way to a costume party, old man?"

"No, sir." The old man arched his eyebrows and chuckled throatily. "That's a gold gun. And it's gonna make you boys rich."

"A gold gun?" said Crane, softly. Thoughtfully, even. But Caleb was scornful and agitated, shifting his big torso with irritation. "That thing ain't gold."

"I didn't say the gun was gold," said the old man. "It's a Neptunian gun. It finds gold."

"It—what?" said Crane. But his tone was more and more thoughtful, and he was looking with open interest at the battered old pistol, even as Caleb shook his head, kept on his mask of incredulousness, said, "if that there is a magical space gun, why's it look like a regular old flintlock pistol from the goddamn Mexican war?"

"Well, why do I look like this? We aliens and our alien devices can't go around showing off our real appearances on your human planet. Your minds would burst and break from the sight of it."

"Hooey," said big Caleb, and he stepped forward and snatched the gun from the old man, who let it go willingly.

Immediately on touching the gold gun, Caleb felt strange. The gun had the weight of the old pistol it resembled, and the cut of the handle felt familiar, like a thousand gun handles he'd held before. But on holding it he felt a radiant discomfort, traveling up his fingertips from the gun, up through his arms, down into his guts. It gave him a rolling kind of feeling in his stomach. He put the gold gun down, and the old man picked it up and tucked it back in his satchel.

"Now," said he. "Here's the proposition."

The gun finds gold, is what the old slow man, the man who said he was from Neptune, explained to Caleb and Crane. The gun finds gold. You take it out, he said, when you're outside, when you're at a patch of ground or a length of creek. You hold it up, and you don't even pull the trigger.

"What do you mean, you don't pull the trigger?" said Crane. Caleb was silent—had been silent since holding the gun and feeling the way it made him to feel.

"I mean just that, son. You hold it, you point it, and it jerks and jumps kinda, it dances, and it points the way to gold. To the real thing."

Caleb and Crane stared at the old man, wide-eyed, rapt.

"So here's what we're gonna do, you and me, boys," said the old man—Caleb and Crane listening intently, chewing on their mustaches, straining their minds. "We spend two days out on your claim, relying upon the alien wisdom of my device, running its powers over your patch of dirt. We pull more gold out of that mudflat than the two of you with your pans and your hands have scrabbled up in the last six months."

"What then?" said Crane.

"What then? We split it, sixty percent to you two, forty percent to me."

"Awfully business-minded, ain't ya?" observed Crane. "For a man from space?"

"I got no choice." The old man shrugged. "What you people call gold, my people call food. And me and my people, we're running out."

"Food?" Caleb broke his silence; this fresh bit of strangeness was too much for him. "You tellin' me that people from the dark side of Neptune, whatever you said, you tellin' me they eat gold?"

The old man nodded, scratched his forehead, and a crust of skin fluttered down to the floor. "Not just the dark side. Lightsiders, too. That's just what Neptunians eat. Back home, son, people'd look just as funny at you, if you told 'em you ate ham and eggs."

Caleb fell silent. Crane, meanwhile, rubbed his furrowed brow, focused agitatedly on the practicalities of the matter. "I don't get it, old man. Your gun's so smart, why'n't you just take the thing out to the claim your own self? Or out to any other claim? Dig up as much as you want and make off with it? Dig yourself up a nice gold feast and leave Earth for good?"

"Would that I could," said the old slow man, looking around the ramshackle cabin. "But I'm tired. Where I come from, a man needs methane in his air, and the atmosphere on this damnable planet of yours, it's got no more methane than a bucket of spit. Wears a man out. I can't even lift a shovel in this heavy soil of your'n. I'm weak. Lookit me! Every hour I spend here saps my strength. Even standing here I feel my bones cracking, my heart pumping too fast to keep me alive! I need a couple of young strong Earthlings to do the digging fer me—and, like I said, I'm willing to pay for it!"

Overwhelmed by this vigorous outburst, the old slow man began to cough, and he coughed so violently that he nearly doubled over in his chair. Then he settled back and closed his eyes, while Caleb and Crane huddled their dusty heads together.

"You know what he wants us for," Caleb said to Crane. "He wants us for mules."

"Yes," Crane said to Caleb, and then paused. "At sixty percent."

A smile played at the corners of the lips of the old slow man. Up they all stood, and down they went to the claim.

The gold gun from space worked just like the old slow man said it would. Why, it worked like the absolute devil.

They walked down to the claim together, the three of them, down to that rutted quarter acre with the twist of creek down the center of it, and stood at the edge. The old man drew the gun forth and pointed it. Didn't even pull the trigger—"you never pull the trigger" he said—and no bullet flew forth. The chamber did not turn. But the gun jerked and danced in the old man's hands, and the muzzle jumped and poked in a certain sharp direction, like the nose of a dog when it's caught a scent. Caleb and Crane watched this performance with astonishment, and when it was done they looked in the direction that the gun had pointed, and saw that over the land in that spot the air seemed disrupted somehow, seemed to twinkle and dance; the air above that spot of land was like tissue paper that had been wrinkled and smoothed out again, and now shimmered prismatically in the daylight.

And there they dug, and there they found gold. Not flakes and small bits, but ounces of it, nuggets, thick gorgeous clots of gold.

"Eureka!" shouted Caleb, and Crane said it, too: "Eureka!"

And then again, and then again, all that cool September morning, the old man would point the gun and its metal nose would jerk and dance; Caleb and Crane would clabber over to where the air above the ground or above the creek was disrupted, twinkling, textured, where the atmosphere had been set to sparkling—and they'd get to it with their shovels and hoes, and out would come the gold—the gold formerly so elusive, revealing itself to them, singing out to them, making itself known, like a coy lover suddenly eager to be taken.

"Eureka," hollered Caleb, every time he heard the satisfying cling of his shovel's edge on a patch of the real deal.

"Eureka," erupted Crane, each time he felt the sharp resistance of metal striking metal down there in the muck, that beautiful jolt traveling up the sinews of his forearm.

The old slow man sat on his haunches on the edge of the claim, aimed his gun, watched it work, watched Caleb and Crane chase the reward. Watched them pour the gold-flecked grit into the cradle, sluice it clean, watched the golden pile grow. And then, after the fourth drawing of the gold gun, with only but a bare eighth of the claim covered so far, under the hot sun and his labored existence, the the old man yawned and stretched and tilted back his head and fell asleep.

Caleb and Crane noted that he was asleep, and looked at him, and looked at each other.

As was so often the case, both of them were thinking the same thing at once—it was only a matter of who would speak it first. It was Crane.

"Forty percent is awful high," is what he said, whispering the words, pushing his wire glasses up the bridge of his nose where they had slipped on the slick of sweat.

"Awful high," Caleb agreed, nodding slowly, clapping caked dirt off his palms.

This was all that needed to be said. Because the gold gun was not the only armament down at the claim that day. Caleb had his hunting rifle tucked up inside his coat, the butt of it down there in his waistband, just as he did every day, in case of wild cats or gold thieves or other predators. Now he drew that old rifle free from his pants and walked up the slope, while Crane stood down in the dirt, nervous, his eye-glasses glinting against the sun. Caleb walked resolutely on his thick tree-trunk legs up the muddy slope of the claim and killed the sleeping old man without ceremony, a single brutal blast right through the center of his head. The body tipped over backwards on the rocking chair and slipped soundlessly down into the dirt.

The thing done, Caleb turned and looked down at Crane, who shielded his eyes against the sun and then slowly trudged up the slope, too, to stand there between his companion and the body of the man he had killed. Caleb looked saddened by what he'd done.

"Do you think—" began Caleb, and then stopped himself, sighed. His eyes were brimming with tears. "D'ya think he was really from Neptune?"

"Yes," answered Crane, speaking softly, like he was speaking to himself. He bent and lifted the gold gun off the corpse of the old slow man. "He was."

"What?" said Caleb.

Crane pulled the trigger of the gold gun and a wash of wild blue fire poured from the muzzle, a blanket of heat and light in the air, surrounding Caleb, smothering him, boiling him alive. In an instant—a flash. Big Caleb died with a scream trapped on his lips, frozen in place as all his organs failed at once as the light washed over him.

No more gold-fever, no more desperation, no more sad glitter of hope for he.

As for Crane, he held the flintlock pistol aloft and looked it over and whistled appreciatively. Those clever bastards from the dark side of the planet were always so much further ahead in the technology department, they really were. They couldn't survive on foreign planets near half as well as lightsiders like him, but dang could they manufacture—a gold gun, indeed!

Crane hunched over, grabbed a handful of glittering metal from the massive pile he and his poor dead partner had gathered up, and chewed it thoughtfully. There was no way around it: this gold gun heralded a major improvement in his lifestyle. Pickings had been so slim, the take so small, that to get enough to eat, he'd needed a partner. But it had been stressful, all the sneaking around—waking in the middle of the night, eating enough of the other fella's share to live on, but not enough to be caught. It had been an anxious, furtive existence, but he'd got by: May to June, June to July, August to September. Now everything would be different. Now he'd bury these two bodies, and then Crane would feast.

—for Nick Tamarkin

HELLFIRE ON THE HIGH FRONTIER

DAVID FARLAND

Wyoming Territory, Circa 1876

Morgan Gray sat alone, peering into his crackling campfire, eyes unfocused, thinking of girls he'd known. In particular, there was a dance-hall girl he'd once met in Cheyenne. What was her name—Lacy? She'd had red hair and the prettiest smile—so fine he almost hadn't noticed that she'd worn nothing more than a camisole, bloomers, and a green silk corset while she lay atop the piano and sang.

For weeks now, he'd been trailing a skinwalker, a renegade Arapaho named Coyote Shadow, but the skinwalker had taken to bear form and lost Morgan in the high rocks of the Wind River Range.

A schoolmarm murdered, her child eaten. Morgan hadn't been able to avenge them.

Sometimes you lose a trail, he knew. *Sometimes you lose the fight. You have to figure out how to keep fighting.*

He downed some coffee, as bitter and cold as the trail.

Out in the rocky hills, a wolf howled. It sounded wrong, a little too high. Could've been a Sioux warrior, hoping to count coup. Morgan would have to watch his horse tonight, sleep with one eye open.

The burning ponderosa pine in his campfire smelled sweet, like butterscotch boiling over in a pan. Some pitch in the heartwood popped. A log shifted, and embers spiraled up from the fire. They rose in balls of red, and seemed to expand, dancing around one another as they sped toward heaven.

Morgan watched them drift higher, wondering when they'd wink out, until time stretched unnaturally, as if the embers planned to rise and take their place among the stars.

Suddenly, The Stranger took form across the campfire, a shadow solidifying into something almost human, sitting on a rock.

Morgan had met him only once, seven years back: a man in a black frock, like a traveling preacher. He wore his Stetson low over his eyes and had a wisp of dark beard. The spurs on his boots were made of silver, with glowing pinwheels of lightning. The cigar clenched between his teeth smelled of sulfur.

Could've been an angel. Could've been the devil. Morgan's gut told him that The Stranger was something different altogether.

"Long way from Texas," The Stranger said in a deep voice, lips hardly moving.

Morgan had no authority outside of Texas. So he kept his ranger's badge in his vest pocket. "Justice shouldn't be bound by borders," he said. "The whole world's gone crazy."

The Stranger smiled. "Got a job for you."

Morgan should never have asked this stranger for a hand. Might have been better to just let Handy drown in the quicksand. With these folks, there is always a price.

But, hell, he'd loved that gelding.

"A job?" Morgan asked. "I catch 'em. Don't necessarily kill 'em." He'd seen too much bloodshed in the war. After more than ten years, the scars were just beginning to heal.

Morgan wasn't afraid of a fight. Once you've stared death in the face a few times, nothing riles you. Yet…

"He's good with a gun," the stranger said. "Few men would stand a chance against him. He's a clockwork gambler, goes by the name of Hellfire. Shooting one of them… it's not the same as killing flesh…"

It should be more like stomping a pocket watch. Clockworks were all springs and gears inside. But Morgan had known a clockwork once, a soldier by the name of Rowdy. Morgan swore that the thing was as alive as any man of flesh and blood. Rowdy had once joked, "Us clockworks, we got souls same as the rest of y'all. Ours are just wind-ups."

"What did it do?"

"Fought alongside Jackson at Chancellorsville," the stranger said, as if to ease Morgan's mind. "Is that enough?"

Morgan had always hated slavers. "The war's over."

"This one still kills," the stranger said. "Not sure why. Some say he took a knock from a cannonball in the war. When the gears turn in his mind, he cannot help himself. The last victim was a boy, sixteen years old.

Hellfire called him out. Before that, he shot a Chinaman, and before that, a snake-oil salesman. Each killing is four months apart—to the minute."

The stranger spat into the fire. His spittle burst into flame, like kerosene, and emitted a rich scent that reminded Morgan of blackberries, growing thick on the vine beside a creek.

Morgan suspected that the stranger was right. This gambler needed to be stopped. But killing a clockwork wouldn't be easy. Their inner parts were shielded by nickel and tin, and you never knew where their vital gears hid. Thirteen Comancheros had had a bout with one down on the border a couple years back. Rumor said it had taken twenty-three bullets to bring him down. Eleven Comancheros died.

Clockworks were quick on the draw, deadly in their aim. The stranger called this one a "gambler," but clockworks had been created to be soldiers and guards and gunslingers.

"What brand?" Morgan asked.

"Sharps."

Morgan ground his teeth. He'd hoped that it might be some cheap Russian model, built during the Crimean War. The Sharps clockworks had a reputation. Going up against one was almost suicide.

Yet Morgan had taken a handout from a *stranger*, and he'd known that there would be a day of reckoning. "Where do I find him?"

"Heading toward Fort Laramie…" the stranger said. "The gambler is like a bomb, with a fuse lit. In four days, six hours, and seven minutes, he will kill again."

The stranger turned into an oily shadow and wafted away.

Morgan hardly slept that night. Gold had been discovered in the Black Hills, and prospectors were crawling all over the wilderness north of Fort Laramie, the biggest supply depot in the West. Tens of thousands were riding in on the new rail lines.

The Indians didn't like it. After getting pushed around for years, Sioux holy men like Crazy Horse and Sitting Bull were on the warpath, trying to drive off the miners, much as they'd tried to hold off the homesteaders and buffalo hunters.

Only this time, the way Morgan figured it, there was going to be a bloodbath. You can only steal so much from a man before he has to push back. Morgan didn't fancy blundering into such a mess. Some Sioux had big magic.

At dawn he rode east toward Frenchman's Ferry, climbing over the hills. A day later, he found a single skinwalker's track between two boulders, in a land covered by worn sandstone rocks and sparse grasses. The creature had been leaping from boulder to boulder, hiding its trail. But it had come to a place where the rocks were too far apart.

Like many skinwalkers, Coyote Shadow had turned himself into a beast once too often, and now he'd lost himself. His print was something halfway between a human foot and a bear's paw. Coyote Shadow had become only half a man.

Much like me, Morgan thought. He'd carried a torch for Sherman, had forced womenfolk from their houses and set entire cities aflame. Sometimes folks had refused to leave their homes, and he'd heard the women screaming in the fires.

He forced down the memories.

Morgan slid from his saddle and studied the print. The dusty ground here had given easily, yielding a deep track with crisp ridges. The track looked fresh—hours old.

Morgan searched the bleak landscape: sandstone thrusting up from broken ground, dry grass and sage, and little else.

During the heat of the day, any sane Indian would have stopped in the shade, though there wasn't much of it here to take solace in.

Morgan's mare nickered and shied back a step, as if she'd caught a dangerous scent.

Morgan sniffed. Between the iron odor of rocks and dry grass, he smelled an undertone—like garlic rubbed in fur.

A skinwalker.

He'd been hunting the creature for months, and now he resented finding it. He was on his way to kill the clockwork gambler.

But justice demanded that he finish this monster.

He searched uphill. A pile of sandstone boulders stood at its crown, with a single rock jutting up from it in a small pinnacle. Yucca plants and a few junipers grew tall in the pinnacle's shadow.

The skinwalker is up there, Morgan realized. *He could be watching me.*

Morgan studied the shadows. Nothing stirred. Perhaps the skinwalker was sleeping.

Morgan tied his pony to a mesquite bush, pulled his Winchester from the saddle holster, and began picking his way uphill, weaving behind rocks and bushes in case the skinwalker tried to take a long shot.

Fifteen minutes later, Morgan reached the rocks, and in the shade of a juniper found some crushed grass where the skinwalker had bedded. He'd left only moments ago.

Biting his lip, Morgan leapt to the far side of the rock and scanned the landscape. He saw the skinwalker, rushing uphill toward the next ridge, a lumbering mound of shaggy fur. His long arms swung with every stride, and he ran low to the ground, like an ape, but Coyote Shadow still wore the scrap of a loincloth. He moved fast, faster than a horse could run.

The creature was more than two hundred yards out, and as he neared the ridge, he turned and glanced back.

Morgan had time for one shot before the sorcerer escaped. He crouched behind a rock and steadied his aim. The skinwalker saw him, whirled, and doubled his speed.

Morgan's hands shook. Mouth went dry. Heart pounded. He gasped. Buck fever.

He didn't want it to end this way—shooting the skinwalker in the back. Morgan had imagined catching Coyote Shadow, taking him to some town where a judge would see that he was hanged proper.

Morgan forced himself to stop breathing, lined the skinwalker up in his sights, and squeezed gently.

The rifle cracked and jumped in his hands. The skinwalker didn't jerk or stumble. Instead, his stride seemed clean, uninterrupted, as he disappeared over the hill.

Still, that didn't mean that Morgan hadn't wounded the beast. Morgan once had seen a rebel lieutenant die in combat—he charged into battle, swinging a sword in one hand and shooting a revolver from the other while bullet holes blossomed on his chest like roses. "Charging Dead," Morgan called it.

So he took note of the place where the skinwalker had stood as Morgan fired, near a large rock with a yucca plant, then hurried to the spot.

He found the monster's tracks and studied the ground for blood, a clump of hair, hoping for or any other sign that the skinwalker was wounded.

Morgan tracked the monster over one ridge, then another.

As the sun began to wallow on the horizon in a leaden sky, and bats wove through the air, he admitted defeat. Not a drop of blood could be found. He'd missed.

* * *

That night, the moon hid beneath bands of clouds, and a south wind from the Gulf of Mexico smelled of rain. Morgan camped without a fire, not wanting to risk setting the prairie alight.

He couldn't sleep. He'd ruined Coyote Shadow's rest, and he worried that the skinwalker might come creeping into his camp, hoping for vengeance. So for long hours, Morgan lay quietly listening for the crunch of a foot in the prairie soil with his pistol in hand, just beneath his blanket.

As the hours stretched, he dozed sporadically, but would wake again with a start. A screech owl hunted nearby, flying low, shrieking every few minutes as it tried to startle mice from their hiding places.

Long after midnight, Morgan decided to relax and put his hat over his eyes. Suddenly it was knocked away, and he rose up and fired blindly, just as the owl winged off.

His hat lay on the ground next to him. The bird had swooped low and struck it. Apparently the bit of rabbit fur on the brim looked too much like a varmint to the owl.

Morgan turned over, indignant, and after many minutes he slid into an uneasy slumber.

He dreamt that he was in a shop, where a tinkerman with a big, white handlebar moustache and penetrating blue eyes worked at piecing together clockwork soldiers.

One soldier lay like a patient on a surgeon's table. The tinkerman had its chest cavity open and was grasping something inside: it was a huge golden coil spring, nearly lost amid gears and pistons. Part pocket watch, part steam engine, the insides of the clockwork soldier were somehow more greasy and filthy than Morgan had imagined they could be.

The tinkerman nodded toward a crate and said in a deep Georgia drawl, "Son, would you be so kind as to fish a heart outta that box?"

The shop had bits and pieces of clockwork everywhere: a shelf of expressionless faces, waiting to come to life; arms and legs hanging from the rafters like dry sausages in a Mexican cantina; tubes and gizmos lying in heaps on counters and on the floor.

Morgan looked into the box. He found dozens of hearts in it, barely beating, covered in grease and oil, black and ugly.

Morgan picked up the largest, strongest-looking one. It throbbed in his grip, almost slipping away. He handed it to the tinkerman.

"Much obliged," the tinkerman said.

He thrust the heart into the contraption, piercing it through with the gold coil, and the clockwork soldier jolted to life—hands flexing, a strangled cry rising from its throat. Its mouth opened, and it whined stupidly, like an animal in pain.

The tinkerman smiled in satisfaction. "Perfect."

Somehow, that pronouncement scared him. Would the clockwork gambler that he was hunting be "perfect?" It sounded presumptuous.

Morgan wondered at that. He said, "When God made man, he only allowed that his creation was 'good.'"

The tinkerman glanced up, lips tight in anger, eyes twinkling. "God, sir, was not a perfectionist. He failed as an organism. We superseded him."

"Superseded?"

The tinkerman smiled cruelly. "He drove Adam from the Garden of Idunn. In some tales, afterward, Adam made a spear and sneaked up on God while he was sleeping…"

Morgan woke, wondering. He'd heard in the war that God was dead. He never heard any legends, though, about how it happened.

Morgan woke with a start, afraid that someone was sneaking up on him. He lay still for several minutes, listening for the crackle of a footfall. Thin clouds filled the sky, which was beginning to lighten on the horizon. Morning would not be far off.

Small birds flitted about in a nearby sage. Here in the desert, most birds were silent, unwilling to call attention to themselves.

Morgan felt that something was wrong.

Suddenly, he realized that he hadn't heard anything amiss. It was what he *didn't* hear that bothered him—his horse. He lurched to his feet, swung his pistol around, and peered into the shadows.

His horse was nowhere to be seen.

Coyote Shadow had circled Morgan, stolen his food, his hat, his rifle, and his horse.

Morgan must have worn himself out, trying to keep watch. The skinwalker could have killed him in his sleep, but this Indian was more interested in counting coup, humiliating Morgan, than taking his scalp.

"Hope you're getting a good chuckle out of this!" Morgan shouted to the horizon.

He turned away from the skinwalker's path and set off for Frenchman's Ferry.

Morgan wasn't the kind of man to chew on regret. In life, he believed that you have to do the best you can. Sometimes you succeeded, sometimes you failed.

He'd lost Coyote Shadow, and by now the renegade was probably heading to join up with Crazy Horse's men; either that or he'd gone up into the aspen forests in the high country. Morgan figured he'd never see Coyote Shadow again.

Yet he began to regret missing his shot at the skinwalker. He wondered about his buck fever—the shaking hands, the dry mouth.

Too many men, when they get in a gunfight, will draw and fire wild, hitting only empty air. That's what gets them killed. A more experienced man will take a moment to aim—half a second, if need be—and thus shoot his opponent.

Morgan was fast on the draw and had a steady aim, but he'd gotten buck fever.

His failure seemed a portent.

The clockwork gambler wouldn't suffer from human debilities. He wouldn't get excited and drop his gun. He wouldn't get a case of tremors. He wouldn't pause because he was having an attack of conscience.

He would just kill.

In some ways, Morgan realized, *he's better than me.*

Morgan survived the next two days off strips of sliced prickly pear cactus, which tasted like green beans, and yucca fruit, which were more like potatoes. The odd jack rabbit added protein to the fare.

Four days after meeting the stranger, Morgan was hobbling along on sore feet, thirty miles from Fort Laramie. If the stranger was right, someone would get killed today. Morgan wouldn't be there to stop it.

When he reached Frenchman's Ferry, down on the North Platte, he spotted a miserable little log shack. Bear traps, snowshoes, and other durable goods hung outside. A pair of dogs—half mastiff and half wolf—guarded the door. Its smokestack was roiling, even in the heat of the day, producing black clouds of smoke.

A bevy of greenhorns had just left the post, heading north into the wilderness.

Morgan hurried inside.

At the counter, an aging squaw sat with a basket of big turkey eggs. She hunched over a lightbox—a box with a mirror on one wall, and an oil lamp in the middle. By holding an egg up to the contraption, a person could check it for cracks or the blobs of half-formed fetuses.

The squaw's blouse was white with red polka dots—a Cheyenne design. But she wore buckskin pants like a trapper, and her perfume smelled imported. She didn't spare him a glance.

"Look around," she offered in that Indian way that was more "careful" than "slow." The shop was filled with merchandise—tins of crackers, barrels of pickles, beans, rice and wheat. On the wall behind the counter were hunting knives, a pair of shotguns—and above them hung Morgan's Winchester.

So the skinwalker had been here.

The gun didn't interest him right now. The skinwalker had stolen it fair and square. He'd counted coup and sold the gun. No sense arguing with the squaw about who owned it. Morgan would just embarrass himself by admitting that it had once been his.

Of everything in the shop, the things that most interested him were those eggs. Hunger gnawed at him. When Morgan was a child, his ma had often sold eggs to folks in town. She'd taught him young how to handle one, to check it for damage.

"Is Black Pierre around?" Morgan ventured.

"Gone for supplies," the squaw said. "Back in three, four days."

The squaw was turning an egg experimentally, studying it. She didn't look up. Morgan could see how judging such an egg might be difficult. Most chicken eggs were a uniform tan in color. Finding blood spots inside was easy. But these eggs were white, with big specks on them— some sand-colored, others more like liverworts. The shells were thicker than a chicken egg.

"I'd be right happy to buy some turkey eggs off of you," Morgan offered.

"Not turkey eggs," the squaw said, "thunderbird! Traders brought them in this morning. Found them in an old geyser vent over in Sulfur Springs."

Morgan had never seen a thunderbird egg before. Back east, they were called "snakebirds" but had been extinct for at least a hundred years. Down in Mexico, the Spaniards had called them quetzals, and some of the tribes still prayed to the critters.

"Want to see?" the squaw asked.

She held an egg to the hole in the lightbox, and Morgan peered in. Sure enough, the light shining through the egg was bright enough to reveal the embryo inside—a birdlike head with a snake's body. Many of its bones were still gelatinous, but he could see its guts forming, a tiny heart beating. Its scales were still almost translucent, just beginning to turn purple.

"Well, I'll be!" Morgan whispered. "Didn't know as there were any snakebirds left. They're fading faster than the buffalo."

"Mmm…" the squaw mused. "The world must get rid of the old wonders, so that it can make way for the new."

Morgan thought on that. He'd seen some of the last real buffalo herds as a child, darkening the plains of Kansas. Now the railroads were coming, and the railroad men were killing the buffalo off. The big herds were a danger to trains.

He imagined the clockwork gambler. Would such things someday replace men?

"Those eggs for sale?" Morgan asked.

"Not to you. They're for the Sioux—big medicine."

"How much you reckon to get?"

"My scalp," she said. "The Sioux slaughtered General Custer last week at the Little Bighorn. I'm going to need some gifts, to make peace."

Morgan didn't have a lot of money. He was able to buy back his pony and his hat at the trading post, but couldn't afford his rifle.

He set off down the Platte toward Fort Laramie, riding overland, well south of the river, far away from the pioneer trails where the Sioux would concentrate their patrols.

When he reached Fort Laramie, the post was full.

People of every kind had taken refuge just outside the fortress walls in tents and teepees—gold miners, fur trappers, homesteaders on the Oregon and California trails, Mormon converts from England and Denmark on their way to Utah, railroad workers of the Chinese, Irish, Dutch, and Negro persuasions, Omaha Indians and a few Comanches, Bible thumpers. Morgan had rarely seen such liveliness on the frontier.

He heard a rumor that there was a plague merchant in town—with bottles of black death and boxes of locust larvae.

Hell, there was even a freak show in town with a three-headed woman, an elephant, and a genuine Egyptian mummy.

The town hadn't seen rain in weeks, and so as Morgan entered the fortress, he found a rainmaker at the front gates—pounding a huge drum that sounded for the world like the crashing of thunder.

"Come, wind!" the rainmaker shouted. "Arise ye tempest, I say! Let your water soak the gnarly ground. Let cactus flowers bloom, while toads claw up from the mud!"

Morgan sat on his horse and studied the slim man—a tall beardless fellow in a fine top hat and tails, who roared as he drummed and stared off toward a few clouds on the horizon like a lunatic, with manic eyes and a grim smile.

The clouds were drawing near, blackening from moment to moment.

Morgan tossed a penny into the man's cup. "Keep your eyes on them clouds, Preach," Morgan said. "Don't let 'em sneak off."

"Thank you, good sir," the rainmaker said, pausing to wipe sweat from his brow with a handkerchief. "There will be rain soon. Mark my word."

Morgan didn't want the clockwork gambler to know that he was hunting for him. But the rainmaker seemed like a trustworthy fellow. He hazarded, "I'm looking for a clockwork gambler. Seen him?"

"You a friend of his?" the preacher asked. His tone became a bit formal, suspicious, and he backed away an inch.

In answer, Morgan pulled the badge from his pocket, a star made of nickel.

"You're too late," the preacher said. "He went on a rampage yesterday. He was sitting quiet at a card table, and suddenly pulled out his gun and shot a showgirl. There was a big row. Some cavalrymen drew steel, and seven men died in the firefight. The gambler escaped."

"See which way he went?"

The rainmaker nodded toward the clouds. In just the few moments since they'd begun speaking, Morgan realized that they'd shrunk and had begun to drift away. "He headed off into the High Frontier, where no one can give chase. There won't be no posse. Major Wiggins has got more trouble than he can handle, with them Sioux."

Morgan had heard tales of the High Frontier, but he'd never been there. Few men had. There had always been stories of castles in the clouds, but truth is far stranger than fiction.

"How'd he fly?" Morgan asked.

"Private yacht. He won it in a poker game."

Morgan wondered. The clockwork gambler was far away by now, more inaccessible than Mexico, almost as remote as the moon.

The rainmaker said hopefully, "Wells Fargo has a new line that goes to the High Frontier. Got to stay ahead of them railroads. Schooner lands next Monday."

"What day is today?" Morgan could guess at the month, but not the day.

"Today's a Wednesday."

Five days to get a grub stake together. Morgan bit his lower lip. He'd seen an airship once, a big copper-colored bulb glowing in the sunset as it sailed through ruddy clouds. Pretty and untouchable, like a trout swimming in deep, clear water.

"The dance-hall girl," Morgan said. "She have any friends?"

The preacher squinted, giving an appraising look, and nodded sagely. "You thinking 'bout going after him?"

It seemed audacious. Hunting a clockwork alone was foolhardy, and few men had the kind of money needed for airfare.

Morgan nodded. "Justice shouldn't be confined by borders."

The rainmaker nodded agreement, then thrust a hand into his pocket, pulled out some bills and change, handed them over. "Here's a donation for your cause, Lawman. Lacy didn't have a lot of friends, but she had a lot of men who longed for her from afar. Check the saloon."

Morgan's heart broke at the mention of Lacy's name. He remembered the red-haired girl, her innocent smile. He'd seen her before. But what was she doing in Laramie?

She'd come here for safety, he figured, like everyone else. Scared of the renegades. They were like sheep, huddled in a pen.

He'd felt so in awe of Lacy, he couldn't have dared even speak to her, much less ask to hold her hand. In some ways, she was little more than a dream, a thing of ephemeral beauty.

The preacher smiled and began pounding his drum with extra vigor. "Come, horrid bursts of thunder!" he commanded. "Come sheets of fire! Groan ye winds and roar ye rain!"

On the horizon, the clouds darkened and again began lumbering toward Laramie.

A week later, Morgan found himself in the gondola of a dirigible.

It turned out that Lacy had had a lot of friends in Laramie. Though none was rich enough to afford passage to the High Frontier on their own, and none was mad enough to shoot it out with a clockwork, Morgan was able to scrape together enough money for his passage.

The balloon above the gondola was shaped like a fancy glass Christmas tree ornament, all covered in gold silk. A steam engine powered the dirigible, providing a steady *thump, thump, thump* as pistons pounded and blades spun.

The gondola swung beneath the huge balloon, connected by skywires. Its decks were all hewn from new cedar and sandalwood; their scent complemented the smell of sky and sun and wind.

City slickers and foreigners sat in the parlor cabin, toasting their good fortune and dancing while bands played.

Morgan could hear their music, smell their roast beef, sometimes even glimpse them dancing. But he wasn't a railroad tycoon or a mining magnate or a politician.

He'd taken passage in the lower deck, in the "Belly of the Beast," as they called it, and had one small porthole in his cabin to peer through.

Still, the sight was glorious.

The dirigible reached the High Frontier at sunset, just as the sun dipped below the sea, leaving the clouds below to be a half-lit mass of swirling wine and fuchsia.

One could only find the High Frontier at that time of day—when the sun had set and the full moon was poised to rise on the far side of the Earth. It was a magical place, nestled in the clouds.

Down below the skyship, a silver city rose—elegant spires like fairy castles, with windows lit up like gemstones. The colored glass in those windows made it look as if sapphires, rubies, and diamonds were scattered over the city.

The skyship landed amid glorious swirling clouds, and the rich folk marched down the promenade, arm in arm, laughing and joking and celebrating their good fortune. On the deck, the band came out and played soft chamber music.

Women *oohed* and *aahed* at the spectacle, while men stood open-mouthed. Morgan imagined that saints might make such sounds as they entered heaven.

The High Frontier had only been discovered four years back. Who had built the silver castles, no one knew. How the cities of stone floated in the clouds was also a mystery.

Angels lived there—scrawny girls with wings, ethereal in their beauty. But they were feral creatures, barbaric, and it was said that when the first explorers had entered the silver city, the angels were roosting over the arches—little more than filthy pigeons.

Some thought that it had once been an outpost, that perhaps angels had once been wiser, more civilized, and that they rested here while carrying messages back and forth between heaven and Earth.

One guess was as good as another. But a new territory was opening up, and folks were eager to be the first to see it. Morgan couldn't figure how a man might make a living here. The sky was always twilit, so you couldn't grow crops. The clouds were somehow thick enough to walk on, but there was nothing to mine.

Just a pretty place to visit, Morgan thought.

When the rich folk were mostly gone, Morgan made his way down the gangplank. A fancy dude in a bowler hat stood at the top of the gangway, smoking a fine cigar that perfumed the air.

He glanced at Morgan, smiled, and said, "*Das ist schön, nicht wahr?*"

Morgan grinned back. "Sorry," he apologized. "I don't reckon we speak the same language."

Morgan walked down the gangplank, his spurs jangling with every step, and trundled through the city. He imagined that madmen had fashioned the soaring arches above the city gate, now planted with vines and lianas that streamed in living curtains.

Maybe a fella could grow crops up here after all, he mused, *though the light is low.* Butterflies and hummingbirds danced among the flowers.

As he entered the silver city, spires rose up on either side. There was something both strange and yet oddly organic about the tall buildings, as if some alien intelligence had sought to build a city for humans. Perhaps dove-men had designed it, or termites. He wasn't sure.

People filed off in a number of directions. It was rumored that many a tycoon had bought houses here—Cornelius Vanderbilt, Russell Sage, along with royals out of Europe and Russia. Even Queen Victoria had a new "summerhouse" here.

All the high-falutin' folks sauntered off to their destinations, and Morgan felt lost.

One fairy castle looked much like another. He searched for an hour, and as he rounded a corner, he found what he was looking for: the wing doors of a Western saloon. He could hear loud piano music inside, and smell spilled beer on its oak floors.

He walked into the saloon and found a madhouse.

On either side of the door were golden cages up over his head, and angels were housed there—small girls, perhaps eight or nine, with fabulous wings larger than any swan's. Their hair was as white as spun silver, their faces translucent.

But their dark eyes were lined with a thick band of kohl, as if they were raccoons. They drew back from Morgan and hissed.

Unbidden, a dark thought entered his mind. When he was a child, Morgan's mother had always told him that when a man dies, the angels come to take his soul to heaven.

He could be walking to his death.

A verse from Psalms came to mind, one of his ma's favorites: "Lord, what is man, that thou art mindful of him? Or the son of man, that thou visitest him? Thou madest him a little lower than the angels..."

As if divining his thoughts, one of the angels hissed at him and bared her teeth. She scooped a turd up from her cage and hurled it. Then grabbed a corn cob and tossed that, too.

Morgan dodged and hurried past.

Inside, the place was alive. Dance-hall girls strutted on stage to clanking pianos and catcalls. Men hunched at tables, drinking and telling jokes. It was much like a saloon, but it suffered from the same miserable clientele as he'd seen on the dirigible—European barons in bright silk vests and overcoats. Eastern dudes. Moguls and robber barons.

The beer wasn't sold in glass jugs, but in decorous tankards, inlaid with silver and precious stones.

The place smelled more of gold than of liquor. Pipe smoke perfumed the air.

But the clockwork gambler was surprisingly easy to spot. In fact, Morgan gasped and stepped back in surprise when he saw him.

The clockwork was obviously not human. His face had been sculpted from porcelain, like the head of a doll, and painted in natural colors, but there were brass hinges on his jaws. When he blinked, copper eyelids flashed over glass eyes.

He wore all black, from his hat to his boots, and sat at a card table with a stack of poker chips in front of him. He had a little gambling kit off to one side. Morgan was familiar with such kits. They held decks of cards for various games, dice made of bone and ivory, and always they held weapons—a pistol and a throwing knife.

The clockwork gambler sat with three wealthy men. By the piles of solid gold coins in front of him, he was winning.

Morgan steeled his nerves, walked up to the table, and said, "You gentlemen might want to back away."

The patrons scattered aside as Morgan pulled back his coat to reveal the star on his chest.

Some men cried out as they fled, and others ducked as if dodging imaginary bullets. The clockwork gambler just leaned back casually in his chair, as calm as a summer's morning. His mouth seemed to have little porcelain shingles around it that moved to his will, so that when he smiled, it created a crude approximation of a grin. The creature's teeth were as white as shards of ice.

"Here to try your luck?" the clockwork asked.

"Your name Hellfire?" Morgan replied.

The gambler nodded, barely tipping his hat.

Morgan felt his hands shaking, and his mouth suddenly dried. He'd never seen a man face death with equanimity the way that this clockwork did. It was unnatural. Almost unholy.

I'm betrayed by my humanity, Morgan thought. *Flesh and blood, gristle and bone—they undo me.*

In that instant, he knew that he was no match for the clockwork gambler.

"Tell you what, stranger," the clockwork said. "Let's draw cards for your life. You get the high card, you get the first shot at me."

Morgan shook his head.

"Come on," the gambler said reasonably. "It's the best chance you've got. Your flesh was created by God, and thus has its all-too human limitations. I was made to draw faster than you, to shoot straighter."

"You might be a better killer than me, but that don't make you a better man."

"When killing is all that matters, maybe it does," the clockwork said.

The silence drew out. Morgan wasn't sure if he should let the clockwork draw first. He didn't know where to aim. The creature's chest provided the biggest target, but it was the best protected by layers of metal. The joints where its neck met its head might be better. But what was a head to this machine? Did thoughts originate there, or elsewhere? The head looked no more serviceable than that of a poppet.

The gambler smiled. "Your human sense of honor bothering you? Is that it?"

"I want justice," Morgan said. "I demand justice."

"On the High Frontier?" the gambler mocked. "There is no justice here—just a pretty tomb, the ruins of a grander civilization. This is Rome! This is Egypt!"

He waved his hands wide, displaying the ornate walls carved with silver, the golden cages with captive angels. "This is what is left of your dead god. But I am the future."

Morgan had heard a lot of talk about God being dead over the years, from the beginning of the Civil War. But the discovery of these ruins proved it to the minds of many.

"Tell you what," the gambler said. "Your legs are shaking. I won't shoot you now. Let's try the cards. I'll draw for you."

The gambler placed a fresh deck on the table, pulled a card off the top, and laid it upright. It was a Jack of Hearts. He smiled, as if in relief.

"I didn't come to gamble," Morgan said. "I came for justice."

"Seeking justice is always a gamble," Hellfire answered reasonably. "Justice doesn't exist in nature. It's just the use of force, backed up by self-righteous judgment."

The gambler cut the deck, pulled off the top card, flipped it: the Ace of Spades.

"You win!" the gambler grinned.

Morgan was all nerves and jitters but pulled his piece anyway, took a full quarter second to get his bearings, and fired. The bullet ripped into the gambler's bowtie, and there was a metallic *zing* as it ricocheted into the crowd.

Someone cried out, "*Mein Gott!*" and a woman yelled, "He's been shot!"

Morgan's face fell. He hadn't meant to wing a bystander. He glanced to his right, saw a fat bloke clutching his chest, blood blossoming on a white shirt.

Morgan ducked low and tried to aim at the clockwork, but faster than the eye could move the gambler drew, aimed, and fired. The bullet took Morgan straight in the chest and threw him backward as if he'd been kicked by a horse.

Morgan fell and wheezed, trying to suck air, but he heard blood gurgling from the hole in his ribs. His lungs burned as if someone had stuck a hot poker through them.

He looked right and left, hoping someone would help him, but all that he saw were frightened faces. He had heard that there was no law on the High Frontier, only money.

No one would stop the killing. No one would avenge him.

As he lay on his back and felt blood pooling on the floor, he fought to stay conscious. The clockwork gambler strode toward him, smiling down, his porcelain face a mockery of flesh.

Morgan realized that he'd been charging dead, from the moment he'd started this hunt. When he'd missed the skinwalker, he should have seen it as a sign.

"Your human tinkermen have made me well, have they not?" Hellfire asked. "You humans, in such a hurry to create. It was inevitable that you would fashion your replacements."

Over the clockwork's shoulder, Morgan saw his angels—leering from their cages. One was grabbing at the lock on its golden door, trying to break free, as if to come for him.

But Morgan was on his way out, like the buffalo, and the Indians, and thunderbirds, and all the other great things in the wide world.

The gambler aimed at Morgan's head. There was no shaking in his hands, no hesitation. He pulled the trigger.

Thus, a new wonder in the world supplanted an old.

THE HELL-BOUND STAGECOACH

MIKE RESNICK

Arizona Territory, Circa 1885

The tall lean man stood alone on the prairie, a thin cigar in his mouth, his Stetson shielding his eyes from the sun. He wasn't sure how long he'd been waiting there, but it couldn't have been too long. It was a blazing hot day, there was no shade anywhere near him, and yet he wasn't sweating.

Finally the stagecoach came into view, drawn by a team of sleek, coal-black horses. They raced over the ground, raising endless clouds of dust, but when the driver saw he had a passenger waiting he eased them first to a trot, then a walk, and at last they came to a stop just as they reached the man.

The man stared at the stagecoach, which was a little fancier than he was used to.

"Climb aboard, climb aboard," said the driver, a small, gnarly man with piercing dark eyes. "I got a schedule to keep."

The man nodded, a door opened, and he climbed into the interior of the coach as the horses started moving again. The only other passenger was a prim, middle-aged woman, her hair starting to turn gray, her dress buttoned all the way up to the neck despite the heat. She held a wicker basket on her lap.

"Good morning, ma'am," said the man, tipping his hat. "My name's Ben, Ben Bradshaw."

"And I am Abigail Fletcher," she replied.

"I'm pleased to make your acquaintance, ma'am," said Bradshaw, extending his hand. She took it in a firm grip and shook it. "Looks like we're going to be traveling together."

She nodded her agreement. "Have you eaten, young man?"

"I truly don't recall, ma'am," he said. "And please call me Ben."

She indicated her basket. "Would you like a biscuit?"

"I'd surely appreciate one, ma'am."

She opened the basket and withdrew a tidily-wrapped biscuit, offering it to him.

"Thank you kindly, ma'am," said Bradshaw, unwrapping it and taking a bite. "Have you come a long ways?"

"Sometimes it feels like it," she responded.

"I meant, on the coach?"

"Not that far."

"Where are you heading, ma'am?"

"The end of the line," she replied. "And you, young man?"

"Ben," he corrected her. "And I'm here for the rest of the trip, too." He looked out the window at the dry, barren landscape. "Hope it gets a little cooler soon."

The driver laughed at that, which surprised Bradshaw, who hadn't thought anything they said in the coach would carry outside to where the gnarly man sat, holding the reins.

"This is a right tasty biscuit, ma'am," said Bradshaw. "I guess I was hungrier than I thought."

"What do you do for a living, young... Ben?" asked Abigail.

"Oh, a little of this, a little of that, nothing very interesting," replied Bradshaw. "I just try to earn a dollar here and there." He paused and stared at her, "What about you, ma'am? If I was to guess, I'd say that you're a schoolmarm."

He couldn't tell if the statement pleased her or annoyed her. Her expression gave nothing away.

"What does a schoolmarm look like?" she asked.

He searched for the right word. "Proper," he said at last, then considered it, nodded his head, and repeated it. "Proper. Like nothing much upsets you, and you've got a handle on everything."

"Well, now," said Abigail, "that could be flattering or insulting. I think I'll choose to be flattered."

"I certainly didn't mean it no other way, ma'am," Bradshaw assured her. He fidgeted uncomfortably for a moment. "Could I maybe trouble you for another one of them biscuits, ma'am? They make powerful good eating."

"I'm very flattered," she replied, almost but not quite smiling. "And of course you can have another." She reached into the basket and handed him one.

"You're sure it's not an imposition, ma'am?"

"I packed enough for a long trip," she said.

"Well, I'll be proud and pleased to ride all the way to the end with you." He took a bite and smiled at her. "You know, usually I'm tongue-tied around women, but you put me at my ease."

This time she did smile. "That's one of the nicest compliments anyone's ever paid to me. I thank you for it."

He looked out the window while he ate, watching a dust storm off in the distance. When he finished eating he turned back to her and found that she was reading a book. He didn't want to disturb her, so he just leaned back and tried to sleep. Sleep didn't come to him, but he relaxed and tried to remember the events of the past few days, which were fast becoming a blur. *I gotta cut down on my drinking,* he thought, *or one of these days I won't even remember my own name.*

Suddenly the stagecoach began slowing down.

"What's the problem?" Bradshaw called up to the driver.

"No problem at all," was the answer. "Got to stop for another passenger."

"Out here?" said Bradshaw, frowning. "Looks like we're fifty miles from anywhere."

"Nevertheless," said the gnarly driver.

"Wonder what the hell he's doing out here?" He turned to Abigail. "Pardon my language, ma'am."

"I've heard worse," she assured him.

The coach finally came to a halt, Bradshaw opened the door, and the new passenger entered. He was dressed all in black—hat, coat, tie, pants, holster, gloves, boots; even his long, drooping mustache was black. He wore a Colt .45 on each hip, and their ivory handles provided the only relief from the blackness that was everywhere else on him.

"Good day, all," he said when he'd taken a seat next to Bradshaw, across from Abigail. "Allow me to introduce myself. I'm—"

"I know who you are," said Abigail disapprovingly. "I've seen your face on enough posters. You're the Wichita Kid."

He smiled. "Do I look like a kid?"

"No," she said. "But you look like a man who's much too handy with *those*." She gestured toward his guns.

"Well, it just so happens that I *am* the Wichita Kid, and I'm more than a little bit proficient with my weapons," he replied. "But out here you have to be. Anyway, I'm too old to be a kid, so please just call me Wichita."

"I'm sure you're proficient," she said. "But if you can get what you want with your brain…"

"Don't argue with him, ma'am," said Bradshaw. "You're not going to change his mind, and it's not worth the effort."

"If you say so, young man," replied Abigail with a shrug.

"You listen to this young man, do you?" asked Wichita in amused tones.

"He's a very nice young man who respects his elders," she said.

"Those who live," chuckled Wichita.

She frowned. "What are you talking about, sir?"

"Don't you know you've been sharing a coach with Bloody Ben Bradshaw? You'd be hard-pressed to name a place from the Dakotas to Texas, or from Missouri to Nevada, that hasn't offered a reward for him, dead or alive."

She stared at Bradshaw for a long moment. "Is that true?"

"I can't deny it, ma'am," admitted Bradshaw. "But don't you worry none. You're perfectly safe with me."

She seemed to consider his answer for another moment, then shrugged. "We're all here together," she said. "I suppose we might as well make the best of it."

"Thank you, ma'am," said Bradshaw. "I certainly don't mean to distress or upset you."

"Nor do I," Wichita chimed in. "I'm just a passenger." His gaze fell on her basket. "You wouldn't happen to have any extra vittles in there, would you, ma'am?" he asked. "I can hardly remember the last time I ate."

She opened the basket and looked into it. "Would you prefer a biscuit, a muffin, or perhaps some home-made bread?"

"Why, a muffin would be just fine, Mrs…?"

"It's Miss," she told him. "Miss Abigail Fletcher."

"And a lovely name it is, Miss Abigail," said Wichita, taking the proffered muffin and biting into it. "This is quite tasty. Certainly better than any I've ever had in a restaurant."

"It's my own recipe," she said, not without a trace of pride.

"There's some kind of berry in it, isn't there?"

She nodded.

"Blueberry?" he asked. "Elderberry?"

She smiled. "My secret."

"Well, the recipe may be your secret, but it's a crying shame that the taste is pretty much a secret too. You should open a restaurant. People would flock to your door."

"Oh, I doubt that."

Wichita smiled. "They would if Bloody Ben and myself were urging them."

She returned the smile. "You know, somehow you two just don't seem like notorious killers."

"I'm a notorious gambler, Miss Abigail," replied Wichita. "I almost never killed anyone who wasn't trying to cheat me or shoot me."

"*Almost* never?" she repeated.

"There are exceptions to every rule, Miss Abigail," he said. "I figure a church lady like yourself must know that."

"Why should you think I'm a church lady?"

"You dress modestly, you sit up properly, you display Christian charity by feeding a hungry man…"

"*Two* hungry men," Bradshaw corrected him.

"Well, I'm certainly flattered by your judgment, Mister…" She frowned. "It seems very awkward to call you Mr. Kid."

He laughed at that. "Just call me Wichita, Miss Abigail. 'Most everyone else does."

"All right, then," she said. "Mr. Wichita."

"Just Wichita will do."

"Where are you bound to, Wichita?" she asked.

"As far from here as I can get," he answered with a smile. "Things were getting a mite unsettled, if you know what I mean—and if you don't, Bloody Ben sure does."

Bradshaw nodded his agreement. "It goes with the territory."

"So where are you headed, Miss Abigail?"

"You know," she replied, "it's the strangest thing, but I can't quite remember."

"Let's find out," said Wichita. "Hey, Driver—how far is the lady going?"

"To the end of the line," answered the driver.

"Hope you brought a bunch of vittles," said Wichita. "I have a feeling this line don't make too many stops."

"It stopped for *you*," she noted.

"I just stood out there and waited," replied Wichita. "I knew that sooner or later there'd be a coach along."

"What happened to your horse?" she asked. "I don't mean this quite the way I'm sure it will sound, but I thought all desperados had horses."

Wichita frowned. "Must have gone lame, I suppose, or I wouldn't have been standing out there waiting for a stage."

"You were all alone out there," she noted. "You must have walked a long way without your horse."

He shrugged. "I suppose so."

"Come to think of it, I can't recollect where I left Diamond," said Bradshaw.

"Diamond?" she repeated.

"My horse, ma'am. Pinto, but mostly white. Now and then, when the sun hits him just right, he glows like a diamond."

"That's almost poetic," said Abigail.

"Are you alright, Miss Abigail?" asked Wichita suddenly.

"Why?" she asked.

"When you turned your head to face Ben, I thought I saw a little blood just behind your temple."

"Really?" said Abigail. She gingerly touched the spot he had indicated, then stared at her fingers. "Whatever it is, it's dried. There's nothing on my hand."

"Turn your head just a bit more," suggested Wichita.

She did so. "Well?" she asked.

"Looks for all the world like a bullet hole, Miss Abigail."

She frowned and blinked her eyes very rapidly. "You know, I vaguely remember telling Ezra—he chops wood and does other chores for me—that if I caught him drinking one more time I would fire him. He went into a rage… and that's the very last thing I remember."

"And you don't feel nothing, ma'am?" asked Bradshaw. "No pain, I mean?"

She shook her head. "Not a thing." She frowned again. "Does that mean I'm dead?"

"I hate to put it this way, Miss Abigail," said Wichita. "But I've never seen anyone survive a wound like that."

She frowned. "Who's going to weed my garden, or get it ready for the next planting season?" She looked across at her two fellow passengers. "If I'm dead, what are you two doing here?"

"Beats me," said Wichita. "Let's have a look." He unbuttoned his black coat and opened it wide, revealing a small, neat hole.

"There you go," said Bradshaw. "One shot, right through the heart."

"Damn!" muttered Wichita. "How about you? You're not wearing a coat, and I don't see any holes in you."

"I'd love to think I got on this here coach by mistake, but I don't suppose it stops for the wrong passengers," said Bradshaw.

"Turn and face out the window," suggested Abigail. "No, not just your head. Your whole body."

"Yep, there it is," said Wichita. "You've been backshot."

"Just my luck," said Bradshaw bitterly. "Now I don't even know who to come back and haunt."

Wichita stared at Abigail for a long moment. "I have enormous respect for you, Miss Abigail," he said at last. "Me and Ben here, we're not surprised to be on this coach, or at least we shouldn't be. We live with death every day, and there's no such thing as an old gunfighter, or even a middle-aged one. But *you*, Miss Abigail—I just admire the way you're taking this, not turning a hair and just worrying about what'll happen to your garden."

"I loved that garden," she replied. "I never had a husband or children, so everything I had went into it."

Bradshaw reached over and gently patted her hand. "I wish there was something we could do, ma'am."

"I appreciate the thought," she said, "but it's a little late to worry about it."

They rode in silence, each lost in their own thoughts, for a few miles. Then Wichita spoke up.

"I always thought one of the advantages of being dead was that I wouldn't be so all-fired hungry all the time—but could I trouble you for another muffin, Miss Abigail?"

"Try this instead," she said, handing him a piece of bread.

"Thank you kindly," he said, taking a bite. He chewed thoughtfully, and got a puzzled expression on his face. "It tastes like there was something sweet mixed into the batter. It's sort of half bread and half cake."

"I'm very proud of it," she replied.

"What's it made of?"

She smiled. "If I told you, then it wouldn't be my own any more, would it?"

"No," he agreed, returning her smile, "I guess it wouldn't."

It seemed to them that the horses had picked up speed, and had been galloping for miles. Then, finally, they started slowing down.

"I was wondering if those horses *ever* got tired," remarked Bradshaw.

"Ain't tired," announced the driver. "Got one last passenger to pick up."

"*Him?*" said Wichita, looking out the window as the figure came into view. "Never expected to see him here this soon."

"Who is it?" asked Abigail.

"Apache Jack Keller," answered Wichita.

"I don't believe I've ever heard of him," she said.

"He's a white man who grew up with the Apaches, ma'am," said Bradshaw. "Fought for Victorio and Geronimo for a few years, then turned in his feathers for a ten-gallon Stetson, and his bow and arrows for a pair of six-guns. He's sent a lot of Indians and a lot of white men off to meet this stagecoach or one of its sisters."

The coach came to a stop, and Apache Jack Keller climbed aboard. He tipped his hat to Abigail, offered her a "Howdy, ma'am," and seated himself next to her. "Well, sure looks like it's Bloody Ben and the Kid from Wichita," he said. "Never expected to find you both on the same stagecoach."

"How are you doing, Jack?" said Bradshaw.

"Not too well, evidently, or I wouldn't be sharing this ride with you," replied Keller with a laugh. "I took quite a while dying—and they always told me that Billy One-Eye was a dead shot."

"Then you know what this coach is?"

"Yeah, can't spend that long dying and not know." He called up to the driver. "Howdy, friend. What do we call you?"

"Scratch'll do," was the answer. The driver tipped his hat, showing off his horns.

"Now wait a minute!" said Bradshaw. "That's got to be wrong."

"You don't think you've done enough sinning to get in?" asked Keller with a smile.

"I done my share and then some, and so have you two," replied Bradshaw. "But Miss Abigail shouldn't be on this here stagecoach. There's been a serious mistake."

"No, Ben," she said. "I belong here."

"I don't believe it!" said Bradshaw.

"It *is* kind of hard to imagine, a nice, proper, well-mannered lady like you," added Wichita.

"It happened a long time ago," said Abigail. "My sister was very much in love with a young man, who betrayed and humiliated her. It broke her heart, so I got a gun and broke *his*. Literally." She sighed. "He had so many enemies that they never even considered that I might have been the one who killed him."

"Well, if you did it, ma'am," said Bradshaw, "I'm sure he deserved it."

He turned to Keller. "You at all hungry, Jack? She's packed some of the tastiest vittles you've ever encountered."

"I'd certainly like to try one out, if you're willing, ma'am," said Keller.

She reached into her basket and handed him a pastry.

"Those look even better than the muffins and the biscuits," said Wichita.

"Have one," said Abigail, handing him one. "Here, you too, Ben." She turned to Keller, who'd already bit into his. "How do you like it?"

"It's just about worth dying for, ma'am," he replied. "If the Apaches could cook like this, I'd never have gone back to living with white folks." He smiled. "Except that none of the white folks could cook like this either."

"Thank you," she said. "You almost made me blush."

"Seems a damned shame, pardon my language, ma'am, that no one else'll ever get a chance to partake of your cooking," said Keller.

"You know," said Wichita thoughtfully, "just maybe we can do something about that."

"Where we're going?" scoffed Bradshaw. "They got a lot bigger oven than she needs."

"Probably they do," agreed Wichita. "But maybe I ain't ready to go there yet."

"None of us are," said Bradshaw. "What's that got to do with it?"

"You know," said Keller thoughtfully, "the Kid's got a point." He raised his voice. "Hey, Scratch—stop the stage!"

"Got a full coach," answered Scratch. "Can't handle any more passengers this trip."

"Stop anyway," said Keller.

"This better be important," said Scratch, bringing the coach to a halt. Abigail leaned her head out the window and saw that the horses were snorting smoke, and their eyes glowed like hot coals. "Okay, we're stopped," continued Scratch, who remained perched atop the driver's seat. "Now what's this all about?"

"We're not ready to ride to the end of the line," said Keller.

Scratch uttered an amused laugh. "Hardly anyone is. But that's where you're headed."

"I don't think so," said Wichita.

"Me neither," added Keller. "I think we'll get off up the road a ways."

"Nosir!" snapped Scratch. "Your souls are mine!"

"I should think you'd be a little more reasonable, given all the souls we've already sent your way," said Bradshaw.

"I thank you for them," said Scratch, "but that doesn't change anything."

"So you insist on taking us all the way?" said Keller.

"Absolutely," said Scratch.

"Got a nice spread, have you?"

"Magnificent," replied Scratch. He uttered a harsh chuckle. "You'll see it soon enough."

"Hey, Ben," said Keller, "how did the Earp Brothers wind up owning the Oriental Saloon down in Tombstone?"

"Pretty much the same way Jubal Pickett took over the Crosshatch Ranch," said Bradshaw. "They ran the old owners off."

"And I hear that's how Red Jim McCabe got hold of half the gambling halls in Denver," added Wichita.

"So if we go all the way to the end of the line with you," said Keller, "and we like what we see, why, we just may take it over."

"After all," said Wichita with a smile, "what are you gonna do—kill us?"

"It's out of the question," growled Scratch.

"You'd better think twice about this, Scratch," suggested Wichita.

"Or you're going to see just how much hell we three can raise," added Keller.

"Just remember," said Bradshaw. "We're *already* dead, so what's the worst you can do to us compared to what we can do to you?"

They couldn't see Scratch's face, but they could hear him muttering and grumbling to himself.

"Well?" said Keller after a couple of minutes had passed.

"Just the three of you?" said Scratch. "No members of your gangs?"

"We don't belong to gangs," said Wichita.

"And it's the *four* of us," said Keller.

"*Her* too?" demanded Scratch.

"Especially her," said Bradshaw.

"Hell, if you want a real chippie, I got a few million at home."

"You insult her once more and I'm gonna climb up there and give you a lesson in manners," said Bradshaw. "Now apologize to the lady."

"You're kidding, right?" said Scratch.

"Lean down, look at my face, and tell me if you think I'm kidding."

Scratch emitted a sigh of defeat. "All right, all right. I apologize, lady."

Bradshaw turned to Abigail. "Is that good enough for you, ma'am?"

She nodded an affirmative.

"All right," growled Scratch. "But I'm gonna want something in return."

"We'll take care of it," promised Wichita.

"Will you sign that in blood?"

"We ain't got no blood, remember?" said Bradshaw.

"All right," repeated Scratch. "I'm sick of the sight of you. Where do you want me to let you off?"

"Next wood and water you come to," said Keller.

It took the horses a hard half hour of galloping, but finally they came to a sky-blue river running alongside a grove of tall Cottonwood trees.

"Remember this spot," said Keller, as the four passengers climbed down. "You're going to be stopping here from now on."

"Why would I ever want to see you again?" demanded Scratch.

"Because even the dead get hungry, and we've got ourselves the best cook they've ever encountered, living or dead," answered Wichita.

They used the timber from the Cottonwoods to build the place, and they called the finished way station—with her permission—Miss Abigail's Rest Stop. Given their particular skills they were able to make sure that everyone behaved, and whenever an outsider wandered in, they sent him straight to Scratch's domain as their part of the bargain. They even added a faro table in the back room. And to this day it remains the most popular way station along the route of the hell-bound stagecoach.

STINGERS AND STRANGERS

SEANAN McGUIRE

Passing through Nevada, Westbound on the Southern Pacific Railway, 1931

"So where exactly are we going, city boy?" Frances Brown infused her words with the sort of exaggerated Arizona drawl that she hadn't possessed in years, if ever. That was a danger sign if Jonathan had ever heard one. He raised his head from the papers he'd been reviewing to see Fran lounging bonelessly in her first-class seat, one foot propped against the windowsill and the other tucked underneath her.

"Boggsville, Colorado," said Jonathan. "Do you think there's any possibility I might convince you to stop giving the porters the impression of your being a woman of negotiable virtue?"

"Well, now. That depends." Fran looked thoughtful. "Would I have to stop letting them pay to put their hands down my shirt?"

Jonathan rolled his eyes and went back to his papers, doing his best to shut out the sound of Fran's raucous laughter.

Anyone peeping into their private cabin would have been struck by the sheer improbability of its passengers. Frances Brown was petite, blonde, and dressed like a farmhand, in wide-legged trousers and a button-down shirt. The empty gun belt at her waist was clearly custom-made, the leather worn smooth by years of handling. She wore no pistols. She didn't need to. While the casual observer might not have known how many ways Frances Brown could kill a man, Jonathan did. His respect for her was unflagging whether or not her weapons were in view.

Jonathan Healy, on the other hand, looked like a visiting professor from some East Coast college, the sort of man who'd never seen a farm, much less worked at one. His suit was impeccable brown tweed, only a few shades darker than the sandy wheat blond of his hair. Glasses perched on the bridge of his nose. He sat ramrod-straight in his seat, barely moving as the train bumped and twisted on the track. It was as if he had considered the laws of physics, declared them undignified, and gone back to what he'd been doing before the question was broached. Currently, that involved reading from a stack of papers, scowling as if they had personally offended him.

Fran watched for a few seconds, laughter fading, before she sighed and turned back to the landscape rolling by outside the window. "It's pretty," she said. "I've missed the desert."

"It's hot, uncivilized, and filled with venomous beasts," said Jonathan.

He glanced up just in time to see her wistful smile. It was directed at the world outside the window; she didn't seem to see him looking. "Like I said: pretty."

"Fran..."

"Don't start, city boy. I'm not going back to Arizona. There's nothing there for me. Besides, what would you tell the mice?" Fran turned abruptly back toward him, smiling that sudden, heart-stopping smile of hers. Even after three long years, it still held all the power of the first time. "You know they'd miss me, and they'd never let you have a moment's peace until you came and talked me into coming back."

"That's true," he allowed, once he could find the words. His family's colony of talking rodents was exceedingly fond of Fran. They would be despondent if she took him up on one of his periodic suggestions that she return to her home state.

If he was being completely honest with himself, so would he. And much like the Aeslin mice, who never forgot or truly recovered from losing the people they loved, he feared that he would spend the rest of his life regretting the moment when he'd let her go.

"So talk to me," she commanded, twisting in her seat so that she was facing him rather than the window. "I'm still not clear on what we're doing out here. Not that I don't appreciate the vacation—I do—but it's not every day I wake up to find you outside my room with a train ticket and a suitcase already packed for me."

Rather than answering, Jonathan fished his watch from his pocket and ostentatiously checked the time. "Eleven hours, twenty-three minutes," he said. "Mother will be most disappointed. She was sure you'd ask me by the end of hour nine."

"I have knives," said Fran.

"I have guns," Jonathan countered. "What we're doing here is attempting to determine the reason that the local Apraxis swarms have been moving during their settled season. The local hunters should be able to find them and burn them out, but instead, the hives are being abandoned before anyone can reach them."

"Uh-huh," said Fran. "I'm guessing that's bad?"

"Yes, it's bad," said Jonathan. "The only good thing about an Apraxis hive is that once it's been built, you know where the swarm is."

"Uh-huh. And what's an Apraxis hive?"

"It's—" Jonathan paused. "I'm sorry, Fran. Sometimes I forget you weren't born to this."

"So educate me." Fran shrugged. "I'm a quick study, and as long as there's something I can shoot at the end, I'm a pretty good student, too."

Jonathan laughed. "You are, at that. Very well, then: let me tell you about the Apraxis wasp. First, picture a yellow jacket the size of a shoe."

"My shoe or yours?" she asked.

"Mine."

Fran shuddered. "Pictured."

"Good. Now, give that yellow jacket human intelligence."

"You're messin' with me," Fran said. "There's no such thing as a bug as smart as a person."

"No?" Jonathan raised an eyebrow. "Wouldn't you have said the same about a mouse, once? If you allow for the existence of Aeslin mice, Fran, you have to allow for Apraxis wasps. Sadly, when nature makes room for the one, she also enables the other."

"Well, ain't that about the least pleasant thing you've said to me recently," said Fran flatly. "So we've got smart wasps the size of shoes. What are we going to do? Beat them to death with brooms?"

"I prefer bullets, but yes, that's essentially the plan. Here's the trouble: the Apraxis don't stop at being intelligent. They're memory thieves."

"What do you mean?"

"I mean they lay their eggs in living flesh and, once the host has been consumed by their larvae, they acquire all the memories of the individual who incubated them. They prefer intelligent hosts. It helps to enhance the hive. Make no mistake, Fran: the Apraxis wasp has no concept of 'mercy.' They're killers, plain and simple, and they destroy whatever they touch."

Fran frowned. "Well, then, shouldn't we be thrilled if something's making them pull up camp and move on? We don't want them hanging out where people live, do we?"

"Well, that depends. What would *you* call something that can make a predator this dangerous abandon its territory in what ought to be its nesting season?"

There was a pause while Fran considered her answer. Finally, her expression hardened. "Bad," she said.

"Precisely why we're going to Colorado to investigate. Now. Let's discuss how we're going to handle the threat, shall we?"

Anyone listening outside their cabin for the next few hours would have been horrified by what they heard. Fortunately for the both of them, no one stopped to listen.

A day and a half later, the train pulled away from the Boggsville, Colorado station, leaving the cryptozoologist and the cryptozoologist-in-training standing on the platform with their bags. "Now where?" asked Fran, turning to Jonathan.

"We're going to want to find a place to sleep while we're here," said Jonathan. "I've written to some of the local cryptozoologists and hunters, to find out what they might know about recent events. It may be a while before we hear from them, and that will be easier if Father knows where to forward any mail."

"Boarding house?" asked Fran.

"I'd prefer a hotel, but honestly, I'll take anything with a bed and a door that locks." His satchel bounced in his hand. He looked down at it and sighed. "A door that locks *very well*."

Fran, whose first introduction to the Aeslin mice had been the result of rodent enthusiasm meeting insufficient locks, hid a smile behind her hand. "Well, then, let's go ask the station agent," she said. "He'll be able to point us in the right direction."

Jonathan nodded and let her take the lead, following her off the platform and toward the low-slung shape of the ticket building. In situations like this, where charisma and natural ease with people trumped knowing seventeen ways to incapacitate a basilisk without getting injured, he was more than happy to let her take the lead. He would have been happier to avoid situations like this in the first place, but beggars, as his father often said, couldn't be choosers.

He was still pondering the frustrating nature of the trip when Fran walked back over to him, cheeks flushed with pride. "There's a boarding house downtown," she said. "Owned by a young widow whose husband went and got himself snakebit before their first anniversary. It's reputable, affordable, and they guarantee no spiders in the privy."

"Fifteen minutes in town and you're back to speaking like a native," said Jonathan, shaking his head.

"Speaking like a native gets us better beds," Fran countered. "So does this place sound like it's up to your rarified city standards?"

Jonathan fixed her with a withering look, earning himself a snort of amusement and a patiently raised eyebrow. Finally, he relented and said, "Yes. If you know the way, please, lead on."

Fran laughed all the way out of the station and into the main street of Boggsville. Then her laughter died, replaced by a look of deepening confusion. Turning to Jonathan, she asked, "Is this how Tempe looked to you when you first came to town?"

For a moment he considered lying to her. Then he relented, admitting, "I suspect it was something similar, yes."

"Damn." Fran took another look around the deserted street. The sidewalks were made of unfinished planks; the buildings all looked as if they could use a coat of paint, a scrubbing, and possibly a structural overhaul—preferably before someone managed to fall through a floor. The sky was the color of dishwater, which was the only reason the heat was less than oppressive: it was coming on too close to winter for a true scorcher.

She sighed. "I've been living in the city too long."

Jonathan's hometown of Buckley Township barely qualified as a city by even the most generous of definitions. Still, Jonathan chose not to argue with her. "Can you find this boarding house?"

"In a town this size? I could probably find it without any directions. Since I've got 'em, we'll be there before the scorpions get us." Fran turned on her heel and strode briskly along the wooden sidewalk, leaving Jonathan to sigh and trot after her.

This was going to be one of those trips.

Dust from the street coated their shoes and the lenses of Jonathan's spectacles by the time they reached the modest two-story home that Fran insisted was the boarding house. There was no sign or other indication that they were in the right place. Jonathan stopped on the sidewalk, eyeing the gingham curtains in the window. "Fran…"

"What's the worst thing that can happen?" she asked, with a generous shrug. "If we're in the wrong place, we move along and try somewhere else."

"The worst that can happen? My guess is that the worst possible thing that could happen is that we discover this is where the Apraxis swarms have been moving, and we're about to be consumed by mind-eating wasps in search of new meat for their larvae," said Jonathan.

"See? That's the way to look for the bright side in a situation." Fran stepped forward before he could protest again, rapping her knuckles on the doorframe.

Jonathan sighed as she stepped back into position next to him. "Forward momentum is the only sort you acknowledge, isn't it?"

"It's the only kind I've got," she said, still smiling.

The door opened.

The woman on the other side could have been taken from an illustration in a medieval bestiary, in more ways than one. She was fair-skinned, with enormous green eyes and long blonde hair that made Fran's lighter curls seem garish, like putting fool's gold next to the real thing. Her clothes were demurely cut, as befitted a widow, high at the neck and low at the ankles, but there was nothing demure about the calculation in her eyes. "Can I help you?" she asked.

"We heard you might have a room to let," said Fran, her smile growing broader and more ingratiating. "We'd rather stay in a nice place like this than in a nasty old hotel, and so here we are, come to throw ourselves on your hospitality."

The woman swept her eyes along the length of Fran's trouser-clad form, clearly not approving of what she saw. She turned her gaze on Jonathan and repeated the process, her frown deepening. "Are you nice folks on your honeymoon?"

Jonathan knew the message in her words all too well, having encountered it repeatedly since Fran began her accidental apprenticeship with his family: it was the "no one lives in sin under *my* roof" judgment beginning. Sometimes he claimed Fran was his sister, which worked poorly if it worked at all. Other times, when the hotels were large enough, they simply checked in on their own and worked things out later. Here, at a small boarding house in a smaller town, he couldn't see where either option was going to work.

Fran surprised him by smiling, taking his hand, and saying, "No, we're traveling to California to see my folks. That was the agreement, wasn't it, sugar-pie? We live on the East Coast with his kin, and once every few years, we take the train out to see mine."

Jonathan tried to follow her lead as best he could, saying, "My Frannie gets anxious if she doesn't see her family once in a while, and I prefer she be as tranquil as a mountain stream." From the way her mouth tensed at the edges when he said that, he was going to pay for it later. He was too amused to be particularly concerned.

"Why aren't you wearing rings?" asked the boarding house owner.

Jonathan gritted his teeth, wishing that the woman's eyesight wasn't so keen. "We left them at home," he said.

The woman's eyes narrowed. "What on Earth would make you do a thing like that?"

Once again, Fran came to the rescue. "We don't want to tempt robbers more than we have to," she said. "I mean, my Johnny's not much of a fighter. If we're going to travel, we're going to do it with as few valuables as possible."

The woman sniffed. "That explains your attire as well. I suppose I have a room for the two of you. Payment is expected up front for the first night; you can settle up at breakfast for any nights you choose to stay after that. Meals are included, but they're served when they're served, and you're not to expect me to hold them for you. I'll thank you to wear skirts while you're in my household, and refrain from any harsh language or lewd behavior. I know how you city folk can be."

"Yes, ma'am," said Fran, with such exaggerated politeness that Jonathan knew she had to be seething inside.

"You folks have names?"

"Jonathan and Frances Healy," said Jonathan. Saying the words aloud was almost startling, like he'd been waiting to hear them for years. The pressure of Fran's fingers laced through his was suddenly very distracting. "And you are…?"

"Eleanor Smith," said the woman. "My daughter, Betty, is at her music lesson right now. I'll thank you not to bother her. She's a good girl." Her eyes flicked to Fran, carrying another silent message: *She's a good girl, and you are not.*

"We wouldn't dream of it, ma'am," said Jonathan. "If we could come inside, we'd love to pay for our room and unpack. It's been a quite long trip."

"Well, come in, then," said Mrs. Smith, as if she hadn't been the one blocking the door. She moved to the side, and Jonathan and Fran stepped into the hall.

A short time later, the two of them were safely locked in their second-floor room, Jonathan sitting on the bed and cleaning his pistols while

Fran paced and the mice—freed from their confinement in his satchel—explored the hidden space beneath the bureau.

"That boorish, judgmental, withered old—"

"Princess," Jonathan interjected, before Fran could go any further.

She stopped dead, her boot heels clicking hard against the floor, which wasn't softened by so much as a rug. "I beg your pardon?"

"She's a princess," he said. "What did you observe?"

Fran scowled. "Johnny…"

"I'm quite serious. What did you observe about her?"

"That she's a b—"

"She's young enough to be seeking remarriage, but she's not. Instead, she's wearing dresses that have been mended repeatedly and running a boarding house that's well maintained, meaning it shows a profit, yet has the bare minimum in terms of furniture and comforts. She has a daughter we've been instructed to stay away from, which should only hasten her toward remarriage. And she demanded to be paid up front."

"Not every woman needs a ring on her finger," said Fran.

Was it his imagination, or did she sound a little wistful when she said that? "Not every woman, no, but a woman that attractive, living in a place like this, with a daughter to care for? I managed to brush against her hand as we took the stairs. She's too warm. Not by much, but by enough, when combined with everything else. She's a dragon princess. They're notorious misers, and highly suspicious of strangers, especially where their children are concerned."

Fran stared at him for a moment before sighing and flopping down on the bed next to him. "Christ above, is there *anyone* human left in this world?"

"Most people are human; you simply notice the non-humans more, since they're the ones most likely to cause us trouble." Jonathan picked up a chamois and began wiping the fingerprints from his gun barrel. "You'd best get some rest. We go looking for the missing Apraxis swarms tonight."

"Oh, that's just what I was hoping you'd say." Fran rolled over to prop her chin on her hand. "What all do I need to keep in mind while we're looking for these Apraxis thingies?"

"Don't get stung," Jonathan replied, and resumed cleaning his pistol. "The ovipositor of the female Apraxis is connected to her stinger, and you don't want Apraxis nymphs feeding on your flesh. I'm told it's one of the most painful experiences possible."

"Don't get stung, got it," said Fran. She eyed Jonathan with some concern. "You gonna get any rest before we go out bug-hunting?"

"I'm going to stand guard." Something about Jonathan's tone forbade further argument. Fran looked at him for a few seconds more before rolling over to face the wall, closing her eyes at the same time. Years of traveling with the circus that raised her had served her well: she was asleep almost immediately.

Jonathan waited until her breathing leveled out before setting his pistol aside and sliding off the bed. He crossed to the bureau, where he knelt and murmured, "The Violent Priestess is asleep."

The mice, who understood the human need for sleep, were quiet as they crept into the open and looked at him with expectant oil-drop eyes. The colony's head priest stepped forward, and asked, in a squeak, "What would you have us do, O Lord?"

"Scatter," Jonathan said, without hesitation. He had long since adapted to the Aeslin tendency to view him as some sort of god, and was content to use it to his own benefit when necessary. "Search. Look for any sign of what moves the wasps. Do not be seen. This is important. We don't know where the Apraxis are; we don't know who they may have infected. If you are seen, you may not return to the colony. Do you understand me?"

"We hear, and understand," intoned the priest.

"Good," said Jonathan. "Now go. Find the wasps."

The mice scattered, vanishing under the bureau. A few seconds later, Jonathan heard the distinctive sound of tiny feet inside the walls. He nodded to himself, satisfied, and returned to his place on the bed, picking up his pistol. Let Fran sleep, for now. He had much to do before the sun went down, and time was not on their side.

Fran woke to find Jonathan standing over her with her gun belt in one hand, and a piece of wood wrapped in strips of cotton in the other. She sat up, squinting at him. "You planning to bash my head in with that thing?" she asked.

"No; I'm fond of your skull in its present configuration. If we're unfortunate enough to find an Apraxis hive, I'm going to set it on fire. Are you ready to go?"

"Just let me hit the privy and rinse my mouth out, and I'm all yours." Fran leaned forward and grabbed her boots. "Anything I need to know?"

"The mice are surveying the town; I've sent a telegram to Father with the boarding house address, but I haven't heard anything back from him yet. I don't expect to for some time, all things considered. For right now, assume we're on our own."

"Aw, city boy." Fran's smile was sharp and sudden. "That's always how I've done my best work." She pulled her boots on and stood, heading for the door. Jonathan followed her. At the bottom of the stairs, she turned toward the hall, while he proceeded into the parlor. Cheapness of the furnishings aside, the boarding house was equipped with indoor plumbing, for which Jonathan was grateful; the last thing he wanted to do with Apraxis wasps in the area was lock himself in an outhouse. Some risks were necessary. Others were simply foolish.

Mrs. Smith was sitting on the couch when Jonathan walked into the parlor. She frowned at the sight of the makeshift torch in his hand, and frowned more when she saw the pistols at his waist. "I don't tolerate late nights or carousing," she said.

"We're not planning on any carousing, and I promise, it is our intent to be safe in bed before the night can be considered 'late,'" said Jonathan.

Her frown deepened. She stood. "Are you sassing me, young man?"

"No, ma'am." The trouble with dragon princesses was their vulnerability: they were essentially human women in all the ways that counted, now that the great dragons they had evolved alongside were gone. That made them suspicious and unfriendly when confronted with anything that looked as if it might threaten them.

But they were also targets for the Apraxis. Jonathan looked at the woman in front of him, with her business and her child to protect, and made a decision.

"My wife and I haven't been entirely honest with you, ma'am," he said.

She sniffed. "That's no surprise."

"We're entomologists. We collect exotic insects from around the world. We heard that you had a wasp problem here, and we thought it might be worth investigating."

Her eyes widened. "If you're here about that, then you're damn fools."

"No, ma'am. We're well-equipped fools, who'd like to remove a threat to you and yours from this town. I just have to ask that you not tell anyone about our comings and goings." Jonathan continued to meet her eyes. "If you know anything about strange disappearances or unusual insect sightings, that information would be useful as well, but really, all we're asking for is a little discretion while we resolve a problem and further our careers."

"What's in it for me?"

"Beyond the removal of the danger? We'll happily pay double for any night when we leave the building after sunset."

He could all but see the equations running in her eyes. Finally, she said, "Fine. If the two of you want to risk your lives on a fool's errand, it's no skin off my nose. But if you're not back by dawn, whatever you've brought with you is mine—I won't hold a dead man's things a minute longer than I have to. It's bad luck."

"I would never ask you to," said Jonathan.

"And don't you dare lead those things back here. I run a respectable establishment."

The idea of "respectable establishment" being determined by whether or not your place of business was regularly attacked by mind-eating wasps was almost ludicrous enough to make Jonathan laugh out loud. He managed to suppress the urge, replying only, "I promise you, we have no intention of leading them anywhere, save perhaps into a killing jar."

Mrs. Smith sniffed, and said nothing. They were still looking at each other when Fran came down the hall, wiping her hands together. She stopped, looking between the two.

"Am I interrupting?" she asked.

"No," said Jonathan. "We were just leaving. Good night, Mrs. Smith."

"Good night," said the dragon princess stiffly.

Jonathan and Fran turned toward the door. Before they could reach it, however, it was opened by someone on the other side, and a young girl—no more than six or seven, with hair the color of sun-bleached corn silk—walked into the room, followed by a woman in her early twenties. Jonathan froze.

The woman was the most beautiful thing he had ever seen, and somehow, he knew that he had known her all his life.

Her hair was black; her eyes were blue; her skin was paler than it should have been, given the desert where she lived and her lack of a bonnet. But none of that mattered. What mattered was that she was looking at him, a smile on her lips, and asking him a question.

Fran's elbow introduced itself roughly to his side. Jonathan snapped back to reality, and realized he hadn't heard a single thing anyone in the room had said since the door was opened. "I—I beg your pardon," he stammered. "Jonathan Healy, at your service. This is—"

"I'm his wife," said Fran, with a thin smile. "Frances Healy, at your service."

"It's lovely to meet you," said the black-haired woman. "My name is Heloise Tapper. I'm Betty's music instructor."

The little girl gave the woman a besotted smile before curtseying to Jonathan and Fran. "It's nice to meet you."

"It's nice to meet you, too, Betty," said Fran. "Your mama's been real sweet to us, but now we have to be going. We've got some sights to see before the night gets too far along. Isn't that right, *dear*?"

Jonathan didn't reply. Fran elbowed him again. He jumped, barely aware that he'd been staring at Heloise, and said, "Yes, yes, of course. We must be going. I do hope we'll see you again, Miss Tapper?"

Heloise smiled. "You can be sure of it," she said.

"Must be going," said Fran, and all but dragged Jonathan out of the boarding house. Even as he stumbled down the steps he was looking back over his shoulder, toward the door, where Heloise stood outlined by the light like a paper cutout.

Jonathan was walking on his own by the time they reached the main street. Fran glanced over, assessed the bewildered look on his face, and continued dragging him along. He pulled away after they turned a corner, putting the boarding house out of view. Fran stopped.

"What was that about?" he asked.

"Funny; I could be asking you the same question," she shot back. "I thought we were here hunting giant death bugs, not so you could make eyes at some black-haired lady who ain't never seen the sunlight. Or is this what you do every time you go out to the desert?"

"What?" Jonathan looked at her blankly. "What in the world are you talking about?"

"I suppose I should expect it. Last time you came to the desert, you brought me home with you. It's past time you went out and got yourself a new pet project. Can't say as I think she'll be half as good with a gun as I am, but hell, maybe you don't like girls who can outshoot you. I swear, Jonathan Healy, you are the most arrogant, idiotic—"

He clapped his hand over her mouth, cutting her off in mid-sentence. Fran's eyes widened, filling first with confusion, and then with the sort of fury he really preferred to see directed as far away from himself as possible.

"Shh," he whispered, before she could pull away or, worse, bite him. "You can be furious later. Right now, *listen*."

Fran glared at him, but relaxed against his hand, doing as he asked.

Then her eyes widened. He pulled his hand away, nodding. Fran nodded back, and the two of them started down the street, moving toward the sound of buzzing wings.

Jonathan's chest tightened as the source of the buzzing came into view ahead of them: the train station. It made sense. The station was the largest standing building in town and, if something was truly upsetting the swarm, it also afforded the most opportunities for a rapid escape. He'd never heard of Apraxis migrating by train before, but he'd never heard of them moving during their settled season, either. If the one could happen, the other also became plausible.

He led Fran up the station steps in silence, wishing he could make her fully understand the scope of the threat. Apraxis wasps were smart. If they'd just been killers, they would have been a horror and a threat, but they wouldn't have been half so dangerous. As it was, he was leading Fran into a building containing an unknown number of flying opponents with human-level intelligence and inborn weaponry.

It was almost enough to make a man rethink his choice of profession.

"Fran, if you don't want to go inside, I would quite understand. You're still an apprentice, and it would be unfair of me to ask you to endanger yourself in this fashion."

"Are you joshing me, city boy?" Knives appeared in Fran's hands, no doubt pulled from somewhere in the lining of her coat. He had long since given up all pretense of knowing how many weapons she carried at any given time. It seemed safer to admit ignorance until she started calling for backup. "You drag me halfway across the country and make me share a house with the Wicked Bitch of the West, and then you try to keep me out of the *interesting* part? You know me well enough to know *that's* not going to work."

"And you know *me* well enough to know that I have to offer," said Jonathan, pulling his own pistol from his belt. "Very well, then. If we're both set on risking our lives before midnight, we'd best get on with it. The clock isn't going to stop while we argue. There are, however, a few rules."

"When aren't there?" Fran asked.

The look he gave her then was so uncharacteristically serious that she quieted, a small frown forming on her lips. "Will you listen?"

"Yes, sir," she replied, all levity gone.

"Thank you. First, you stay behind me. It's not simply a matter of my trying to cover for you—Apraxis often attack from the rear, and we're going to need the cover if we're going inside. So stay behind me, and watch my back. In exchange, I'll watch yours. Agreed?"

"Agreed."

"Second, if I say run, you run. Don't take one more shot. Don't decide that I'm being overly cautious. *Run.* I've seen what the Apraxis do to their victims. You haven't." With any luck, she never would. With even more luck, he never would again.

"Anything else?"

Jonathan sighed. "Please try not to die. There aren't any convenient circuses to steal a replacement trick rider from."

"I'll keep breathing if you'll do the same, city boy," said Fran.

"It's a deal," said Jonathan, with a brief-lived smile. Then he began advancing on the train station, his pistol held ready. This time, Fran followed him, not into the streets of Boggsville, but into Hell itself.

Night and darkness had transformed the station from a bright, airy building into a cavern filled with suspicious shadows and sounds that had no obvious source. The buzzing was constant, so loud it seemed impossible that the entire town wasn't coming to investigate. Fran crept along at Jonathan's heels, and decided that anyone who was still alive and living in Boggsville must have learned to ignore the buzzing, because to do anything else was to deal with the question of its source.

Jonathan continued forward until they reached the middle of the station's main waiting room, where the sound was at its loudest. He stopped there, gesturing for Fran to do the same. She nodded and turned, locking her shoulders against his back. Then, and only then, did the pair look up toward the rafters, and the sound of thousands of wings beating in unison.

It took a moment for their eyes to process what was in front of them. The ceiling seemed to be pulsing, like it was breathing in time with the humming of the wings. Jonathan's mouth went dry. It was a living curtain of bodies—some small, proving that the Apraxis were continuing to breed, while others were almost a foot in length, wasps grown far past the point which Nature intended. The only mercy of the scene was that the darkness sapped the brilliance from their colors, turning them into gray-banded shadows. Seeing them in the light would just have made it clearer that they were never intended to exist.

He felt, rather than heard, Fran's indrawn breath. There was no need to motion her to be quiet; she knew as well as he did what would happen if they baited the apparently sleeping beasts above them. The wasps must have taken shelter in the train station for the night. They would remain there until morning, unless startled. Slowly, Jonathan reached back with his free hand and gestured toward the door. He and Fran needed to exit. Reconnaissance was complete: the hive existed, and could be tracked. Now it was time to decide what to do about it.

A normal Apraxis hive would contain ten to thirty individuals. When he'd heard the sound of wings, he'd believed that was what they were moving toward: a single hive, ready to be examined and exterminated. He hadn't been expecting to discover all the missing hives from the area clustered together in a single place, apparently united against whatever had caused them to move.

Fran nodded, once, before starting to walk back toward the door. Jonathan matched her steps, trusting her to guide him out. He didn't want to turn around; he didn't want to do anything that might risk his losing sight of the pulsing mass that was the hive for even an instant.

They were almost out when a rock hit the station window. The sound echoed through the room like a crude imitation of a gunshot. The buzzing stopped a split-second later, like the monstrous wasps were holding their breath in anticipation.

"Run," whispered Jonathan.

Frances ran.

Jonathan ran after her, and behind him came the roar of wings as hundreds of Apraxis wasps launched themselves from the ceiling and swept down upon the perceived threat to their hive. Fran reached the door first, grabbing for the knob. It refused to turn.

"The door's locked!" she shouted, all pretense of stealth abandoned.

"Find a way to unlock it," Jonathan snapped back, before turning, pulling the second pistol from his belt, and opening fire on the descending swarm.

The first several Apraxis to dive toward him were greeted with bullets which shattered their fragile exoskeletons and sent them careening to the floor. The next wave veered off, choosing to attack from the sides instead. He shot three of them down. The fourth encountered a hastily-flicked knife as Fran caught the motion out of the corner of her eye. All the wasps they hit went down. But there were more—so many more—and their weapons were limited.

The third wave paused in their attack, hovering overhead and moving in a complicated interweaving pattern, like a deck of cards being shuffled by a pair of skillful hands. Jonathan tried tracking them with his pistols, and found that he couldn't keep a single wasp in his sights; they were moving too fast. He might hit one or more if he fired into the body of the swarm—they were tightly packed enough to make that possible—but he might also miss entirely, and bring the full weight of their wrath down on his head.

"Frances, if you're taking your time out of a misguided respect for the property of others, this is the time when you stop being considerate and start smashing things," he said, out of the corner of his mouth.

"I'm trying," she hissed back.

The swarm overhead was beginning to dip lower, still moving in that complicated, coordinated pattern. It was almost hypnotic in its way, like watching fire consume a log. Jonathan blinked, trying not to let himself be mesmerized by the swirling sea of wings and bodies. He didn't dare look away. Looking away would be an invitation to the end.

"Fran—"

"Almost…" There was a loud splintering sound. "Got it!" Then the door was shoved open, and she was dragging him out into the night, away from the swarm. Fearing the escape of their prey, the Apraxis dove. Too late; Jonathan and Fran were already outside. The wasps pulled up short at the threshold of the station. Then they vanished back up into the rafters, leaving only the steady drone of wings to mark their presence.

Jonathan, who had half-fallen against Fran, got back to his feet. "Well," he said, re-holstering his pistols before removing his glasses and wiping them against the front of his shirt. "That was bracing."

"Is that normal for giant demon wasp things?" asked Fran. She moved to stand beside him. Her knives were already gone, vanished back into her clothing.

"Not in the slightest. We should be dead now." Jonathan replaced his glasses. "They won't leave the building. Enough Apraxis to kill everyone in this town, and they're hiding in a single defensible location."

"Meaning what?" asked Fran.

The look Jonathan gave her then was enough to make her blood run cold. "Meaning there's something out here that the Apraxis are afraid of."

"See, I was really worried that you were going to say that." Fran looked back to the doorway. "Now what?"

Jonathan didn't have an immediate answer.

* * *

"Things don't add up," said Jonathan an hour later, as he sat on the edge of their shared bed, flipping one more time through his father's notes. "Apraxis wasps depend on swarm intelligence. Collectively, they know everything that any of their victims knew. Depending on the size and complexity of the swarm, they can have the intelligence and memories of hundreds of humans. Swarms have even been known to exchange members when they were missing information that they thought might be beneficial."

"What does that have to do with anything?" Fran continued oiling her knives, testing their edges one by one before sliding them back into their sheaths.

"A healthy Apraxis swarm isn't afraid of *anything*, because the lives of individuals matter only when the swarm is reduced to the point where they risk losing vital information. This swarm is a… a collective. They're not at risk of losing anything. So why would they refuse to leave the station?" He threw the notes down in disgust. "They have no natural predators. They have no known illnesses. Their behavior makes no *sense*."

"Now hold on there, Johnny. I think you're missing something."

Jonathan looked toward her. "How so?"

"When we met, you didn't know that there were Questing Beasts in Arizona, and I didn't know that there were talking mice in Michigan," said Fran. "An' neither one of us knew that there were little green snakes with wings living in Indiana."

"They're a sub-species of coatl," said Jonathan. His interjection lacked heat; he was already getting the distant look that meant he was considering the implications of her words.

"Whatever they are, they're little green snakes with wings that no one knew existed. So how about you stop saying the giant wasps have no natural predators, and tack on a weasely little 'that we know of'? Then all we have to do is look around until we know what we have to shoot. Besides the several hundred giant death wasps."

"Frances Brown, you're a genius." Jonathan was suddenly on his feet and heading for the door, leaving Fran to blink bemusedly after him.

"Was it something that I said?" she asked, of no one in particular.

Jonathan's pounding brought Eleanor Smith to her bedroom door, the high collar of her dressing gown clutched tight around her neck. Her eyes widened when she saw him, and she stepped out into the hall, closing her door—but not before he could see the mound of gold chains and ore covering her mattress.

"I don't have time for pretty pretense or lying to you," he said, cutting off her protests before they could begin. "I am here to find out what is upsetting the Apraxis hives and endangering lives in this town, including yours and your daughter's. As I have no idea how to contact the local bogeyman community, any information I acquire will have to come from you. Now: when did this start?"

Eleanor stared at him, open-mouthed, for several seconds. Then she lifted her head, took a breath, and said, "I'm sure I don't have any idea what you're—"

"You're a dragon princess," he said. "Your species used to live symbiotically with the great dragons, until they became extinct. You've been hiding amongst the humans ever since. I'm not here to endanger you, but I'm not going to allow you to lie to me, either. There's too much at stake."

"Mama?" Betty's voice was sleepy. Her head appeared around the edge of the door as she rubbed at one wide blue eye with the heel of her hand. "Hello, Mr. Healy."

"Hello, Betty." He looked back to Eleanor. "I know it's got to be hard for you to be here without a Nest to help keep you safe. I truly have no intention of making things harder. But I need to know when the Apraxis started behaving like this."

"Go back to bed, Betty," said Eleanor, and gave her daughter a gentle nudge back into the room. "I'll be in soon." She closed the door again. Her eyes all but spat fire as she said, "If you're lying, I'll see you hanged for casting aspersions on my character."

"Ma'am, unless Colorado is a strange state indeed, 'the Widow Smith isn't human' is less casting aspersions and more a sign of insanity on my part. Still, I'd be grateful for anything you could tell us. We saw the swarm tonight, and it was…"

"Bigger than you thought it'd be?" Eleanor chuckled mirthlessly. "If I had a penny for every man who's ever said that—I'd still be running this boarding house. Where'd you leave your wife? I don't want you people asking me questions more than once."

"She's in our room," said Jonathan. He wasn't going to correct her about Fran not being his wife. Eleanor had just admitted she wasn't human; he wasn't going to make her cope with the idea of unmarried couples sharing a bed beneath her roof. Besides, he wasn't sure how he was going to cope with that either, once the time for sleep arrived. "Come with me."

Fran was cross-legged on the floor when he returned to the room, with Eleanor close behind him. The mice were clustered in front of her in a semi-circle, apparently in the middle of a report. They froze when the door opened. When she saw the mice, Eleanor did the same.

"There are vermin in my home," she announced, in the calm, overly measured tone of a woman who was deciding how loudly it would be appropriate to scream.

"They're with us," said Fran. "Mice, y'all say hello to Mrs. Smith. This is her place we're staying at."

"HAIL, MRS. SMITH, OWNER OF THE PLACE!" piped the mice obligingly.

Eleanor's expression transformed from horror into simple disgust. "Oh," she said. "They're *Aeslin* mice."

"Yes, ma'am," said Jonathan, closing the door behind her as she finally stepped into the room. "We're sorry we didn't mention them when we were checking in, but I'm sure you can see where the topic would have been difficult to raise."

"I don't allow pets anyhow," said Eleanor. She folded her arms, looking from Jonathan to Fran. "You wanted to ask me about the wasps. So ask."

"My question is the same as it was before: when did this behavior begin? Apraxis swarms shouldn't be moving this time of year, much less grouping together. There's no recorded reason for this behavior."

"It started about three months ago," said Eleanor. "There'd always been reports of large insects in the canyons and the hills, but they mostly didn't bother you if you didn't bother them. We had a few ranchers and prospectors go missing every year or so." She didn't need to say the words "no great loss"; her tone conveyed it for her. "Then the sightings started getting closer to town, and not long after that, folks started to disappear."

"And the more people vanished, the larger the swarms became," ventured Jonathan.

"You'd think, but it was almost the opposite for a while. It was like they were takin' people just to keep their numbers up. We kept finding these bits of broken wing in the street. Something's been killing them.

Or was—it stopped a few weeks back. It hasn't been safe to walk out alone since then."

"Thanks for stopping us from going out," said Fran. "Or trying, anyway."

"I can't stop the suicidal from doing what they will," said Eleanor. "Anyway, the swarms started grouping together about then. I suppose it's their way of defending themselves."

"No matter how good a predator is, it would have to be foolish to cross a swarm the size of the one we saw tonight," Jonathan agreed. "Did anyone new arrive about the time the swarms changed their behavior?"

"New people come and go all the time around these parts," said Eleanor.

"Anyone who stood out?" pressed Jonathan. "Maybe someone who asked questions that made you uncomfortable, or seemed overly interested in the wasps?"

"You mean like the two of you?" asked Eleanor sweetly.

"How about somebody who didn't stand out," said Fran, saving Jonathan from the need to come up with a response. "Was there anybody who showed up and did their best to keep a low profile? Maybe tried to stay out of sight?"

"Yes," said Eleanor. "Wait—no. Wait... I don't know." She blinked, looking perplexed. "Why don't I know? I know everything that goes on around here. I make it my business to know. Why don't I know?"

"Mrs. Smith, take a deep breath and think back to when the wasps began to change their behavior," said Jonathan. His voice was suddenly soothing. "What else changed around then? Anything at all, no matter how small it might seem, could tell us where we need to start looking."

"Well, there was a good barley crop. We had the harvest festivals about then, put out the usual offerings of offal and ground bone meal for the chupacabra and the black dogs in the hills. Betty started taking music lessons. I had a lodger who ran out without paying for his last two nights—"

"Wait," said Fran. "Back up a bit. Why didn't Betty start music lessons until this past fall?"

"There was no music teacher," said Eleanor automatically. Then she paused, blinking. "But that can't be right. Miss Heloise has been here for years."

"Except for the part where she wasn't here before this past fall," said Jonathan. He looked to Fran. "I suppose it's time we go have a talk about music lessons, and why someone decided to lock us in the train station."

The mice cheered.

"Do dragon ladies have memory troubles?" asked Fran, as she and Jonathan walked down the main street toward the music teacher's house.

"Dragon princesses, and no," said Jonathan. "They're usually quite canny. They have to be, if they want to survive without the dragons to protect them."

"Never had a dragon to protect me," said Fran. "I find a sufficient number of knives handles the situation nicely."

Jonathan smiled. "Yes, Fran, but you're one of a kind." He might have said more, had they not found themselves standing at their destination.

Miss Heloise Tapper's music studio was tucked into a storefront off the main street. From the light in the window overhead, she lived and worked in the same place. Jonathan produced a length of wire from inside his vest and bent over the lock. A moment later, the latch opened with a click, and he nudged the door open with the toe of his boot.

"I love it when you break the law," murmured Fran.

"Shh," Jonathan replied, and stepped inside, moving as quietly as possible. Fran followed. They automatically fanned out, putting a space of about three feet between their bodies. Then they stopped, both frowning as they tried to make sense of the empty room around them.

Finally, Fran asked, "Shouldn't there be some kind of... I don't know... music stuff here?"

"You'd think." Jonathan touched his temple, looking perplexed. "This is very odd..."

"Sweetheart?" Heloise Tapper's voice was followed by the appearance of Heloise herself on the stairs. She was wearing a dressing gown, and looked ever-so-slightly rumpled, like she'd just gotten out of bed. "Did you catch the intruder?"

Jonathan's hand dropped away from his temple. His pistol was suddenly in his hand, aimed at a wide-eyed Fran. "Yes, dear," he replied. He scowled at Fran. "You'd best be prepared to face constabulary justice, young woman."

"Oh, swell, she's a mind-scrambler. You couldn't have said somethin' about that?" Fran's own guns appeared in her hands, drawn almost too fast to follow. One was aimed at Jonathan; the other at Heloise, who looked startled, and not a little angry.

"Young woman, you are being *rude*," she snapped.

"Don't reckon so, but I'll take that under advisement," said Fran. "What in tarnation are *you*? Some kind of super-wasp? You're prettier, but I don't see as you're any nicer. Now get the hell out of Johnny's head, or it's not going to end well for anybody in this room. Deep down, he knows that I'm the faster shot, no matter what you've done to him."

Heloise pressed a hand to her chest. "What makes you think *I've* done something?"

"Because he's holding a gun on me, and that's not something my Johnny'd do."

"Ah." Heloise dropped her hand, eyes narrowing. "Now the question is, why isn't it working on you?"

"I don't know. Maybe 'cause I'm too damn stubborn to be mind-scrambled." Fran cocked back the hammer of the pistol aimed at Heloise. "Let him go."

"Make me," Heloise snapped.

"Suit yourself," said Fran, and fired. Jonathan pulled his own trigger half a heartbeat later.

Fran's bullet flew clean and true, catching Heloise in the breast. It should have pierced her heart; it should have taken her down in an instant. Instead, the music teacher screeched wordless fury before turning and running up the stairs. Jonathan's aim was a little less clean, perhaps because he didn't actually want to kill Fran; his bullet hit her right shoulder, knocking her back a step. She shouted, bringing both guns to bear on him.

"Johnny, don't you make me shoot you," she half-begged. "I don't want to shoot you. You know that, don't you?"

"You shot my wife," he snarled.

"What is it about this town and you and fake wives?" demanded Fran. "She's not your fake wife, I am! You don't have a wife, you idiot!"

There was a flicker of confusion in Jonathan's eyes. "I don't know what you're talking about," he said, shaking it off. "Heloise and I—"

"Johnny, *I love you.*"

Jonathan froze. "What?"

"You think I stuck around your house for the past three years because I was bored? Any circus in this country'd be glad to have me, and your monster-hunting's fun, but it ain't everything. I stayed for *you*. I love *you*. Don't you let some cheap Snow White-lookin' bitch make all that work be for nothing."

"I…" Jonathan shook his head, like he was trying to get rid of something buzzing in his ear. "I…"

"Aw, hell." The buzzing wasn't just in Jonathan's ears: Fran could hear it too, and it was getting closer. "Hate to stop there, but think you can shake off your delusions long enough to play shooting gallery with me? I think we're about to have company."

And the Apraxis burst through the window, cutting off all further conversation.

It was the sort of battle better described than lived through. Jonathan and Fran wound up backed against the wall, shooting down as many wasps as they could—Jonathan's aim was better, Fran fired faster, and the swarm was packed so tightly that neither had the advantage—before the bullets ran out. Fran began flinging knives, while Jonathan looked frantically for an escape route.

There was a single interior door. It might lead to a dead end. It was their only chance.

"This way!" he shouted, and grabbed her hand, hauling her behind him as he ran. For her part, Fran was glad to go. The wasps were starting to get past her defenses, and their stingers burned like pokers when they pierced her skin.

The door led into the shop's small kitchen. Fran slammed it shut, listening to the dull impacts of Apraxis wasps against the wood. "What the hell is going on in this town? I do *not* approve!"

"No one does." Jonathan stepped away from the door. "Fran, help me look for things to burn."

"Oh, so I'm Fran again, am I? Not the wife-shooter? Because I was—" Her words were cut off by his mouth slamming down against hers, kissing her with all the intensity of a decade of frustrated waiting. After a split-second of shock, she kissed him back, just as fervently. Then she pulled away, slapped him across the face, and started rummaging through Miss Tapper's shelves.

"I suppose I deserved that," said Jonathan, grinning a little, and followed her.

In a matter of minutes, they had piled every flammable thing they could find in front of the door, liberally dousing them with lamp oil, kerosene, and cooking fat. "Johnny?"

"Yes?"

"We gonna die?"

"Oh, quite probably. Fran?"

"Yes?"

"Will you marry me?"

"Oh." Fran blinked, and then smiled at him, radiant as the sun coming out. "Quite probably. Now light that match, city boy, and let's have us a bonfire."

The flames were just starting to consume the door when Jonathan heaved a chair through the kitchen window. He and Fran tumbled out into the street, landing in a heap amidst the broken glass and dirt. They heard footsteps.

It was really no surprise when they looked up to see the town sheriff standing there, gun drawn.

"I suppose we're under arrest," said Jonathan wearily.

"You suppose correct," said the sheriff.

The town was small enough that there was only one jail cell, which they were allowed to share after they swore, again, that they were married. Jonathan had managed to beg a pair of tweezers and some gauze, insisting that it would be easier than waking the doctor. Fran sat on the bench in front of him, shirt bunched around her shoulders, wincing as he dug the tiny Apraxis eggs out of her flesh. The gunshot wound in her shoulder was already wrapped in a thick layer of bandages.

"What'n the hell happened back there?" she asked, as quietly as she could.

"That Tapper woman—whatever she was—she scrambled my head," Jonathan said. "I remembered being with her for years. I remembered our *wedding*."

"So how'd you break out of it?"

Jonathan extracted another egg from Fran's arm. "You mustn't laugh."

"Johnny, right now, I'm not in a laughing mood."

"I couldn't remember a single mouse ritual having to do with her. That simply wasn't believable. And then you were there, and you... I remembered the mice celebrating *you*."

Fran laughed.

"You promised."

"City boy, no one could hear that without laughing." Fran grimaced as he removed another egg, and then asked, "So why did she scare the wasps so bad?"

"She manipulated my memory. Apraxis colonies are nothing *but* memory. To them, she must have seemed like the greatest predator the world had ever created. If she could do to them what she did to me…"

"Well, isn't she a great neighbor? Remind me to hate her a little more." Fran was quiet for a minute. "Did you mean that back there?"

"Yes. Although not until we get home. My parents would murder me if we got married in a Colorado jail." Jonathan paused. "Assuming you meant your acceptance?"

"Only took you three years."

"Touching as this is, I'd like you to leave." They turned to see Eleanor Smith standing outside their cell, hands clutched primly in front of her. "Your bail's been posted, and since it seems you burned down an unoccupied building, you're free to go."

"But what about—"

"Most of the town doesn't remember her. I suspect I only do because I've been paying for music lessons." Eleanor's mouth pursed. "She never taught Betty a note. Now come collect your things—including your vermin—and go."

"Why are you doing this?" asked Fran, pulling her shirt back into position. "It seems awfully nice of you."

"I don't like you," said Eleanor. "I liked the wasps even less, and the ones that didn't burn to death seem to have left. Good job. Now go."

"Thank you," said Jonathan. He stood, helping Fran to her feet. Eleanor turned, waving to someone. The sheriff appeared a moment later to unlock the cell.

Leaning on each other, battered, bloodied, and feeling oddly victorious, Jonathan and Frances limped out of the jail and into the blazing, wasp-free light of the Colorado dawn. There would be research to do, and the question of what the Tapper woman had been would need to be resolved, but for now, they were alive, they were free, and they were finally together.

Perhaps, Jonathan thought, trips west weren't so bad after all.

He kept the thought to himself.

BOOKKEEPER, NARRATOR, GUNSLINGER

CHARLES YU

Lost Springs, Wyoming, 1890

It starts as a twitch.

Or that's what I thought it was. At first.

A jitter in my thumb. Then it's in my wrist, a jolt of energy running up my arm. All at once, too fast to know exactly where it had come from. *There it is,* I would start to think, but it was over before I had finished the thought, and there I was, gun in hand, smoke weeping from the barrel. Forty paces in front of me, a dead man in the dirt. He never had any idea it was coming. That made two of us: I was as surprised as he was.

I'd never been known as fast before, never been a man other men knew to steer clear of. Every now and then, a new gun would ride into town, preceded by his reputation, infamous for being mean and quick. And when these troublemakers came through, most of the other gunfighters, myself included, well, what can I say? There was a lot more of us looking down at our boots, or off toward the painted, bloodshot red mountains to the south. Anywhere but in the eyes. You could see them, just looking for it. Someone to step in front of them, someone to spit on the ground within fifty yards. Any excuse to start a fight, a fight that would end with one guy dead and the other guy moving on to the next town, his legend a little bit bigger.

But even these assholes knew who was who in our town. A lot of towns have a fastest gun. We had three: Fallon, Ratface, and Pete. But never mind their names, because it was Pete who looked like a rat. Fallon was the ugliest of the three. And Ratface, well, he was actually a good-looking fellow.

Fallon and Pete were friends, until they had a falling out over a woman, the only woman who ever took a liking to Pete and his rat-ugly face. Pete caught Fallon sniffing this woman's wet undergarments, which wasn't great, sure, but wasn't that big a deal, really, except that the woman was still wearing them at the time.

"I'll see you tomorrow at noon," Pete said.

Fallon said, "Where?"

Pete said, "Are you kidding me? At the, uh, place. You know, the main drag. Oh God, why am I blanking."

"Just think about something else," Fallon said. "It will totally come to you if you think about something else."

"Fallon what in the hell is wrong with you? Shut up."

"I'm just saying. It totally works for me if I think about a cactus or a rock and then I remember what I was trying to..."

"Goddammit, Fallon, you ruined the moment. Just meet me in the place where guys like us go and draw our guns."

And then Fallon started laughing at Pete, and Pete tried not to laugh, tried to do his best to stay angry, but that never works, and the harder Pete tried not to laugh, the more he laughed, until Pete didn't want to kill Fallon anymore.

But then later that night, Pete was lying awake, alone, and looking up at the stars, and realizing he was sleeping close to his horse just for heat and the skin contact, and he didn't want to be ugly anymore, but there was no way around that, so he got his boots on and walked over to Fallon's little shack on the edge of town and roused him out of bed with a gunshot to the moon.

"Pete?"

"Yeah."

"What can I do for you? It's an hour before dawn."

"I don't want this ugly face anymore."

"Well, nothing much I can do about that. Your face is your face. Can't change it."

"I know. So instead, I'm going to do the next best thing."

"What's that, Pete?"

"Kill you."

"Oh. That all?"

"I mean it. I'm going to kill you dead."

"Now that's just redundant."

"In front of the whole town."

"And dramatic."

"If you're done, Pete, I'm going back to sleep."

Word spread fast. By sunrise, all the boys in town were placing bets on Fallon vs. Pete. This was a big deal for the town. Ratface was the fastest gun, not just here, but within a hundred and fifty miles, at least by most people's accounts. But Fallon and Pete were clearly number two and three, in some order. And now we were going to find out what that order was. Two would probably be standing, and three would certainly be dead.

At about quarter to noon that day, people started lining the center of town, like they were waiting for a parade to come through. Mothers kept their small babies inside, but you could see the little heads peeking out from the windows, straining for a glimpse.

Pete and Fallon stood facing each other, forty paces apart, starting the stare-down.

"I reckon you got what's coming to you, Fallon."

"That's how you talk, man? That's now how you talk."

"Yeah. Why? How do you talk?"

"Like a regular person."

"What do you mean? I reckon that was an insult."

"That's what I mean. Reckon. Who says that? Stop saying reckon."

"I can say reckon if I want. Reckon. Reckon. Ah reckon. Ah dew reckun."

"Real mature, Pete."

"Reckon, reckon, reckon."

Then Ratface walked out from the saloon, whisky still in one hand, half a glass of beer in the other.

"You two idiots," he said. "You both know I'm faster than either of you. How about this? Whoever wins, gets me next. So then you'll both be dead, and I'll be out a bullet. How do you like that? That's what I thought. Now get your asses in the saloon and let's play some cards."

Fallon said, "Get out of the way, Ratface. This is between Pete and I."

And that, to my great and everlasting surprise, is where I come into the story.

So there I am, look at me, I am standing on the porch of the general store, leaning on a post, arms crossed, just observing, like I always do.

That's my job. I guess you might call me the narrator of the town. I sell sundries, do a little bookkeeping on the side, and watch everyone come and go, keeping a mental ledger to go along with my ledgers full of numbers. The town and its people and their stories.

I've never had any problems with anyone, certainly not any of the gunslingers, including Fallon.

But for some reason, I just can't let this one go.

Fallon says, "Excuse me?"

Ratface just starts laughing, like he knows I'm a dead man.

"Correct grammar is Pete and me. You said… Pete and I."

"I know what I said, bookkeeper."

"It's a common mistake," I say.

Pete says, "Come on, Fallon, he doesn't mean any harm."

But it's already too late. Pete vs. Fallon has been cancelled, and replaced with the new matchup: Fallon vs. me.

By noon the next day, people are lining up again, but this time there aren't any bets being taken. People either feel sorry for me, or think I am incredibly stupid. Or both. I guess those things aren't mutually exclusive.

We stand face to face, about forty paces. We do the stare-down thing. Fallon stares hard. He has a good gunslinger stare. What I do is more like squinting. It is bright and hot and dry and dusty, so you can imagine I am squinting pretty hard.

I close my eyes for a second, half wishing it could just be over with, wishing I could lie there in the dirt like the dumbass I was, half feeling like I deserve this, for being so stupid as to be giving unsolicited grammar lessons to someone like Fallon, someone with the dangerous combination of being both a prick and really quick on the draw.

And then this is what happens, in some order. I will tell you what order it feels like it happens, which is not necessarily the order in which it actually happens:

I hear a scream.

I hear everyone in town gasp all at once.

I open my eyes.

I look down and see my gun in my hand, smoke curling out of the barrel.

I come to understand that Fallon has screamed.

My brain figures out what my body has known for a while: my hand has fired my gun. My bullet has found a resting place between Fallon's dark eyebrows.

I hear another scream, this one escaping from my own mouth, as I realize there is a dead guy. And I am not him.

It's later, over a beer, that Ratface tells me Fallon never screamed.

"Think about that," he says.

It's even later that night, while drifting off to sleep, that I realize Fallon did scream. Just not out loud.

It isn't long before guys start showing up.

Sometimes they ride in alone, sometimes in twos and threes. They don't want Pete. He's small potatoes now.

And even though everyone still figures Ratface to be the guy to beat, they don't want him either.

They want to test themselves against me. The guy who shoots with his eyes closed.

It's the same thing, every time. Stranger rides into town. Looking for trouble. Can't find it—and I'm certainly not going to give it to him.

I stop going to the saloon, stop going anywhere I don't need to go. But sooner or later, they all find me anyway. It might take a day or two, but eventually they find a way to cross paths with me.

I continue to work at the general store. Which makes it easier on them—they just wait for me there until I close up shop for the day, catch me on my way home.

Their first reaction is usually relief. Then a smirk. I don't much look the part of town gunslinger. Killing me, they figure, is going to be easier than they thought.

So then I even stop going to the store. Doesn't matter—they come to my home, make up some story, some imagined slight, something an uncle of mine did to them in the past, just whatever it takes to start a fight, and then, the next day at noon, there we are, stranger dead, me with my eyes closed, trying to remember how I did that.

This can't possibly last, I think. And so everyone else in town privately agrees. You don't just get this fast overnight. You are born with it, or you aren't, and I wasn't. Bad eyes, bad hands, bad reflexes. There's a reason I'm the town bookkeeper.

So if not skill, then it must be some kind of luck. Some kind of quirk that happens, once a century, in some small town, some coin-flipping in the cosmos, coming up heads a hundred times in a row. There is just no way I could have killed all these killers, these bad men, men who can shoot two holes in a silver dollar before an average man has his gun drawn.

It's the twitch. The jitter in my thumb, the jolt running from my wrist to my shoulder. It's just some freak of my body, gaining some kind of ability, a hidden gift that just happens to be manifesting itself now. It has to be, right?

Except, maybe. It isn't. Except, maybe it has something to do with the fact that I close my eyes, something to do with that scream I heard from Fallon, a scream that didn't come from his mouth. Came from somewhere inside of him. Unless, maybe, it isn't my body at all that was fast.

But that's just hooey. This can't last. Any day now, I'll get killed. Any day now, some really fast gun will ride into town, and put a bullet in me, and end this lucky streak once and for all. That's what everyone in town thinks. I can hear them thinking it. At least that's what it feels like.

I see Ratface once in a while. He's usually at the bar, seeming bored by it all, and possibly, and I can't quite believe I'm even saying it, possibly a bit envious of me. Of me. The bookkeeper. But he's always been good. Or if not good, decent. At least to me. So I give him a wide berth, while he watches me with curiously intense interest.

And then, Deke comes riding into town. He doesn't even try to pretend he's come for any reason other than to kill me. He rides straight up to the store. It's early in the morning, I've just opened up shop, and he walks in, draws his gun, and leads me out to the place where I killed all those other men, just like I'm going to have to kill Deke.

Maybe this time will be the time. Everything feels wrong. I'm standing with the early morning sun in my eyes. I haven't even fully woken up yet. And the night before, I drank myself to sleep, thinking of all the men I have killed, men who'd asked for their own death sentences by wanting to draw against me. My legs felt heavy, my whole body was sluggish.

Deke did the staring thing. And I am thinking, what is with the gunslinger staring thing? Why do we have to do this? And my mind sort of drifts off and maybe it's because I am lost in thought that I don't close my eyes this time, but for whatever reason, I have my eyes wide open which means I am looking at Deke's butt-ugly face and I see exactly how it happens.

"Now," Deke says.

Don't do it, I say.

Except when I say it, Deke hears it, in his head, hears me, responding to him, even though he hasn't said a word, and although his hand is reaching for his gun, the sound of my voice inside of his head freezes Deke, just like three dozen others before him, freezes him in terror at the feeling of someone else inside his head, and in that instant, my gun is out, my finger already squeezing the trigger.

After Deke, it just gets worse.

On the one hand, I have become the town hero. The de facto sheriff. Can I say de facto, in this kind of story? Aw, hell with it. It's my story. I can say it if I want to. Women come to me every week, asking me to kill their husbands for beating them. Bad men come through town looking to exact revenge, and I am the designated guardian of our population. I have a cheering section. I have fans. Hell, I have a *job*.

My fans get a little cocky, knowing their guy is always gonna be the winner, knowing that in just a second, I'm going to wipe the smug grin off of the stranger's face. Knowing, but not knowing anything. Just knowing their guy is going to win.

And that feels good. I'm not going to lie: it is nice to be loved.

But the feeling doesn't last long.

I win. But I don't feel good about it. Now they're coming with faster guns, bigger guns. People want me to close my eyes. People are placing bets. It's not fun, and it's not fair, and I don't feel good. This is murder, what I'm doing, even if it looks like self-defense. But what am I supposed to do, turn down the gunfights? Turn my back on my town, my fans? Live looking over my shoulder? Wait until someone catches me in a bathtub, or asleep in my bed?

I try to shoot some of them in the hand. I'm a good shot, but I'm not that good a shot, and some of them die anyway. And the ones who live through it are madder than hell and demand we go again as soon as their hand heals.

And before long, the town turns, too. They've gone beyond asking for protection. They developed a thirst for it, for the sport of it. Boys line up, imitate my style. The women, now freed from their abusive husbands, look at me different. I get dirty propositions. Sometimes more than that.

Some of the men who were my fans now sneer at me. I walk into the saloon, and the music stops. People look at me, whisper. Made a deal with the devil. Some kind of witch. Saw him going into an Injun tent and come out without a soul.

Now the kills are piling up. There are hardly any gunfighters left to come challenge me.

I walk through town now, alone again. I go back to working at the store. People pretend none of it ever happened. Pretend I didn't save their asses. People forget quickly.

I almost forget myself. Almost.

And then comes the day. This day.

It starts early, with the moon looking out of place, and rain falling from a cloud, there must be a cloud, but it's nowhere to be found. Maybe up high and thin, a very diffuse cloud, but whatever it is, there's water cleaning our roofs, there's a half moon in the morning sky.

The stranger who rides in today is different. He doesn't seem to be looking for a fight. At least not in the way the other ones all have.

And I'm minding the store, selling picks and shovels. Selling dreams and tools. Selling snake oil and stories from my ledger. Keeping the books, feeling the judgment, hearing the thoughts.

The stranger—and this one is a she—she is just out there, on her horse. Not bothering anyone. Not looking for me. I'm not even sure why she's here. It's been so long since we've had a sincere visitor that I almost don't know what to do.

So the two of us are in agreement: no fight. I feel sure she feels the same, although it's not quite yet clear why.

And then I hear it: the town, goading us on. It's the town who does this, who pushes us together for their amusement.

They push us together, me and this mysterious woman.

We are forty paces from each other. The sun seems to have gone into hiding (maybe behind the invisible cloud). But for whatever reason, everything seems wrong again. Like against Deke, but more intense.

I look over at Ratface.

Come on. You gotta be my help, back me up.

This is your battle, he says. *I'm here to help.*

It takes a second for it to occur to me what has just happened.

Oh, that's what happened. Ratface never opened his mouth while saying any of that to me.

—*You too, I say?*

—*Yeah.*

—*And you've known all along. You've just left me out here, to kill all these poor...*

—*Hold it right there. Those men came looking for you. They asked for your best, and they got it.*

—*But you could have at least told me. Helped me puzzle through this.*

—*That's all part of your learning. Your training, if you will.*

—*My training? I've killed half a hundred gunslingers.*

—*Those men had it coming. You did the world a favor by taking them from it. Gunslingers don't seek each other out like that. They respect each other. Generally. Like me giving you space. To work it out. Those men weren't real gunslingers.*

—*If they weren't, then who is?*

—*She is,* Ratface says, pointing to the woman forty paces from me.

The town's whooping and hollering for a fight now. So loud I can barely hear when this stranger puts her lips right up to my mind and says, *Welcome to the club, buddy. You thought you were the only one?*

Ratface says, *There's a lot of evil out there, outside of our safe little town, outside of your organized little general store. Welcome to the new world—you ready for it?*

I look back at my opponent, and square off. I don't do the staring thing, and neither does she. We're both silent, on the outside, and the inside. I wonder how many others there are like us out there, wonder why a quiet little bookkeeper. But then I think, why not me? People think it's your hand, that's what makes you a gunslinger. Or it's your eyesight, your reflexes. And sure, it is. It's about who can do the stare-down, about people who don't flinch. But it's also about this, right here. This little moment, in between moments. When you and the other person are just waiting. It's about a moment, knowing what a moment is. It's about picking the right moment. Knowing that a moment is a coin, you flip it, on one side is death. The other side: life. For one more day. For one more moment.

HOLY JINGLE
A MAD AMOS MALONE TALE

ALAN DEAN FOSTER

Carson City, Nevada Territory, 1863

San Francisco was beautiful in the spring, Malone reflected, as he and his horse Worthless ambled toward town. Unfortunately, the town was Carson City, Nevada. Wild, seductive San Francisco still lay many days ride to the west, over the imposing crest of the Sierra Nevada. Malone didn't brood over the time required, however. He would get there soon enough. He always got there, wherever *there* happened to be.

Heading down the last bit of forested hill into the city proper, they were closely watched by a pack of gray wolves. Lying in wait for something small, opportune, and filling, the wolves instead glimpsed Malone and Worthless and, so glimpsing, held their peace. Wolves were intelligent critters, and this pack no less so than the average. Or maybe it was the wolf's head cap that Malone wore that caused them to shy off, or the fact that the cap turned to look at them with glowing eyes. Instead of the howls of outrage that might have been expected to resound from the pack upon encountering such a sight, there arose from the cluster of close-packed predators little more than a few intimidated whimpers. Also, one or two peed themselves.

It had to be admitted that there wasn't much *there* to Carson City, but its civilized surrounds were a considerable improvement on the vast desert wilderness Malone had just crossed. He was tired and thirsty and hungry and thirsty and sleepy and thirsty. Leaning forward, he gave his mount an encouraging pat on the side of its massive neck.

"Oats a'comin, Worthless. Oats and a soft straw bed. Enough o' the former so's you won't be tempted to eat the latter, like you did that time in St. Louis."

As the steed of impressive size and indecipherable breed turned its head to look back at Malone, the mountain man noted that the leather strap across the animal's snout was bulging again. *Have to attend to that*, he told himself. Wouldn't do to get the locals gossipin'.

Room and stable stall arranged, Malone repaired to the bar in the front of the hotel, sequestering his odiferous enormity at the dimly lit far end of the counter so as not to unduly panic the other patrons. The husky mustachioed bartender with the wide impressionist apron waited upon him with good cheer, which the mountain man downed steadily and in copious quantities.

That was where Hank Monk found him. The stagecoach driver noted the impressive number of empty bottles arrayed like so many ten-pins on the wooden bar in front of the slumped-over giant, carefully appraised the looming imbiber's degree of sobriety, and determined to embark on the potentially risky business of conversation. While the whip was somewhat smaller than the average man and Malone a bit larger than the average bear, the driver was possessed of the surety of someone who made his living guiding rickety, rattling coaches pell-mell down ungraded mountainsides. He was cautious but not intimidated as he cleared his throat.

"Have I the pleasure of addressing Mr. Amos Malone?"

Thundercloud brows drew together and eyes like mouths of Dahlgren cannons swiveled 'round to regard the supplicant. "Don't know as how many folks regard it as a pleasure, but unless there be another hereabouts sportin' the same name plate, I'm him."

Monk smiled politely. "I have heard it tell that you are a bit mad." The man seemed fully prepared to chuckle or bolt for the front door, depending on the response.

The giant shrugged, the action jostling his expansive salt and pepper beard. "So have I."

"But not to your face." Monk stroked his own, far more neatly trimmed, beard. "It would take a brave man to say that."

"More usual-like they're addled. I ignore all that they say. Actually, the entire species is crazy. Mr. Darwin failed to note that observation in his book. I called him on it but have yet to receive the courtesy of a reply."

This response, like the name Darwin, held no especial meaning to the stage driver, so Monk continued with his petition. "I would beg your assistance in a small matter of considerable urgency, Mr. Malone."

Turning away, the mountain man picked up a bottle with a

particularly garish label rich with Spanish words of false promise, and proceeded to down the remaining quarter liter. This explained, Monk now understood, the absence of glasses on the bar.

"I don't much cotton to beggin'."

Monk pursed his lips thoughtfully. "Well then, I'll pay you."

Malone set down the empty bottle. "Better."

"I'm presently a bit low on ready cash." Monk dug into a vest pocket. "But I'll give you this."

Intrigued, Malone turned sideways and leaned forward to inspect the pocket watch. It was beautifully engraved and chased with raised images of horses and a coach. "A fine example o' the timekeeper's art, Mr. Monk. Real gold, too."

Monk looked proud. "Was given to me by Mr. Horace Greeley of New York, for getting him on time to a meeting in Placerville everyone said he couldn't make. I'll give it to you in return for your help." He nodded at the timepiece. "Worth five or six hundred dollars, I'm told."

Malone examined the watch a moment longer before handing it back. "I reckon you've used that watch as collateral in more than one dealing, Mr. Monk, and I expect there'll come a time you'll need it again. What need is so desperate, then, that you'd be willin' to hand it over to a stranger like myself with no guarantee o' receiving its worth in return?"

"I've a shipment to deliver to California and gold to bring back. The only man in either state who I trust to ride shotgun messenger on such a trip is John Barrel. He has been rendered indisposed by an affliction for which I am unable to find a cure. From what I've heard whispered and rumored, Amos Malone might be the one man with the wherewithal to bring him back to his duties."

"I see." Half-hidden beneath the lower lip of the wolf's head cap, furrows appeared in the granitic prominence of the mountain man's forehead. "And would there be a name for the nature o' this affliction?"

Monk nodded curtly. "Love. Or more properly in this instance, infatuation. One so fast and unbreakable that poor John appears unable to move from the proximity of the woman who has caught him fast." The driver's expression darkened. "A woman of the East, no less."

"New York?" Malone mused aloud. "Chicago? Dare I say Boston?"

Monk shook his head sharply. "Were that it were so, Mr. Malone, were that it were so. The east to which I refer is at once less and more civilized than those fine upstanding American cities. There are over a thousand Chinee in Carson City, sir, and this woman is of that country that supplies to us both labor and mystery. She has enchanted my friend, Mr. Malone. Bewitched him from the blond curls of his young forehead to the accumulated fungus between his toes. No argument, no logic, no reason or threat or promise of wealth has proven sufficient to bestir him from her quarters. I am not the only one who finds it more than passing strange. If there is not more to this than the straightforward draw of the loins, sir, I'll gnaw the hindquarters off a northbound polecat!"

Malone considered. "If your need be so urgent, and the attraction so unambiguous, why not go with a few armed companions and drag him out by the heels?"

"I thought to do just that, sir, but this woman has friends and a respected employer. Somehow, she commands others with words as well as with movement, to the point that those who might help find themselves dissuaded in her company and depart her presence wondering what became of their senses. I have felt a touch of it myself. The sensation is akin to drunkenness, but without the vomiting. Also, it smells strongly of jasmine."

The mountain man sighed and turned back to his drinking. Monk looked on anxiously. As the whip teetered on the cusp of certainty that his appeal had failed, Malone turned back to him once more and rose. He had been slumping on his bar stool in a courteous attempt to somewhat mute his mass, and, now, standing, his head nearly scraped the ceiling. Conversation in the room grew quiet, as though an unearthly presence had suddenly made itself known.

The djinn was out of the bottle, Monk realized. Or rather, out of the bottles. There was no backing down now. It occurred to the driver only briefly to flee. He was a brave man, having in the course of his employment faced down everything from starving catamounts to desperate bandits. All these paled, however, in the shadow of the immense and ripely unwashed simian shape that now stood, swaying ever so slightly from having ingested a truly prodigious quantity of liquor, before him.

"Let's go and see if we kin speak some sense to your pal, Mr. Monk. I make no promises. Of all the drugs that befuddle a man's senses, love is by far the strongest."

"Stronger even than, dare I say, sex?" Monk inquired as the room cleared precipitously before them.

Malone stared solemnly down at the driver. "We have yet to ascertain under which particular affliction your friend reposes. Does he say nothing of his circumstances?"

"I've not seen him in weeks, sir, and despite my most sincere efforts have succeeded in drawing no closer than the door to the rooms where he now resides. I did not see him, and could hear him shouting but one thing over and over before I was summarily ejected. 'Holy jingle!' he kept bawling. 'Holy jingle!'"

"Interesting," declared Malone as the two men, one traveling in the umbra of the other, exited the bar. "If naught else, we can believe that whatever has inveigled him is nothing if not costly."

The building to which Monk brought him in the open buckboard was one of the more substantial structures of Carson City. Several stories tall, it was fashioned of local stone and boasted fine glass windows imported from San Francisco.

San Francisco. It called to Malone. For a scion of the mountains and the plains, he was inordinately fond of the occasional draught of salt air. Soon enough, he promised himself. Tilting back his head, he let his eyes rove the numerous windows, eventually settling on one on the topmost floor. Light from oil lamps within, the hue of soft butter, lit the rectangular opening. He nodded knowingly.

"That one. There."

Mouth agape, Monk stared up at him. "Now how could you know that, Mr. Malone? You've never been here before."

Nearly buried beneath an incautious bramble of rabid, unkempt whiskers, a prodigious nose contorted. "I kin smell jasmine. And lotus essence, sandalwood, and other emollients most foreign to this part o' the world."

Frowning, the driver inhaled deeply. "All I can smell is street muck and night soil."

Malone grinned. "I once spent some time in Paris sojournin' with a master parfumerie and have retained a bit o' that knowledge." He started forward.

Monk contemplated the swaying, rolling gait of the giant before him and tried to imagine a connection between the mountain man and the tiny crystal bottles of mostly floral scent he had occasionally seen in rooms occupied by ladies of the evening. Failing quite thoroughly in the attempt, he set the unresolved contradiction aside and followed grimly in the big man's wake.

Not all the way, though. He was stopped inside by the redoubtable Bigfoot Terry, the madam of the house, who was quick to inquire as to their purpose in visiting. The question was rhetorical, as her establishment dispensed one class of goods and one kind only. "The best in Nevada," as the hefty owner was oft heard to declare. She glanced only briefly at Monk, her attention immediately drawn to his companion, her Carolina accent as thick as her thighs.

"Ah declare, suh, you strike me as a man in need of some serious service." Blue eyes twinkled amusedly. "The question is, can a sizeable but roughhewn bumpkin like yourself afford the finery for which my establishment is famed?"

Malone was not looking at her, his gaze drawn instead to the wide walnut stairway that cleaved the back of the parlor as opposed to cleavage of a more neighboring but no less sturdy kind. Brushing past her without a word, he headed directly for the stairs.

Startled by his indifference, the proprietress seemed about to summon forth the men of unpleasant mien whom she kept on retainer to cope with just such discourtesy. Monk hastened to forestall her.

"I will pay for my friend. Despite your assessment, it is hoped his visit will be brief, and accounted accordingly."

Adjusting the feathers that encircled her shoulders and neck like the boa for which the adornment was named, the madam calmed herself. Her attention turned to the smaller and more voluble visitor. "Fair enough." She proceeded to name the figure for a standard visit. Monk nodded his understanding and reached into a pocket.

"I am at present a mite short of coin, but I have this watch…"

The chamber was at the end of the hall on the top floor. As he passed the intervening rooms, Malone listened for the sounds of commerce. There were none to be heard. Did Madam Terry reserve this entire floor for one employee because she was special? he wondered. Or could it be that her fellow courtesans were fearful of working in the stranger's vicinity? Did they perhaps shun her because she was Chinese? He already suspected that there were things at work here that transcended love and sex, and that was saying something.

To any other inhabitant of Carson City, the smells that emerged from beneath the solid wooden door would have reeked of exoticism. Malone, however, was familiar with them, being as he was rather more widely traveled than anyone save his horse suspected. Inhaling their familiarity, he identified one fragrance after another. Shanghai and Hong Kong, Kuching and Singapore, Calcutta and even Lhasa. No wonder this woman had so thoroughly enchanted the man called John Barrel. She had taste. She had reach.

It was time to find what else she had.

He knocked. Softly at first and then, when ignored, harder. A voice from the other side mewed, "Come in—it is not locked." Turning the knob, he pushed against the wood and entered Paradise.

Or so it would have seemed to the unsophisticated, uninitiated miners and drovers and businessmen likely to frequent such an establishment. Heavy carpets on the floor were cartographies of interwoven patterns: lanterns and birds, dragons and Chinese characters, all rendered in finely wrought wool. Tables sculpted from dark wood supported oil-filled lamps and incense burners. In one corner, a pair of ceramic Ming lions glared ferociously. A rainbow waterfall of glass beads separated one room from another. Densely arrayed on the walls were paintings rendered in pale watercolor, in fine ink, in bird feathers and butterfly wings. The room was aswirl with luxury.

There was movement behind the beaded curtain. The shape of a woman eased into the room, the smoke parting around her like a diaphanous veil. Malone had seen much in his time, but the sight made him draw in his breath.

This was not going to be easy.

Glistening black hair was drawn tightly back into a single braid. Her face was as blemish-free and pure as a bowl of cream, save for the double crimson slash of her lips, which were as red as the wound from a cavalryman's saber. Packed into the glittering sequined cheongsam she wore were breasts more substantial than might have been anticipated, a narrow waist, and hips whose curves would have troubled Newton. When she smiled, the whole room seemed to sigh.

"What have we here?" She approached him. He held his ground as one hand reached out to stroke his arm. "I sense need bottled as tight as hundred-year-old brandy, and just as hot. Relax to me and I will release it."

He swallowed. Safer to be facing a troll in the Arctic or a shark in the sea, he thought. Monk was right to be worried about his friend.

At that moment, a moan came from a back room. It was weak, yet not an expression of pain. Back there, out of sight, a man was dying slowly. But not painfully. Malone nodded in its direction.

"You are entertainin', if that's the right word, a guest name o' John Barrel. He has been here a long time. Too long. You speak o' need. Well, his friend needs him… now and right quick."

A second hand reached out to slip between the mountain man's right arm and his waist. Fingers dug in hard, clutching, trying to penetrate the thick buckskin. The lacquered nails did not break.

"But I need him, too. I need him *more*."

Malone frowned. "His friend needs him to ride shotgun. What d'you need him to ride?"

The irresistible lips parted, eyelids fluttered, and there came a whisper that was part pure physicality and entirely feral. "He is a fine young man, healthy and strong. Being Occidental you will not understand, but I need what moves him. Call it a lifeforce. Say it is an Oriental obsession."

Malone shook his head to clear it. The room, the incense, the nearness of his hostess were making him dizzy. Hips were moving against him with a strength that would have impressed the Krupps. Resistance was not futile, but it was becoming increasingly difficult. He struggled to keep his senses about him.

"I thought you only worked for money. Lifeforce is a demonic obsession that spans all continents. 'Tis something far from exclusively Asian."

A growl escaped her throat as she stepped back from him. He was quite certain it was a growl; low but not heavy. "Who are you, to speak of such things, far less to know of them?"

"A traveler. One with needs less immorally acquisitive than your own."

"Do not judge me, master of stinks!" Regaining her poise, she replayed her smile. "You want to free the youth? Very well. I will trade you."

The mountain man hesitated. "What could I possibly have that you would want?"

When she smiled this time, sharp points seemed to flash briefly from the tips of her teeth. "You. I will trade John Barrel's lifeforce for yours. Come and lie with me and I will take what I need. You will feel no pain." As she turned to walk away from him, the oceanic roll of her backside caused his eyes to water as if they had been doused with pepper. She looked back over her shoulder, her inviting smile at once coquettish and carnivorous. "Come, big handsome devil. Are you afraid?"

"Let Barrel go first."

She shrugged. "Will you then run out on me? I think not." Obsidian eyes flashed. "You are intrigued. Of course you are. Having set eyes on me, you have no choice."

It took Hank Monk plus one of Bigfoot Terry's men to get John Barrel out of the building. Monk was shocked when he saw his friend. Normally stout and muscular, the shotgun rider had been reduced to a shrunken shell of himself. It was as if someone had stuck a straw into his body and sucked out half the juice.

"A steak." Monk spoke worriedly as the madam's man helped load Barrel into the back of the buckboard. "Two steaks. With potatoes, and bread, and ale. We'll have you fixed up right quick, John. Be back on your feet in a day or two." Climbing up onto the front of the buckboard, Monk took up the reins and set it in motion. Lying in the open bed behind him his companion moaned, his voice barely audible.

"Holy… jingle…"

"No need to worry about money now, John. Don't let such things worry you. We'll soon have you right."

As they passed the far end of the building, Monk glanced upward. The light from a window on the top floor was flickering oddly. He chucked the reins a little harder, urging the team to a faster pace.

If the greeting room was overflowing with objects d'arte and seductive smells, the bedroom into which Malone found himself escorted redefined opulence. A beveled mirror on the ceiling reflected a rumpled bed that had been made up with sheets of French silk trimmed with Irish lace. Embroidered pillows rode the plush mattress like manatees on a rippled silver sea. Lamps glimmered while cherubs sculpted of wood and gilt parasitized the walls. Everywhere was crystal and smoke.

Then his hostess dropped her cheongsam, and everything else vanished from view.

"Too late now," she murmured. In her perfect nakedness, she turned and waved a hand, whispering something in Chinese so ancient only a few of the most eminent scholars of the Forbidden City would have understood.

Aromatic smoke swirled and danced. An unsourced sigh at once cosmetic and cosmic filled the bedchamber. Whisked away by a zephyr, the bedsheets were replaced by new and fresh that smelled of roses fresh plucked. As she moved toward the bed, the walls rippled around Malone. Unbidden, he found himself starting to remove his own clothes. Given the number of layers and the quantity of grease and other dried fluids they had absorbed, this was a considerable process.

She did not so much lie down on the silk sheets as spread herself across them like honey on lavosh. Utterly unabashed, she turned to face him. One hand gestured and he found himself drawn toward her. He did not remember walking: just floating an inch or so above the floor. Wisps of incense-laden smoke massaged his body as he traveled, cleansing him more thoroughly than any bath, perfuming him as the Aztecs would a particularly important sacrifice.

"You will sustain me far longer than that youngster John Barrel," she murmured. "You will renew me for many months, perhaps even years, until all has been used up. And you will enjoy every moment of it."

He felt himself rising up over the bed, over her. Then he was descending, the great mass of him descending as gently as an autumn leaf, until he became one with her.

She howled.

Blocks away, the door of a stable stall shattered when its occupant burst through the barrier as if it were made of cardboard. The nightwatch stable boy barely managed to fling himself aside as Worthless turned the main doors to kindling. Pounding through the streets, the fiery-eyed runaway scattered late night drunks and sober pedestrians alike.

Very soon, the stallion found himself outside a singular stone structure from whose topmost floor lamplight danced and twitched as if imbued with a life of its own. Whinnying and rearing, sending ordinary horses stampeding in panic from where they had been tied, Worthless stomped back and forth in front of the building. When two men managed to get a lariat around him, one twitch of the muscular neck sent both of them flying into a nearby water trough. Raising a rifle, a third prepared to bring the maddened mount down. One look from his intended target caused the visiting rancher to drop his weapon and sprint for the nearest available doorway.

In front of the furiously pacing horse, men and women were spilling from the building's main entrance. Though some wore few articles of clothing and others none at all, their nakedness was not of as much concern as escaping a heretofore solid structure that seemed on the verge of collapsing. Indeed, as they gathered themselves in the street, a few turned to marvel at the quivering multistory building. Given the range of motion in which the outer walls were presently engaged, it struck all as impossible that they were not crumbling before their stunned eyes. Yet though it shivered and shook like a gelatin mold placed atop a steam engine, the building did not collapse.

Despite the grinding and rumbling of shaken stone, another sound could be heard. It was a roaring, a shrieking, a howling scree as if a pack of demons was being tormented in ways unimaginable to mere human beings. It was the sound of an evil spirit being hoisted by its own petard.

Or in this case, that of Amos Malone.

The bed, with its luscious silks and enveloping pillows and hand-wrought steel springs, was slowly disintegrating beneath its present occupants. The room was, quite literally, heaving in time to their synchronized movements. Locked against each other, they were unaware of their physical surroundings. Engaged in oneness, they became the universe while the real one disappeared. It was the totality of tao.

Beneath the immensity of Malone, the courtesan's eyes widened.

"Not possible! It is not possible! How can you...?" He moved suddenly, a certain way, and her eyes closed. Her nails dug at his back, much as those of an animal might dig at the ground searching for prey. She whined, she whimpered, she threw back her head and howled. As she did so, her mouth opened wide. Determined, resolute, Malone kept moving even as an ethereal redness began to emerge from between her lips.

"I know the way," he muttered even as he strove to maintain the effort. "I know the places to touch, the moves to make. You are done in this time and place, vixen. Be off with you, says I! Take yourself elsewhere and find another to feed upon. I'm Amos Malone, and I'm afraid I got to hang onto all the lifeforce I've got. Might need it later." With that he thrust his hips forward as hard as he could, in a most distinctive, ancient, and thrice-forgotten manner.

"Holy jingle," Barrel had kept mumbling, over and over. Not being conversant with old Mandarin, the driver's enunciation had been only an approximation. But from the man's semi-coherent sputtering Malone had been able to divine the correct pronunciation—and its true meaning.

"Huli jing!" poor Barrel had been trying to say. It was not an exclamation, but a warning.

The courtesan's mouth opened wider still. Wider than humanly possible. Around them, the overheated air shuddered as the Huli jing spirit was expelled from the human woman's body. Hovering in the air by the head of the bed, the nine-tailed fox-shaped apparition spun and whirled helplessly, bereft now of its human host. It snapped at him once, barking half in anger, half in amusement, almost biting his nose. In the far corner of the room, atop his pile of discarded clothes, Malone's wolf's head cap snarled, and its eyes glowed red with fury at the sight of its hereditary enemy.

The Huli jing growled a last time, whipped its nine tails once across Malone's face, and was gone.

Malone collapsed.

The air in the room grew still. Walls ceased their shaking and behaved once more as stone. Crystal ceased singing and the flames in the oil lamps calmed themselves. Outside on the street, a manic horse quieted, huffed, and ambled over to a recently vacated water trough to drink long, heavy, and noisily. Beneath an utterly exhausted Malone, black eyes flickered, focused, and gazed up at him in wonder.

"Who... who are you, sir? What has happened here?" Raising her head, she regarded her elegant if unsettled surroundings. "I remember last being sold and being put on a ship. I remember a place, a port..."

Worn as he was, Malone still managed to muster a thoughtful response. "That would not, by any chance, be San Francisco?"

"Yes!" A small trill of excitement underlined her words. "San Francisco, yes. I remember being delivered and then... nothing." Her gaze returned to him, searching his features. "You have a dangerous face but kind eyes, sir. What will you do with me?"

Letting out a groan that shook the foundations of the building one final time, he rolled off her. There was silence in the room for a long minute. Her expression expectant, she eyed the mountain of man beside her but forbore from interrupting his recovery. Then he exhaled heavily, sat up, clasped hands around knees the size of small boulders, and looked down at her.

"If it's all the same to you, ma'm, I'll take you back to San Francisco. There are good folk there o' your own kind, folks who will find a decent place for someone like yourself. One where you won't have to worry about bein' possessed. Because that's what you were, ma'm." The great sweep of his beard framed a surprisingly reassuring smile.

She looked away, neither demure nor embarrassed by her nakedness. "You call me 'ma'm.' My name is Meifeng."

Malone nodded approvingly. Outside the closed window, a horse could be heard whinnying insistently. He started to rise. A hand, strong but graceful, reached out to restrain him.

"Before you leave to prepare for our journey, sir, I would show you my thanks for saving me, though I have but small and inadequate means of doing so."

"I really ought..." he began. But she was insistent, and begged him, and her dark eyes were now filled with the kind of earnest soulfulness it had always been his misfortune to be unable to refuse. Besides, despite all he had endured, he was always a fool for knowledge.

After all, Meifeng does mean "beautiful wind."

THE MAN WITH NO HEART

BETH REVIS

Arizona Territory, 1882

Ray Malcolm never shot first.

It ain't that he were slow, or yellow, or no-count. Ray was a betting man, and he bet that the man who shot first would miss. He'd been right so far. Whenever a fight went from fists to bullets, the man who pulled his gun first was too quick with the trigger and missed. Maybe not miss all the way—Ray had a scar on his shoulder and a bullet still in his leg to prove that—but miss enough to not kill him.

And that was enough. Because the men who shot first needed more than one bullet, but Ray never did.

It's not like Ray went looking for trouble. But he *was* a betting man, and he liked his cards. And he was good at 'em. A bit too good, often enough. And when you're a bit too good, some people take offense. And when some people take offense, they shoot.

Flagstaff wasn't much of a town. Ray counted ten buildings, but one of them was a saloon, and that was all Ray needed. He pushed open the wooden door and breathed in the scent of rotgut, whiskey, and sawdust. With a nod to the barkeep, Ray accepted a shot of whiskey and leaned against the bar, surveying the room. Four men and a saloon girl grouped around the other end of the bar, talking and drinking. A few old 'uns were playing twenty-one on a rickety wood table; not gambling, just flopping the cards over in a bored sort of way. There were others, at the tables along the far wall, who were taking the games much more seriously.

Ray had been known to make a living off of cards, and while it wasn't always green pastures, he typically made enough to be happy about it. He'd started out in Chicago, but couldn't abide the number of people there and progressively moved west. Ray was in Arizona now, thinking about maybe going on to California, or maybe head south instead. He needed to move soon, that was sure enough true. He hadn't found any of the answers he was seeking here.

"I told you, it t'weren't real!" a man said on the other side of the bar. Ray looked up. A crowd had formed around a short feller holding something up in the flat of his hand.

The man touched whatever the thing he was holding was, and Ray saw a flicker of movement. The saloon girl screeched and shied away, and the men roared with laughter. An older man bought the lady a shot to ease her nerves, and she tossed it back so quickly Ray would bet that while the barkeep charged the old man a full fifteen cents for the liquor, there was nothing in the glass but water.

Ray left his empty on the bar and moved closer to the crowd.

"It *looks* real," the saloon girl said, leaning over the short man's shoulder.

"Ain't," the man said. He touched the thing again, and it stopped moving.

Ray finally had a good peep at the thing—a spider, about the size of a double-eagle gold piece, all black and spindly legs. It was motionless in the man's hand now, and Ray could tell the man hadn't been lying—it wasn't a real spider. But when the man stroked the back of it again, the spider jumped to life, scuttling over his hand and between his fingers.

"You wanna hold it?" the short man mocked, holding the spider out to the saloon girl.

She smacked his hand, and the spider leapt from the short man's palm right at Ray. Ray instinctively raised his hand to protect his face, and he felt the light tickle of the spider on his skin. Pulling his hand down, he looked at the thing. It *felt* like a real spider, but Ray could hear the faint sound of metal clacking against metal as the spider's legs danced along the back of his hand.

Ray hadn't noticed how quiet the bar had gotten until he looked up and saw the short man right in front of him.

"It's mine," the man said, his voice lower than when he was teasing the saloon girl.

Ray shrugged and turned his hand over so the spider dropped into the short man's hand.

"Where'd you get that?" Ray asked.

The man looked suspiciously at him. "From an In'din," he said finally.

"Which kind?" Ray asked.

"What you mean?"

"There's more than one kind of Indian. Arapaho? Hopi? Ute?"

The man narrowed his eyes. "Why so curious?"

"Ain't," Ray said, shrugging. "I only came here for cards, anyway."

He moved away from the bar toward one of the tables near the window, where there was gambling. A couple of men were crowing over a faro table, but Ray steered himself to the on-going poker game instead. It was getting on in the day, but the bar wasn't as crowded as it would be later. Only two men were playing, and the poorer of them was eager to get fresh blood in on the game. Ray sat down. Opposite him, the short feller pulled up a chair. The mechanical spider scuttled out of the man's hand and then froze on the edge of the table, unnaturally still.

"I ain't never seen nothing like that before," the man dealing cards said, his attention half on the spider.

Ray could tell that the short man was torn: show off the spider and let everyone envy him, or protect it and hide it away. His pride won out.

Soon, though, everyone's attention went back to the cards. Ray bet sparingly in the first few hands. He *was* a betting man, and he was good at what he did, and what he did was pay attention. He had a friend— back before the War killed him, more than fifteen years ago—who would sometimes accuse Ray of cheating. But Ray never cheated. He just watched.

And after a while, he started betting.

It didn't take long for one of the men to bow out. Soon enough, it was just Ray and the short feller.

"What's your name?" the short feller asked, peering over the cards.

Ray didn't answer. The short feller only talked when his hand was bad, though, so Ray pushed some more money into the pot. The short feller folded.

At the next hand, the short feller asked, "You with the railroad?"

"Railroad?" Ray asked.

"Some surveyors came in 'bout a month ago," one of the men who had quit the game said. "Atlantic and Pacific Railroad, gonna be just a bit south o' here."

Ray grunted and folded his hand.

The short feller didn't say a word at the next hand. Finally, he had something worth betting on, Ray could tell. He glanced at his own cards. A pair of fours and three deuces. Low cards, but a good hand.

"I bet everything on the table," Ray said, sweeping his money into the center.

The short feller's eyes widened for a second, then shot down to his own cards, then back to Ray. Ah. A good hand, but not that good.

"Well?" Ray asked softly.

"All in," the short feller said.

"Everything on the table?"

The short feller nodded and slid his money toward the pot.

"Let's see 'em," Ray said.

The short feller flipped his cards over. Two kings.

Ray allowed himself a tiny tilt in the corner of his lips, the closest he came to smiling.

"If I win this pot," the short feller said, "I reckon I'll have enough money to keep going south. If you're headin' that way, stranger, I'll take you to the place where I got the spider."

Well, shit.

Ray folded his hands without showing his cards. "Looks like you won," he said.

The short feller got his supplies that evening, and Ray helped him pack his horse the next morning. "Heard there might be gold, up past the Big Canyon," he said. "If you think you can find any, you're welcome to it. Too many In'dins there, and it's damn hard to navigate anyway."

Ray helped the man sling the last pack onto the horse's back, then turned to his own mount.

"That all you got?" the short feller asked.

"It's all I need," Ray said.

Ray figured it was a good thing the short feller liked the sound of his own voice, as that was the only sound either of them could hear the whole ride. They went southeast, through some logging land that gave way to sandier ground and scragglier trees.

"This here's Walnut Canyon," the short feller said. "I thought I might get lucky around here; my pa always said if you want to find gold, you gotta go by the canyons. But I reckon he might not've known what he was talking about, seeing as how he weren't sober since 'fore I was born, and when he died the undertaker said his blood stank of whiskey. I was heading up to the Big Canyon, but maybe I should just do what other folks are doin' and hit the California Trail."

Ray ignored the short feller, staring out at the canyon. "This is where you found the mechanical spider?"

The short feller shifted in his saddle, and for the first time since they left, he didn't seem like he wanted to talk. Ray turned to stare at him, waiting for his answer.

"Well," the short feller finally said, "not 'xactly *here*."

"Then where?"

The short feller heaved a sigh. "Come on," he said, leading his horse down the trail.

"Some In'dins used to live here, that's what the Spaniard said. Called 'em Sinaguas."

Ray had no idea who the Spaniard might be, nor had he ever heard of a tribe called the Sinagua. As soon as the horse rounded the corner into the canyon, he knew why: whatever Indians had once lived here were now long gone. The cliff dwellings were carved directly into the rock, each house hollowed out of the stone side of the canyon. But there was nothing here now beside rocks and dust; no sign of life or civilization.

Or clockwork spiders.

Ray pulled his horse up and turned to look at the short feller.

"I ain't lying," the man said immediately.

Ray narrowed his eyes.

"In there." The man pointed to one of the few cliffside dwellings that it would be possible for someone to enter without a ladder. Ray got off his horse and grappled up the rocks.

He could smell death before he saw the corpse.

"That In'din there," the short feller said, "weren't bein' fair. I tried to make a fair bargain with him, and he tried to trick me."

"So you killed him and robbed his body?"

"He woulda killed me, if I didn't shoot first!"

Ray knelt beside the stinking corpse and examined his clothing. "He wouldn't have. This man's a Hopi. One of the most peaceful tribes."

"An In'din is an In'din," the short feller said, his voice rising.

"Most Hopi live near Black Mesa," Ray said. "What was he doing all the way out here?"

"Well then, see, he probably weren't no Hope-pee then," the short feller said immediately. "This one said he was from the Big Canyon. Didn't never mention Black Mesa."

Ray frowned.

"Well," the short feller said. "I've held up my end. I'll take my leave."

Ray stayed with the corpse of the Hopi man long after he heard the hooves of the short feller's horse galloping away. He had been looking for answers for a long time, and he wasn't happy that the one man who might have had some for him was dead and stinking on the floor of an abandoned cave.

It wasn't hard to find the Big Canyon—due north until a giant rip in the ground stopped him. He stood on the edge at the highest part of the canyon at dusk, watching as the colors of the sunset blended in with the colors of the canyon. Yellow, red, orange. And at the bottom, the Colorado River, sparkling like a line of diamonds.

"Whelp," Ray said to no one, looking over the edge, "I ain't getting down there on horseback."

As the sun set, Ray set up camp. The air was cool and dry and still too early for snakes, so Ray gathered some firewood. Before he had a chance to light it, though, he was out cold.

He woke up when he smacked himself in the face.

"The hell?" he muttered, sitting up. A scuttling sound clacked past his ears.

Spiders.

And not just any spiders: mechanical ones. They were all heading north, toward the canyon's edge. Ray pushed himself up and stumbled after the click-clack of dozens of clockwork arachnids.

"Are you the man who killed my brother?" a deep voice rang out through the cool night air.

Ray froze, his hand already on the butt of his gun. "I've killed a lot of men, might've been your brother," Ray said. "Might not have been, though."

The clouds shifted, and the moonlight grew. Ray saw the outline of a man on the edge of the canyon. The mechanical spiders scuttled past the man's feet, over the edge, into the unknown.

Ray stepped forward, his hand still on his gun. The man wore a simple tunic and loose trousers, a wide band of dark cloth around his head, and a beaded necklace. Around his waist hung a heavy belt decorated with silver ovals that didn't hide its true purpose: on one hip, a gun; on the other, a knife with a horn handle. The gun looked to be a Colt, with a well-worn grip. The cartridges in the man's belt loops showed it was a .44-40. Within reaching distance of the man lay a '73 Winchester, obviously of the same caliber.

"I didn't kill your brother," Ray said, his voice strong.

"How do you know this?" the man asked, his voice lilting in an elegant accent. "If, as you have stated, you have killed many men, how do you know you have not killed my brother? He was in the south, and you rode up from that direction."

"I ain't never killed an Indian," Ray said.

"My people are peaceful," the man said. "But we know the scent of death. It clings to you now."

"I did see a dead man today. Indian."

"But you did not kill him?"

Ray shook his head.

"You know who did?"

"A short man, heading south."

"Why?"

Ray shook his head again. It could have been over the mechanical spider, or it could have been some other matter, but whatever made the short feller kill the Indian was none of his business.

"I have said," the Indian continued, "we are a peaceful people. We must now ask that you peacefully leave this place."

Ray frowned. "I can't do that."

The Indian didn't move. "Why can you not?"

"I have a powerful curiosity 'bout them spiders."

"So you intend to follow them into the bottom of the Big Canyon?"

"If that's what it takes."

"There are more than spiders within the canyon," the Indian said.

Silence wove around them for a heartbeat, then Ray said, "I'm still going to find out 'bout them spiders."

"Why do you care so much?" the Indian asked.

Ray didn't answer. He had his reasons, he just didn't much feel like sharing them. He hadn't told hardly anyone, not in all his long, long life. Ray didn't look half as old as he really was, but he felt the years, and the distrust they'd given him twisted in his gut.

The Indian stepped closer. Ray's fingers pressed into the cool ivory at the butt of his gun, but he didn't think the Indian meant to threaten him.

"You are a man with two-hearts," the Indian said finally. "You do not listen to the heart you carry here—" He poked Ray in the chest "—but instead you listen only to your heart here." He thumped Ray on the head. "This is dangerous, to be of so many hearts."

Ray barked in laughter. "Funny you say that," he said, no humor in his voice. "Most people reckon I ain't got no heart at all."

Ray intended to follow the spiders into the canyon, but not in the middle of the night. He didn't think the Indian would hurt him—Hopi were known to be peaceful, and it was against their way for undue violence. Still, he slept with his boots on and his gun nearby.

When the sun rose, he made his way back to the canyon's edge. The Indian was already there, kneeling, his face toward the sun. Ray thought for a moment that he was praying, but the man ducked down and Ray saw he was drawing in the dusty earth. He leaned over, trying to see what the man drew, but he could barely register the shapes outlined in the dirt before the Indian stood, sweeping away the drawing.

"You are still here," the Indian said.

"I aim to go down the canyon."

"The spiders are no longer there."

"I aim to go down the canyon anyway."

"If you are not looking for clockwork spiders," the Indian said, "what are you looking for?"

"Answers."

This surprised the Indian. "Come. Sit with me." The Indian opened a sack near him and pulled out bread and dried meat. He passed it to Ray before taking any for himself.

"My name is Cheveyo," the man said. "My brother's name was Hania. Together, we have been guarding the Canyon."

"Guarding it from what?"

"People like you."

Ray swallowed. "I told you I didn't kill your brother. I'm peaceful, like your people."

"You are here, and you do not intend to leave. That is dangerous enough." Cheveyo held a piece of bread in his hand, but Ray noticed he did not eat it.

"I would be very interested to know where you came from," Cheveyo said when Ray didn't reply.

"So would I," Ray said.

Cheveyo watched Ray intently, like a bird of prey watching a mouse.

"What was your brother doing south, if y'all were supposed to be guarding this canyon?" Ray asked. If they were going to talk, at least they could talk about someone other than himself.

"He went to the land of the Ancient Ones, seeking answers."

"Answers?"

Cheveyo didn't reply. After a while, he put away his uneaten meal and turned to face the edge of the canyon. "This is sacred ground, White Man."

"It's a canyon."

"It is the birthplace of the world."

Ray swallowed the last of his bread and rolled his eyes at the Indian's back. He didn't need any of Cheveyo's religious nonsense.

"It is, in fact, the *sipapu*, from which all worlds originate."

"All worlds?" Ray scoffed, wiping his hands on his pants as he stood.

"All worlds," Cheveyo repeated. "This is but one of four."

"Oh, four worlds?" Ray said, unable to keep the sarcasm from his voice.

"You think those spiders are from this one?" Cheveyo challenged.

Ray paused. The mechanical spiders were unlike any he had ever seen. A perfect recreation of a spider, but mechanical. Clever clockwork... or otherworldly?

Ray shook himself. He didn't have time for that.

"Thanks for the meal," he said. He turned away from Cheveyo, looking for a place to safely start his descent into the canyon.

"No mere man can reach the bottom!" Cheveyo called behind him. "Do not attempt it."

"Will you try to stop me?" Ray asked. His fingers went to the gun at his hip, just touching the cool ivory of the grip.

"No," Cheveyo said. "But you will be stopped."

Ray wasn't sure if Cheveyo's threat implied monsters or not, but he was having a hard time just navigating the canyon itself. Perhaps it would have been better to try to reach the bottom of the canyon by going west or east, at Lee's Ferry or some other point where he could take a boat through the Colorado River. But this was where the spiders were, and the canyon was far too vast. It would take days, maybe weeks to reach one end of the canyon or the other, and Ray was tired of waiting. Besides, the river wasn't safe. A decade or so ago, the government had sent out a steamboat through the canyon, but it had crashed. The river wound around like an angry snake and had viper's teeth along the bottom to boot. So Ray had taken his tack from his horse and hid it, then let the horse go, shouldering a small pack and descending into the canyon Cheveyo had said no man could conquer.

At midday, Ray stopped. He traveled light—a little food, two canteens, his knife and guns. As he drained the first canteen, he paused to consider that he might not be up for such an expedition. He let himself collapse along the path he'd discovered—nothing bigger than the barely-there trail of a deer or a goat. His feet dangled over air, and a rock jutted into his back, but it was the best rest he'd had all day.

A spider dropped onto his shoulder. Ray could just barely hear the whirring of the gears inside it. He held out the flat of his hand, and the spider scuttled into his palm.

Ray held the creature up to his face. A part of him wanted nothing more than to crack it open and look at the gears that made the thing work. Ray liked knowing how things worked. That's why he was so good at cards, at shooting. He watched, he learned, he figured out the way people worked, the number of cards that had been played, the calculated chances he took. Inside a man was a beating heart and pumping lungs and stomach and guts, but those things were just squishier versions of gears and clockwork, far as he could see.

Ray let the spider down on the ground beside him. It paused, raising two legs at him, then turned and scurried down the path. Heaving a sigh, Ray pushed up from his seat and followed.

It didn't take long for him to notice something sticking to the bottom of his boot. At first he tried to scrape it off in the dirt, but whatever it was stuck. With one hand against the canyon wall, Ray looked at the sole of his right boot.

Something… shiny. Like string. But sticky. Ray picked the filaments from his boot, and the thread stuck to his fingers… and kept going. Now that he was looking for it, Ray saw an almost invisible line of thread stretching down the path, farther than he could see.

Spider web.

The mechanical spider had left a web. And not just a normal spider web, one that could break with a single tug. This slender thread of web was unbreakable, cool to the touch like metal, as flexible as a blade of grass but stronger than an oak. Ray wrapped the string around his fingers and tried to pull it apart, but the strong web tore his skin before he could break it.

Ray tugged. The web was more than just an unbreakable string… it was also a path. One that led directly to the spiders.

To answers.

Following the web proved a good idea. It took him down paths he didn't think were possible, and twice he had to hold on to the unbreakable string for balance as he scrambled over perilous gaps in the path. But finally, finally he reached the end of the string.

There was no spider in sight. The thread stopped at the mouth of a cave. Ray carefully wound the last bit of string around his hand and slipped the bundle into his pocket. Such string could be useful in future.

As Ray debated whether he should go into the cave or wait till morning, he heard rustling movement from just beyond his sight. Something big—much bigger than a spider.

"Cheveyo," Ray said as the Indian emerged from the cave.

"You are not supposed to be here," Cheveyo said. "I told you, this place is sacred."

Ray noticed that Cheveyo's hand was on the .44-40 at his hip, his fingers wrapped around the grip, ready to draw. Ray took a breath. He couldn't pull his gun out before Cheveyo could shoot. But that was fine. Ray never shot first anyway.

"How did you find this place?" Cheveyo shouted. His voice was no longer peaceful, contemplative. He was starting to sound mad.

"It should have been impossible for one such as you to come here," Cheveyo continued. "I cannot let you into the heart of the *sipapu*."

Behind the Indian, in the darkness of the cave, Ray could hear a loud *clack, click, clack* sound. Cheveyo's grip on his gun tightened.

"How did you reach this cave? And in one day? Are you part god? Are you from one of the other worlds?" Cheveyo's voice was hysterical now, panicked. "Are you even a man?"

Ray looked down his front languidly. "I got man parts, don't I?"

A crooked, evil grin spread across Cheveyo's face. "If you are man, then you can die like one."

He shot. Ray only had the sense of gunpowder and smoke wafting in the breeze before he felt the slug hit his chest. The force was so powerful it knocked Ray off his feet. He lay in the dusty ground, the stars twinkling above him, and he knew the hit had been direct. Cheveyo's aim had been true. The bullet had hit his heart.

Or... it would have hit his heart, if Ray had had a heart. He sat up, still struggling to catch his breath, and reached into the bloody, gaping hole in his chest. Without his flesh covering it, Ray could hear the *whrr-chrr*, the mechanical sound that he had instead of a heartbeat.

"What are you?" Cheveyo whispered.

"I got man parts," Ray said, "but that's not all I got."

He stood, and Cheveyo could finally see what had once been covered by flesh: a metal pump, embedded with glowing wires.

Ray reached his finger into the hole in his chest and felt the dent where the bullet landed. He tried to pick the lead out, but couldn't.

Ray dropped his bloody hand to his side and drew his gun. "You shot me," he told Cheveyo. "Seems only fair that I return the favor."

Enough. The word was not spoken aloud, but seemed to reverberate through Ray's skull. He dropped his gun, clutching the sides of his head.

Cheveyo's eyes widened. "You hear the voice of Grandmother, too?"

This man is Pahana, the voice inside Ray's head said. *Let him pass.*

"Pahana?" Ray asked, still clutching his head.

"You are the lost white brother," Cheveyo said. He reached a hand out to Ray. "And Grandmother wants to see you."

Ray had expected "Grandmother" to be an old Indian woman, shriveled like a fig.

He had not expected a giant spider, easily eight feet tall, with long legs tapping along the back and sides of the stone cave so big that it disappeared into the darkness, only the sound echoing from the black.

You are not of this world, Grandmother said inside their minds. *I sent out my children to bring you back.*

Ray glanced at the cave walls. Hundreds of mechanical spiders clung to the walls, clacking their tiny, geared legs.

"He is a man that is not a man," Cheveyo told the giant spider.

That was a bit harsh, Ray thought. But also true. He had known for some time that he was different. The way he could calculate cards, read people. The way he always knew exactly when to pull the trigger.

And there was the matter of his heart. Not just his heart—when he had been shot in the leg, he'd discovered metal instead of bones. He had gears inside him, just like the spiders.

He didn't know where he came from, or why. He'd been wandering the West for years now, trying to figure out why he didn't age when his friends did. Why he was never sick. Why he couldn't be hurt.

But he'd never thought he'd find the answers in a giant spider in a cave at the bottom of a canyon.

There are four worlds, Grandmother spoke in their minds. *And you are from the second, Pahana. You slipped through. And you left a hole that could not be closed.*

"Is that where the spiders have come from, Grandmother?" Cheveyo asked. He held out his hand, and one of the small clockwork spiders crawled onto his palm.

The giant spider inclined her body toward Cheveyo. *It is. They are from the second world, too. They have sought you, Pahana. They wish to bring you back.*

"Back?" Ray asked.

To the second world. Your home.

"My brother and I have been trying to discover why the *sipapu* was open," Cheveyo said, turning to Ray. "More and more spiders have emerged. And other things. Some dark. Some good. But none of them belong in this world."

"And neither do I, is that what you're saying?" Ray's voice rose, anger weaving in and out of it. He had known from the moment he saw the spider that he wanted to learn more. It was like him, part real, part mechanical. But he hadn't known that discovering the truth would mean leaving this world. Panic rose in his throat. This world was his home, the only home he knew.

The second world is your real home. You will find others like you.

Cheveyo stepped forward. "I and my brother were the gatekeepers. My brother is no more, Grandmother."

The giant spider lowered her body in a way Ray knew meant sorrow.

"If this man is Pahana," Cheveyo continued, "then he is a brother, too. He has crossed the plains of the worlds."

"But I don't remember it..." Ray said, his voice weak. "I don't remember any of it. My earliest memory is far from here—not in another world, I mean, but in the East. How could I have come from this place, from another world?"

The paths across the worlds are complicated and long.

"Perhaps his path was meant to end here, rather than begin," Cheveyo said. "Perhaps Pahana is meant to be a gatekeeper with me. With my brother dead, we need another. One who can cross into the other worlds."

This is true, the great spider said. *Is that what you would like, Pahana? Rather than go through the door to the second world, you would be able to open and close the doors to all four worlds. You would protect them, with your brother Cheveyo.*

"First time I had a brother who shot me in the chest," Ray said.

Cheveyo grinned. "The second world is mechanical, and its people have discovered ways to longevity. Each world has its advantages. Would you like to discover the rest of them?"

Ray thought about what this would mean. He had once believed the West was the great unknown, the hidden heart of America that might show him the answers to who and what he was. Now he realized that the unknown lay just beyond this giant spider, through the gates to whole other worlds.

He could think of nothing he would rather do than explore them all.

WRECKING PARTY

ALASTAIR REYNOLDS

Arizona Territory, 1896

We caught him wrecking the horseless carriage on Main Street a little after two in the morning. It was a hard rain that night, the kind that keeps most folk indoors. Hardly ever rains in Arizona, but when it does it comes down like something Biblical. Our wrecker must have thought he had the town to himself. But Doctor Hudson was abroad, returning late from attending a birth at the ranch in Bitter Springs. He had already attempted to remonstrate with the wrecker. This earned him a powerful swing from an iron bar, the kind gangers use to lever up railroad tracks. The Doctor dodged the bar, and after scrambling up out of the mud he came to my office, where Tommy Benedict and I were sipping lukewarm coffee and wondering if the roof would hold against the rain.

I buckled on my holster and revolver, leaving Benedict in charge of the office.

"You recognize this man, Doctor Hudson?"

"Haven't seen him before, Bill. Looks like a wild man, come down from the hills. Smells like he's got half a gin house inside of him, too. He's riled up about something."

It didn't take us long to find the wrecker still at work in front of Quail's saloon. The horseless carriage was already in a sorry state. Under the violence of the bar, the machine clanged like a cracked bell. Pieces of it were already in the mud. One of its lamps had buckled, turning it squinty-eyed. I couldn't help but think of a dog being beaten, cowering against the next blow. It was stupid because the horseless carriage was just a thing, made by men from metal and rubber and leather. It didn't have a soul or a mind. But it looked pathetic and whimpering all the same.

"Be careful," Hudson warned as I neared the scene.

Mindful of what had nearly befallen the Doctor, I drew my revolver and held it up to the sky, the barrel catching the rain like a chimney spout. "This is the Town Marshal!" I shouted. "Stop what you're doing!"

But he didn't stop, not even when I'd fired a warning shot. The man just kept swinging away at the machine, seemingly more enraged with each strike. One of the mudguards had come off now.

I told Hudson to go back to the office and summon Tommy Benedict. I circled around the wrecker, peering through the rain as it curtained off the brim of my hat like Niagara Falls itself. Not that it excused the wrecker's actions, but it was a fool thing of Parker Quail to leave his horseless carriage out there like that, in the mud and rain, letting everyone know he was rich enough to own that fancy German toy.

I kept a wary eye on both the wrecker and the saloon. I didn't want Parker Quail or his men getting mixed up in this. Chances were good they were all sound asleep after a heavy evening of drinking and carding. But I watched the windows all the same.

If I could just time things, get that bar off of him. But I wasn't quick on my feet these days. Even less so on a cold wet night, when the bullet in me started wriggling around.

I took a lurch for the bar and missed. My leg buckled under me, and I went down in the mud. Lightning flashed, lighting everything up in black and white. The wrecker really did look like a wild man, all rags and beard and crazy long hair. Enraged by my attempt to spoil his fun, he lunged at me with the rod. Thinking fast, Doctor Hudson grabbed my shoulder and tugged me sharply out of harm's way, my posterior skidding on the mud.

"That wound playing up again, Bill?"

I pushed myself to my feet, now just as muddy as the Doctor. "You did the best you could for me. Dig any deeper, you'd have come out the other side of my leg."

Hudson nodded—we both knew I was lucky to have kept that leg at all, after that Union bullet went into me in '62. Better men than me were walking around on pegs. But on a damp night that Yankee shot sure did like to remind me it was there.

Thankfully, Benedict was quicker than either the Doctor or me. Before he signed on as deputy, he'd wrangled cattle. Now he came with his rope and had it around the wrecker on the first try, like they were both part of the same circus act. Hudson seized the chance to scoop up the iron bar. Benedict and I got hold of the wrecker and hauled him like a sack of horse oats back to the office. He put up a struggle all the way back, and Benedict and I lost our footing more than once. By then it really didn't matter how much more mud we had on us.

I thanked the Doctor and told him to go and get some shut-eye.

"Why'd you do it?" I asked the wild man when we were indoors and Benedict was fetching the keys to open the cell. "What has Parker Quail done to you?"

"Never heard of no Quail," mumbled our man. Inside the office, the fight had gone out of him. He was slumped down in the chair we'd pushed him into. He seemed more worn out than angry now, all his rage gone from one moment to the next, the way it often did with drunks. He gave off a stench like a barrel of vinegar.

"You were smashing private property," Benedict said evenly, opening the cell. "That horseless carriage belongs to Parker Quail, as if you didn't know."

"Doesn't matter who it belongs to," the man said resignedly. "Had to smash it. That's what you do. You smash 'em. Smash 'em to pieces, so they can't move, can't do nothin'. Smash *them* before they smash us. It's just another kind of war, just like the one between the States."

I tried to gauge the man's years. "You fought?"

"Sure I fought. Did you?"

I nodded. "Hampton's Legion, under Hood's Brigade. My war only lasted 'til Antietam, though. Guess I was lucky to get out of it with just a limp."

"You were Legion?"

"What I said."

"I was Legion as well."

I looked at him skeptically. "This far west, that's some coincidence."

He truly did look like a wild man come down from the hills. Hair so long and straggly it fell all the way down his face, so you couldn't tell where hair ended and beard began. No hat, and clothes that were halfway to shreds. Boots that were hanging off his feet. Smelled like he hadn't been near any kind of water, warm or otherwise, in years. Hard to guess his age, too. The grey hair made him look old, but the eyes that looked through the hair, where it allowed, were sharp and attentive. They were clear, too. If he had been Legion, he couldn't be much younger than me. But the war between the States was thirty years gone.

All of a sudden, I felt a shiver of recognition.

"You got a name?" I asked, with a tingling feeling going right through me.

"You know who I am, Bill. Didn't realise it was you, 'til you mentioned the Legion. But what are the odds of two southern boys fighting in the same infantry unit, windin' up in the same one-horse town in the Arizona Territory? Unless we came here together?"

"Abel," I said quietly, almost as if I didn't want Benedict to hear me. "Abel McCreedy."

"Been a while, Bill."

Benedict sauntered over. He had splashed his face in the basin and washed most of the mud off. "You two acquainted, Bill? Thought you didn't recognize him."

"I didn't, at first. But it's been—what—twenty odd years?" For Tommy Benedict's sake I added: "Abel and I shipped west after the war was done. Tried to make a living as bounty hunters. When that didn't work out, we signed on with the Pinkertons. Later, I ended up deputizing for a marshal in Eloy. Abel stayed with the Pinks... least, that was the last thing I heard."

"Worked out for a while," Abel said philosophically. "But you know how it is. Always been better on my own. Tried to go freelance."

"And?"

"Got myself into some trouble, Bill. Big trouble." He raised his filth-caked hand slowly, and pushed the hair away from his face. He still had the beard, but there was no doubt now. I was looking at my old partner.

Big trouble. I guess it had to be.

"You're in a whole heap more of it now," I said.

"I got carried away out there," Abel said. "But I had my reasons, Bill. I'm as sane as the day we parted."

"What brought you into town now, after all this time?"

"Things built up. I guess I was kind of hopin' our paths would cross, Bill—figured you'd help out an old friend. But then I saw that man's horseless carriage and it all boiled up inside me and I couldn't stop myself."

Benedict was watching us, arms folded. Abel's story about not recognizing me was obviously a lie, if he'd been looking for me from the outset. "Want to lock him up yet?"

"Hear me out," Abel said. "Then do what the hell you want."

I nodded to Benedict. "Stroll over to Quail's saloon. If no one's awake, leave it that way. Otherwise, do what you can to placate 'em."

"And if Quail decides to send some of his friends over to have a word with the man who smashed up his horseless carriage?"

"They'll be breaking the law."

"Ain't stopped them in the past, Bill."

"McCreedy's in custody now. That's all Parker Quail needs to know. Any problem with that, he can take it up with me."

I waited until Benedict was out of the office. Parker Quail was a constant thorn in our sides. He had made a lot of money from his gambling and whoring businesses, money that he liked to flaunt as often as possible—the horseless carriage was a prime example. He also had a streak of mean in him that would have made a pit viper timid. On two occasions, Quail's men had broken into the Town Marshal's office and busted men out of jail. Once to free an associate, another time to enact brutal justice on a man who had crossed Quail. Neither of those things had been during my time as marshal, and I was not going to let it happen on my watch.

Still, I cast a wary glance at our new fortifications, the improved locks and reinforced window bars. Would someone be able to get in?

"For your sake, Abel, you might be better off in the cell. At least until tempers have died down."

"I don't care about… who'd you say the man was?"

"Parker Quail," I said slowly. "You mean this really wasn't about getting back at him?"

"Told you, Bill. It was about the *machine*, not the man. It's always about the machines. They're all that matter now."

This is what Abel McCreedy told me, while he was still in custody.

I've never been sure of how much to believe, even allowing for what happened with Tommy Benedict later that night. Or of what happened to Abel, come to think of it. None of it, maybe. Perhaps just a little. But in all our time in the Legion, in all the years we bountied together, during our time under the Pinks, I never knew Abel McCreedy tell a lie or bend a truth. He just wasn't the lying or exaggerating type. Never thought of him as having too much in the way of imagination.

"It started with the wreckin' parties, Bill."

"The wrecking parties," I said, as if this was meant to mean something.

"The train wrecks. The ones they put on, for the show. Started as a fad, like it was going to come and go, way these things generally do. But there was money behind it. Money and power. Too much to stop, even when people started gettin' maimed and dyin' over it."

I knew about the train wrecks, although it had taken Abel's prompt to jolt my memory.

It was a lunatic thing to do, when you thought about it. Started in Texas, maybe Ohio—someone getting it into their head that there could be profit in staging train wrecks before a paying audience. They laid out maybe four miles of railroad track, straighter than an Apache arrow, and near the middle, where the two trains were due to collide, nature had seen fit to provide a natural amphitheater from which several tens of thousands of paying customers could view proceedings. They laid out more tracks to bring people in to watch, put in a new depot and telegraph station just to cope with the number of spectators. They put in a grandstand for VIPs, only two hundred yards from the rails, and a press box for photographers half as close again. Mister Edison even came with his new motion picture camera. There were medicine shows, hucksters, a bandstand, even a purpose-built jail. They hitched up cars behind the two locomotives and sold advertising space on the sides of them. They promoted the thing for months.

It was a grand success, and also a disaster.

They brought the trains together, then backed them off until they were two miles apart. Their engineers started them going then jumped off before they had got up too much speed. Soon the locomotives and their trains were rolling faster than a man could run. Then there was no force on Earth capable of stopping them.

During my time in the Legion, shortly before that shot at Antietam put me out of commission, I saw a Union munitions dump go up. I was a mile away and I have never heard, nor care to hear, a louder thing. They say there was twenty tons of explosive in that munitions dump. When the locomotives ran into each other, it was as if that dump contained fifty tons, maybe more. Their boilers were not meant to explode, but they did anyway. Pieces of metal landed half a mile away. People died. Not many, it was true, out of all who came to watch, but enough that there was an outcry. They sacked the promoter. There was a move to ban organized train wrecks.

"But someone didn't want 'em banned," Abel said. "A Utah Congressman tried to push through the necessary legislation. They found him dead. His brother tried to find out what happened. He disappeared. Then the brother's wife hired me to dig a little deeper." Through his beard I made out the cock-eyed smile of a man able to look back at his own mistakes with some detachment. "I shouldn't have taken the case.

I learned things, Bill. Things that you can't never unlearn. Things that brought me here."

"You're not making much sense, Abel. What does train wrecking have to do with Parker Quail's horseless carriage?"

"It's machines, Bill—don't you get it? It's all just machines. They're comin', rollin' toward us like those locomotives. There's nothing we can do to stop them."

"Still not making sense, sorry."

Abel closed his eyes. I could almost feel him trying to organize the crazy clutter of his mind. "I followed the money. What you always do, right? I wanted to know who was willin' to murder and intimidate government officials to keep these wrecks happenin'. And I followed it almost all the way. That's when I met *her*."

"Her."

"The woman. Said her name was Miss Dolores C. Steel. Ten years and I can see her like she's standin' in front of me now. Dressed all in black, like a widow. Black silk gloves, black veil on her hat, always carried a black parasol." Seeing the mental picture he must have thought he was painting, he added: "But she wasn't old and dowdy, like one of them war widows. I'd have said she wasn't no older'n thirty. Still a very comely woman, dressed in the latest Boston styles. Had a very particular way of speakin', too. Had me wonderin' if she wasn't from our shores."

"Where did you meet?"

"At a wreck in Idaho. But I'd seen her more than once before, at other wrecks. She was obviously close to the money. At first I thought that was because she was involved. Then I found out she was like me, *tryin'* to get close to it."

I nodded. "I'm guessing the woman—this Miss Steel—was connected to one of the victims. Either someone who died at one of the wrecks, or someone who got in the way of the next one happening."

"What I thought as well. But it wasn't like that." Abel hesitated in his narrative, as if debating how much he dared tell me. "You knew me well in the old days, Bill. Would you say I had a level head?"

"None leveler."

"Then make of this what you will. The day we met properly, before we'd even spoken, I followed Miss Steel into a huckster's tent. I meant to speak to her quietly, to warn her that she was getting close to dangerous men. But she'd tricked me. There was no one in that tent save the woman herself—she'd been meaning for me to follow her! As soon as I'm inside, she spins round like a cornered cat. I start to raise my hands, let her know I mean her no harm. But I can't! I'm totally frozen! I want to move but nothin' happens. And I don't mind telling you, Bill. I felt the fear of the good Lord run through me." Again there came that hesitation. "I knew I was in the presence of somethin' that wasn't natural. That woman wasn't a woman at all. Ten years ago and it feels like yesterday. You ever had that feeling before a thunderstorm, Bill? As if the air itself is all charged up and crackly?"

"Once or twice."

"That was how I felt around Miss Steel. And it was comin' off her. She lifted her veil, let me see her face properly. And then she did the thing I'll never forget, not so long as I have another breath to draw."

"Which was?"

"*She took off her face.*"

I repeated his words, in the hope they might make more sense coming out of my mouth than his. "She took off her face."

Before Abel could answer there was a loud bang as Benedict came back through the door, flinging it wide open. I'd seen that determined look on his face and I knew it meant a particular breed of trouble.

"Something up, Deputy?" I asked, tearing myself from Abel's crazy narrative.

"Exactly what you feared, Bill: Quail's men are up out of bed and spoiling for a fight." Benedict went straight to the armory and took out his favorite Winchester shotgun, which he kept loaded and ready for occasions such as this. He strode back out with the Winchester held like a staff, barrel to the sky. My revolver still holstered from the earlier business, I followed him outside. It was still raining like Noah himself would have needed a second ark.

Benedict and I stood on the wooden sidewalk, head and shoulders above the men who had followed Benedict back to the office.

"We know you've got him, Bill!"

I nodded at the man who had spoken. "Go back to your bed, Parker. All of you."

Normally Parker Quail dressed like an East Coast businessman, with his pinstriped suit and bowler hat—the very model of civic respectability. Tonight, dragged from his slumbers by news of the vandalism wrought on his horseless carriage, he had slipped a heavy coat on over a striped nightgown and jammed his trouserless legs into a pair of boots. His hair was uncombed and greasy.

I didn't much care for Quail—never had. He knew it, too. He'd made his money through every form of skullduggery and intimidation known to man. His men were thugs, only now they were well-dressed thugs with friends in the right places.

"Word is your prisoner's a friend," Quail said. "Folk saw him drinking before he started off on his wrecking spree. Overheard him boasting about being Legion. Now who else do we know who fought in the Legion?"

I shrugged, still keeping my hand on my holster. "Friend or no friend, he'll get the same treatment everyone gets."

Quail spat into the mud. "What's to say he won't be gone by sun-up, spirited away so he won't have to face justice?"

"My word as marshal."

"Maybe your word isn't worth as much as you think. McCreedy made a pretty mess of my *auto-mobile*." I had never heard that expression and it did not sound as if it came naturally to Quail, more that he was trying it on for size, like a new style of hat.

"It's just a machine, Parker. They'll make you a new one. Now get back home!"

"Give us McCreedy, we'll give it some consideration!" Quail said.

I glanced at Benedict. Benedict nodded and let off the shotgun, aiming it into the sky. Now none of these men were strangers to gunfire, or easily impressed. But when a lawman lets off a powerful firearm like that, a lawman that you know has the right and authority to employ that weapon within the city limits, it carries a certain conviction. Quail's mob, yellow-bellies to a man, began to disperse.

"This ain't over!" Quail called back to me, smearing a hand through his hair.

"Is that a threat, Mister Quail?" I relieved Benedict of the shotgun, made a point of lowering it so that the barrel wasn't exactly aimed at Quail and wasn't exactly *not* aimed at him either. "Think it over," I said quietly.

I hoped that was the end of it, but experience told me it probably wasn't. Quail and his men would retire to their saloon and drink until their rage and thirst for retribution overcame what little good sense they possessed. It was a pattern Benedict and I were already more than familiar with.

I closed the door, told Benedict not to bother racking the shotgun for now.

"Feeling we've got a long night ahead of us." I examined the cold contents of my tin mug. "You want to set some fresh coffee on, deputy?"

Abel McCreedy was still in his chair. "Heard you give 'em both barrels, son," he said, nodding appreciatively at Benedict, as the younger man went to light the stove.

"I doubt it made much difference," I answered. "You really could have picked someone else to make an enemy of, Abel."

"Told you, it wasn't nothin' to do with Parker Quail."

"Right," I said, trying to pick up the thread of what we'd been discussing. The woman in the huckster's tent, that was it. "So tell me about the lady without a face," I said, thinking it would pass the time to daybreak, if nothing else.

Benedict looked over his shoulder. "Lady without a face?"

"Never you mind," I growled.

Abel waited until I gave a nod for him to continue. "She reached up and pulled it away, like it was a paper mask. Only it wasn't no paper. There was no join there, no line around her face, and yet it just came away in one piece. Mouth, nose, eyes—and the worst part of it was, the mouth and eyes were still movin' even as she took her face off, holdin' it in her fingers all dainty and lady-like, like this was the proper thing, like takin' off your hat in church."

"And what was under the mask?"

"Nothin'. That was the worst, I think. I was lookin' down a kind of tunnel, the same shape as her face. Went on and on, like a rifle barrel, stretchin' too far into the distance. It should have come out the back of her head, but it didn't! And there were things around the walls of this barrel, all movin' and tickin' like gears and levers... but the way they was doin' what they was doin', I could only look at them for a second before my eyes started hurtin'. I wanted to look away. Lord knows I tried. But my head wouldn't move. Even my eyes wouldn't move! God have mercy, she put her face back on. Makes a squelch like a boot in mud. Just pushed it back into place, and there's no line, no gap, where it joined back up. And she says: 'I find it helps to get to the point, Mister McCreedy.'"

"She knew your name?"

"I don't know how. Then she says: 'We have been taking an uncommon interest in each other. I understand your concern for me.'" Abel spoke these words slowly and clearly, like he was making a special effort. "'But I must warn you that the concern should be for your own well-being. You are meddling in forces beyond your narrow comprehension.' Then she allows me to speak. I feel as if she's reached into my head and pulled a lever, like in the cab of a locomotive. I say: 'Who are you?' And she answers: '*What* are you would be more appropriate, sir. I am a *machine intelligence*, Mister McCreedy. A mechanical woman. Think of me as a kind of clockwork automaton, if that helps you.'"

I smiled. Like it or not, he was painting a strange picture in my mind. "Did it?"

"What do you think? She had me doubting my sanity, Bill. Even now, I know how this has to sound. But ask yourself: does a mad man ever 'fess up to doubting his own sanity?"

"Not in my limited experience."

Benedict came over with three tin mugs of coffee, done the way we usually took it: black as night and strong as a mule's kick. "Seems quieter out there now," he said, "but reckon I'll keep a watch on things just in case."

"Good idea," I said, accepting my mug and offering the second to Abel.

Benedict went out the door, not taking the shotgun this time, just his holstered revolver and a mug of coffee. I didn't doubt that we'd have more trouble from Parker Quail before sun-up, but an armed and alert deputy is a fair deterrent for most kinds.

"Miss Steel told me she was here to put things right," Abel said. "'The rule of law is being broken,'" she said, 'and I have come to enforce it. Unfortunately I travel alone, and my resources are extremely limited.'"

"Did you ask her where she came from?"

Abel let out a little laugh. "She told me she came from the Moon."

"And you believed her?"

He shifted. "Not exactly. Thing is, she wasn't made of no clockwork, either. Something else, something stranger." He took a cautious sip from his coffee. "Reckon she was sugarin' the pill for me, Bill."

"So the truth was something *stranger* than her coming from the Moon?"

"Now you put it like that…"

"Guess it's no madder than a woman who can take her face off and calls herself a *machine intelligence*. This 'rule of law' she came to enforce. What in blazes did it have to do with the wrecks?"

"That's where it gets weirder. She said there were others like her, other *machine intelligences*, only these other ones had come down from the Moon or wherever, to do something bad, something that was against their law. Like gamblin' or whorin' is against ours. And this woman…

thing… this Miss Dolores C. Steel… was a kind of agent, like a Pinkerton, operatin' for her government, tryin' to track these outlaws down, only she was on her own and she needed to disguise herself up so she could walk around and sneak up on them, because they were tricked out like she was, made to look like ord'nary men and women."

"She was happy to tell you all this?"

"Said it didn't matter to her one way or the other whether I believed a dang word of it. Just that it was better for me if I kept out of things. She said she didn't want people like me gettin' hurt because of *their* differences."

"And these differences… what these clockwork Moon people were falling out over… they somehow centered on train wrecks?"

"Machines, Bill—like I said right there at the start. According to Dolores C. Steel that's all there is out there. Just machines. Clockwork folk like Miss Steel herself. Machine intelligences. Folks like you and me, made of flesh and blood, we're a creek that don't run nowhere. She said it's like that on all the planets, wherever you go. Life starts out all creepy-crawly, with birds and bees and flowers, and monkeys and rattlesnakes and men and women. Then folks get lazy and start fashionin' themselves all kinds of tools and accouterments—fancy ploughs and waterwheels, then steam hammers and riverboats, then locomotives and telegraphs and horseless carriages. Get so lazy they can't even *walk* to see a spectacle, so they settle for lookin' at photographs and Mister Edison's vitascope instead. And it don't stop with horseless carriages, neither. Miss Steel says that's just the start of things—the first word on the first page! Before long there are flyin' machines and talkin' machines and machines makin' more machines! And once that happens, it's like setting the throttle on a steam locomotive, and jumpin' off while she's still movin'! You can't stop it! Can't slow it down! It's *techno-logical progress*, Bill. Starts off seemin' like a good thing, but it ends with machines takin' over. Ain't room for two kinds of folk, and the clockwork kind always win. Kill us, squeeze us out, just plain outlive us—don't matter in the long run."

"You still haven't got to the wrecking."

"That's easy—or at least Miss Steel made it seem that way. She says there are good machines and bad machines out there. The bad ones, they're always lookin' out for a world like ours. Got to come at the right time. We're like an apple that's just turnin' red and juicy—ripe for picking. They see our machines and see what they used to be—all steam and pistons and oil and smoke. To them it's like animals, or little children."

"I still don't…"

"Bill, it's like this. There are men who'll pay to see bears and dogs fight each other to the death. Men who'll pay to see terrible things done to other people, too—pay to see people do things to people, if it comes to that. All kinds of violence and depravity, things that'll make any God-fearing soul sick to the pit of their stomach, there's someone out there who'll *pay* for it. Well, it's no different for the machines. But they have their own laws and civilization, too. And places where the law don't stick. Like here."

"So the wrecks… that's like cockfighting, or bear-baiting, to these people?"

"Near as Miss Steel could make me understand it. And she said that violence being done by one machine to another was the *worst thing* she could imagine, and that it was important to track down the machine intelligences who were behind all this, yankin' our chains to keep the wrecks happenin', because if she didn't, they'd only go on to worse things."

"Worse things," I repeated.

"It's like a disease. Sign of somethin' not right in their heads. Miss Steel's here to catch 'em, take 'em back home. Back to their own justice."

"But our machines… they're just metal and rivets and bolts. They move because of steam and fire and men pulling levers. There's no mind inside of them."

"I asked Miss Steel that. She said I was lookin' at things from a 'biological perspective.' To them, there ain't no line in the dirt twix' one machine and another. A woman that talks and takes off her face, a telegraph machine, a Colt revolver, an iron bar, it's all just a question of degrees. They don't see themselves as standin' apart from all the other sorts of machines. They're all kinfolk. And when they see a holy abomination bein' done to one of their kind, it makes 'em full of righteous indignation!"

That made no sense to me, that a machine could see all other machines as being kin, but then I thought back to the wrecking of the horseless carriage, how it had looked pathetic to me, like a dog being beaten.

"Then I truly don't understand, Abel. She told you all this, and yet I still found you smashing up Parker Quail's machine?"

"She made me *believe* it, Bill, but that don't mean I had to like any of it. I believe in the Devil—don't mean I dance to his tune, neither. Miss Steel told me that the machines will always triumph, sooner or later. Gonna happen here, too—and men with their horseless carriages, they're only hurryin' it on!"

"So you wrecked Quail's carriage to stop the machines taking over?"

"Knew it wouldn't make no difference, Bill, but if everyone did the same thing, then maybe it would... or least ways slow it down some. Why'd we have to stampede into this? Ain't the future coming fast enough as it is, without giddyin' it along like the Pony Express?"

I thought about the changes I'd seen, just since the war between the States. You owned the world when you were a young man, felt it like it was fashioned to fit your hands. You could do anything with it you wanted to. But the world kept changing, and sooner or later there came a day when it didn't feel like you were the one the world was interested in anymore.

"That's just old age talking, Abel."

"Maybe it is. I'll tell you this, though, Bill. Whatever you think of me, I didn't imagine Miss Dolores C. Steel. I was talkin' to her plain as I'm talkin' to you now. Told you that was ten long years ago. Ain't been a day since then when I haven't ruminated on her words. She put things in my head, made it hard for me to feel at home around decent folk. Won't say I didn't seek solace in the bottle, either. But even liquor couldn't wash away what she'd made me believe. I didn't mean no harm by Parker Quail. But when I saw that horseless carriage, something in me snapped. I had to do my part, Bill. I had to slow things down."

"If you're right, it won't make a shred of difference. Not in the long run. But then, I suppose, what does?"

"You gotta help me, Bill. I know I did a rash thing out there. But it ain't Parker Quail or his men I'm worried about."

"Who?"

"They're still out there. The machines Miss Steel was tryin' to find." He shook his head ruefully. "Should've listened to that woman. She told me not to go pokin' my nose into what I didn't understand, but I thought I knew better... I couldn't help myself, Bill. I had to know if what I'd seen in that tent was real. So I kept on, tryin' to get close to the men at the heart of things... and I got *too* close. They know about me, know what I know... and I know one day they'll find me."

"Maybe you should've stayed out of harm's way, instead of making a public spectacle of yourself."

My words seemed to wash through him. "You can get me out of here, Bill. Over the state line. I'll make it to Mexico. You won't never hear of me again."

I thought of what Parker Quail had said, of how I'd look after my friend. "I can't do that, Bill. We both know that. But you'll be safe here. What you've done ain't exactly a swinging crime."

"Help me, Bill."

I made to answer when something crashed against the window, as if it had been hurled from the street. The glass shattered, but the iron bars prevented the object from going any farther.

"Don't go anywhere," I said, placing down my coffee mug. I wasn't surprised that someone had hurled something at the office, but I was annoyed and puzzled that there'd been no reaction from Benedict, no shout or warning shot.

Something compelled me to fetch the shotgun. I cocked it, opened the door, and stepped onto the sidewalk. A fist-sized pebble lay at my feet. Two shadowy figures were slipping away, ducking down the narrow alley between the land office and Kimball's hardware store. It was still raining like the ocean itself was over our heads, draining out through the clouds.

"Benedict!" I shouted. "Where in heck are you?"

"Over here, boss!"

Benedict was running down the street, coming back from the wrong direction. He had his revolver drawn. "Thought I had 'em!"

"Must've been more than two of them," I said, figuring that they'd meant to draw Benedict in the wrong direction. I was cross, but I couldn't hold it against my deputy. It was hard to see much on a night like this, and Parker Quail's men were sly and numerous enough to give us the runaround if they so wished. "Guess I didn't make my point strongly enough." I began to negotiate the steps down from the wooden sidewalk.

"Where you going, boss?"

"Quail's saloon. See if I can talk some sense into that snake-mean sonofabitch."

Benedict paused halfway up the sidewalk, the light from our window catching the gleam of his boots.

"You want back-up?"

I shook my head. "Keep an eye on Abel McCreedy until I'm back. All this over a horseless goddamn carriage!"

"My mammy always said no good'll come of such things," Benedict said, slipping past me.

I didn't know what kind of a deal I was going to have to make with Parker Quail to keep the peace, but just the thought of it was already leaving a taste in my mouth like I'd sucked snake venom. I'd made my promise to Abel, though. I couldn't shield him from the law, but I could shield him from lynch mobs.

But I was halfway to Quail's saloon when it felt like a little lever had just clicked in my head.

Something wrong about Benedict.

Not the fact that he'd mentioned his mammy, which was unusual. But his boots. Gleaming in the window light. There hadn't been one damned speck of mud on them as he came up those steps. Almost as if the mud didn't want to be on them, like it had better places to be hanging around.

He'd looked dry, too. Even though it was still bucketing down. I was already soaked clean through.

Feeling a deep foreboding, I turned around and headed straight back to the office. It couldn't have been more than two minutes since I'd stepped off the sidewalk. The door was ajar, a crack of light spilling out onto the sidewalk. I readied myself, prepared to use that shotgun, and kicked the door wide.

McCreedy was still there. Nothing had happened to him. He was still sitting in the chair, facing me with a kind of slack-jawed look about him, as if it was odd for a man to come busting through a door with a Winchester shotgun, which I suppose was a fair reaction.

"I thought..." I started. Then: "Where's Benedict? Did you see Benedict return?"

Abel didn't answer. He was still looking at me, but nothing on his face had changed. His mouth was still open. A long line of drool began to ooze its way out between his lips, down into the uncharted territory of his beard.

"Abel?" I asked. "Abel? What in hell's gotten into you?"

He made a sound. It was a series of dry clicks, made with the back of the throat, the kind that people make in their sleep when they're halfway to snoring.

I set down the shotgun and rushed to Abel. I knew then that something was wrong with him, something beyond the capability of any doctor or surgeon to remedy, but I didn't want to believe it. He was still alive, still breathing, and I couldn't see a scratch or bruise on him that hadn't been there before. But someone or something had got to him, I was sure of that.

"Abel, talk to me," I said, holding his head in my hands.

He just kept up that clicking. His eyes were looking into mine with a powerful fear, as if he knew just as well as I did that there was something terribly wrong. But there was nothing he or I could do.

Behind me, the door opened.

"Boss!"

It was Benedict, as muddy and soaked as his earlier apparition should have been.

I still had my hands on Abel's head. "Where you been?"

"Heard a commotion around the back, went to look. Wasn't no one there, so I came back. Why are you looking at me that way?"

Benedict didn't need to know what I'd seen only a few minutes earlier. It didn't help a man to know his double might be walking around. "Something's happened to Abel."

"You mean someone got in?" He was standing in the doorway, half in half out. "How could they, boss? One of us would've been here."

"Something happened," I said. "That's all I know."

I don't suppose the dry facts add up to much. Abel McCreedy, a man of my acquaintance, was caught wrecking someone else's property. The man was detained and found in possession of an outlandish story, unquestionably the product of a mind losing its hold on things. Threats were made against the man, and my deputy and I took pains to assert our authority against an organized lynch mob under the influence of Parker Quail, owner of the damaged property. In the course of events, on a dark and rainy night, there was a momentary confusion of identities. Someone may or may not have gained entrance to the Town Marshal's office by posing as my deputy Tommy Benedict. If they did, they left no trace of their presence save a man turned mute and fear-struck. Of course, when a man has spent ten years of his life staring down a bottle, that sort of thing can happen to him without outside assistance.

Doctor Hudson certified that Abel McCreedy had suffered damage to his wits, damage that was serious and irrevocable enough to render him totally unfit for trial. Unfit for anything, in fact. Abel McCreedy, son of Georgia, soldier, bounty hunter, Pinkerton, private detective—and good friend of mine—was sent to end his days in the county asylum. He remains there today. I have it on excellent authority that he has never uttered an intelligible word, although he is said to be given to screaming in his sleep.

Mostly, I have tried not to think about Abel, or his story of machine intelligences. It has not been too hard. There is always more work for me and my deputies. Each year seems busier than the last, and each year goes quicker, too. None of us get any younger. At times it is almost too much. One learns to snatch the quiet hours when they come. Tommy Benedict has long since moved on, but I soon taught my new deputy the way I take my coffee. When there is a chance, I like to read the newspaper. They have photographs in them now, and advertisements for automobiles. No one calls them horseless carriages anymore.

I am reading about some brothers in North Carolina, bicycle makers, when there is a knock at the door. A woman enters, dressed all in black, and there is something electric in the air, like the premonition of a thunderstorm.

"Miss Dolores C. Steel," I say.

"You know my name."

"I heard about you from Abel McCreedy. He told me you met in a huckster's tent."

"That was a long time ago."

"But you don't look any older than the way he described you. I shouldn't be surprised, should I?" I fold my newspaper carefully. "Have you come to turn me mute as well?"

"That wasn't my doing, Marshal. I wanted the best for your friend, but he wouldn't listen. Unfortunately, he came to the attention of the wrong sort of people. I don't know how they found him so quickly. They must have been waiting… knowing he would seek your assistance sooner or later. I would have liked to help, but I was… elsewhere. I'm truly sorry about what happened."

"Can you make Abel better?"

"No, that's not within my gift. But I understand you did your best that night."

"It wasn't much."

"Have you had cause to ponder on the things Abel told you? The other things, I mean."

"How do you know he said anything at all?"

"Intuition, Marshal. And the way you're looking at me now." She raises a hand. "I've not come to do you harm. Far from it. I just wanted to put your mind at ease. The people who did that to Abel… they needn't concern you now. They've been brought to account."

"Here, or on the Moon?"

The tiniest smile cracks the masklike perfection of her face. "A little farther than the Moon. But they won't be back here. And I'm sorry for the trouble that was caused."

"To me?"

"Let's just say there'll be no more... interference."

I nod at this, but my qualms won't settle that easily. "But what Abel told me, it all still holds? The triumph of the machines? That's all still going to happen?"

"I've seen it a thousand times. I wish I could say otherwise."

"You almost sound sympathetic, Miss Steel."

"Perhaps I am. I've spent a lot of time around the organic. It's hard not to form attachments." She pauses and extends her hand. The fist is closed, but it opens slowly. "The thing that was troubling you, since the war between the States? I took the liberty of removing it. I hope you won't consider that an impertinence."

She leans forward and places the little black pellet on my desk. It's impossibly tiny. How can a thing that small have given me so much unpleasantness? It doesn't seem fair.

"When did you remove it?"

"A few moments ago. I needed only to be in this room. The rest was... well, I'll spare you the details." She cocks her head in an oddly clockwork manner. "I could put it back, if you'd like."

"No," I say. "Please don't."

"I'll be leaving soon. I just wanted to make your acquaintance..."

"Thank you, Miss Steel."

"See me to the street, Marshal?"

I stand, and for the first time since that bullet went into me, I don't feel the slightest twinge. I wonder if it's a trick, a kind of hypnosis. That little black thing on my desk could be anything, just some grit she found out on the road. I won't know for certain that she is what she says she is until she does that thing with her face. But I can't very well ask that of a lady.

Even in these times of automobiles and flying machines, there are limits.

HELL FROM THE EAST

HUGH HOWEY

The Free Territory of Colorado, 1868

My path to sickness began the day General Lee surrendered his sword. That coward laid down his arms, and so me and my brother took our rifles and headed west. Wasn't sure where we was heading, just away. My brother didn't make it far. He survived the Battle of Sharpsburg but was brought down by a persistent cough. Fell off his horse and never got back up. I'd seen more dead than any vicar, but that don't make me immune to its sad effects. Many a drink and several fistfights later, I found myself in a new army. They gave me a uniform I was more familiar shooting at than buttoning across my chest, and somehow slid from a war between brothers to this frontier life hunting natives. It was all about killing a man you didn't know. That made it easier, keeping them strangers. Knowing them makes the killing hard.

My father had raised me and my brothers in the pine-studded hills of Virginia, just outside of Staunton. Pa gave me my first rifle, pointed at a squirrel, and told me to shoot. Men more dear to me than my father have been handing me guns and directing my fire ever since. I still find it strange how a man can lose at a war and then enlist in another with his enemy. But there are no real sides in this life except the barrel of a gun and the butt of a gun, and I know where I prefer to stand.

After enlisting, they stationed me at Fort Morgan. This was years before that unfortunate incident at Wounded Knee Creek. It was before the world heard of the Ghost Dance that was driving the natives mad. What we would one day call the Messiah Craze, and would lodge in my ear like a starving tick, had yet to cause trouble on those plains.

Fort Morgan was a lot like the endless Confederate encampments I had endured while serving. The only difference was that the fort didn't relocate in the morning; it had far fewer men moaning and dying in tents; and it was less prone to abandonment at night. I reckon Colorado was a long way for a man to run home from. Most soldiers out there had already done their running, and Fort Morgan was where they'd ended up. Their final resting spot was a scrabble of tents and rickety shacks ringed by a shoddy wall of pine stumps where the best that could be said was they fed you twice a day. Two muddy tracks came in straight as an arrow from the east, cut right through Fort Morgan, and disappeared out the other end toward the west. In one direction, a flat nothing where only the dust stirred and a creek petered out and was swallowed by the cracked earth; in the other, ancient and impossibly tall mountains stood with white tops like old men. The hell in-between was our home.

In the spring and all through the summer—when the gray brows on those granite men to the west receded with the melts and the creek raged—an endless caravan of poor people with rich dreams appeared along the twin-rutted road from territories east. They passed through on their way to California, and our sworn duty at Fort Morgan was to see that their scalps moved right along with them.

Those were the melts and the busy months—spring and summer. Autumn and winter were a harder time at the fort. Men took to cards and more drink than the Good Army allowed, and each of us spent our share of nights in the pen sobering up and feeling like asses for mistakes we barely remembered. Those were the hard months—and in the eighteen hundred and sixty-eighth year of our Lord, they got suddenly harder.

I was out with Private Collins taking in a pair of deer when Lieutenant Randall took the sickness. The Lieutenant had been away from the fort for near on eight weeks. A trail scout, he spent most of his time up in the hills living in a tent like a native and looking for less damnable passages between those brutish mountains. He was always a bit peculiar, but nothing to presage him wandering back into camp and murdering five good men in cold blood. Yet that's just what he did; four of his fellow enlisted men were shot dead, plus a half-Indian cook named Sammy. Randall shot each of them in the head before someone managed to wing him and put an end to the slaughter. Why they didn't kill him on the spot, I'll never know.

Private Collins and me returned from our hunt too late to help with anything but the digging. Saw the aftermath, though: brains and skull and hair that took me right back to the war. They was already mopping it up, and so we were handed shovels. Now, nobody consulted me for my legal expertise, but Justice would've been served by shooting Lieutenant Randall right there on the spot. But the good Army of the United States of America has its own sense of justice. There are trials and spectacles afforded a man before his chest is riddled by a firing squad. There are nights spent in the pen. Which is how I found myself nursing a blister from the shoveling, sitting there on a hard bench outside the holding cell, taking my shift at watching Lieutenant Randall so that he weren't shot dead by some enterprising fellow before dawn.

On the bench across from me was my hunting partner and shovel mate, Private Collins. I surmised that his presence was to make sure I didn't scratch that itch of justice, either. I was keeping an eye on him and he on me, and both of us on the Lieutenant. Randall, meanwhile, snored and babbled like only the guilty and outright crazy could manage on the eve of their probable execution. What could make a man break camp one morning and ride in to shoot his comrades in their skulls? Morbid curiosity had me itching to know. I tried to discern some of what he was saying in his sleep—but couldn't make out a word.

"That's Red talk," Collins told me.

I turned to the Private and realized I'd been leaning forward on my bench, my face scrunched up in concentration. I tried to relax. "You understand what he's mumbling?" I asked, keeping my voice down.

Collins chewed on the end of an unlit cheroot, and then spat a dab of tobacco between our feet. "Arapaho," he said, matter-of-factly. Private Collins had that air about him, that supreme confidence that got on some men's nerves. He had also bagged both deer that morning, firing before I had the chance. Still, I liked him.

"What's he saying?" I asked. The only Indian I recognized was their war cries, when the hair on the back of my neck was translation enough.

Collins shrugged and sucked on his cigar. "Used to take an Arapaho whore in Mason," he said. "I know what their language sounds like, can catch a few words, but unless he starts talking about how thick my member is…" He smiled. And not for the first time, I wondered why I liked this man yet despised so many others.

"Why the hell is he dreaming in Arapaho?" I asked, still whispering. It was strange that I wanted the man in that pen dead but cared not to disturb his sleep. Collins turned toward the dimly lit cell.

"Reckon he done and gone native. Happens. Too much time up in the hills. Or maybe he's been heading into Mason and taking up with my whore." Collins laughed, but Randall didn't stir.

I settled back on my bench and marveled at a man who could sleep through what might be the last night of his life. More than justice, I was thirsty for answers. I decided, come morning, I would ask the Major if Collins and I could go hunting for something up in those hills besides deer.

Major Jack Lawson was a peculiar leader of men. Part eccentric and part mountain man, he was the reason Fort Morgan had a grand piano and a small library but no decent latrine. Music and books—and somehow shitting in bare holes in the dirt—were all apparently good for our souls.

Turned out the Major was just as curious about Randall's sudden madness as we were. He gave us his blessing to ride out in search of clues.

Collins knew where Randall had set up camp the previous autumn, and so we followed an angry stream up through the pines and aspens and cottonwoods that made up the scruff around the old mountain's neck. Stumbling on a native camp, it took a moment to realize that it was in fact Randall's place. An army-issue tent lay draped across a lean-to of woven branches. A half-finished structure of limbs and sticks jutted up nearby, a rough circle with a tall pole in the center. Around the camp, every tree within a hundred feet had been felled, the trunks radiating outward as though they'd been knocked over by a terrible blast. Gnawed stumps stood out everywhere. I noticed how cleanly they'd been hewn, not an errant strike to be seen, none of the work of a madman.

"Took down enough trees for a second Morgan up here," I remarked. I peered inside Randall's abandoned tent and found nothing amiss. The bedroll was laid out like it expected to be slept in, a set of pots and cutlery innocently nestled in one corner. It smelled of leather and sweat and man, even with the air cold enough to fog my breath. Collins poked a smoldering log in the fire pit with a stick and was rewarded with a flight of embers, like bees startling from a hive.

"Don't think he was after the timber," Collins said. He left the pit alone and headed past the tent to the half-completed structure that'd made me think this was an Indian campsite. Shielding his eyes, he glanced up at the autumn sky. "I reckon he was out to fell the shade, is what."

I looked up as well. The morning sun slid shyly behind a bank of clouds. "'Fell the shade?'" I asked.

"It's a sun hut." Collins waved his arm. "They dance in it. The Arapaho do."

There was a loud snap in the woods. We both turned toward the sound. There was a flash of white as a deer bounded away from us and through the cottonwoods. I turned to Collins, who I suspected knew more of the Arapaho than the moans of a Mason whore.

"What kind of dance?"

Collins watched the deer a moment longer, then scanned the woods. Finally, he turned to the odd structure, whose walls curved upward like an unfinished dome. A pole sat in the center that I figured was bound to support an arching roof; but I would find out later that the hut was finished just as it stood.

"All I know is what little I've heard. Pretty sure it started with the Arapaho, but other tribes have taken part. Spreading like those damn Mormons, like some kinda religion." Collins pointed to the sky. "They dance around a pole and stare up at the sun for days. They see things. Hear voices. And then they probably get drunk on peyote and shove feathers up their arses for all I know."

He shrugged and pulled out his cheroot. To my amazement, Collins bent and grabbed a smoking fag from the fire and lit the thing with noisy puffs. Maybe he figured we'd already chased away the deer and to hell with the smoke. Or maybe he'd seen enough death the day before to stop saving the thing for a morrow. Or perhaps the talk of ghosts and whispers had stirred his nerves. I watched his white exhalations rise toward the clouds, and the sun reemerged to peer down at us.

"I guess you were right," I told Collins.

He raised an eyebrow and threw the fag back in the fire.

"I think Lieutenant Randall has done and gone native. Maybe fell for some squaw and started seeing us as the enemy."

The private pinched something off the end of his tongue and inspected it. "Maybe," he said. But it sounded like he doubted it. He smoked his cheroot like it would be his last and studied the sky as if the sun up there knew something we didn't.

The two of us shared our findings with the Major later that morning and handed over Randall's tent, bedroll, and mess kit. Collins drew a straw for the firing squad; I didn't. The both of us had missed the court martial, which hadn't taken long. Three witnesses said he did it, and Randall hadn't uttered a word of defense. We heard he stared at the ceiling the entire time before being led back to the pen.

I should have gotten some sleep before lunch—only had a few hours the night before—but I volunteered to ride out with some others to see about another rustling, a strange disappearance of cattle from a rancher to the east.

On the ride out, I sidled my horse next to John McCall's. McCall had grown up in the Arizona territory, had missed the war entirely, and knew as much about Indians as any of us. He used to keep a feather stuck in his cap until the major told him to lose it. When pressed, McCall admitted he'd heard of the Sun Dance. He was surprised to hear about the hut near Randall's tent, said he thought it must've already been there. I told him about the felled trees. McCall didn't have much to say after that. We rode along in silence, the sun beating down on us, the horses growing warm, the featureless landscape making it feel like we hardly moved.

While the others went to talk to the rancher about his missing cattle and the burn marks some lightning strikes had left in the grass, I rode the fence line looking for a break in the thorny wire. I was sure the rancher had already checked his fence, but in my experience the most likely culprit to make off with a few head of cattle were those few head of cattle. I expected to see them milling about on the side of the trail where the grass grew tallest. It was getting on noon, and the flies buzzed something fierce. Amazing it could be cool in the morning up in the hills and so damn hot come afternoon on the plains. My mouth was dry and tasted of the dirt kicked up by my horse. Shaking my canteen, I decided to take it easy on the water. Before long, I found a drooping wire in the fence and dismounted to take a closer look.

Was only the top wire amiss. A sprightly cow might make the jump, but unlikely. Wiping my neck, I glanced up accusingly at the high sun. Not a cloud in the sky. I remembered something I'd learned early on in Kansas: there were tribes who would only come at you in the morning from the east. They would ride in, and you couldn't see their arrows in the glare. Before they attacked, one of their scouts would sit on a hill every morning, high on his horse, feathers blazing, and would be as good as invisible. Ghosts, bringing hell from the east. They would keep an eye on their enemy until it was time to rain death. Devious sons a'bitches.

The sun shone bright that day as I scanned the sky—and finally I had to look away. I didn't believe what Collins and McCall had said about dancing around and looking up at that fiery beast. A man couldn't stand two seconds staring at it. And maybe I was delirious from lack of sleep; or thinking about a man I had known who was at that moment being shot in the chest by my compadres; or maybe it was the sight of those I'd buried the day before; or I was just being powerfully curious and not thinking straight. But I felt an ungodly tug… and so I looked up and tried to return the gaze of that great yellow monster in the wide blue sky.

The burn was intense and immediate. It made my brain hurt somewhere deep between my brows. The squinting was involuntary. My horse made a sound and pawed at the air with one hoof. "Steady, now," I told him, taking the reins and turning away, unable to take it any longer. Blinking tears, I could see a green image in my vision, a disk the color of fresh grass. I wondered if this was what they claimed to see, those who danced and saw what weren't there.

The wire fence drooped like it was melting in the sun. A faint wind blew dust across my boots. Back toward the fort, mountains rose from the flat desert, impossibly tall, the white on their tops growing with the cold months. I blinked and blinked and wondered what in the hell I was doing out there. How could anyone dance around for three days and stare at the sun? Determined, I gave it another try. I would go for the count of twenty, pain be damned. If an Arapaho could do it, so could I.

Throwing my head back, I squinted at the sun and met it like a man. Again, the feeling was like claws raking my eyeballs. There was a primitive urge to look away, like a thumb on a hot pan. I forced my eyes open wider, muscles in my face quivering in complaint, tears streaking down my cheeks. I lost count. I swayed, my balance funny, and reached for a fencepost to steady myself. As my horse clomped down the road, I ignored him. There was nothing but white and heat, both penetrating straight into my brain. I hopped in place and cursed nothing in particular, just said "shit" and "damn" while the tears streamed out, but no bright light was stronger than this Virginia boy.

I had to've gone to a count of twenty, but I decided to keep going a bit more. I had the water in the canteen, could dump that in my eyes after and put the fire out. There was no thought of going blind. That fear would come later. I was just enduring the pain because goddamnit it wasn't going to beat me.

My neck cramped up, but now something had taken hold of me, some wild thought that this was the right thing to do, to stare at the sun for as long as I was able. Releasing the post, I drifted around in circles there in the dirt, admiring the shapes and colors as they spun in my vision. I saw purple. I saw strangers swim through the sky. When my lids clamped down involuntarily, I used my fingers to pry them open again. The burn and pain went straight through me until it felt like an itch being scratched. I spun and spun and felt the barbed wire catch at my trousers. The fence would keep me in. I thought of Collins spinning around in his little Indian hut. The barbs were suddenly those sticks, poking at me, corralling me. The light shone right through my eyes, down to the base of my skull, and deep into my neck where words are formed. My face grew warm, but now the bright light was cool as it swam through me. I could hear myself laugh. The horse drew away further, and I cared little.

When the vision came, it was a thunderclap. A sudden roar, though I realized the words had been there before. They were the buzzing in my brain, nonsense words, but I knew what they meant. I saw them like shapes and things, like swirling dreams. There was shouting, someone on the road with me, a man with my own voice. Crying and crying, fingers pinned my eyes open, and I never wanted to look away from the sun again. I loved it in that instant. I wanted it to fall out of the sky and enter me through my eyeballs; I wanted to let it blow me across the prairie and set everything on fire, to burn that land ahead of its coming, to make room. I saw men and women and children fall before me. I saw an infant thrown into the flames, blood in everyone's eyes. And the voices, these words foreign and understood that came like pictures directly into my head, this voice on the road that spoke as I spun and spun between the barbed wire and my skittish horse, they sounded like the tongue of a Red Man.

I woke up and men were dead. My men. Something told me there had been a killing. My head throbbed like my heart was trapped in my skull, had swollen up, and needed out. It took a moment to realize my eyes were open but I wasn't seeing anything. I could barely make out a shape in front of my face when I waved my hand before it. Groping about, I felt a bunk beneath me, a wall of steel bars behind. I was in the pen. I could feel the firing squad lined up, instruments of death aimed at my chest, could see the men I'd killed.

"Sir, he's done stirred."

Voices and shuffling feet. I had Arapaho on my tongue, the taste of silver and fire, words like pictures drawn in the dirt, telling me what to do. Something alien had communicated with me. A part of it lived deep inside.

"Drink some water, son."

There was a hand on my wrist, a hand reaching through the bars. A tin of water was pressed into my palm, sloshing cool on my forearm. My lips stung as I drank. I pulled the cup away and touched my mouth, found my lips swollen and cracked. My throat burned. But the horrible throbbing in my eyes and my brain drowned out these lesser hurts.

"What the hell happened to you?"

"Major?" My voice was a pale shadow of its old self. I drank more, ignoring the sting of my fouled lips. "What did I do?" I asked.

"They found you face up in the dirt, babbling like you had a few too many. Your horse came back to the fort without you."

"I can't see."

"That's what you've been sayin'. Doc said to put you in here where it was dark, that it should come back. You rest up, okay? Can't afford to lose any more of my men."

"How many?"

I could hear the boards creak as the Major shifted his weight. "How many of what, son?"

"Did I... how many dead?" Memories and visions were mixed up in my head. Words I knew and words I didn't. There were flashes of green and swimming lights in my eyes like an angry campfire. Something was telling me to kill or that I already had, hard to tell which.

"Get some rest. I'll send some food over."

I nursed my water and decided I hadn't done the things I thought I had. But I could feel the urge. Some silent screaming beneath my skin, something directing my bones. I was reminded of a visit to Richmond when I was a boy. A friend of my mother's was a pastor there, took us to his great big church. There was a belfry terribly high off the ground, a circuit of rickety stairs, and at one corner you could peer down at the street like a bird. And something in me felt this urge to jump out and go plummeting down, something so strong that I had to back away and clutch my father, even though I was too old to be holding his hand. And now this demon was in my blood again, but this time to hurt others.

Long after the tin cup was dry, I continued to pass it back and forth between my hands. It was Collins who brought me my supper.

"You gone and blinded yourself," Collins said, a voice in the darkness. Hinges peeled as he let himself into the pen, and I realized the door had never been locked. I hadn't killed no man. Not that day, anyhow.

The plate was warm as he rested it on my knee. A fork was pressed into my palm. "You manage all right?" he asked. "See anything yet?"

I shook my head. I saw things, but not like he meant.

"I blame myself," Collins said. "But what was you thinking?"

"I weren't," I admitted. "Just started and couldn't stop."

Collins laughed. "Most take a glance and know it's a bad idea."

I groped around the plate with my fork, found some resistance, some weight. Took a sniff of potatoes and blew on 'em in case they was hot. How anyone lived with such blindness, I couldn't fathom.

"I heard voices," I told Collins. I wasn't sure I'd ever tell anyone, but it just came out. "Voices and… I had a vision." I swallowed the potatoes and shook my head. Patches of murk swam in the darkness, a vague discernment of shapes. I'd welcome just seeing my own hands.

"You heard voices. You mean when they scooped you off the road?"

"Before." I peered at where I thought Collins stood, where I heard him. "They were telling me to do awful things. I think Randall was poisoned by the sun."

"Randall was poisoned by the Arapaho. He was babblin' that nonsense right up until we shot him. You just need some sleep is all."

I nodded and ate, and Collins gave me silent and invisible company. By nightfall, it felt as though some of my eyesight was returning, but not much. I fell asleep on that cot for drunkards, madmen, and murderers— and wondered which one of them I was.

When I awoke, it was not yet dawn. My internal clock had unwound from the late shifts and lack of sleep. But I could see my hands, and my lips only part ways stuck together. Groping about, I let myself out of the pen and sought my own bunk.

Along the way, with my fingers brushing cedar clapboards to keep from spinning in circles, I noticed the pinpricks of tiny lights in my vision. It was pitch black across the fort, and it was like somehow the brightest of stars were able to penetrate my blindness. But no: it was my eyesight returning.

I stopped and marveled at the tiny spots of light in that infinite darkness. The voices were out there, straining to be heard. There was a madness in my soul, an invader.

It hadn't taken a full hold of me, but its claws had left marks. It was the same madness I'd seen in the war cries of the natives we fought with. It was the madness Randall had seized upon. A cry from some distant throat telling me that this land was someone else's and that a reckoning was coming. That was the sight I'd seen: a land wiped clean and taken by those who didn't belong, a land of dead and missing cattle to starve us the way we'd done with the buffalo, a time of great sickness and men dying beyond counting, with infection rained down from the heavens like some poisoned blanket.

This was the calling. I heard it clearer that night than I ever would again. I stood there for what felt like hours, searching for those pinprick stars and marveling at how our own sun was said to be one like them. Our sun, where native tribes stood sentinel in the morning so we couldn't see them coming, where they would watch and watch and plan their deadly raids. Many a time, they had brought hell on us from the east with the rising of the sun, the Arapaho and the Sioux and the Apache, but I reckoned we'd done the same and that others might do it to us one day. Generations back, a man with my name had crossed a wide sea and brought his own hell from the east. Others would come. It were folly to think we'd be the last.

That was my vision, what I saw clearly that night in my blindness and with an earful of strange voices. I saw the night and its lights like never before. There was a far and dark sea out there, hanging over me. A dark sea that ships sailed on, scouts arriving at dawn to watch over us, vast fleets to rain down by dusk. But it was not yet dusk. It was early yet. And those stars were like campfires impossibly distant where strange men spoke in strange tongues and conjured war. They spoke with words that I could not fathom but could see like scratches in the dirt, could see like a calling to do bad things on their behalf.

I tried to explain this to whoever would listen, but they would only lock me up for my troubles. They would lock me up before I ever got the chance to heed those voices the way Lieutenant Randall had. I was locked up years later and therefore not a part of that massacre at Wounded Knee Creek, which put an end to the war with our red kin. I was locked up while more cattle went missing and a great sickness swept the land, millions and millions of people dying like my brother had. It has not yet come, this thing from the east that whispers for me to clear the land in preparation. It has not yet come. But something stirs and will talk to those crazy enough to look and listen. There is something across that dark sea, across that expanse of space that men saner than me say no one will ever cross, but I wager my red brother thought the same thing of the deep blue Atlantic that lapped their former shores—and here we are.

We who hailed from the east, who came from that rising sun too bright to see, who came first with scouts across the pitch black, standing tall and ignorant and proud atop some deadly ridge.

SECOND HAND
A CARD SHARP STORY

RAJAN KHANNA

Wyoming Territory, Circa 1874

Quentin Ketterly stood in the Gold Star Saloon and lit his cheroot with one hand, the other resting lightly on his hip, very close to his waistcoat pocket. He stared across the room at the five men playing poker at a nearby table. His eyes tracked the movement of the cards that they held and played, though his mind was on another set of Cards entirely.

The lion's share of his attention was focused on one Hiram Tetch—an itinerant and idiot, who happened to be Quentin's charge. Not for the first time, Quentin cursed the promise that had led him to become… what? Hiram's teacher? His chaperone?

Whatever the title, he had promised the old man that he would look after the lad, and without the old man, Quentin wouldn't have become a Card Sharp and wouldn't have discovered the Cards. Taking care of Hiram was payment for that debt. That the old man had a halfwit for a son was just part of the price.

The dealer dealt out a fresh hand and Hiram looked surreptitiously at the cards, then tugged at the brim of his bowler hat. Quentin recognized it as one of Hiram's tells. It meant he had a good hand. Unfortunately, the money in front of him was meager. He could have gone all in, but that likely would have scared off the skittish players at the table. Hiram liked to draw out the play, reel in the others, then clean up.

Hiram reached into the inside pocket of his dusty black coat and removed a gold cigarette case. He held it down in his lap and fitted a cigarette to his lips. As he struck the match on the underside of the table, Quentin saw two lights flare—one from the match, the other from inside the case. Quentin stifled a curse and his hand moved closer to his waistcoat pocket.

Quentin couldn't see the Card Hiram had just Played, the one that had come from inside the cigarette case, but he would bet it all that it had been a Diamond. Diamonds were associated not only with wealth, but with trickery. Illusion. What in the damned Hell was the boy playing at?

A moment later, Hiram reached into his coat pocket (an outside one this time) and removed a small pouch of clinking coins. Quentin knew with certainty that the pouch had been empty just moments before. "My emergency supply," Hiram said and spilled shining coins onto the table. The other men grunted, but seemed pacified. They had no reason to know of Hiram's notorious lack of foresight, his inability to look even an hour into the future.

The hand continued.

Hiram reeled them in.

When all was said and done, Hiram had more than tripled the money he'd started with. He sat back, a wide grin etched on his face. He looked at Quentin and winked. Quentin frowned back. It was an expression all too familiar to him these days.

A cry went up from one of the other men at the table. While Hiram had won back most of his "emergency supply," some of the coins had made their way into the others' piles, and the man who had cried out held one of these between two grimy fingers, his face puckered into a grimace. The coin flexed between his fingers, to the astonishment of everyone except Quentin and Hiram.

Then the room erupted into chaos.

Hiram swiped at the paper money in front of him, scooping up as much as he could, then ran for the front door of the saloon as his fellow players reached for their guns.

Quentin cursed and tossed the cheroot, his hand reaching to his waistcoat pocket and his Deck. It was a reflex action in times of stress, but he would be damned if he would waste one of his Cards on that fool of a boy.

Still, his hand stayed near his pocket.

The men ran after Hiram, and Quentin chased after them. Hiram bolted across the street and around the side of the tailor's shop, running for the fringe of scrub that rimmed the town of Stillwell like thinning hair. Quentin winced as a shot rang out. It would serve the kid right to get a bullet in the ass as a result of his play. And for generally being a burr in the seat of everyone's pants.

Quentin pulled out the Five of Spades, held it tightly between his fingers. Ahead, Hiram dove for a small bush, and Quentin saw a flash between the sparsely-filled branches.

The two pursuers held their guns out, but as they prepared to shoot, the gun barrels twisted, curving until they were black and silver snakes in the men's hands. Both men screamed and dropped the snakes to the ground. Then, with a look at each other, they bolted.

Quentin waited a moment, then strode to where Hiram was hiding. "I don't know where to begin," he said. "With your damn fool decision to cheat or with your poor job in doing so." He pulled the young man up by his collar.

Hiram's expression turned serious. "I don't cheat," he said. "Conjurin' up more coins don't mean I cheat at cards."

Quentin rolled his eyes. "You couldn't hold the Play."

Hiram flushed. "Just a moment longer and it would have been fine." He shrugged off Quentin's touch and brushed the bramble from his coat. "Only, well, I used a Four."

"How many coins did you conjure?"

"Forty-nine. I mean, I know that the numbers should match, but, well, it was still in the range of four..."

Quentin slapped the back of Hiram's head. "Idiot," he said. "I taught you better than that. Never mind. We need to get off this street in case those men come back."

Quentin grabbed Hiram's arm and pulled him down the street. "When are you going to learn some sense?" Quentin said. "Wasting Cards on a card game?"

"What do you care?" Hiram asked. "They're my Cards. You can't use 'em."

"*You* should care," Quentin said. "Once they're gone, there are no more."

"But I did good with those pistols, right?" Hiram asked.

Quentin spit. He would have liked to say the Play was no good. Instead, he admitted, "Yeah, kid. That was good."

Hiram pulled away from Quentin and went back to where the altercation had taken place. When he returned, he was tucking one of the six-shooters, now reverted to its original form, into his belt.

"What you going to do with that?" Quentin asked.

Hiram shrugged. "Maybe next time I won't need to use my Cards."

Quentin shook his head. "We're not here to start useless fights. And we're not here to win money at cards."

"I know," Hiram said. "We're here for the list, but we need money to keep us going, right?"

Quentin gritted his teeth. The boy was right. They'd been chasing down a list of names that the old man had kept inside his battered traveling case. So far, it had yielded little but had eaten through a lot of their resources—Cards and cash both. The last name had brought them to Stillwell, but they'd only had enough money to pay for one night in the hotel.

"You head back to the room," Quentin said. "I want you lying low in case those card players are still about."

"What are you going to do?"

Quentin narrowed his eyes. "I'm going to see if we can't turn this hand around."

The last name on their list was just "Gunsmith." Quentin asked about, as discreetly as he could. The boy at the stables turned his luck. "Don't know no Gunsmith, but there is a gun shop in town."

It sounded right to Quentin. If this were a card game, it would be enough for him to bluff. He returned to the hotel, grabbed Hiram, and dragged him to the gun shop. They stood outside looking for a moment at the plain, wooden building.

"Guess we should go inside," Hiram said. Before Quentin could stop him, he bounded up the steps leading to the shop door and burst inside.

Mumbling curses, Quentin followed.

The store wasn't very different from other gun stores that Quentin had been to, though he had only seen a few. Sleek, oiled pistols and rifles lined glass cases, with a few models mounted on the walls.

Standing behind the counter, wearing a leather apron, was a woman. Her sandy hair was streaked with gray and pulled back into a ponytail. Her eyes were a startling blue, but tired. She raised an eyebrow at Quentin. "You looking for a gun?" she said.

"No," Quentin said. "I'm actually looking for someone who might go by the name of Gunsmith. You know anyone like that?"

The woman's eyes narrowed. "And what might you be wanting with this Gunsmith?"

"Just to talk," Quentin said. "We think he might have known a friend of ours."

"My father," Hiram said. "Though he was never no friend to me."

One of the woman's hands came up with a black revolver. "Well, there's no Gunsmith here. And unless you're looking to buy a gun, I think you'd better just leave now." She eased the hammer back with her thumb.

Quentin's hand jumped to his waistcoat pocket. "Now hold on," he said. "No need to get jumpy."

Hiram reached for his Cards, too, in their cigarette case, and the woman swiveled the pistol toward him.

Quentin pulled the Five of Spades.

The woman's eyes flashed between the two of them, then she thumbed the hammer back into place and lowered the revolver. "Wasn't expecting you to be slinging Cards," she said.

Quentin's eyes widened. "You know about the Cards?"

The woman nodded. "I'm Gunsmith."

Quentin nodded and slid the Five of Spades back into his pocket. He moved forward, excited. "I'm Quentin Ketterly. And this is Hiram Tetch."

"Real names, huh? You must be greenhorns. Most seasoned Cardslingers use nicknames."

"Oh," Quentin said.

Hiram elbowed Quentin lightly in the ribs. "I'm going to call myself the King of Aces."

"No," Quentin said. "You're definitely not." He turned to Gunsmith. "We've been looking for you."

Her eyes narrowed again. "I get that. Why?"

"To learn more about the Cards," Quentin said.

"And you expect me to learn you? Why would I do that?"

Quentin paused, taken aback. "I just thought…"

"That we're all one happy family? You *do* have a lot to learn. There are some that would kill you just for showing your hand. Hell, I almost killed you myself."

"Why?" Quentin said.

"I made a lot of enemies in my time with the Cards," Gunsmith said.

"You're using a six-shooter, though," Hiram said. "Reckon that's so you can save your Cards?"

"In a way," Gunsmith said. She held up the pistol and, without it being pointed at him, Quentin saw that it was one of the finest revolvers he'd ever set eyes on. "This here's a Colt Peacemaker," Gunsmith said. "In the right hands, a Peacemaker'll kill a man dead. But this here Colt will kill anyone dead with just one shot. Anywhere. Graze a man on the ear, and he'll die. Guaranteed."

"How?"

Gunsmith smiled. "The Six of Spades. I infused the power into the revolver. Good for six shots. And, well, you know Spades…"

She held up another six-shooter made from a darker metal. "This one was the Six of Clubs. Each shot is a small explosion. First pistol won't hurt anything other than a person. But this one can blow in doors."

"You have them for the Six of Diamonds and Six of Hearts, too?" Hiram said.

"I used to," Gunsmith said.

"So you harness the power of the Card," Quentin said, "but defer the effect until later."

"Exactly," Gunsmith said.

"Can I do that?" Quentin asked.

"Well, not without practice," Gunsmith said. "It took me years to master it."

Quentin shook his head. There was so much he didn't know about the Cards. So much he hadn't even considered. He certainly had never imagined being able to infuse their power into other objects.

"I don't usually go heeled," Quentin said, "but a gun like that…"

Gunsmith raised an eyebrow. "You in need of killing someone?"

Quentin looked at his boots. "Not anymore."

She let this pass. She looked at Hiram. "So I guess your father was Jeb Tetch?"

Hiram nodded.

"When I met him, he was going by the name 'Hoyle,'" Quentin said.

"Hoyle?" Gunsmith said. "The nerve of that man. He used to go by Cannonball. As in 'all the subtlety of.' The man was a brute, but—" Her eyes squinted in recollection. "—boy could he dance."

Quentin looked at Hiram, who shrugged.

"So, I take it you're now teaching this one." She indicated Hiram.

"As much as I know," Quentin said.

"And how is that going?" she asked Hiram.

"Well, ma'am," Hiram said, "he's about as fun as a bucket of mud, but I think he's learning me just fine."

Gunsmith eyed them both, shaking her head. "I should send you both packing."

"But you're not," Quentin said, picking up on her reticence.

Gunsmith sighed. "No. Against my better judgment I'm not." She looked at Hiram. "As a favor to your father. He wasn't all bad."

Hiram shrugged. "If you say so."

"Besides," she continued. "You remind me of better times, of my own apprentice." Her face darkened for a moment. Then she smiled. "Why don't you boys come by tomorrow. We can have lunch. Will that suit?"

"Yes," Quentin said. "Thank you. We'll see you then."

Quentin couldn't deny something like a thrill as he dressed the next morning. He couldn't wait to meet with Gunsmith, couldn't wait to hear more about the Cards. He had twenty-six left, but he hoped to learn a way to use them more wisely. Or even just learn more about where they came from. How they worked. He had promised the old man that he would teach Hiram. This would help. And then, when he was done, he could start using the Cards to help people. To do good instead of violence. Hell, maybe they both could.

He went outside for a quick smoke, then went to fetch Hiram, who was already two drinks deep at the bar. "Isn't it a bit early?" Quentin said.

"Just needed a little fortification," Hiram said. "I'm good now."

"Good. Because we have an appointment today."

"I know," Hiram said. "The old lady."

"You be respectful," Quentin said. "We could learn a lot from her. You'd do well to pay attention."

"I'd love to get my hands on one of those Colts," Hiram said. "D'ya think she'd give us some kind of discount?"

"No. And no asking her neither. Be polite."

They stopped by the fancy store up the street, the one that carried imported goods, and walked out with some tea from back east and some biscuits. Then they went over to Gunsmith's.

There was no answer when Quentin knocked, so he knocked again. Then again.

"Do you smell smoke?" Hiram said.

Quentin sniffed the air, then kicked in the door.

The interior of Gunsmith's shop was in disarray, glass cases broken into shards, pistols and rifles and instruments strewn across the place, curtains torn down, tables overturned.

"What do you think—?" Hiram said.

Quentin shushed him, his Deck already out in his hands. Hiram followed suit. They crouched down and stalked through the store. The place was silent save for the sound of their own steps, and whatever had been burning had been doused already, so there was no immediate danger.

At the back of the shop, they found Gunsmith. She lay on the ground, stiff, her arms and legs contorted, her face twisted in a permanent expression of complete pain.

"Good god," Hiram said, and turned away.

Quentin crouched by the body. Touched one claw of a hand. It wouldn't budge. Then he searched the woman's pockets, her apron.

"God, man, be decent," Hiram said.

"I'm checking for her Cards," Quentin said.

"Why?"

"Because I can't imagine she would let this happen. And—" He didn't finish the sentence. He needed to be sure.

His search turned up nothing. No Cards. None even littered the ground. As an afterthought, he checked her boots. Hiram's father had taught Quentin to keep his Jokers there, since their uses were unpredictable. Quentin had taught Hiram to do the same.

Gunsmith's boots were empty.

"Maybe she didn't carry them with her," Hiram said.

"You know what the Cards are. How special they are. Would you keep yours anywhere but on your person?"

"No," Hiram said. "But… maybe she was empty. Dry. No more."

The thought chilled Quentin. "She did use the power in her guns. Maybe she *had* run out."

"Shit," Hiram said. "What do we do now?"

Quentin clenched his jaw. He knew that they should just move on. Someone good enough to take out Gunsmith, to make this kind of Play, might be more than they could handle. But this was the end of their trail. If they walked away now, they might never find another person who knew the Cards.

"I don't want to spend too much time here, but I say we do some quick exploring. Might be something here that could help us out."

Hiram nodded. Quentin gritted his teeth. He hated going through the woman's things—it felt too much like looting—but anything that would help them, any more information on the cards, would be a boon.

This wasn't what I bargained for, he thought. *Skulking around like a criminal. Yet, the Cards are too important.*

He closed Gunsmith's eyelids and rose to search her shop.

* * *

They found the Spades revolver in one corner of the room, and the cylinder had only two bullets left in it. "She used this," Quentin said.

"But it didn't help her," Hiram said.

"No. And since there's no other body here, we'll have to assume she didn't hit anyone."

Hiram took the pistol and tucked it into his belt. "No use leaving this behind," he said. "Not with the magic in it."

Quentin winced at the word. He hated thinking of it like that. But Hiram always named it so.

Quentin ran his fingers along the edge of his Deck. He could rustle up something to help track the killer, but it would use up a Card. He'd dealt out half of them while pursuing revenge against his uncle—payback for the death of his father. He'd hoped to honor his father by doing something better with the Cards afterward. And he would, once he'd finished schooling Hiram.

He could ask Hiram to make a Play. The boy would put up a fuss, but in the end he'd probably do it. But that idea left a bad taste behind it.

That was the thing about the Cards. As wondrous as they were, they made one a miser. Like an old man clinging to a dwindling fortune.

"I don't like this," Quentin said. "Whoever killed her didn't seem to take much. Most of the weapons are still where they belong. Save for those that got knocked over."

"And it weren't no gunfight," Hiram said. "Not with that smell in the air. If it weren't her Cards, then maybe someone else made the Play?"

Could that be it? Quentin thought. *She had said she'd made enemies. Did one come back to kill her?* "Let's go upstairs and see if we can find anything."

They moved through Gunsmith's rooms, pulling open drawers and pawing through chests and bureaus.

"What are we looking for, exactly?" Hiram said.

"I don't know," Quentin replied. "Something to give us direction."

In the end, they found nothing beyond what a woman of Gunsmith's age might have in her house—clothing, some toiletries, and linens—plus an assortment of tools in an old chest. But nothing about the Cards. No notebooks or diaries, either.

"Let's get out of here," Quentin said.

"Okay," Hiram said. "Just give me a minute. I want to check on something."

Quentin descended the stairs… and froze when he saw a woman standing in the room beside Gunsmith's body. She was young, blonde, with piercing blue eyes; she wore traveling clothes and held a deck of cards (he had to assume they were Cards) in her hand.

Suddenly, she noticed him. "Who the hell are you?" she said. She stepped back.

Quentin's eyes flicked to her Deck. "Now hold on," he said.

The woman's eyes narrowed. "D'you kill her?"

"What? Me?" Quentin said. "No, I—"

She pulled a Card from the top of her deck, though Quentin could only see the red back of it. He raised his own Card. But something held him back.

"Let's not be hasty," he said, moving slowly forward. "This could all be a misunderstanding."

"What isn't a misunderstanding," she said, "is that my mother's dead. Murdered. And I find you robbing her house. No, there ain't no misunderstanding."

"Wait, your mother?" Quentin said. "She never said she had a kid."

"Oh, and you knew her so well, did you?" She still held the Card out in her shaking hand. All it would take was some concentration and she could rain fire down on him. Or something else. He could try to counter, but there was no knowing what card she held. Quentin would either have to Play one of his highest or risk going down.

Hiram's arrival broke the moment down into pieces. The woman's eyes jumped to him. Quentin moved. He pumped his legs, closing the gap, and tackled the woman to the ground. He placed one hand across the woman's eyes, hoping it would momentarily break her concentration. Then he hissed in her ear, "We didn't kill your ma."

"How do I know you're telling the truth? Why should I believe you?"

"We came here to meet with her. She was going to talk to us. About the Cards."

"What about them?"

"We're... we're new to this. We thought she could teach us something."

The woman looked from Quentin to Hiram. She narrowed her eyes. "That does sound like her."

Quentin let go of the woman and got to his feet, offering his hand to her. "I'm awful sorry about your mother. If there's anything we can do to help, we'll try."

Her face softened, then she took his hand and he helped her to her feet. She turned back to where her mother still lay and took a moment to compose herself. "When did you get your Deck?" she asked, brushing off her skirt.

"His father gave it to me." Quentin indicated Hiram. "As a favor."

"That's some favor."

"Well, it wasn't all kindness. He asked me to train this one."

"Hey!" Hiram said.

"My ma gave me mine," the woman said. She extended her hand. "I'm Clarice."

"Quentin." He shook her hand. She had a good grip. "This here is Hiram."

Hiram tipped his bowler hat. "Ma'am."

"Do you know who might have wanted to hurt your ma?" Quentin asked.

"I know she'd made enemies," Clarice said. "I'd heard tell that someone was gunning for her. One of her friends down in Abilene got word to me. I just… got here too late."

All of them turned when they heard the loud voices outside the front door. Quentin peeked through the curtained windows. "The Law," he said and grabbed Hiram's arm. "We have to go. Looks like someone heard something. Clarice, if you need us, you can find us at the Sovereign Hotel."

"No," Clarice said. "I'm going with you."

"Why?"

"The sheriff's not going to believe my ma was killed by a deck of playing cards. And I can't waste time here with those dullwits while her killer is still out there. I'll go with you now and deal with the law later."

Quentin nodded. "Okay. If that's how you want to play it. Let's go."

They slipped out the back and made their way to the hotel. Quentin had to stop himself from barraging Clarice with questions. He'd thought his hopes for more knowledge about the Cards had died with Gunsmith. But now he'd found someone else. Only there were more important things to focus on now. But once they were done…

He pushed the thoughts away. They entered the hotel, and Quentin turned to Clarice. "Why don't you stay down here, maybe get a drink, and we'll head up to our room for a minute, then we'll come back down and join you."

"I'll come with you," she said.

"But—" Quentin said, exchanging a glance with Hiram. Surely she would be concerned about propriety.

"My ma just died," she said. "I need to do something."

He shrugged and the three of them walked up the stairs to the room the two men shared.

Clarice sat on the bed, and Hiram, without being asked, poured her some whisky from the bottle they kept in the room. Clarice took a long draught. Quentin took off his hat, poured some water into the basin, and threw it over his face and neck. Dust and grit colored the water.

"How many do you have left?" Hiram said behind him.

"Not enough," Clarice said, and left it at that. Curiosity burned brightly in Quentin's mind. Was that part of the etiquette? Don't let others know what you have? It certainly would be safer.

"Did your mother have any Cards left?" Quentin said, toweling off his face.

"I… I don't know," she said. "She did last time I saw her, but…" She shrugged.

"I guess she either'd run out or she used what she had left trying to fight off her killer. If we're lucky, that means he will have used a few Cards of his own."

"There could have been more than one of them," Hiram said. "If I wanted to take down a veteran Card Sharp, I'd have sent a few men after her."

"We don't know enough," Quentin said. "If the killer just came here to kill Gunsmith, he might already be on his way out of town."

"Then we should be checking and maybe asking around to see who might be new in town," Hiram said.

"I'll do that," Quentin said. "I don't want to chance you running into your friends from the Gold Star Saloon."

"What should I do then?" Hiram said.

"You and Clarice see what you can turn up. Maybe ask around here? It might even make sense to talk to the sheriff."

Hiram grimaced, but Clarice nodded.

Quentin gave Hiram a pat on the back, a pat that the younger man seemed to find uncomfortable, then he left.

The bright light of Stillwell's main road brought second thoughts. *What are you doing, Quentin? Risking your life and maybe your Cards for something that doesn't concern you?*

But he had wanted to do good with the Cards. Wasn't stopping a killer doing good? Wasn't righting injustice worth the risk?

He stopped first at the other side of Stillwell at the Alder Hotel where the stagecoach departed from. The next stage wasn't for at least an hour, and no one was there waiting.

Next, he stopped by the town stables and asked around if anyone had left in a hurry. No one seemed to have done so. Quentin hung around the stables for a spell nevertheless, until he felt stupid watching for someone who might never come.

On his way back to the Sovereign, he detoured past Gunsmith's place. Outside of it, he pulled his Deck from his waistcoat pocket and flipped through it. Hiram had wanted a special case for his—the cigarette case—but Quentin liked to have his pressing up against him, easily accessible.

Of all the Cards in his deck, he had more Diamonds than anything else. Cards from the other three suits had been burned up in his vendetta against his uncle.

He found he suddenly wished for a pistol like the one Hiram had picked up. Perhaps the boy had it right. Maybe it was a way to hold on to the Cards a little longer. No wonder Gunsmith survived for as long as she did. Finding a way to make the Cards last was a miracle. Once they were gone, they were gone. It was the one absolute truth he knew about them.

The lawmen had left Gunsmith's house some time ago by the looks of it, probably to cart off the body to the undertaker. He wondered what they would think of her death; there were no real wounds on the body—whatever had killed her had been from the Card Sharp's Play.

Quentin reached for his Diamonds. He hadn't been intending to use a Card for this—it wasn't even his business, any of this. But finding out what happened to Gunsmith felt right. And Clarice might be more willing to exchange information if he helped find her mother's killer.

Making a Play was tricky and never a guaranteed thing. If you tried for something beyond the value of the Card, it wouldn't work. And you would waste the Card nonetheless. So he thought carefully.

He needed to sharpen his senses. He flipped to the Five of Diamonds. It seemed right—five senses, after all. But before he drew it, he flipped ahead to the Six and pulled that out. Five normal senses, sure, but there was that elusive sixth. And Diamonds was the suit of vision and also of earth, of buried secrets.

He entered the house through the open back door and sat down where they'd found Gunsmith's body. Then he focused on the Six of Diamonds, shaping his desire, feeling the power gather as it always did, and he willed the Card to life. It flared in his hand, burning away to nothing.

He gasped as his vision swam and the room around him seemed to thicken, as if he were underwater. A shape, like dark smoke, coalesced before him. As he stepped back, it sharpened into Gunsmith. Or at least an approximation of her. Her features were muddied, unclear. But he knew it was her.

The vision went beyond sight, though. He could feel her boots upon the wooden floor. Could smell the scent of her—oil and leather and something herbaceous.

She was bending down, lining up some pistols in a glass case. The door opened. She rose and reached for the Spades pistol. The figure in the doorway was black smoke.

Quentin caught the momentary image of a Card in the figure's hand. Then a charge ran through the room and the glass case in front of Gunsmith shattered, throwing glass around like sparks from a fire. Gunsmith rose, firing—once, twice, then the pistol went flying from her grasp.

She reached down to a holster beneath her apron, coming up with a Card.

The vision blurred as intense energies filled the room. Though he was removed by the veil of time, Quentin thought he could feel Gunsmith's attack raise the hairs on his arms.

Gunsmith reached for another Card, but maybe she was injured, or just too slow. Whatever the reason, she never used it. An unseen force gripped her, arching her back and contorting her face, and then she toppled to the ground, still in the same awkward position.

The attacker moved into the room. And as she neared, as the room saw her, felt her, her features resolved so that Quentin could see who it was. His skin went cold.

Clarice.

As he watched, she bent down over the dead form of Gunsmith and removed the Card from the still-clutching hand, then retrieved the rest from the holster at the dead woman's side. It was a thin stack, but she took them, and put them in her own coat pocket.

I've been a damned fool, Quentin thought.

He ran upstairs, back into the bedroom. He remembered a photograph from before, in a tarnished silver frame. He picked it up. There was a younger Gunsmith and Clarice, no more than a girl. Why would she kill her own mother?

He was just leaving the bedroom when a gunshot rang out downstairs.

Quentin ran down the stairs and barreled into the shop. Clarice stood over a limp, dark figure on the ground, holding a still-smoking pistol. Gunsmith's Spades pistol. Quentin recognized Hiram's bowler hat rolling away on the floor. Clarice held Hiram's Deck of Cards in her free hand.

Clarice turned and leveled the pistol at him. Quentin's Cards were still in his pocket.

"Why?" Quentin gasped, reeling as he spoke the words. *I'm sorry, old man—I failed you. I let your son die.*

"For these," she said, holding up the Deck.

Quentin shook his head. "But you can't use another man's Cards!"

Clarice grinned with one side of her mouth. "Are you certain of that fact?" she said. Quentin began to move, but she cocked back the hammer of the pistol. "Uh-uh."

"Do you really think you can make them work?"

"Oh, I know it to be true," she said. "It's clear you're milling about on the ignorant side of the fence—and to be fair, most of us are—but there are ways out there, secret ways, that only a few know. One trick lets you take another's Cards and make them your own."

Quentin gasped. The old man had taught him that there was only ever the one Deck. Once you used that up, the power was gone. Never to return. To be able to get more…

"Why kill him?" he said through clenched teeth.

"Don't you understand how it works? The Cards are linked to us when we take them. When we use them. I can't take these if the owner is still breathing. The ritual that tethers them wouldn't work otherwise."

"Ritual?"

"Yes," she said, her smile widening. "Once I find it, I'll—"

"You don't even have it yet?" Quentin said, incredulous. Without even meaning to, he moved forward, and then stopped when Clarice took a step toward him, gun arm fully outstretched, violence sparking in her eyes.

"No," she said, the smile now gone. "Not yet, but I will. Ma got it from one of her old pals. Only I had to kill him when I made my escape. Believe me, every day I spent chained up in her cellar… I don't regret it one bit. Though it did make this part more difficult. The sad thing is that the cost, in Cards, is high. But with your two Decks, and Ma's, I should have plenty leftover after."

Quentin shook his head. "She tried to take your Cards?"

"I was so happy when she told me about them, when she made me my Deck. I was adopted, you see. I felt like this was her passing on her legacy to me. Only I don't know if she did it because she wanted to share them, or if she knew this is how it would end. I think she gave them to me just so she could take them back again."

"My God," Quentin said. "Why?"

"Why?" she repeated, a wild gleam in her eyes. "You know why. So much power, but always fleeting. She spent most of her life trying to make them last longer. Putting their strength into objects. But, as you know, they dwindle. They go. She started getting weird in the head. Paranoid. She kept saying that old enemies were coming for her. She needed more. I guess… I guess I made things easier, unsuspecting as I was."

Quentin thought back to the old man training him. If he knew barely anything now, he'd known literally nothing then. The old man could have easily killed him and taken the Cards back. "How did you manage to survive?"

The smile returned. "She had to learn me something," she said. "I think that's how the magic works. She couldn't just take them from me right away. Even so, it wasn't easy. I used one of my Jokers and that gave me an opportunity. I ran away and never came back. 'Til now."

It made sense. Jokers, as Wild Cards, had unpredictable results. He'd in fact used one to similar advantage.

"Thing was," Clarice said, "I was really gunning for you and your friend. I picked up on the two of you going around to some of the old-timers, asking questions. I figured you'd be easy marks. I never expected you'd lead me back here. I ought to thank you. Lucky I got to you before she did."

Realization dawned in Quentin's mind. If she was right, Gunsmith wouldn't have taught them about the Cards. She would have taken them. Still, it didn't matter much. Clarice was going to do the same.

She smiled. "Now, toss your Cards to me."

"No," Quentin said. "You're going to kill me anyway. I'm not gonna make this easy for you."

"Fair enough," she said. The gunshot rang out even as Quentin felt the slug strike his left shoulder. He fell backward, his chest erupting into pain.

This was it, then, he thought. Death at last. Still with some Cards remaining. The Cards she would take from him. From his corpse.

He fell to the ground, the impact hard against his body. He'd been expecting a quick death, thought that's how the gun would work, but it was taking its sweet time. He hurt too much—it was sadistic.

Clarice moved toward him.

Quentin found himself wishing that the bullet would take effect, would kill him before she took his Deck away. To have to watch…

She stood above him now, her eyes greedy.

Then the room exploded into a flurry of butterflies—fluttering, delicate wings of every possible color flitting and flying through the space.

Clarice turned in surprise and started swatting at them as they flew at her.

Quentin pushed aside his astonishment and moved. Whatever the reason, the bullet had yet to take him, and he still had his Cards. Ignoring the pain in his shoulder, he rose to his feet and took out the next Card from his deck, the Seven of Diamonds. His perceptions from the previous card were still lingering, and he reached out through them, feeling roots tangling beneath the wooden floor, coiling through the earth there. The Card flared in his hand and with a creaking, then a cracking, the roots shot up through the wooden floor, suddenly animated, wrapping around Clarice's legs.

The pistol went tumbling from her hands, and she reached for her own Deck, drawing a Card, which quickly burned away in her hands. The roots that gripped her suddenly took fire, sizzling away into blackish smoke that blew across the flying butterflies.

Quentin flipped out another Card, the Eight of Spades this time, and focused his thoughts, throwing a thunderbolt across the store's space. It flared bright blue-white, incinerating a wide swath of butterflies in its path as it arced toward Clarice.

But the light from a Card in Clarice's hand was already fading, throwing up a reddish, transparent shield, and Quentin's thunderbolt danced across its surface without reaching her. It crackled, trying to penetrate it, but she held it back, her Play at least as powerful as his own.

They stood like that for a moment, him pushing his power, Clarice holding it back.

Quentin fumbled for another Card even as Clarice reached for her own, but his wound made his arm tremble and blood had run down onto his hand. He grabbed for one, any one, staring at it so that he could focus on a meaning. Something, anything to take Clarice down.

He drew the Seven of Hearts, and his mind reached out desperately for the first meaning that appeared. The heart. Life energy. He grabbed it and seized it and in his mind pictured Clarice's heart, willing his fear and anger at it.

She had already drawn her Card, but then the hand holding it dropped and her other hand went to her chest, her eyes wide in fear and shock.

He pushed with all of his willpower, carrying the Play through to its end.

Clarice fell to the ground, terrible gasping sounds coming from her throat.

He ran to her, crouched down over her. She looked up at him, tears spilling from her eyes. Then she was still.

Quentin went to Hiram, who stirred on the ground. "How are you not dead?" Quentin asked. "How am *I* not dead? Did Gunsmith's pistol fail?"

Hiram, clutching at a wound in his thigh, shook his head. He pointed across the room to what looked like Gunsmith's Colt lying in a corner.

"But—" Quentin said.

"I laid a glamour on it," Hiram said. "Made the plain one look like the special one and vice versa."

"Didn't trust her?"

Hiram smiled. "I just wanted to keep it for myself." He crawled his way over to Clarice's body, wincing in pain, and roughly retrieved his Deck. "Bitch," he said. "Luckily, I remembered the Jokers in my boots."

"Butterflies." Quentin shook his head. "Unpredictable."

With his Cards returned, Hiram pulled out one of his own Hearts and fixed up the wound in his leg. Then, in a rare moment of generosity, he used one on Quentin's wound as well.

They left the body where it lay, though Quentin removed Clarice's Cards. It would be up to the sheriff to figure out what had happened, if he could. Quentin knew that they would have to gather their things and move on. Both of them with their Decks lighter than they'd been when they arrived in Stillwell.

Using a key they found on her body, they visited Clarice's room at the Avery Hotel. Quentin wanted to open her suitcase but in a rare moment of insight, Hiram thought it might be trapped. "Gunsmith could put a Play inside a pistol, why not one inside a bag?"

So it was one more Play each (a Diamond to detect and identify the protection and one of Hiram's Spades to counteract it) before they could safely open it. Inside they found six Decks of varying sizes. These they carefully placed into their own bags.

Quentin also found a journal filled with names and locations in a feminine scrawl. "Another list?" Hiram said.

Quentin shrugged. "Got to play the hand that we've been dealt."

* * *

Quentin fingered Clarice's journal as they sat on the train heading west. Dusty brown land dotted with scrub passed by outside the window.

"Did you believe what she said?" Hiram asked. "That you could get more Cards by taking them away from a person?"

Quentin looked at his hands. "I don't know," he said. "It seems an awful horrific thing to do." *And yet*, he thought, *the Cards flee so quickly*.

"In any case," he said, "none of us know the secret. And I think that's for the best."

"Oh, most certainly," Hiram said, an odd note in his voice.

They looked at each other uneasily. The rest of the ride passed in silence.

ALVIN AND THE APPLE TREE
A TALE OF ALVIN MAKER

ORSON SCOTT CARD

The State of Hio, 1820

It's not certain now whether Alvin Smith was on his way to Hatrack River for a visit to his own birthplace and his wife's people, or on his way west from such a visit, but the hamlet of Piperbury isn't more than two days' walk for a man with shoes, three days barefoot, and half a day for Alvin when he ran through the woods with the greensong in his heart.

Coming or going, when Alvin came to a covered bridge spanning a brook so narrow a lazy man could step over it, he knew he was on the road his father and brothers had traveled not long after Alvin himself was born. They left no stream unbridged in those days, as a kind of vengeance on the Hatrack, which had served the Unmaker by taking the life of the family's oldest boy, Vigor.

"You seem to be touching that bridge like a half-forgotten friend," said a man's voice.

Alvin turned and saw him then, resting his back against the trunk of a tree with his feet in the cold water of the stream.

It wasn't often a body could sneak up on Alvin. But since he was sitting still I suppose he wasn't sneaking. He was as still as if he had grown like moss on that tree. Alvin could ordinarily sense folks, especially White folks, who didn't often blend in proper with the living things around them. But this man did. Or rather, it's more like he didn't exist at all, for all Alvin had noticed of him till he spoke.

"You seem to belong here," said Alvin, "yet your worn-out pack and the calluses on your feet say that you're a traveler who walked long today."

"And you're not even out of breath," said the traveler, "and yet you ran out of those woods so fast I thought you to be a hare in a hurry."

"That's because my shoes are so fine," said Alvin, "I have to run."

"But you ain't wearing any shoes," said the traveler.

"My shoes are so fine," said Alvin, "that only I can see them."

The traveler lifted one dripping, naked foot out of the water and rubbed the rough and horny sole. "You can see I'm wearing shoes, too, but coarse and homey ones. I never asked the Lord for any better, though."

"I think we have a cobbler in common, sir," said Alvin.

"Your clothes are homespun and your feet are bare," said the traveler. "May I ask if you're primitive Christian, sir?"

"I've been called primitive," said Alvin, "and I try to live as a Christian, but I think when you put those words together they took on a new meaning and I don't know it."

"We're the Christians who try to live the simple life the Master led. Shoeless, in coarse raiment, living from handfuls of corn in the field and the wind-harvested fruit of the tree."

Alvin thought about that for a moment. "I'm not sure if it says in the gospels, sir, that Jesus chose his simple clothing, but rather wore the best he could afford."

"He also said to sell all you have, give it to the poor, and come follow him."

"Did you sell all you had? Did it fetch a good price?"

"I gave it to my brother and left it all behind. Now I travel from place to place with my bag of apple seeds and the word of the Lord."

"Then I have a name to put to you, sir, if I'm not mistaken. Are you John Chapman, the one they call Appleseed, who has established apple nurseries in towns from east to west and north to south?"

"Not much east and even less south, but north and west of here, I'm sometimes called John Appleseed, or Johnny when they drink a toast to me with the cider made from the sour fruit of my seed-grown trees."

"Seed-grown always?" Alvin asked, for he had heard some faint emphasis in the way John Chapman said those words.

"The gentle fruit for a rich man's table is made from a grafted tree, delicate sweet-bearing trunk sprouting from a hardy sour root. But here in this country, I plant the seed-grown tree that's honest from root to leaf, the kind of apple tree that a working man can keep, because he doesn't have to climb up to pick the fruit when it's unblemished and pretty. A working man comes to my tree and gathers the fruit from the ground, too ripe and tart to go into the mouth, but just right for the cider barrel. I plant drinking apples, my friend."

Alvin laughed, because he liked a brag and a tale as much as any man. So he stayed and jawed and bathed his feet with the man and they traded stories, some of them nigh on to true.

But the best stories, Alvin reckoned, were the ones about the apples John Chapman planted. That's because Alvin, being a Maker, had a way of seeing into most folks' knacks, puzzling out exactly what it was they did, and when John Appleseed got to talking about how he put the pollen from one tree into the blossoms of another and found the best mix, Alvin understood his treeknackery better than any other soul was likely to.

For John Appleseed didn't just blow the pollen into the blossoms. John Appleseed breathed the pollen into his lungs and there he came to know the grains, the deep inner secrets of them, in the few moments of a held breath. Then he puffed out onto the blossoms only the pollen grains that he wanted them to know, and so the apples that came forth were like the animals from Noah's Ark, ready to go and propagate the world, each after its own kind.

"You're a man with a marvelous knack," said Alvin, "for talking and for growing things. But I don't see a jug of cider in your kit."

"A man who's had the pure pollen in his nostrils has no need of the fermented cider," said John Chapman.

And because Alvin was an honest man, and didn't expect to hear any more lies than he would tell himself, he took him at his word. And, as far as it went, that word was true. John Appleseed was no cider drinker. He ate the tart apples as they came, sharp to the bite, and otherwise he ate cornbread like other folks.

The sun was at midafternoon when they parted, Appleseed for a place he'd camped before, the time he came to plant his nursery here. "And you go on into Piperbury, my young smith. It's a godly town."

"The whole town?" asked Alvin. "That *will* be a sight. Every other town I seen has its good and bad people all mixed up together."

"In Piperbury, they have a keen awareness of the goodness of God and the low poor condition of the human soul," said John Appleseed. "Every living soul of them. It's why I love it more than any other place where I've set up a nursery of my trees. It's why I keep on coming back."

From this, Alvin wasn't quite sure what to expect as he crossed through the bridge and walked on into Piperbury. Would they be a pious group, proud of their humility, critical of any who weren't as humble as they? Or would they be genuine Christians, their hearts filled with compassion and generosity? From what he found, Alvin figured, he'd know a good deal more about John Chapman.

What he found was a mournful procession in the hamlet. It's hard to put on a good funeral show when there's no more than twenty families altogether, but this was the most ragged bunch of grievers Alvin had ever seen. It's not that they weren't sad enough—he couldn't remember seeing a group more downcast. It's that they also seemed so very tired, plodding along as if at the end of a long day's work.

Well, of course they were. It was late in the afternoon, and Alvin doubted that anyone except the immediate family had taken the day off work.

Alvin doffed his cap, as he knew would show respect, and then fell in at the back of the procession. Up ahead, the plain box rested on the shoulders of six men, and Alvin wondered if they were the dead one's family or if the hamlet was so small that the same six men carried everyone who died.

But before he could ask anyone that question, he had to establish himself. So he spoke quietly to the prentice-age boy nearly at the back. "You mind a stranger asking whose burial we're headed for?"

The boy didn't even glance up. "Why? You didn't know her."

"Well right there that's something I didn't know. A woman. Or a girl?"

"A woman as should have knowed better," said the boy, and then he sped up his walk and left Alvin behind.

"Move on through this hamlet, mister," said a middle-aged woman. "We got nothing for you here."

"Not even a bite of supper? I can work for it or pay, if need be."

"You don't want to spend even a night here," said the woman. "It's the wickedest place in all the world." Tears streamed down her face.

"This little place?" asked Alvin. "It's too small to be wickedest. You don't even have all the equipment."

"We are burdened with our sins," said the woman, "and we don't have time to take you on."

"Maybe I can help with your burden," said Alvin. He was beginning to get an idea of the kind of Christianity that John Chapman loved.

"There's no helping us," said the woman. "Jesus only hung for a day on the cross. That wasn't time enough to atone for me." And then she burst into tears and, like the teenage boy, she sped up her pace and left Alvin behind.

Well, Alvin knew that a funeral wasn't a place to discuss theology. And for all he knew they might be right. A town was bound to know itself better than any stranger could, especially one who just walked in and meant to walk right out again next day. What was he going to tell them, that they'd listen to?

And yet they did all seem burdened, and not just by bearing a box on their shoulders, or grieving for the dead. It became clearer when he got to the hilltop cemetery. For they took turns speaking over the grave before throwing a handful of dirt onto the coffin, and they all said just about the same thing.

"Nedra died convinced of her damnation, but I'm more damned than she could ever be. There was the day she had a new bonnet, and I said, 'Would Jesus think that money was well spent? Remember the widow's mite.'"

The other mourners groaned, sharing her apparent agony.

"I judged her and I know it broke her heart. I pray God to forgive me, for I helped put her down there."

Others had different tales, some longer, few as short. How they'd done this or that to offend Nedra. But the pattern was soon clear. First, the offenses were all of a sort most people did without thinking. They could be bad, but they didn't seem intentional.

Second, they mostly consisted of saying things that might cause Nedra to judge herself harshly. Which seemed oddly circular. There they stood, each in turn at the head of the grave, explaining how their terrible sin was to make Nedra feel more sinful. Seemed to Alvin she would have fit right in.

By the end, Alvin was beginning to think that the woman at the back of the procession had been half right. This town *believed* itself to be the sinfulest place, but the sins were all those of piety.

Usually when people were full of such condemnation, they spent it to condemn others; but in Piperbury everyone condemned himself— and what they condemned themselves for was harsh judgment of others. Yet Alvin wasn't really sure he believed that people so sensitive about judgment would all have committed the same sin... of judging.

So he finally spoke up, when the woman from the procession's end was done with her confession and self-condemnation.

"Forgive a stranger, ma'am, but the words you say you said to Nedra seem awfully condemning. You don't seem to be the sort of woman who would say such a harsh thing."

The group was silent, and the woman he was talking to seemed abashed. "Well of course I didn't say it *out loud*," she said.

"But if you didn't say it aloud, then Nedra couldn't have heard your words, and if she didn't hear them, how could your offense have put her in the ground?"

The woman burst into tears. "I should have said them aloud! Maybe we could have talked. Maybe I could have been a true friend to her!"

Alvin turned to face the largest group of mourners. "She's not the only one, is she? Did *any* of you say your sinful thing *out loud*, where she could hear?"

"Goodness no!" said the preacher.

"We try so hard not to hurt anyone," said the weeping woman. "Yet she felt our rejection and our condemnation, and she could bear it no longer. She is on our conscience! We slew her in our hearts, every one of us!"

And there arose then such a wailing that Alvin fled from before it, walking halfway down the hill and trying to puzzle out just what was going on here, and what sort of Christianity this was. He'd never heard of an all-damnation, no hope of atonement version of the faith. Nor could he believe that the cheerful, witty fellow with the knack for apples that he met outside of town would find this place anything but disheartening. Yet he had loved it.

He sat unobtrusively a ways back from the lane when the mourners came down to return to their lives in the hamlet. No one met his gaze, until at last the woman he had spoken to brought up the rear. She stepped aside and went to him.

"I thought you'd still be here," she said. "I think I've left you more confused than helped, and that's a sin."

"No, it's not," said Alvin.

"Let's not argue," she said. "You're a stranger and it's too late for you to go on to the next town, though that would have been a better plan. So you can come to my place. I'm a widow now, alone in the house, but you look to be an honorable young man."

"I'll do any jobs as need doing," said Alvin. "I have a way with stuff needs fixing."

"Lives?" she asked. "Souls? Do you have a knack with those?"

"Only one who ever had such a knack as that," said Alvin, "and I'm not him."

"Come with me. You'll have food and a nice place to sleep. My son's bed lies empty. It'll be good to have someone in it again."

"Has he been away for long?" asked Alvin.

She shook her head. "Near two year ago. Half cut his own leg off with a scythe and bled to death. The tourniquet was too late. Or maybe someone was deliberately slow, to help him on his way."

"Are you saying someone helped to kill him?"

"It's the only mercy we have left—to get to hell sooner, before we rack up any more sins."

"What's wrong with you people?" asked Alvin. And then, remembering himself, he said, "Of course I mean that in the nicest possible way."

"It's our knack, I think," she said. "We have a knack for recognizing our own sins and confessing them. Other people in other places may commit worse or coarser sins, but what is within our reach, we do, mostly by hurting each other."

They were already in the town square now—not much of a square, but not much of a town, either. There was a church there, and behind it a large and lovely garden of a graveyard.

"I wonder why you moved it," said Alvin. "The cemetery. This one doesn't look half full yet."

"Plenty of room there, in the churchyard, on hallowed ground, where a godly soul might go to rest until the resurrection day," she said.

"So why did you move the cemetery out to that hill?"

"Because you can't bury a suicide in hallowed ground," she said.

"She killed herself?" asked Alvin. "No one mentioned that."

"No one had to. We knew where we were burying her, and we knew why."

"There are so many others up there," said Alvin. "More graves than here. They can't all be..."

But they could. She gave him a glance that said all.

"Every one of them by their own hand?" asked Alvin.

"Because we drive them to it," said the woman.

"The things you all told about up there by the grave—none of you even *said* those things."

"Some did."

"Most didn't," said Alvin. "What she didn't hear *couldn't* drive her to commit such a terrible sin."

"Sin it is," said the woman. "The worst sin. But when you finally come to understand that your soul is so filthy that even Christ can't save you, then what does it matter if you add one more sin to the burden, if by doing it, you can *stop* your miserable life of abomination?"

It was the ugliest sophistry Alvin ever heard. Peggy had taught him to recognize such false reasoning. But his own experience had taught him not to bother arguing. Most people's logic was invented to explain why they could only do what they already meant to do. Her logic for suicide was meant to explain why so many had taken their own lives. But arguing wouldn't save a one of them.

Oh, it got worse. Turns out the woman—Mrs. Turnbull—kept a table for seven different men of the hamlet—which was a high percentage of the total. Every one of them had lost his wife, and so she cooked for them, having lost her husband and her son and her two daughters.

"Did they all…?" Alvin knew it was prying and rude, but he had to know.

"No," she said bitterly. "My husband killed himself, but my two wicked daughters fled the town like Jonah, thinking they could hide their sins from the Lord."

Alvin couldn't help but think they had the right idea. Especially when he found out one more piece of information.

At supper—an adequate meal, but Mrs. Turnbull was no great shakes as a cook, except the apple pie—Alvin could hardly believe it, but Mrs. Turnbull told them about Alvin's curiosity. He started to apologize, but they seemed intent on begging *his* forgiveness—for what, he didn't know—and then each man in turn told about his wife's suicide, and they weren't halfway around the table before Alvin realized the worst thing of all. Most of the suicides sounded like accidents to him.

He said so.

They all nodded knowingly. "Yes, that's what Satan would like us to believe."

"They seized the opportunity of the moment," another one explained. "I don't want to say they *planned* it. They were just ready to die, and took the first opportunity."

"It's still self-slaughter."

That night Alvin lay down on Mrs. Turnbull's dead son's bed, covered with his clean white sheet and a blanket lovingly laid down. "You look right in that place, young man," said Mrs. Turnbull, kissing his forehead like a mother. "How I wish I hadn't driven him to his death." Then she left the room weeping.

This was definitely not the most sinful place he'd ever been, but he'd never known people who felt guiltier. And it was also not the most perfectly Christian place he'd been, either, unless your idea of Christ was about condemnation.

Yet this obsessive guilt did not seem like anything that John Appleseed would love. He had spoken of the New Church, whose members should go about like Jesus, doing good, and that it was your collective good works that earned you a place in Christ's forgiveness. Nobody here talked about good works, or expressed the slightest hope that the good they did could ever balance out, let alone overcome, their terrible, nonexistent bad deeds.

The most common sin was driving people to suicide by unspoken criticisms and unperformed acts of spite. Everyone in fact treated each other well, if a bit dolefully. And all the suicides Alvin heard of might well have been accidents or illnesses—and might have been recovered from, except that nobody bothered to take care of the sick or treat the injuries or even stop the bleeding from a seeping wound. Alvin wanted to scream, He might have lived, if you had only kept feeding him! Broken arms heal, it doesn't mean she tried to kill herself and failed! The sin here is that you all want to die, and you keep allowing each other to do it, needlessly!

With these thoughts in mind Alvin tried to go to sleep, but his mind kept spinning around and around.

Who am I to judge these people? I saw none of these accidents, none of the illnesses. How can I say that any action of theirs might have made the slightest difference? It's easy for *me* to talk of healing or curing or helping or saving, because I have the Maker's knack, I can reach inside folks with my doodlebug and fix whatever's wrong with them. Who else can do that? How dare I, with my great gifts, judge people who don't have them?

And then worse thoughts, as the hours grew later. They'll know that I judged them. I already let them see that I thought they should have tried to save their loved ones' lives, and now my condemnation rests on them like a burden. Of course it will be unbearable; how could he put something like that upon them?

What if every man at that table kills himself tonight, what if Mrs. Turnbull herself is dead by morning? Whose fault will it be but mine, for having judged them so harshly, so unfairly?

And unlike them, I didn't even have the decency to keep it to myself. I spoke right up, I said my say. I'm the worst of all of them.

By morning, Alvin was so full of despair, of the dark weight of his own sins, that he found himself thinking of ways to die.

Accidental ways. As if he could trick God into not recognizing his subterfuge and thinking that he died naturally. In his mind Alvin played out many stories of his unintentional death, and now he understood why everyone knew that the suicides were really suicides, however they might look: everyone had these thoughts, these nightmares.

But why do *I?* he asked himself. I don't believe the way they believe. I don't live here. If there's some guilt disease they all caught, I don't have it. I haven't done anything wrong, at least not lately, and yet I'm so ashamed of myself, so guilty before God that I can hardly bear it and it makes no sense at all.

Does somebody have a knack for causing other folks to have bad dreams?

Is there something about the bed pillows or mattress ticking in Piperbury?

And he kept thinking about John Appleseed. Calling this the most righteous town—no, no, what were his words? "A keen awareness of the goodness of God and the low poor condition of the human soul," that's what he had said. "Every living soul of them," he had said.

John Chapman has seen what I see, and he approves. There's an unsanctified cemetery filling up with bodies of purported suicides, and everybody in this town thinks they're worthy of nothing better than death and hell. And John Chapman said, "It's a godly town."

Alvin thought back to the only meal he had eaten in the place, and the only part of the meal worth eating: Mrs. Turnbull's apple pie. It wasn't made with windfall cider apples. These were delicious to the taste, even baked in what he had to admit was a very mediocre crust. What was good and memorable about the pie was the apples.

He didn't take any of the offered breakfast. He especially didn't take any of the apple scones. "Will you hold my place for me, Mrs. Turnbull?" he asked. "I hope to be back before the day's out, but I have an errand to run."

"What business could you possibly have around here?"

"The business isn't around here," said Alvin, "but your house, and your son's fine bed, will be on my way back from it."

"It's not as if there's anyone clamoring to stay here," she said. "But if you don't mind paying me the bit that you promised afore you go."

Alvin paid it, preferring money to chores when he had some traveling to do, and then he set out briskly along the path back to the main road, which skirted Piperbury about a mile and a half south.

He came to the place where he had chatted with John Appleseed, and then began to look for the way the man had gone. He had stayed with the road, it seemed, for Alvin saw no sign of disturbance on the left hand or the right, and invisible as Chapman might be when sitting still, he was a White man and he wasn't going to turn off the road without leaving a mark.

Alvin would make better time getting off the road and running through the forest with the greensong in his heart. But then he'd see no signs of Appleseed. So he loped along on the road, getting a little benefit in speed and smoothness from trees leaning over him most of the way.

After only a half-hour's run, Alvin found a turning, and the place where Chapman had spent the night. It would have been a two-hour walk for him, no doubt, being older than Alvin by twenty-five years or so. And however early Chapman might have risen that morning to resume his trek—he left no sign of having cooked anything for breakfast—he could not be all that far ahead.

Chapman gave a yelp of fright when Alvin touched his shoulder and said, "Beg pardon, Mr. Chapman."

"How did you come up behind me without my hearing?"

"You must have been lost in thought, sir," said Alvin. "I had a question to ask you, and I ran from Piperbury this morning to see if you had an answer."

Chapman looked very skeptical. "From Piperbury? This morning?"

"Spent the night in Widow Turnbull's house. In the bed her dead son left behind."

"Her son gone? And her husband, too?" Chapman looked sincerely grieved.

"All part of the godliness of the town, it seems to me," said Alvin. "Does it seem that way to you?"

Chapman stared hard at him, and then suddenly tears started dripping from his lower eyelids and running down his cheeks. "I deserve to go to hell for this."

"Quite possibly," said Alvin, "but this morning, after last night's dish of apple pie, I felt that my life was so evil and dark that death and hell would come as a relief. I think that feeling is familiar to you."

"I walk through the world with such a dark awareness of my sins," said Chapman. "I've tried all the good works that Swedenborg called for New Christians to embrace. I live simple, I dress simple, and go about planting trees. It's more than the apples, you know. When I leave a nursery behind me, the local farms can transplant those trees to meet the legal requirement of planting fruit trees on their land to prove their title.

They can do that instead of clearing and planting five acres—six trees are as good as five acres in the law, because they're an orchard."

"No one doubts that you do good work, John Chapman," said Alvin.

"I doubt it!" he cried, with anguish so deep it made Alvin's own heart hurt to hear it. "I see the work but nothing feels good to me, or not for long, or not good *enough*."

"What did you do to the apples in Piperbury?" asked Alvin, getting to the point. "Was that supposed to be a good work?"

"It was supposed to serve God," said Chapman miserably. "I saw all these… these *happy* people, paying no attention to the sinfulness of the world."

"The apples," Alvin prompted him.

"I thought about the Tree of the Knowledge of Good and Evil. When Adam and Eve partook of it, they were expelled from Eden. But it says the *reason* for their expulsion was so that they wouldn't eat of the Tree of Life and live forever. Once they'd eaten of the fruit of the Tree of Knowledge, that wasn't forbidden any more. God didn't mind if they ate more of *that*."

"Doesn't exactly say so, but it might be true," said Alvin.

"Yet here were all these people, utterly without knowledge of the evil that they do in the world. But I have that knowledge. To my bones I know it. So I thought that I should try to bring that great tree back into the world of men. Not the Tree of Life! That would be blasphemous! But a fruit that, when men eat it, they can see and understand evil—I could do that."

"How odd, then, that you made it so delicious."

"Well who would eat it, if it was nasty?" said Chapman. "I found that knowledge of evil in my own soul, and I put it in the pollen, and I gave it to an apple tree with a strong root. Then I took the pollen of the trees that grew from that, and gave it to an apple with a perfect fruit, sweet and hearty. And the trees that grew from that pollination, they grow now in every orchard in Piperbury."

"Strong so they live long, sweet so they're good to eat, and filled with damnation."

"No!" cried Chapman. And then: "Yes. But that's not how I meant it. It was supposed to turn them toward righteousness. It was supposed to make them…"

"Like unto you," said Alvin.

"As *aware* as me."

"But you forgot to give them the knowledge of good. It's supposed to balance, in that tree."

"They knew good!" cried Chapman. "They were so…"

"Happy."

"I've never been happy," he said. "Not for more than a few minutes at a time. I make a wonderful blending of two apples and I feel good and then I think, this is the sin of pride, I'm such a wicked man to be proud of the workmanship of mine own hands. So I leave the nursery behind me and go on to another place and try again, but my sins follow me everywhere."

"You have those moments, though," said Alvin. "These Piperbury folks, they've got none. No taste of goodness any more. No speck of joy."

"They die from *accidents*," said Chapman. "I've asked. All those suicides, they're just accidents or illnesses."

"And yet there are so many dead," said Alvin. "Because their hopeless friends and family members don't help them, don't heal them, don't even feed them in their extremity, because they know that death will come to them as a relief."

Chapman dropped to the ground, curled up, and wept.

"I don't know about evil," said Alvin, "but right now you're pretty useless."

"I can't fix it," said Chapman. "Even if I cut down every tree in Piperbury, the pollen has already spread into the world. Bees have carried it to other towns. The crossbreeds aren't as powerful—not as delicious, not as sturdy, not as…"

"Pernicious."

"Effective," said Chapman. "But it's loose in the world and there's no calling it back."

"Well, we can stop sending out the pure pollen, can't we?" asked Alvin.

Chapman groaned in agony at the very thought, and Alvin realized: even this Tree of the Certainty of Evil, he can't bear the thought of cutting it down.

"You love even the wicked trees," said Alvin.

"They're the only children I have in the world," said Chapman.

"You could have married and had the flesh and blood kind," Alvin said.

"The only woman I ever wanted to ask, I got there and she had agreed to marry someone else the day before."

"And all other women were monstrous?"

"They all become monstrous after you marry them. I've seen how married people are. I don't know why I ever thought even one would be different. They're always... telling you things. Demanding things from their husbands. Having opinions. Being disappointed or angry or *crying* in order to make you do things."

Alvin could see now why John Chapman wandered the world. Like everybody, he needed the company of other people, but only for a short time. He had to leave before people began expecting things from him.

"You can't leave this one behind," Alvin said to him. "We've got to kill those trees."

"I come back here to try new pollens on them. Pollens to undo what I did. I look at happy people out in the world and I try to find that place in them and make a pollen that will grow an apple that will give them that—"

"No," said Alvin. "That's wrong. An apple that makes you *happy*? Then all that people would do all day is eat those apples."

"So you agree that misery is a necessary—"

"I agree that happiness and misery ought to be earned. You've forced guilt on people who don't deserve it. How will it make it better to force an equal certainty of the goodness of everything they do on people who also don't deserve it? A body should feel good because he *did* good, and feel bad because he *did* bad. Your tree isn't giving anybody knowledge, it's giving them *certainty*."

"That's the same thing," said Chapman, surprised.

"Certainty is how you feel about your opinions. Knowledge implies that you're pretty sure, but that you're also right. Certainty doesn't require that you be right."

"That's more philosophy than I can handle," said Chapman.

"It's not philosophy, it's common sense," said Alvin. "The Tree of the *Knowledge* of Good and Evil isn't about making people *sure* they're wicked whether they are or not, nor about making them *feel* bad. It's about letting them see *clear*. What's really good. What's really evil. To *know* what each of them *is* when they see it. To help them make choices, and understand the choices they made."

"Well I don't know how to make a fruit that can do *that*."

"That's because you don't have to," said Alvin. "Eve and Adam already ate that fruit, and passed the knowledge on down to us. We're born with it, all but a few sad and broken people."

"Like me," said Chapman.

"That's foxfeathers, my friend," said Alvin. "You know what good and evil are. You just got the mistaken notion that it's evil to be proud of accomplishing something good."

"Pride is a sin!"

"Pride in a good thing is a good thing," said Alvin. "The sin is when you're proud of *stupid* things. Like being born to rich parents. Or figuring out how to cheat other people of more than your right share of money. Making other people ashamed of themselves so you can feel proud of being better. Those are sinful kinds of pride. Being proud of worthlessness. But being proud of having *worth*. Of bringing apple trees to farmers who need them—for cider, for pies, or for proving out their claim—that's something to be righteously proud of."

"And why should I believe you?" demanded John Chapman.

"Because you have the knowledge of good and evil inside you," said Alvin, "and you know I'm right. Even if the Unmaker whispers to you that it isn't so, your first response to what I said—your heartfire leapt up when I said it. You recognized Good when you heard it."

"I recognize it," said Chapman. "But it's still out of my reach. I put this tree into the world and it's killing people, and making them so unhappy that they're grateful to die."

"Well, we can't stop it," said Alvin. "And we're sure not going to make an opposite tree, that forces people to be proud and happy for no reason. And there's no way to make a Tree of Good Sense."

"Well now," said John Chapman. "Maybe…"

"John Appleseed," said Alvin, "if you had any sense inside you, you'd never have made this tree in the first place."

"No, no, there's no way to put good sense into an apple," said Chapman. "Or if there is, only God can make that tree. But good sense isn't what we need here."

"It's hard to think of a time when that statement is even slightly true," said Alvin.

"I meant only that a *tree* of good sense isn't—"

"I knew what you meant," said Alvin. "I'm just a wicked man and I'm ashamed of myself for making a joke."

"What my tree makes them feel is despair," said Chapman. "It's the tree of despair. The certainty that nothing is good and it will never be good. So the tree I need to make is the Tree of Hope."

"Well, now, that's a thought. Can you do it?"

"I'm not a hopeful man."

"When you set out to crossbreed two apples, don't you *hope* you'll come up with something useful?"

"Usually I don't."

"But sometimes you do. So you *hope* that at least now and then you'll get a good result."

"That's not much."

"You don't *feel* much hope," said Alvin, "but you *act* on your hope. You have enough hope to go on trying. To go on living. To leave this town and go on to the next. To plant these seeds and *hope* they'll grow, even though you leave them behind in another man's care."

John Chapman closed his eyes. After a while he shook his head. "I don't feel it."

"It's not a feeling," said Alvin. "It's a decision. It's the part of you that decides to try again. Not the part that gave up on all women ever. The part that made you *once* go to ask a girl to marry you."

"The foolish part."

"The part that acted in spite of fear. The part that dared."

They got back to town well before dark. I asked Alvin myself whether he took John Chapman by the hand and ran with the greensong through the wood, but he just shook his head and laughed and told me that he wouldn't remember a thing like that. "You don't remember the greensong," he said. "While you're in it, you're someone else, and when you're back from such a journey, it passes away like a dream."

But he's taken *me* into the greensong and I remember it. Each time I ran with him like that, I remember it. I don't think he's lying. I think it's that he's always just on the edge of the woodland, in his heart. So stepping over into the greensong isn't such a wrenching change for him as it is for other folks.

However they did it, by greensong or with a footsore wornout Appleseed, they were back in Piperbury by dark, and Alvin watched as John Chapman called them out of their homes and said, "Don't you eat any more apples from these trees I gave you."

Not understanding how the fruit of those trees was killing everyone they loved and any chance of happiness, they refused. "It's the one good thing left in our lives!"

"If you won't stop eating them I'll burn them all and chop them down," cried Appleseed, "or the other way around!"

"Then you'll just have to do that," said Mrs. Turnbull, "because them apples is the only thing that makes my cooking any good at all."

Chapman turned to Alvin, sitting on a bench at the edge of the public square. "What can I do?" he asked.

"Eat from the Tree of Good Sense," Alvin replied, which meant nothing at all to the people gathered there, but it made John Chapman smile just a little.

"How about this," said Chapman. "The apples you've got stored up from this fall, destroy those the way you'd shoot diseased cattle, to save the rest of the herd. But the new apples that come this year, they should be all right."

"What's wrong with them?" asked a man.

"They make you believe things that ain't so," said Chapman.

"Like what?"

"You wouldn't believe me if I told you," said Chapman. "Because you're a fallen, sinful man."

Since that was what everyone in town already believed about themselves, nobody gave Chapman any more argument.

They brought out their apples and had a fire. Smelled like an apple roast. Smelled like a party. But Alvin and Appleseed watched to make sure that nobody ate any of the cooked apples. If mice got into the mess that night or next morning, and then in despair went out for the hawks or the owls to get them, Alvin couldn't begin to guess. He warned the mice not to eat those apples, but if they couldn't resist the smell, he couldn't very well change their nature, which was all appetites, even stronger than their fears.

When the fire was down, Alvin and Appleseed went around from tree to tree. They weren't in blossom yet, but that's where Alvin's knack came in handy. Appleseed had made the pollen for apples filled with hope— not a crazy hope when there was no reason for it, but the hope that makes a man act to do something good even when he thinks it probably won't work. A measured hope. A teaspoon of hope to counteract a bucket of despair.

Alvin looked inside that pollen and saw the deepest seed at its heart, and then took that pattern and reproduced it in the tree. Tree after tree, working as fast as he could, it took him an hour with every tree, or maybe a little more or maybe a little less. Alvin didn't carry a watch and time passed differently for him when his doodlebug was out working in the world.

In three days he was done. There weren't *that* many trees. Or maybe it took less time than he thought, per tree.

I know what you're thinking. If he could change the trees to add hope to the pollen they'd produce in their blossoms in the spring, why not change them to take away what Appleseed had done to fill them with despair?

"I once took away something from a boy with a powerful knack," said Alvin. "I took it away from the deepest seed inside him, because that was the part that the Finders tracked. I did it to save his life. But it killed a part of him. It killed his knack, or weakened it, or broke it. When you take something out of a man, you take something out of his soul."

"I can tell you that this boy you're talking about, whatever you took, he doesn't miss it," that's what I told him.

And he said, "Just because he doesn't miss it doesn't mean it isn't gone."

"A tree's not a man," I said to him.

"Trees were John Chapman's children. I wasn't going to kill them. I just added something to them. A gift. That pollen still spread out into the world. A lot of people feel guilty for things that aren't bad. But a lot of people feel guilty for things that *are* bad, and it helps them stop from doing such things. What matters though is that with that pollen, with those apples, they also get them a dose of hope. So whatever they might feel guilty of, it doesn't take away their hope. It gives them more."

"I don't know that I've ever eaten such an apple," I said to him.

"That was years ago, and the bees've been busy," said Alvin. "In the past five years you've never eaten an apple that *didn't* have that pollen in it, his first change and then the second one. Not a new tree rises from the ground without those blessings in the fruit."

"Blessings," I said to him, thinking of the graves in the Piperbury cemetery.

"They started having babies in Piperbury again," said Alvin. "They started bringing children into the world."

"Well I suppose that *is* hope," I said. "What about John Chapman?"

"He kept on planting apple nurseries with seed of his own making," said Alvin. "But I don't believe he ever again tried to make an apple that would change human nature. I think he decided to leave that up to God."

"So you're saying he *despaired* of such a thing," I said, trying to goad him a little.

"I'm saying he put his hopes in God, and set about making fruit that was delicious to the taste, but left a man his freedom."

So yes, I had it from the mouth of Alvin Maker himself, in the happy days in Crystal City. He didn't make a copy of the Tree of Knowledge of Good and Evil, the way some folks say, and he certainly never made a Tree of Life. But he made it so every apple in America, by now maybe every apple in the world, comes from a Tree of Hope and Despair, and so we all swing back and forth between the two.

MADAM DAMNABLE'S SEWING CIRCLE

ELIZABETH BEAR

Seattle, Washington, 1899

You ain't gonna like what I have to tell you, but I'm gonna tell you anyway. See, my name is Karen Memery, like memory only spelt with an e, and I'm one of the girls what works in the Hôtel Mon Cherie. Hôtel has a little hat over the o like that. It's French, so Beatrice tells me.

Some call it the Cherry Hotel. But most just say it's Madam Damnable's Sewing Circle and have done. So I guess that makes me a seamstress, just like Beatrice and Miss Francina and Pollywog and Effie and all the other girls. I pay my sewing machine tax to the city, which is fifty dollar a week, and they don't care if your sewing machine's got a foot treadle, if you take my meaning.

Sure, fifty dollar'd be a year's wages back in Hay Camp for a real seamstress, and here in Seattle it'll barely buy you a dozen of eggs, a shot of whisky, and a couple pair of those new blue jeans that Mister Strauss is sewing. But here in Seattle a girl can pay fifty dollar a week and have enough to live on and put a little away besides, even after the house's cut.

You want to work for a house, if you're working. I mean… "sewing." Because Madam Damnable is a battleship, and she runs the Hôtel Mon Cherie tight, but nobody hits her girls, and we've got an Ancient and Honorable Guild of Seamstresses, and nobody's going to make us do anything we really don't want to unless it's by paying us so much we'll consider it in spite of ourselves. Not like in the cribs down in the mud beside the pier with the locked doors and no fireplaces, where they keep the Chinese and the Indian girls the sailors use.

I've never been down there, but I've been up along the pier, and you can't hear the girls except once in a while when one goes crazy, crying and screaming. All you can hear up there is the sailors cursing and the dog teams barking in the kennels like they know they're going to be loaded on those deep-keel ships and sent up north to Alaska to probably freeze in the snow and die along with some Eastern idiot who's heard there's gold. Sometimes girls go north too—there's supposed to be good money from the men in the gold camps—but I ain't known but one who came back ever.

That was Madam Damnable, and when she came back she had enough to set herself up in business and keep her seamstresses dry and clean. She was also missing half her right foot from gangrene, and five or six teeth from scurvy, so I guess it's up to you to decide if you think that was worth it to her.

She seems pretty happy, and she walks all right with a cane, but it ain't half hard for her to get up and down the ladders to street level.

So anyway, about them ladders. Madam Damnable's is in the deep part of town where they ain't finished raising the streets yet. What I mean is when they started building up the roads a while back so the sound wouldn't flood up the downtown every spring tide, they couldn't very well close down all the shopping—and all the *sewing*—so they built these big old masonry walls and started filling in the streets between them up to the top level with just any old thing they had to throw in there. There's dead horses down there, dead men for all I know. Street signs and old couches and broken-up wagons and such.

They left the sidewalks down where they had been, and the front doors to the shops and such, so on each block there's this passage between the walls of the street and the walls of the buildings. And since horses can't climb ladders and wagons can't fly, they didn't connect the blocks. Well, I guess they could have built tunnels, but it's bad enough down there on the walkways at night as it is now and worth your life to go out without a couple of good big lantern bearers each with a cudgel.

At Madam Damnable's, we've got Crispin, who's our doorman and about as big as a house. He's the only man allowed to live in the hotel, as he doesn't care for humping with women. He hardly talks, and he's real calm and quiet, but you never feel not safe with him standing right behind you, even when you're strong-arming out a drunk or a deadbeat. Especially if Miss Francina is standing on the other side.

So all over downtown, from one block to the next you've got to climb a ladder—in your hoop skirts and corset and bustle, that ain't no small thing even if you've got two good feet in your boots to stand on— and in our part of town that's thirty-two feet from down on the walk up to street level.

When the water table's high, the walks still flood out, of course. Bet you guessed that without me.

They filled up the streets at the top of town first, because the rich folk live there—Colonel Marsh who owns the lumber mill and such. And Skid Row they didn't fill in at all, because they needed it steep on account of the logs, so there's staircases up from it to the new streets, where the new streets are finished and sometimes where they ain't. The better neighborhoods got steam lifts, too, all brass and shiny, so the rich ladies ain't got to show their bloomers to the whole world climbing ladders. Nobody cares if a soiled dove shows off her underthings, I guess, as long as the *underthings* is clean.

Up there some places the fill was only eight feet, and they've got the new sidewalks finished over top of the old already. What they did there was use deck prisms meant for ships, green and blue from the glass factory on the north end, set in metal gratings so that when there's light the light can shine down.

Down here we'll get wood plank, I expect, and like it. And then Madam Damnable will just keep those ruby lamps by the front door burning all the time.

The red light looks nice on the gilt, anyway.

Our business mostly ain't sailors but gold camp men coming or going to Anchorage, which is about the stupidest thing you ever could get to naming a harbor. I mean, why not just call it "Harbor," like it was the only one ever? So we get late nights, sure, but our trade's more late afternoon to, say, two or four, more like a saloon than like those poor girls down under the docks who work all night, five dollar a poke, when the neap tide keeps the ships locked in. Which means most nights 'cept Fridays and Saturdays by three we're down in the dining room while Miss Bethel serves us supper. She's the cook and barkeep. She don't work the parlor, but she feeds us better than we'd get at home and she keeps a sharp eye on the patrons.

Sundays, we close down for the Sabbath, and such girls as like can get their churching in.

I don't remember which day it was exactly that Merry Lee and Priya came staggering into the parlor a little before three in the morning, but I can tell you it wasn't a Friday or Saturday, because all the punters had gone home except one who'd paid Prudence for an all-night "alteration session" and was up in the Chinese Room with her getting his seams ripped, if you take my meaning. The rest of us—just the girls and Crispin, not Madam Damnable—were in our robes and slippers, faces scrubbed and hair down, sitting in the library when it happened. We don't use the parlor except for working. Beatrice, who's the only one at the hotel younger than me, was practicing reading out loud to the rest of us, her slim dark fingers bent back holding the big ivory-bound book of Grimm's fairy tales.

We'd just settled in with tea and biscuits when there was a crash down the ladder out front and the sound of somebody crying like her leg was broke. Given the sound of the thump, I reckoned that might not be too far from the truth of it.

Crispin and Miss Francina gave one another The Look, and while Beatrice put the ribbon in her book they both got up and moved toward the front door. Crispin I already said about, and the thing about Miss Francina is that Miss Francina's got a pecker under her dress. But that ain't nothing but God's rude joke. She's one of us girls every way else, and handy for a bouncer.

I followed along just behind them, and so did Effie. Though I'm young, we're the sturdiest girls, and Effie can shoot well enough that Madam Damnable lets her keep a gun in her room. Miss Bethel kept a pump shotgun under the bar, too, but she was upstairs in bed already, so while Crispin was unlocking the door I went over and got it, working the breech to make sure it was loaded. Beatrice grabbed Signor, the deaf white cat who lives in the parlor—he's got one blue eye and one yellow and he's loud as a ghost when he wants something—and pulled him back into the library with the rest of the girls.

When I got up behind Crispin, it was all silence outside. Not even anymore crying, though we all stood with our ears straining. Crispin pulled open the door and Miss Francina went striding out into that burning cold in her negligee and marabou slippers like she owned the night and the rest of us was just paying rent on it. I skin-flinched, just from nerves, but it was okay because I'd had the sense to keep my finger off the shotgun triggers.

And then Miss Francina said "Sweet child Christ!" in that breathy voice of hers and Crispin was through the door with his truncheon, bald head shining in the red lantern light. I heard him curse too, but it sounded worried rather than angry or fearful, so I let the shotgun muzzle droop and walked up to the doorway just in time to grab the arm of a pretty little Indian girl—Eastern Indian, not American Indian—who was half-naked and in hysterics. Her clothes had never been good, or warm enough for the night, though somewhere she'd gotten some lace-up boots and a man's coat too big for her. All she had on else was a ripped-up shift all stained across the bosom, and I could tell she weren't wearing nothing under it.

She was turned around, tugging something—another girl's arm, poking out frontward between Crispin and Miss Francina where they were half-dragging her. Once they got both girls inside in the light, Effie lunged forward and slammed the door.

"Here, Karen," Crispin said in his big slow molasses voice. "You take this little one. Bring her after. I'll get Miss Merry here upstairs to the sickroom."

Miss Francina stepped back and I could see that the girl between them was somebody I knew, at least by reputation. Not a girl, really. A woman, a Chinese woman.

"Aw, shit," Effie said. Not only can she shoot, but Effie's not real well-spoken. "That's Merry Lee."

Merry Lee, which was as close as most American tongues could get to her real name I guess, was half-conscious and half-fighting, batting at Crispin's hands while he swung her up into his arms. Miss Francina stuck her own hands in there to try to hold her still, where they looked very white against all the red on Merry Lee's face and arms.

Effie said, "She's gunshot. I guess all that running around Chinatown busting out crib whores finally done caught up with her. You know'd it was sooner or later going to."

"You hush about things you know nothing about," Miss Francina said, so Effie drew back chastened like and said, "I didn't mean nothing by it."

"Go and watch the door, Effie," Miss Francina said. I gave Effie the shotgun. Effie took it and did, not sulking at all. Effie talks without thinking sometimes, but she's a good girl. Madam Damnable don't tolerate them what ain't.

The girl in my arms wanted to get loose of me—she pulled away once and threw herself at Crispin, but Miss Francina caught her and gave her back, and honest she was mostly too light and skinny to put up a good fight once I had a grip on her. I tried to talk to her, tell her she was safe and we were going to take care of her and Merry Lee both. I didn't think then she understood a word of it, but I found out later her

English was pretty good so I think it was mostly that she couldn't hardly have been more upset. But something got through to her, because after a minute of twisting her wrists and getting blood all over my good pink flannel she stood still, shivering, and let me bundle her up the stairs after Crispin and Merry Lee while Miss Francina went to fetch Miss Lizzie.

We followed them down the long rose-painted hall to the sickroom door. Crispin wanted to take Merry Lee in without the Indian girl, but the girl weren't having none of it. She leaned against my arms and keened through the doorway, and finally Crispin just looked at me helplessly and said, "Karen honey, you better bring that child in here before she cries down the roof."

She was better inside, sitting in a chair beside the bed while Crispin checked over Merry Lee for where she was hurt worst. Effie was right about her being gunshot, too—she had a graze through her long black hair showing bone, and that was where most of the blood was from, but there was a bullet in her back too and Crispin couldn't tell from looking if it had gone through to a lung. It wasn't in the spine, he said, or she wouldn't have been walking.

Just as he was stoking up the surgery machine—it hissed and clanked like a steam engine, which was never too reassuring when you just needed a boil lanced or something—Miss Lizzie came barreling up the stairs with an armload of towels and a bottle of clear corn liquor, and I knew it was time for me to be leaving. The girl wasn't going anywhere, but she didn't look like interfering anymore—she just leaned forward in the bedside chair moaning in her throat like a hurt kitten, both hands clenched on the cane arms.

Crispin could handle her if she did anything. And he could hold down Merry Lee if she woke up that much.

I slipped through the door while Miss Lizzie was cutting the dress off Merry Lee's back. I'd seen her and that machine pull a bullet before, and I didn't feel like puking.

I got downstairs just as somebody started trying to kick in the front door.

In all the fuss, Effie hadn't thrown the bolt, which should be second nature but you'd be surprised what you can forget when there's blood all over everywhere and people are handing you guns. The good thing was that I had handed her the gun, and when the front doors busted in on their hinges she had the presence of mind to raise up that gun and yell at the top of her little lungs, "Stop!"

They didn't, though. There were four of them, and they came boiling through the door like a confusion of scalded weasels, shouting and swearing. They checked just inside, staring from side to side and trading glances, and from halfway up the stairs I got a real fine look at all of them. It was Peter Bantle and three of his bully boys, all of them tricked out in gold watch-chains and brocade and carrying truncheons and chains along with their lanterns, and you never saw a crew more looking for a fight.

The edges of the big doors were splintered where they'd busted out the latch. So maybe they'd have broken out the bolt trying to get in anyway.

"I said *stop*," said Effie, all alone in her nightgown in the middle of the floor, that big gun on her shoulder looking like to tip her over.

Miss Francina wasn't anywhere to be seen, and I could tell from the sounds through the sickroom door that Crispin had his hands full of Merry Lee. Madam Damnable, bless her heart, was half-deaf from working in dance halls; she might have gone up to bed and even if Miss Francina had headed up to fetch her it would take her a minute to find her cane and glasses, which meant a minute in which somebody had to do something.

I didn't think on it. I just jumped over the banister, flannel gown and quilted robe and slippers and all, exactly the way Miss Bethel was always after me about for it not being ladylike, and thumped down on the red velvet couch below the staircase.

I stepped off the couch, swept my robe up like skirts, and stuck my chin out. "Peter Bantle," I said, real loud, hoping wherever Miss Francina had got off to she would hear me and come running, "you wipe your damn muddy feet before you come into my parlor."

Now I ain't one of the smaller girls—like I said, I'm sturdy—and Peter Bantle is like his name—a banty and a peckerwood—which is probably why he struts so much. I'm plump too—the men like that— and I'm broad across the shoulders, and when I came marching up beside Effie he had to look up to meet my eyes. I saw him frown a little on the size I had on him.

The three in front of him were plenty big, though, and they didn't look impressed by two girls with a single pump shotgun between them. Bantle's men had all kinds of gear hung on them I didn't even recognize, technologics and contrivances with lenses and brass tubes and glossy black enamel. Bantle his own self had a kind of gauntlet on his left hand, stiff boiled leather segmented so the rubber underneath showed through, copper coils on each segment connected by bare wires.

I'd heard about that thing; I talked to a girl once he made piss herself with it. She had burns all up her arm where he'd grabbed her. But I didn't look at it, and I didn't let him see me shudder. You get to know a lot about men in my work, and men like Peter Bantle? They're all over seeing a woman shudder.

I don't take to men who like to hit. If he reached out at me with that gadget, I was afraid I'd like to kill him.

He didn't, though. He just ignored me, and looked over at Effie, who he could get eye to eye with. He sneered at her and through a curled lip said, "Where's Madam Damnable?"

"She's busy," I said. Only reason I didn't step in front of Effie was on account of she had the gun, but the urge to was that strong. "Me and Effie can help you. Or escort you out, if you'd rather."

Miss Bethel would have cringed at my grammar, too. But right then I couldn't afford to stammer over it to make it pretty.

Effie settled that gun on her shoulder a little better and lowered her eye to sight down the barrel. Bantle's men looked unimpressed so hard I could tell they was a little nervous. One hefted his black rubber truncheon.

"You got one of my whores in here, you little chit, and that thieving outlaw Merry Lee." Bantle's voice was all out of proportion with his weedy little body. Maybe he was wearing some kind of amplifier in that high flounced collar of his. "I aim to have them with me when I go. And if you're lucky and give them over nice and easy, my boys here won't bust up your face *or* your parlor."

Rightly, I didn't know what to say. It wasn't my house, after all; Madam Damnable gives us a lot of liberty but setting the rules of her parlor and offering sanctuary to someone else's girls ain't in it. But I knew she didn't like Peter Bantle, with his bruised-up, hungry crib whores and his saddle shoes, and since he had come crashing through the front door with three armed men and a world of insolence, I figured I had a little more scope than usual.

"You're going to leave this parlor now," I said. "And shut the door behind you. And Madam Damnable will send somebody around in the morning so you can settle up for the lock you busted."

"I know they came in here," Bantle said. "There's Chink whore blood all over your hands and the floor here."

Oh, I knew the answer to that one. I'd heard Madam Damnable say it often enough. "It's not the house's policy to discuss anyone who we may or may not be entertaining."

Then the thing happened that I ain't been able to make head nor tail of. My head went all sort of sticky fuzzy, like your mouth when you wake up, and I started feeling like maybe Bantle had a point. That *was* one of his girls upstairs, and Merry Lee *had* brought her here—or vice versa maybe—without asking. And didn't she owe him, that girl, for paying to have her brought over from India? And there was Effie pointing a gun at him.

Bantle was pointing that glove at me, finger and thumb cocked like he was making a "gun." I had another skin-flinch, this time as I wondered if Bantle could *shoot* electricity out of that thing. His eyes sort of… glittered, with the reflections moving across them. It was like what they say Mesmeric—I think Mr. Mesmer was the fellow's name?

"Do it," Bantle said, and God help me didn't I think it seemed like a good idea.

I was just about reaching over to grab the barrel of Effie's shotgun when the library door eased open off to my left. Through the crack I could see Beatrice's bright eyes peeping. Bantle saw her too, because he snarled, "Get that Negra whore out here," and one of his standover men started toward her.

I had just enough warning to snatch back my reaching hand and slap my palms over my ears before Effie jerked the gun up and sent a load of buckshot through the stained glass over the door panels that didn't never get no sun no more anyhow. The window burst out like a spray of glory and Bantle and his men all ducked and cringed like quirted hounds.

I just stood there, dumbfounded, useless, as full of shame for what I'd been thinking about doing to Effie and Madam Damnable as some folks think I ought to be for whoring.

"I got four more shells," Effie said. "Go on. *Go and get her.*"

The bully who'd started moving couldn't seem to make his feet work all of a sudden, like the floor'd got as sticky as my head had been. Without looking over at Beatrice, I said, "Bea sweetie, you take Pollywog and go run get the constable. It seems these gentlemen have lost their way and need directions."

When it was coming out of my mouth, I couldn't believe it. The words sounded calm and smooth, the opposite of the sticky fuzz I'd been feeling a moment before. I even saw one of the bully boys take a half-step back. It didn't impress Peter Bantle, though, because while the library door was closing across Beatrice's face he started forward. Effie worked the pump on the shotgun, but he looked right at her and sneered, "You don't have the *balls*," and then he was reaching for me with that awful glove and I didn't know yet if I was going to scream or run or try to hit him, or if Effie was really going to have to learn to shoot him.

But a big voice arrested him before I had to decide.

"Peter Bantle, just what the hell do you think you're doing in my house?"

Peter Bantle didn't have the sense to turn around and run when he heard the ferrule of Madam Damnable's cane clicking on the marble tile at the top of the stair. He did let his hand fall, though, and stepped back smartly. I heard Effie let her breath go. I looked over at her pale, sweaty face and saw her move her finger off the trigger.

She really had been gonna shoot him.

I stepped back and half-turned so I could watch Madam Damnable coming down the stairs, her cane in one hand, the other clenching on the banister with each step.

She was a great battleship of a woman, her black hair gone all steel-color at the temples. Her eyes hadn't had to go steel-color; they started off that way. Miss Francina was behind her on the one side and Miss Bethel on the other, and they didn't look like they was in any hurry nor in any mood for conversation.

"You got one of my girls in here, Alice," Peter Bantle said.

She reached the bottom of the stairs and Miss Bethel fanned off left to come take the shotgun from Effie.

"You speak with respect to Madam Damnable," Miss Francina said.

Bantle turned his head and spat on the fireplace rug. "I'll give a tart what respect she deserves. Now are you going to give me my whore back or not?"

Madam Damnable kept coming, slow and inexorable, like a steam locomotive rolling through the yard. She was in her robe and slippers, like the rest of us, and it didn't one wit make her less scary. "I'll give you your head back if you don't step outside my parlor. You may think you can own folks, Peter Bantle, but this here Seattle is a free city, and no letter of indenture signed overseas is going to hold water. The constable's on his way, and if you're not gone when he gets here I'm going to have him arrest you and your boys for trespass, breaking and entering, and malicious mischief. I pay more in taxes than you do, so you know how that's going to end." She gestured to the broken door and the busted-out window. "The evidence is right there."

"Your own girl shot out that window!" Outrage made his voice squeak.

I had to hide my laugh behind my hand. Effie squeezed the other one. She was shaking, but it was okay. Madam Damnable was here now and she was going to take care of everything.

Peter Bantle knew it, too. He had already taken a step back, and when you were faced with Madam Damnable, there was no coming back from that. He drew himself up in the doorway as his bully boys collapsed around him. Madam Damnable kept walking forward, and all four of them slid out the door like water running out a drain.

Their boots crunched in the glass outside. He couldn't resist a parting shot, but he called it over his shoulder, and it didn't so much as shift Madam Damnable's nighttime braid against her shoulders. "You ain't heard the last of this, Alice."

"For tonight, I think I have."

He took two more steps away. "And it's Hôtel *Ma* Cherie, you stupid slag!"

We heard the boots on the broken ladder before Madam Damnable breathed out, and let herself look around at us. "Well," she said cheerfully, "what a mess. Effie, fetch a bucket. Miss Bethel, put that gun away and find the broom, honey. Karen, you go tell Crispin when they're done with the Chinese girl he's to come down here and board up this window and sweep the glass up. He'll just have to sit by the door until we can get in a locksmith. Miss Francina, you go after Beatrice and Pollywog and tell them we won't need the constable."

Miss Francina bit her lip. "Are you sure, ma'am?"

Madam Damnable's hand glittered with diamonds and rubies when she flipped it. "I'm sure. Go on, sweeties, scoot." She paused. "Oh, and ladies? That was quick thinking. Well done."

When I came back up the grand stair with coffee in the china service, the sickroom door was still closed, but I didn't hear any screaming or any steam engine chugging through it which could only be a good sign. If Merry Lee was still under the knife, she would have been screaming and the machine would have been whining and wheezing away, and if she had died of it, I thought the girl would be screaming instead. So I rapped kind of light on the frame, on account of if Crispin or Miss Lizzie was busy in there I didn't want to startle them. It took me two tries to make my hand move, I was still that ashamed of myself from downstairs.

His voice floated back. "It's safe to come through." So I set the tray on my hip and turned the knob left-handed, slow in case there was somebody behind the door. The sickroom's different from our other bedrooms. There's no wallpaper and the sheets aren't fancy, and the bedstead and floor and all is just painted white. It makes it easy to just bleach or paint over again if there's a bad mess, and you'd rather paint stained wood than rip up carpet with puke or pus or crusted blood in it any day. The knife machine kind of hangs in one corner on a frame, like a shiny spider with all black rubber belts between the gears to make the limbs dance. It's one of only three or four in the city, and it needs somebody skilled as Miss Lizzie to run it, but it don't hesitate—which when you're cutting flesh, is a blessing—and it don't balk at some operations like other doctors might. And you always know its tools is clean, because Crispin boils 'em after every use.

When I stepped inside, that whole white room looked like it had been splashed about with red paint, and none too carefully. Crispin looked up from washing his hands in a pink-tinged basin with clotted blood floating like strings of tidepool slime around the edges. Merry Lee was laid sleeping or insensible in the bed on her side, clean sheets tucked around her waist and a man's white button shirt on her backwards so you could get to the dressings on her back. There was a mask over her face, and Crispin's other big enamel-knobbed brass machine that handles all those sickbed things that the steam-powered knife machine doesn't was kind of wheezing and whirring around her, its clockworks all wound up fresh and humming. The bloody sheets were heaped up in the basket, and the Indian girl was perched on the chair by the head of the bed, holding Merry's sallow hand clutched between her olive ones and rocking back and forth just a tiny bit, like she was trying with all her might to hold herself still.

I picked my way between smears of blood. Crispin looked up, grinning instead of grim, so I knew Merry Lee was going to be just fine unless the blood poisoning got her.

"Karen honey, you are a delivering angel." He nodded to the tray. "This here is Priya. She helped me change the sheets."

I got a good look at her and Merry Lee while I set the coffee on the cleanest bureau. Merry was a lot younger than I would have expected from the stories, fresh-faced and sweet as a babe in her sleep and maybe seventeen, eighteen—not more than a year or two older than me.

Given she's been a thorn in the side of Peter Bantle and Amrutar—who's like Bantle's older, meaner, richer, Indian twin—and the rest of those cribhouse pimps for longer than I've been working, she must have started pretty young. Which ain't no surprise, given some of Peter Bantle's girls—and boys too—ain't no older than your sister, and before she got away from Amrutar, Merry Lee is supposed to have been one of them.

The Indian girl had taken off that coat and Crispin or somebody must have given her a clean shift. Now I could see her arms and legs and neck, she was skinnier than anybody ought to be who wasn't starving to death. I sat there watching the knobs of her wrists and elbows stick out and the tendon strings move in the backs of her hands. I guess sailors and merchantmen don't care so much if the slatterns they visit are pretty so long as they're cheap, and it's dark in a whore's crib anyway; plus, I guess if Peter Bantle underfeeds his girls they're cheap keepers.

Still, as I sat there looking at her, her bloody tangled hair and her cheekbones all sharp under skin the color of an old, old brass statue's, it more and more griped me thinking on it. And it more and more griped me that I'd been going to let Bantle have her.

And what the hell had I been thinking? That wasn't like me at all.

There was plenty coffee in the pot, cream and sugar too, and I'd brought up cups for everybody. But it didn't look like the Indian girl—Priya—was going to let go of Merry Lee's hand and pour herself a cup.

So I did it for her, loaded it up with cream and sugar, and balanced all but one of the biscuits I'd brought along on the saucer when I carried it to her.

She looked up surprised when I touched her hand to put the saucer in it, like she might have pulled away. She wasn't any older than me either, and this close I could see all the bruises on her under the brown of her skin—layers of them. There was red fresh scrapes that would blossom into something spectacular, that might have been from dragging Merry Lee bleeding across half of Seattle. There was black-purple ones with red mottles like pansy blossoms. And there was every shade of green and yellow, and you could pick out the hand and fingerprints among 'em. And the red skinned-off slick-looking burns from Peter Bantle's electric glove, too, which made me angry and sick in all sorts of ways I couldn't even find half the words to tell you.

She was a fighter, and it had cost her. My daddy was a horse-tamer, and he taught me. Some men don't know how to manage a woman or a horse or a dog. Where a good master earns trust and makes a partner of a smart wife or beast—acts the protector and gets all the benefit of those brains and that spirit—all the bad ones know is how to crush it out and make them cringing meek. There's a reason they call it "breaking."

The more spirit, the longer it takes to break them. And the strongest ones you can't break at all. They die on it, and my daddy used to say it was a damned tragic bloody loss.

He probably wouldn't think much of me working on my back, but what he taught me kept me safe anyway, and it wasn't like either of us asked him to go dying.

Priya looked up at me through all those bruises, and I could see in her eyes what I saw in some of my daddy's Spanish mustang ponies. You'd never break this one. You'd never even bend her. She'd die like Joan of Arc first, and spit blood on you through a smile.

My hand shook when I pushed the coffee at her.

"I can't take that," she said, and that was my second surprise. Her English wasn't no worse than mine, and maybe a little better. "You can't wait on me. You're a white lady."

"I'm a white tart," I said, and let her see me grin. "And you need it if you're going to sit up with Miss Lee here. You're skin over bones, and how far did you carry her tonight?"

I thought she'd look down, but she didn't. Her eyes—you'd call 'em black, but that was only if you didn't look too closely. Like people call coffee black. And her hair was the same; it wasn't not-black, if you take my meaning, but the highlights in it were chestnut-red. I knew I wasn't supposed to think so, but she was beautiful.

"She got shot coming out from under the pier," she said. "She told me where to run to."

Which was a half-mile off, and uphill the whole way. I poked the coffee at her again, and this time she let go of Merry Lee's hand with one of hers and lifted the cup off the saucer, which seemed like meeting me halfway. I leaned around her to put the saucer and the biscuits on the bedside stand. I could still hear Crispin moving around behind me and I was sure he was listening, but that was fine. I'd trust Crispin to birth my babies.

She swallowed. "I heard Mister Bantle shouting downstairs."

There was more she meant to say, but it wouldn't come out. Like it won't sometimes. I knew what she wanted to ask anyway, because it was the same I would have wanted if I was her. "Priya—did I say that right?"

She sipped the coffee and then looked at it funny, like she'd never tasted such a thing. "Priyadarshini," she said. "Priya is fine. This is sweet."

"I put sugar in it," I said. "You need it. In a minute here I'm going to head down to the kitchen and see if Miss Bethel can rustle up a plate of supper for you. But what I'm trying to say is Madam Damnable—this is Madam Damnable's house Merry Lee brought you to—she's not going to give you back to Bantle for him to beat on no more."

I'm not sure she believed me. But she looked down at her coffee and she nodded. I patted her shoulder where the shift covered it. "You eat your biscuits. I'll be back up with some food."

"And a bucket," Crispin said. When I turned, he was waving around at all that blood on rags and his forceps and on the floor.

"And a bucket," I agreed. I took one look back at Priya before I went, cup up over her face hiding her frown, eyes back on Merry.

And then and there I swore an oath that Peter Bantle was *damned* sure going to know what hit him.

On récolte ce que l'on sème. That's French. It means, "What goes around comes around." So Beatrice tells me.

STRONG MEDICINE

TAD WILLIAMS

Medicine Dance, Arizona Territory, 1899

It was late afternoon, but it had rained the night before and the scent of creosote bushes still hung in the air. Lost Angel Mesa loomed behind the town, its eastern flank shadowed sage-purple. I stopped first at the graveyard on the edge of town to pay my respects, then I hoisted my trunk onto my shoulder and walked down Fore Street toward the Carnation Hotel. I had a feeling that's where people would be on the day before Midsummer, and I didn't want to seem like I was trying to sneak into town.

Of course, Sheriff Hayslip didn't recognize me at first, but he and the other men gathered around the hotel bar certainly noticed that a stranger had walked in. As I lowered the trunk to the dusty floor, they all looked me over.

"What brings you to Medicine Dance, stranger?" the bartender asked. He didn't sound like he was asking out of pure neighborly friendliness, but under the circumstances I didn't really blame him.

"Just visiting," I said.

"Don't get many visitors," another man said, a brush-bearded fellow who looked like he'd never got over the disappointment of being a couple of decades late for the Civil War. "Don't particularly want any, either." A few of the others grunted in agreement.

The sheriff was examining me. His paunch and thick mustache made him a bit hard to recognize, but I finally found the youthful face beneath all that unfamiliar window-dressing. He seemed to catch on to something too, because when I met his gaze his eyes widened, then he nodded slowly. "You've been here before, ain't ya?"

"A while back."

"Long while." Hayslip nodded his head. "I remember. You'll be needing a place to stay, then. Neddie, you finished with your drink?"

A slender young man sitting nearby stopped staring at me to turn to the sheriff. The irritated crease on his forehead suggested he didn't like being asked, but it could be he just didn't like being called "Neddie." "Uh, yes, sir, I reckon so."

"Why don't you take this gentleman over to the Widow Denslow's. She's got plenty of room."

The young man looked surprised, maybe even a bit alarmed. "Denslow's? You sure?"

Hayslip dropped one right into the spittoon from three feet away. "'Course I am. I know this gentleman—he's been in town before. He's all right." He looked at me. "You take care, now."

The young fellow shrugged and got up. He wore a gun on one hip, but his holster looked brand new. He eyed my trunk. "You want some help with that?" He bent and grabbed one handle, then lifted. He didn't lift it far before he whistled in surprise and let it thump back down. "Heavy!"

"I've got it." I hefted it up onto my shoulder, making a show of effort.

"Where's your horse?" the young man asked as we walked out of the hotel. "Even better, you got a wagon, or you gonna carry that box of anvils all the way out to the Denslow place?"

"Don't have a wagon. Don't even have a horse."

His jaw almost hit his chest. "How'd you get here?"

"Walked."

He shook his head. "Lost it in the desert, huh? Lucky to be here at all. I'm surprised you stopped with just one drink—I'd be powerful thirsty if I'd just got in out of the sun like that."

I didn't bother to tell him I'd never had a horse in the first place. I've learned over my previous visits that if you don't absolutely, positively have to explain something, it's easier just to keep your mouth shut.

My silence made him restless. "Sheriff says you've been here before."

"Yes, but it's been years. Before you were born."

He stared at me, surprised. "You don't look that old."

"Yes, I've been told that."

The main street of Medicine Dance, Arizona was pretty much what you'd expect: a row of commercial buildings with tall, painted fronts masking the much less impressive structures behind them—the hotel, the feed store, the post office, the bank. A couple of horses were tied to the rail in front of the bank, but other than that the town might have been deserted, about to smother in the growing shadow of the mesa. Day before Midsummer was usually like that in Medicine Dance: even the people who didn't know anything about it could sense something and tended to stay close to home.

Just past the post office, we left the main drag, heading southeast across town. The houses were simple structures for the most part, though a few were a bit more substantial. We were headed toward one of the biggest of them. When the Denslow house was first built, it had stood by itself, but now the town had grown out to surround it. It was more impressive than most of the others—two stories, gabled roofs, and painted trim. It even had a bit of a garden, and the window boxes were full of flowers. Somebody had to have a pretty green thumb to get that much color out of an Arizona June.

"By the way, my name is Edward Billinger," the slender young man said as we approached the house. He stuck out his hand. I gave it a brief shake.

"Custos," I told him.

He frowned and nodded, an odd effect. "Huh. That some kind of Spanish name?"

I shrugged. "It's Latin."

"Uh-huh, uh-huh. Didn't study that the way I should have in school. Might be more than a railroad clerk if I had." He was looking around and licking his lips now, as if there was something in the house that made him nervous. He led me to the porch, took a deep breath, then knocked on the front door. "Mrs. Denslow?" he called. "Catherine? Anybody home?"

Something growled underneath the porch.

"Shut it, Gally, it's me," Billinger told the unseen dog. "What are you doing under there, anyway?"

A white-haired woman opened the door. She was at least seventy, but stood ramrod straight, with fine, high cheekbones that suggested she might have some American Indian in her ancestry. Her eyes lit on me first, narrowed a little, then shifted to my companion. "Oh, good day, Neddie. What brings you by?"

I felt Billinger tense beside me: he truly didn't like being called that. "Sorry to bother you, Mrs. Denslow, but this is Mr. Custos. The gentleman needs a place to stay for the night and Sheriff suggested I bring him over here."

She invited us both in, but Billinger begged off. He lifted his hat to the woman, asked to be remembered to Catherine, then sauntered away, thin as the gnomon of a sundial. Mrs. Denslow watched him go. "Always was a bit shy of new things, that one," she said. "Should have left, gone off to make a life in Tucson or somewhere." She turned to me. "Now, what are we going to do with *you*?" There was more in the question than just the matter of a spare bed.

She offered me some tea, which I took, although I wasn't thirsty. It gave me a chance to look around while she went to fix it. She kept the place nicely, all the surfaces and the glass spotlessly clean, which wasn't easy to do in the middle of windy, dusty grassland. Other than the flowers in vases all around the parlor, the house didn't look a whole lot different than the last time I'd seen it.

She gave me my tea, then took hers to her rocker; once seated, she looked me up and down as if I were something she was planning to bid on. "Now it's your turn," she said.

"You want me to make you some tea?" It wasn't meant to be a joke. Sometimes I'm a little slow to understand what people mean.

Mrs. Denslow gave me a look I had no trouble interpreting. "No, it's time for you to tell me why you're back after all this time."

"You know why I'm here, Mrs. Denslow. You know how long it's been. What tomorrow is."

"Why is it you can remember what tomorrow is after all these years, but you can't remember my name? What's all this 'Mrs.' nonsense?"

"I remember your name, Marie."

She was silent for a moment. "That's something, I guess. Land, you make me ashamed to have got so old. Where have you been all this time, Custos?"

Before I could answer, the front door swung open and a girl—a young woman, really, but just barely—bounced into the room in a whirl of skirts and smelling of lavender soap. "Oh, Grammy!" she said, "I was so worried I wouldn't get back before dark..." She broke off when she saw me. She was very nice to look at, golden-haired and pretty, but with a politely determined jaw that reminded me of someone else. "I beg your pardon," she said, coloring ever so slightly. "I didn't know..."

"This is Mr. Custos," the old lady said. "He's in need of a bed, so he's going to stay the night in the spare room." There was a distinct suggestion of *so let's just keep our mouths shut, shall we?* in her tone, and that suggestion was aimed at me. "Mr. Custos, this is my granddaughter, Catherine Denslow."

I rose and extended my hand. "Please to meet you, miss." Her skin was soft—softer than mine, anyway.

She shook politely, but she was clearly puzzled by me. "Goodness, I've got to put these things away," she said, heading for the kitchen. "Mrs. Pritchard sent some butter and eggs, Grammy. Little Oscar seems a lot better, though. What a time to have Doc Babbit out of town…!"

The old lady watched her go, then turned back to me. "She's a lovely girl."

"She is indeed," I replied.

"Listen, Custos, I'm happy to have you stay here, for… for old time's sake. But I'm sure you understand me when I say that I'm not going to let anything—*anything*—happen to that sweet child. She's only seventeen."

I nodded. "I feel the exact same way about her, believe me. Protective. Like a family member."

The look Marie Denslow gave me then was the strangest yet, but her reply was surprisingly soft. "Her real father's been dead fifteen years. She scarcely knew him at all."

"She has my sympathy. It's tough to be separated from the ones you love." I finished my tea, then carefully set the cup back down on the plate. "If you don't mind, I'll go to my room now. I had a long walk to get here and I'm a mite tired."

An hour later, we sat down to a very respectable chicken and dumpling supper, good enough for a Sunday meal, though it was only a Wednesday. I didn't eat much.

Young Catherine seemed as excited as if there was a weekend dance on down at the local grange hall (although I doubted Medicine Dance was big enough to have anything like a grange, even now). The girl could hardly sit still. She was up and down a dozen times during the meal, and twice that many afterward, clearing up and making coffee. She even produced a fruitcake that had been hidden away in a cupboard since Christmas. ("We got it all the way from Abilene!" she said proudly.) It was clear that her grandmother didn't particularly approve of the girl's almost feverish excitement, and she kept looking at me as if she wanted to make sure I understood that.

After dinner, I went back to my room, lay down, and thought.

Sometime not long before midnight, I heard a noise downstairs. I hadn't been asleep, so I went down to investigate.

"Mr. Custos!" said Catherine, surprised. She was standing at the window, looking out over the moonswept town, such as it was. (Nobody would ever suggest Medicine Dance was anything more than tiny.)

"Just 'Custos,' Miss Catherine," I told her.

"Well, I don't think I'm allowed to call *you* by your first name, not on such a short acquaintance. Gram… my grandmother wouldn't approve, I'm pretty sure."

"I'm pretty sure you're right." I smiled. I didn't remember how to do it very well. "But you'll have to trust me when I tell you it's just Custos."

"All right, but I'm sure I won't be able to say it." She turned back to the window. "It's a beautiful night." Several silent moments passed before she said, "Why are you here?"

"Here in this town, you mean?"

"You know what I mean. This town, tonight. You know what tomorrow is, don't you?"

"The longest day of the year—the Summer Solstice, they call it. June the twenty-first, 1899."

"That isn't all, and we both know it. Why would you be here, elsewise? And why would my grandmother be so worked up about it? She's frightened, that's what. I know that dear old lady better than I know my own self, and she's frightened. Not of you, but of… tonight. What's going to happen." I could see the girl peering at me from the corner of her eye as we both looked out at the neighbors' houses, the broad sky and all the stars. It was like we were standing on a table, looking out over the world like God Almighty Himself. At least, that's what a man other than me would have thought.

All I said was, "Yes, I know what night this is. And I also know that the finest calculations of the Royal Observatory over in Greenwich, England say that there's just a little less than an hour left before midnight." And tomorrow was going to be a big one, I felt pretty certain—something truly strange. Midsummer's Day in Medicine Dance was always a bit odd, but this was going to be the kind that only happened every thirty-nine years. I don't really understand the reason for the thirty-nine year cycle myself, but I once knew a man who did. "So maybe you should get back to your room," I told Catherine, "and lock the door while we wait to see how bad it's going to be."

"Shows what you know," she said, scowling. "I don't even have a lock on my door. And you still haven't answered my question, so don't try to send me off to bed like some silly kid."

I didn't have two smiles in me that night, but it was close. "My apologies, Miss Denslow. You're right—I didn't answer the question. I'm here because of a promise I made somebody. That's the best way I can put it. I don't mean you or your grandmother any harm."

"I never thought you did," she said, then climbed back up the stairs, but she showed me by the way she did it that she was acting under protest.

I waited a few minutes, then leaned close to the open window and inhaled the warm June air. It tasted like what nearly every such night had probably tasted like since the last Ice Age. But that would change.

I went upstairs at last, only because I knew it would be easier for the women to fall asleep if they knew I was back in my room. But I also knew I'd be too restless to stay there long.

Mrs. Denslow herself came down a bit after four in the morning. I was back at the window, watching the stars wheel slowly across the sky.

"Where have you been since last time, Custos?"

I didn't answer her directly. "What do you remember about that?"

"Snow everywhere. That was the first time I realized how strange this place really was. We'd always been lucky on Midsummer before, I guess. Just some differences in climate. You know, suddenly more humid because the river was a lot wider. Things like that. Used to see some pretty strange looking birds, too, a few unusual animals. But then that last time you were here, what was it, 1860 it must have been, and we had the snow, and that was... Well, you remember."

"I remember lots of things. What do you remember?"

"It was like being on the moon." She laughed. "Heavens, not that I've ever been there! But it felt like that, it was so different. I woke up that morning and my youngest son was crying—cold, poor little tyke. Everything was so strange. White as far as you could see, and the mesa was lower than it ordinarily is. The whole valley was snowed in. I saw an elephant!"

"A mammoth. If it was as snowy as that, it was a mammoth."

"You didn't see one yourself?"

"I was busy."

"Well, who wasn't? But I remember you. Papa and Mama didn't have a spare room, so you slept over at the Dahlers' place in their barn, but in the morning you helped Papa shovel the snow and ice off our roof so it didn't collapse. You helped a lot of other folks, too." She turned toward me. She'd lost her slightly brittle air. "But how can you be here again? And looking just the same, almost?"

"You should get some sleep, Mrs. Denslow." I caught her look. "Marie, I mean. Tomorrow may be a long day."

"Do you think we'll get the snow and the elephants again?" She sounded almost hopeful. "That was something. But there were wolf tracks, too, big as dinner plates! I hope we don't see those."

Dire wolves. No, we definitely didn't want to see any of those, or cave bears, or sabertooth tigers, or any of the other giant predators of that era, creatures that made cougars look like kittens. But maybe we'd get lucky. Maybe we'd get nothing worse than twenty-four hours of Devonian ocean at Medicine Dance's doorstep, nothing but interesting fish and insects, then a sunset we'd never see the likes of again, a wide sky empty of birds. But it was equally possible we'd get the dire wolves again or worse.

Which was why I'd brought so many guns.

It wasn't snow this time, and there weren't any mammoths or dire wolves, but that's about where Medicine Dance's luck ended.

I was oiling my guns as the first rays of light snuck in between the closed curtains. Mrs. Denslow had finally gone back to bed an hour or so earlier, and Catherine was still asleep. I had been about to go out and look around before they woke up, thinking I might save everyone some difficulty that way, but instead I heard a loud knocking on the front door.

I couldn't quite imagine a dire wolf doing that, so I only took my pistol as I headed down to see who it was. Marie Denslow appeared at the top of the stairs behind me with a lantern in her hand and a shawl around her shoulders.

It was Edward Billinger, looking quite shocked. The young man wasn't wearing a shirt collar, and it was pretty obvious he'd dressed in a bit of a hurry. "We're drowned!" he declared.

"What are you up to, Ned?" called Mrs. Denslow. "Don't exaggerate, now. No one's drowned—not here, anyway."

"May God strike me dead if I'm exaggerating!" Billinger was wound tight as a spool of sewing thread. "Come look! Come on! You've never seen the like!"

I followed him outside, Mrs. Denslow a few cautious yards behind me.

The view had certainly changed since the day before, but it took me a moment to figure out why. At first I thought the distant eastern hills had risen, then I realized that they were gone altogether, that the heights I could see beyond the town were new mountains, taller and farther away. I turned and looked west. Lost Angel Mesa, the background of the town since the first cabin was built, had simply vanished. Strangest of all, though, was what had happened to the rest of Brujado Valley, twenty miles or so of grassland stretching south from the town to the usual mountains. It appeared now to have become an ocean.

It truly was a bit startling, even to my unusual sensibilities.

"Where did all this come from?" asked Billinger, waving his hands like a drunkard. To be fair, I don't think he was a jot less than utterly sober; seeing one of the thirty-nine year cycles in action for the first time can do that to a man. Human beings aren't meant to see big things change that fast.

"It's not so much *where* it came from as *when*," I explained. "And it's not so much when it came as when did we come to it. Because we are the ones who are out of place, Mr. Billinger."

"Call me Edward—or even Ned," he told me. He was terrified, but doing his best to be courteous. "Because if we're all going mad together, then we likely don't need to be too formal."

I found myself liking the young man, but knew that might mean adding another responsibility. I wasn't at all certain I could afford to do that.

"Can you explain it to him, Mr. Custos?" Mrs. Denslow had come up behind us. Even though dawn was spreading light all across the wide water and the distant mountains, she still held up her lamp like Diogenes on the hunt. "Because I can't—and this is my second time."

"I can't really understand everything myself, but I'll do my best to tell it the way I heard a smart man do it." I turned to Mrs. Denslow. "Maybe we should wake up Catherine and get it explained to everyone all at once now, while things are peaceful. Might be a bit busy for it later on."

Mrs. Denslow agreed and strode back to the house, still following her lantern like a worried miner.

"What do you mean, 'a bit busy later on'?" Edward Billinger was still staring in utter astonishment at the scene before us. "Is there something I ought to know?"

I imagined that when one had looked at a huge mesa all one's life, and were now suddenly without that mesa and staring out at an ocean that hadn't been there the day before, one might find it a bit disconcerting. Didn't Billinger have any family? Hadn't anyone warned him what might be coming?

"I'll get to that when I get to that." I didn't want him running off again until I could figure out whether I'd need him here. "Maybe you should come inside, Mr. Billinger. You had any breakfast?"

He looked at me as though I had just asked him if he'd ever seen a pig fly. "Breakfast? I woke up and there was an ocean outside my window."

"Come on in and get some," I said. "You'll thank me for it later."

The greenish light of dawn gave way to a harsher, whiter, more ordinary looking world (except, of course, for the new body of water) as we finished up the griddle cakes and bacon that Mrs. Denslow had been good enough to make. Well, I say we, but I didn't eat much. I never do.

"A long time ago," I began, "Mrs. Denslow's grandfather, Noah James Lyman, came from England and settled here in Medicine Dance. He was a bit of a scientist, as rich men sometimes were back in the old country, and he chose this part of Arizona because of things he had heard about it—stories the local Indians told—and some curious artifacts found by the earliest pioneers. The very name of the place, Brujado Valley, meant 'enchanted,' or even 'cursed.' Over the years, Doctor Lyman became more and more convinced that the place was special and began a series of experiments that he expected would prove just how special it was."

"Special how? And what sort of experiments would those be?" Ned sounded a bit skeptical. I was glad, because I'd seen how he kept looking at Catherine, and I would have hated to think a serious admirer of hers could turn out to be stupid.

"I don't have the scientific knowledge to explain," I said, "except that Doctor Lyman believed that this area… Well, his way of saying it was that Medicine Dance 'sat very lightly in time.' Those were his words. And Noah Lyman was a very, very smart man. He thought he could figure out a way to understand what was special about the place and… harness it, I suppose you'd say. Like the way you'd fasten the tow-rope of a river barge to an ox-bow, then let the ox do the work of pulling the boat."

"So he was going to use the town to pull a barge?"

"Ned, hush now," said Catherine. "You're just making fun, but you certainly can't explain all that *water* out there. Let Mr. Custos speak." I was glad to see that she didn't put up with any nonsense from him, either.

"Not exactly," I replied to Billinger's question. "More like he was going to try to find what it was that made the place special and then redirect a little of it. Like digging a channel off a big, fast-moving river to get some of the water to flow somewhere else and turn a water wheel."

A dog was barking outside, loud and getting louder. I cocked an ear.

"I apologize, then," Billinger said, "but I'm afraid you've lost me, sir."

"Doctor Lyman built a machine that he thought could find the *frequency* of this place, which is a bit like the way a string or a bell makes music, a pattern of vibration. When he finally discovered that frequency, he tried to duplicate it artificially. But it didn't quite work."

The dog was still barking loudly, with a frightened edge to it now. Catherine stood up to look out the window.

"Whatever are you doing, Catherine?" Mrs. Denslow said. "And what's got into that dog? I confess it's fretting me."

"It's... I'm not sure, Grammy. There's something on the fence down at the far end and it's bothering poor Gally to distraction. I think it's a hawk, but it's awful big."

"Don't say 'awful,' say 'awfully.' We call that an adverb, dear."

Billinger was up now, looking out the same window. "It may be an adverb, as you say, ma'am, but it ain't no hawk. Crane, maybe. I've seen a few of those down in Sulphur Springs..."

I climbed to my feet. "That's no crane. Fact is, that's no bird at all. And there's a lot of them."

Now everyone crowded the window to watch the things wheeling through the sky. Most of the winged creatures were spinning lazily along the edge of the new ocean, but a few were right above us.

"Oh!" said Catherine as the one on the fence launched itself across the yard. It glided past the window before banking on its leathery wings and heading toward the water. "It's... it's horrid! What is it, Mr. Custos?"

"I'm not certain," I told her. "The wings look like a bat's, but..." The creature had a long beak, but not a feather to be seen. "Some kind of... reptile?"

I didn't have long to wonder. Only a few moments later, another of the nightmare creatures glided down from the sky on leathery wings that must have spanned close to a dozen feet. It landed not twenty yards from our window, and the barking of Mrs. Denslow's watch dog suddenly jumped to an entirely different level of frenzy. The reptile-bird seemed offended: it opened its long beak and hissed, then leaped up into the air, flapping its huge wings, and glided toward the side of the house where the dog was tied up, just out of our sight. The barking became a yelp of panic.

"Galahad!" cried Catherine. "Oh, no! That thing is hurting him!" She dashed toward the door, but I reached out and caught her as gently as I could.

"Don't go out there," I said. "Not until I've—"

"I'll save your dog, Miss Catherine!" shouted Billinger, who was beyond my reach. Before I could do anything, he unholstered his pistol and ran out the front door, which he left open behind him. I heard the young man shouting, then I heard him fire his gun—I prayed he was shooting into the air. But even as I headed for the door, his cries turned from anger into alarm, then into shouts of pain.

As I rounded the edge of the house, I could see Billinger and the flying creature engaged in the most fantastic battle the world had perhaps ever seen, although it was nothing compared to what was to come later that day. The monster had apparently tried to seize the dog like a hawk takes a hare, and had partially succeeded, snapping the animal's tether, but either Galahad was too heavy or young Billinger's arrival had prevented it from escaping with its prey. The creature had one of its talons caught in the dog's collar, but Billinger was holding the collar too. As the shrieking reptile-bird struggled to rise, wings flapping with a noise like someone beating wet clothes on a flat rock, the poor dog dangled by its neck, whining piteously.

"My gun!" Billinger shouted when he saw me. "I dropped it! Over there!"

I had a gun of my own, but didn't intend to use that either if I could avoid it, in part because of the danger to the young man and the innocent hound. Instead, I swung a broom which I had grabbed on my way out and hit the creature hard enough to startle it, but it didn't let go of the dog's collar, so I waded in, shoving and swatting with the broom to keep the thing distracted. When I got close enough, I dropped the broom and pulled my buck knife to cut the dog's collar. Poor Galahad fell to the ground, then ran back toward the house with his tail firmly clenched between his legs and crawled back under the porch. The reptile-bird, free now, flapped up to the edge of the Denslows' roof and crouched there, squawking at us like a giant crow. Billinger retrieved his gun and began firing, though I shouted for him to stop. A moment later, the hideous, beaked corpse lay half off the roof, drizzling blood.

I meant to retrieve the creature's body, but was distracted by Catherine running out the door. When she found out her dog was under the house, apparently whole and safe, the girl threw her arms around both of us in gratitude. "Oh, you are true heroes! But what was that horrible thing?"

"A creature from another age," I said. "One of Mr. Owen's 'dinosaurs,' I believe, if you read the popular newspapers. I think our flying monster is something from Earth's distant past."

"Then how has it survived so long?" said Catherine, eyes wide.

"It's not the dinosaur that's out of its time, Miss," I said. "I'm afraid it's the rest of us." I looked to her grandmother. "Doesn't she know?"

The old woman shook her head. "Like everyone in the town, she knows that strange things happen at Midsummer—but that's all."

"Here now, what is all this?" said Billinger. "Stop talking in riddles, will you?"

"Tell them," said Mrs. Denslow. "They need to know."

"It's Medicine Dance," I said. "It's the town itself. Thanks to Mrs. Denslow's grandfather, Noah Lyman—your great-great-grandfather, Miss—and the experiment I already mentioned, once a year on Midsummer's Day the entire town becomes unstuck from one dawn to the next and wanders in time. How it feels to us is that the town stays the same, but the surroundings change, a little or a lot depending on how far it moves through time. That's how it was explained to me, anyway.

"Most years Medicine Dance doesn't wander far at Midsummer— sometimes I'm sure the change is scarcely noticed. But every thirty-nine years, the movement is more... violent. Last time, as Mrs. Denslow can tell you, the townsfolk here woke up to find themselves in an icy age full of strange creatures, some of them quite dangerous—"

"Do you mean the June Blizzard?" Billinger was staring at me intently. "I know of that. It was a freak storm that happened when my parents were courting..."

"It was no storm. It was the town itself that slipped through time to an era many thousands of years ago, when ice and snow covered all this territory."

"That seems a long claim," said the young man.

"Then tell me what you just fought in the front of the house?" I asked. "A parrot, do you think? Ask Mrs. Denslow what she once saw out there, where today an entire inland sea lies in front of you...? What did you see in the snow that day thirty-nine years ago, Marie?"

It shocked the old woman a bit, me using her first name in front of the others. "An... an elephant," she said at last. "It was covered in long, shaggy hair. It was huge! I saw it right there, plain as the nose on your face."

Young Catherine looked quite overwhelmed, but Billinger was frowning. "I don't like to call any lady a liar, Mrs. Denslow—" he began.

"Then you'd better stop right there, Edward Billinger," she said, but before she could make clear exactly what the penalty would be if he didn't, we heard more noise from the front yard. This time it was shouting.

"That sounds like young Tim Winkens," said Catherine. "What's he doing?"

"Running," said young Billinger as he looked out the window. "Looks pretty het up, too."

I headed for the door. On a thirty-ninth Midsummer, nobody was likely to be running around just for exercise.

"Help!" the boy shouted as he scrambled over a gate he could have unlatched in a second or two. He was perhaps twelve years old, all elbows and knees. "Come help! The Dahlers' house is on fire! Some big animal knocked it over! Hurry!"

"Oh! You're not really going... out there, are you?" Catherine said, frightened. "Not out with those dreadful creatures?"

"We must," I told her. "At least *I* must. It's why I'm here. But perhaps Mr. Billinger could remain to watch over the house..."

The young man drew himself up straight. "Do you mean to insult me, sir?" he asked. "My neighbors need my help—how can I remain here?" I decided I liked him pretty well, although I would have preferred that he stay with the women.

We left the ladies locked in, armed with two of my smaller pistols and a cavalry saber of Noah Lyman's that had hung on the parlor wall. I took two more pistols for myself out of my chest, and also the big Springfield Trapdoor rifle. At Mrs. Denslow's suggestion, we grabbed buckets and shovels as well. When we opened the front door, the dog Galahad quickly emerged from beneath the porch and traded his hiding-hole there for one inside the house.

Tim Winkens had only stopped to catch his breath and was already trotting toward a cloud of black smoke rising over the northern end of town, but he had run a long way already and we quickly caught up with him.

"You said something about a big animal," I said.

"Huge! Bigger than any circus elephant! Karl Dahler told me it was Leviathan, right out of the Holy Bible!"

I couldn't help wondering if maybe I should have brought the dynamite, too, but decided that it might not be the best thing to carry to a fire.

We reached the Dahler property in just a few short minutes, along with several other people from the town. The house, which had once sat beside Angel's Creek, now stood at the edge of a marshy estuary bordering the new ocean. We could see many strange creatures in the trees and in the water, but no sign of Karl Dahler's Leviathan. There was, however, a track that had been made by feet and a dragging tail. The footprints were each more than a yard across, and the creature had also left a pile of dung as big as a wheelbarrow, now being swarmed by beetles as big as dinner plates. It was easy to see how the Leviathan's massive tail might have knocked down the side of the barn, almost crushing the farmer in the process as he sat on his milking stool, and tipping over the lamp to cause the fire, which had already caught one wall and the barn roof.

The air, while still summer hot, was so much thicker and damper than normal that I could see some of the men were having trouble with it, coughing and spitting as if they had contracted a chill. Despite the moisture, though, the flames seemed to burn even hotter than usual; there wasn't much we could do to save the barn, but we did what we could to keep the fire from spreading. While some formed a bucket brigade to bring water from the swamp, Billinger and I helped others to dig a firebreak, then knocked out the walls that still stood so as to collapse the ruined barn and make it easier to fight the flames. When we had saved the other buildings, Karl Dahler went from group to group, thanking everyone and trying to describe the thing he'd seen, which he said had been straight out of scripture.

"He had a neck like a giant snake!" Dahler said, then pointed at the wide, muddy track the creature had left behind. "Look, just like it says in Job—'His undersides are jagged potsherds, leaving a trail in the mud like a threshing-sledge.' And it's true!"

As Midsummer's Day wore on, we were called onward from the Dahlers' place to one emergency after another. Smaller reptiles no bigger than cats, creatures that went on their hind legs, got into barns and cellars all over town, causing havoc, but the upset they caused was as nothing to the terror inspired by the winged sky-creatures and the (fortunately peaceful) long-necked giants. There was talk of fiercer creatures attacking livestock.

Noon came and went without food or rest as Ned Billinger and I went where we were needed.

Late in the afternoon, as we tramped back through the heart of town for what must have been the fifth or sixth time, the church bells on Spring Road began chiming over and over, as though some ill-behaved child was swinging on the bell rope. Half the people in town seemed to have gathered in front of the clapboard church. The ringing stopped as the preacher climbed down from the little belfry and walked out to stand on the front porch like a politician addressing his constituents. I didn't know the man, and didn't know what exactly he was going to say, but I felt pretty sure it wouldn't be much different than what I'd heard thirty-nine years ago from another minister. That had been mostly outraged fulminations against the ungodliness of Medicine Dance and the bizarre weather God had punished the town with, but this time the central feature was the unholy ocean which had seen fit to suddenly spread itself along the town's flank without so much as a by-your-leave from the preacher, the mayor, or the town council. The preacher felt this was clear evidence of some kind of punishment on the town for sinfulness.

I quickly grew impatient. God might very well have caused all this—I wasn't equipped to say one way or the other—but even if He had, it didn't help solve it. Also, I was beginning to worry about what might be going on back at the Denslow place, even though it was on the opposite side of town from most of the strange creatures we had encountered. I told Billinger I thought it was time to get back to Catherine and her grandmother.

We left the rest of the citizens arguing about why exactly the Devil had brought the sea to Medicine Dance and made our way back along the shore on the edge of town, reptile-birds wheeling and croaking high above us.

We paused for a moment to watch a bunch of boys—Clay Hopyard's sons, Billinger told me—who had made themselves a raft out of stripped saplings and were wading it out into the water. The young sailors were being watched by a half dozen men taking some rest, who said they'd been chasing the springy little lizards out of nearby houses for the last hour, but I was concerned. I shouted to the boys to come in, but we were still too far away for them to hear. As they listened to me, the men watching seemed to realize that this new ocean might contain things bigger than the fish they were used to pulling from the local streams, but before they could do more than look thoughtful, a long neck suddenly came coiling up out of the water near the children, silver in color and as long as a horseshoe pitch. The boys screamed when they saw it, and all of them ran to one end of their raft, which promptly capsized.

This time I did take out my guns, pulling both pistols and firing them in the air as I ran down toward the edge of the water. Those of the other men who had guns did the same. We must have seemed like a low-lying thunderhead full of lightning as we hurried down the slope toward the splashing and screeching.

It was a stroke of luck that the raft had capsized in relatively shallow water, so that after only a few strokes most of the boys could get their feet beneath them again. A couple of them were already dashing up the bank toward us, screaming that a monster snake was attacking their friends. I could see the creature's huge body just beneath the surface, an expanse of hide as long and wide as a whale's carcass, but I didn't bother to tell them this beast was no mere serpent. Instead, I began firing in a more concentrated way as the creature tried to get at the last two boys where they cowered in the water behind the overturned raft. The raft was not going to stay afloat much longer—already the thing was beginning to come apart under the hammering of the creature's fierce, fanged head.

It was not my intention to kill when I didn't need to—the old man had taught me that these creatures were no more at fault than the people were—but neither was I going to stand idly by and watch two children eaten, one of them no more than six or seven years old. I had left my rifle lying back on the shore, but I needed to make an accurate shot, so when I had waded out into the water past my thighs, still a good twenty yards away from the splintering raft, I holstered one of my pistols and aimed the other one as carefully as I could, resting my gun-hand on my other wrist. I waited until the water-monster lifted its head high above the boys, poised to strike, then I pulled the trigger.

At the noise of the shot, the creature snapped its head to one side as though startled, but I saw a spray of blood before it dove down into the water again. I truly hoped I had not given it a mortal wound, but I was relieved I had stopped it. The boys' father was running down the beach toward us—a beach that had not been there when he went to bed the night before, beside an ocean that had never existed in Arizona during the memory of man—and he let out a terrible cry of fear as the creature sent the water splashing high into the air. A moment later his fearful shout turned into a cry of gladness as he saw his other two sons staggering out of the water, the older carrying the six-year-old, who was, most understandably, crying loudly.

Sheriff Hayslip, who had been one of the men watching, waved to me and called, "God bless you, sir. It's good to have you back."

The worst over, I felt even more strongly that Edward Billinger and I needed to get back to the Denslow women. As we hurried across pasture land toward the Denslows' side of town, we saw many other strange animals, some of them so big as to beggar imagination, although I still hadn't seen anything likely to have been Karl Dahler's Leviathan. The closest was something that had smashed through John Pratt's fence, a giant that looked like a cross between a tortoise and a pile of rocks. It went on four legs and was bigger than a Wells Fargo coach, but like Dahler's Biblical beast, it seemed to have caused the damage without intending to; when we spotted it, it was grazing contentedly, mowing down grass as swiftly as an army of field hands while Pratt watched it from horseback beside his broken fence. He had wisely decided to let the creature do what it wished.

Deeper in the field next door, out at the edge of the town and almost on the edge of a low forest of huge ferns, we encountered a whole group of long-horned creatures, each big as a house, also grazers from what we could see. They had beaked noses like turtles, and their heads were protected not just by the impressive sweep of horns, but also by a raised shield of skin-covered bone that protected their necks. We got close enough to see that some of them had young—I could only think of the little ones as "calves," despite their reptilian skin and tails. I was glad that they seemed harmless, because even a buffalo gun seemed unlikely to stop such a huge beast, or even slow it. In all seriousness, I believe it would have stamped an African rhinoceros flat.

As I gazed at these wondrous creatures, I saw a stir of movement in the nearby forest and realized something else was watching the horned giants. It only made sense, of course: where grazing animals were, there also would be predators. The buffalo of America's plains had been hunted by catamount and wolf long before the Indians arrived, and on the prairies of Africa the aforementioned rhinoceros would be watched by hungry lions. But even a lion found a rhinoceros difficult prey, and from what I knew would only attack the sick ones, even when the lions had numbers. What could possibly be fierce enough to prey on something like these giant, horned cattle-lizards?

I caught a momentary glimpse—only a flash—of the massive, toothy thing in the low forest, but that was enough. I turned to Billinger and said in a quiet voice, "We need to make more speed, Mr. Billinger."

He shook his head. "I don't understand."

"Don't move suddenly, but look over there. These giants are being hunted by another giant."

For a moment, he saw the predator clear between the trees. He blanched and almost dropped his gun. "Oh, merciful Lord," he said. "What kind of horror is that?"

"I could not tell you," I said. "But I have just remembered that we left the bloodied carcass of one of those winged monstrosities dangling from the Denslows' roof." I did not mention that he was the one who had shot it, quite unnecessarily. "And I imagine that both the hunting creatures and the scavengers will eventually come to smell it, if they haven't already."

Billinger turned white in a way that even the most terrifying events of the day had not accomplished.

"Oh, my sweet Lord," he said. "Hurry!"

We did not dare run, not with that huge thing crouched bright-eyed in the trees nearby, but we walked away quickly. A little farther on, a pack of what looked at first like some kind of terrible bird had surrounded a cow in the Vandeleurs' pasture, the property next to the Denslows'. These creatures were nothing like the size of the monster we had just seen, but they were still terrifying: they were covered in feathers, and went on their hind legs like roadrunners, but were bigger than any earthly bird except perhaps an African ostrich, and they had the toothy mouths of lizards. The poor cow was already bellowing in pain as the creatures nipped at it like a pack of pariah dogs, but then one of them jumped up onto the cow's back, extending its stubby, clawed wings for balance like a man riding an unbroken horse. This small murderer darted its head down to bite at the back of the cow's neck, and blood ran down the lowing beast's shoulders. As if the blood had set them off, two more of the creatures leaped onto the cow, which was running in circles now, making terrible sounds of despair as it was bitten to death by the feathered wolves.

As we hurried toward the Denslows' gate, we nearly ran into another group of the terrible pack-hunting lizard birds as they feasted on the remains of another cow, their mouths covered in blood so that they looked like a troop of deranged circus clowns. It was all I could do to restrain Edward Billinger from shooting at them. I was afraid we would need all the ammunition that remained to us.

I was right to be fearful.

As we ran around the edge of the Denslow house, we saw a huge shape, a twin to the thing I'd seen in the swampy forest, crouched only a few yards from the front door. When it heard Ned's shout of alarm, the monster turned toward us, the stringy remains of Billinger's reptile-bird dangling from its jaws. To our horror, we saw that the creature had trapped young Catherine Denslow on the porch.

The beast was more awful than anything a modern human can imagine, I am certain. I have no name for it, but it was as if one of the feathered beasts of Vandeleur's field had been made many times larger by some cruel god, some deity more interested in the limits of grotesquerie than common sense. It must have stretched twelve yards or more from the tip of its great tail to the end of its fanged snout, and it had a raised, spiny ridge along the top of its back that reached higher than the Denslows' roofline. Just its head alone was as long as a man is tall, with rows of knifelike teeth in its jaws that would have done any shark proud. Like the feathered lizards, the monster went on its hind legs, which were massive things, since they had to hold so much weight. Its front limbs looked scarcely useful at all, but even those small legs ended in claws as long as my head.

"Catherine!" shouted Billinger. "Don't move!" Before he could charge forward (to almost certain death), a loud report echoed from the front door of the house, and I heard the hiss of pellets flying past me. Marie Denslow stood there with a very old rifle, a blunderbuss that had almost certainly belonged to her grandfather, and which looked like it might last have been fired at British tax collectors. Her courage was advanced far beyond her aim: I am not certain that even one bit of shot touched the monster, but she had definitely singed me in a few places with hot metal.

"Mrs. Denslow, don't shoot!" I cried. "Edward Billinger and I are out here!"

For some reason, the sound of my voice did something that our appearance and even the old woman's blunderbuss had failed to do, which was excite the monster to action. It tossed its head back, swallowing the bony remains of the flying creature with a single gulp, then sprang heavily toward Billinger and me where we stood at the edge of the garden. The young man immediately began firing his pistol, but although I saw at least two of his shots strike its thick hide, the wounds barely bled and did not slow the monster reptile down. As he retreated, Billinger stumbled, which meant I had no time to aim, load, and fire my long Springfield. Instead, I dropped the rifle on the ground and ran toward the thing, shooting my pistol in the air to attract its attention, which distracted it just long enough for me to hack at its leg with the fire ax. This drew an impressive splash of blood, and the creature's bone-rattling bellow assured me that I had caused it pain. I did not want to injure these strange beasts, let alone kill them, but neither could I let them harm those I was bound to protect.

I swept up Ned, who was a bit surprised by how easily I lifted him, then hurried with him back to the porch. "Get Catherine inside!" I said. "I need to go back for my rifle."

The monster, which had been watching our retreat with sour suspicion and sniffing at its own bleeding ankle, roared when I left the shelter of the porch but hesitated before attacking me (perhaps because of the injury I'd just dealt it), which allowed me to snatch up my Springfield and hightail it back toward the Denslow house.

If it had ended there, all would have been satisfactory, since the wound I had given the great beast was thin and clean and would likely heal. The massive creature remained near the house, but for the moment did not seem inclined to attack again. It was clear, though, that the downstairs rooms were no protection against something that could easily push its entire head through a window and grab anything in those rooms in its grisly jaws, so I herded Mrs. Denslow, Billinger, and Catherine upstairs to the second floor landing, where we all huddled. Catherine was crying, not from fear so much as a sort of exhaustion. Mrs. Denslow told us that the girl had gone outside because she thought she heard us coming back, and had been caught on the porch by the unexpected arrival of the monster. She had spent the best part of an hour huddled there, too terrified to move, while her grandmother tried to find the powder to load the old blunderbuss. I told Catherine she had done the right thing by remaining still, and she composed herself enough to thank me, then remembered to thank Billinger too, which restored a great deal of the young man's spirit.

After an hour or so, I snuck back downstairs to get some food from the kitchen for the others. It was growing dark outside, but I could still see the shape of the monster outside the house, moving restively back and forth, huge head held low to the ground as if it were still trying to puzzle out where we had gone.

Those who were up to eating made a joyless supper out of bread and some cold bacon. I could not help wondering how many other families in Medicine Dance were huddled in their own houses this way, terrified and helpless, like people waiting for a cyclone to strike. At least Medicine Dance's strange Midsummer phenomenon would end sometime near dawn. Frustrated by my own uselessness, certain that Noah Lyman would have been disappointed by my failures, I could only hope that all the townsfolk would survive the night.

Somewhere in the last hour before dawn, when the other three had finally dropped into ragged sleep and my only company was the shuddering light of a lantern nearly empty of kerosene, I heard a strange and ominous sound from downstairs, a scratching as of some very large dog asking to be let indoors. Since the only dog, Miss Catherine's Galahad, was still under the bed in her room, I knew that hunger had finally overwhelmed caution for the great killer we had fought in front of the house.

An instant later, there came a great splintering crash from downstairs, followed by the tinkle and click of falling glass. The creature had clearly decided to come through the front room window, although I felt sure that opening wasn't large enough for it.

"Oh, merciful Lord, what now?" cried Mrs. Denslow, who had been startled awake with the others.

"Stay here." I climbed to my feet. The noise of destruction grew louder as the creature shoved its head and more of its body through the space it had made. I couldn't imagine it would find the downstairs parlor very comfortable, since the creature itself was fully as large as the room, and indeed I could hear its oversized body reducing everything in the room to splinters—furniture, pictures, and Mrs. Denslow's fancy china that had been displayed on the mantle. But this creature had more on its mind than destruction, and despite the half-terrified, half-outraged cries of the two women, I knew that the worst was yet to come.

"Billinger! Take the ladies and barricade yourselves in Miss Denslow's room," I ordered. That way everyone, including the dog, would be in one place, which would make things easier on me.

He argued, but I pointed out that his gun had already proved too small to stop such a beast, and at last he reluctantly agreed to go with the women. "But what will you do?"

"Try to stop it," I said. "But I doubt I will succeed. I hoped the Springfield would stop anything we might encounter, but clearly Professor Denslow's effect will bring us dangers even he could not entirely foresee. Next time, I must prepare better."

"Next time? What are you talking about?" he demanded, but I was busy breech-loading my rifle and did not have time to satisfy his curiosity, even had I wished to.

As soon as Billinger and the ladies disappeared into the bedroom and I could hear them piling furniture against the door, I put my back against the frame and lifted the rifle to my shoulder. I guessed I would get two shots at the most. I knew very little about the monster reptiles, but the thing's narrow, horse-like skull made me cautious—who could guess how much bone lay between me and the creature's brain? But I also knew that shooting even a large animal such as a bison or elephant in the heart might not stop it for several steps, which meant that even if I somehow managed a mortal shot to the chest, its two or three tons were still likely to land on me, or perhaps even crash through into the room where the others hid. If I did have time for two shots, I decided I would try both head and chest and hope for the best.

Like the dragon Fafnir of Germanic legend, the monster suddenly poked its great, grinning head into the stairwell, darting it forward and back as if it did not know what it might find waiting there. I held my fire until the nightmare had swung back into the light of the dying lantern again, its mouth opening as it peered at what must have been a blinding glare. I pulled the trigger. The Springfield roared, and the monster jerked back with an answering bellow. I could hear it smashing things at the base of the stairs, where it could scarcely have room to turn, but instead of the thing falling dead with a four hundred and five grain bullet in its skull, it began trying to climb to the landing to destroy the annoying gnat that had just stung its face. I could see a tattered flap of skin and a crude, bloody hole below its eye, but otherwise it seemed unmoved by my first shot.

As it got its massive, clawed foot up onto the first few steps, and just as I finished loading the second cartridge and slammed the breech shut, the stairs cracked and broke beneath it, canting the creature sideways as it struggled for balance in the wreckage. I took advantage of its loss of balance and fired again, right into the exposed ribcage. This time I saw black blood pulsing strongly from the wound, but I also saw that the injury was by no means fatal. The thing splintered the remains of the steps and a good deal of the stairwell as it struggled for footing, but even if it couldn't climb, it was still tall enough to reach me with those immense, snapping jaws. Before I could fumble another cartridge into the long rifle, I was snagged by the toothy mouth and the gun was thrown from my hand. It shook me like a terrier with a rat, smashing me against the wall, then tossed me down to the first floor, where I landed like a pigeon full of birdshot.

The deadly beast put one of its massive hind feet on me, pinning me flat and helpless. I could feel my ribs buckling as the snarling mouth turned sideways and tilted down toward me, a vast bear trap full of carrion stink, its teeth as big as skinner's knives, then suddenly the massive thing grew faint and shadowy. For a moment I thought life was fleeing me as my organs ceased working, but then, only a few seconds later, the creature simply vanished, and I was lying by myself in the soft pink light of dawn as it streamed uninhibited through the shattered wall of the house. With the rising of the sun, Midsummer's Day had finally ended.

Medicine Dance had been lucky—*very* lucky. Despite the extent of the catastrophe, there had been no deaths other than livestock, though a few other families had suffered damage as great as the Denslows. Some of the houses had been knocked entirely from their foundations by Dahler's Leviathans, huge grazing creatures with serpentine necks that some excited souls swore were almost a hundred feet long. Determined not to be driven out, even by such bizarre happenings, the rest of the townsfolk immediately began to rebuild. Everyone chipped in, whether their own houses had been damaged or not. Even the preacher did his best to help his flock during this trying time, but everyone could tell that the man's faith had been severely tested. (Indeed I later learned that he did not last the year in Medicine Dance and was gone long before the next summer came, taking himself to Tombstone to ply his trade, a place whose sins were many and whose problems, though grave, were more familiar.)

Two days after Midsummer, Mrs. Denslow brought a pitcher of lemonade out to me and Ned Billinger and the local men who were helping repair her house. As the rest of the men shared it, she took me aside. We paused in the shade of the very lemon tree that had supplied the fruit.

"I remember that distracted look from last time, Custos," she said to me. "You're going to be on your way soon. I don't suppose it would do any good to ask where you're headed?"

"I'm afraid not, Ma'am."

"Will we see you again? I mean, before thirty-nine more years pass?" She smiled sadly. "Because I don't suppose I'll still be around when that happens."

"Don't underestimate yourself," I told her. "You Lymans have a rugged constitution."

"Which means no. I hope you said goodbye to Catherine. She's become quite fond of you."

I looked out to where Catherine had brought a glass of lemonade to Ned Billinger, who had taken personal charge of the rebuilding of the Denslow house. "She's fonder of him—and that's the way it should be."

"I was very taken with you myself, when you were here last." The old woman wouldn't quite meet my eye. "I'd just lost my husband the year before, and I thought you quite handsome and mysterious."

"That's very flattering, Mrs. Denslow."

Her smile was sad. "But you're not for the likes of me or even my granddaughter, are you?"

"No, Ma'am. That's not why I'm here in this world."

"I didn't think so." She stood on her tiptoes, shy as a little girl, and kissed me on my cheek. "What cool skin you have!" she said. "Are you the Lost Angel, Custos? Are you the angel that our mesa was named for? Is that why you don't change?"

"I'm no angel, Marie." I don't know why I called her by her Christian name, the name I had known her by first, but I did. "I promise you that's true."

I bid goodbye to Catherine after supper, then asked Edward Billinger to come with me while I gathered my things.

"Here's a list of items I need," I told him, handing him the list I had drawn up on brown paper, then I took a bag of gold Liberty dollars from the crate and gave that to him as well. "Use this to pay for it all."

"But this is a fortune!" he said. "There must be two or three thousand dollars here!"

"Buy those things for me, then keep the rest to start your life with Catherine."

He stuttered his thanks, then said, "But what do I do with all these items after I purchase them? And what on Earth would you want with a Gatling gun? Are you going to come back for them?"

"Eventually. But you don't need to worry about that. When you have collected them all, bring them to the cemetery."

"The... cemetery?"

"Don't be frightened—it's a place I know they'll be safe. There is a grave not far from Noah Lyman's—a stone crypt above the ground. The marker reads 'C. Denslow' with no date. It's empty. Open the crypt and store the weapons and other supplies there."

"C. Denslow..." He stared. "Is that you, Custos? Catherine's grandmother told me she met you before, long ago. Are you some member of the Denslow family, then, returned from beyond the grave to protect them from the professor's ungodly experiment?"

"I swear I am no ghost," I told him. "Good luck, Edward… Ned. Take good care of Catherine and her grandmother."

I left him there, shaking his head, the bag of gold and the piece of brown paper clutched in his hands like holy relics.

I walked out of town and made my way along the riverbank, looking out over the dry lands that only a few short days ago had briefly but memorably been an inland sea. When the darkness began to fall across the valley and I felt sure nobody could see me, I struck out across the open grassland toward the jut of Lost Angel Mesa. When I reached the crumbling, rocky butte I began to climb, by ways only I now knew, until I reached a place high on the side of the mesa, sheltered from view of the town that had grown so distant below. A row of caves looked out over the valley as they had for thousands of years—not quite back to the days of the reptiles which we had so recently visited, but since long before white men had first walked here. Now the caves were empty, or nearly so, the aboriginal men and women who had lived there long gone.

In the third cave from the left lay the passage that led deep into the Earth. I climbed down the difficult slope in darkness. I needed no lantern to find my way—I was home now—but when I reached the bottom, I lit a candle. The machinery was delicate and I wanted to make certain all was left as it should be when I returned to sleep.

If the high cavern with its odd, nearly silent machines seemed a little strange even to me, how much stranger would it have seemed to Ed Billinger, Marie, or Catherine, despite the fact that all the devices had been built by Noah Lyman, the Denslows' ancestor? I sometimes wondered if Doctor Lyman, who had taught me all I knew and made me what I am, might himself have wandered to England and then to Medicine Dance from some farther future—certainly I knew that nothing like his machinery existed anywhere else, either the device that had originally loosed Medicine Dance from the normal strictures of space and time or the machinery that enlivened and supported me. But that was something I doubted I would ever discover. All the information Noah Lyman had given me was, of course, still with me and always would be, even though the doctor himself was long dead. But Noah Lyman's great mistake would never go away, and that was why I would always be here, too, protecting Medicine Dance and Lyman's descendants.

I was tired. I could feel the magnets inside me, which ordinarily spun so fast that I did not even notice their existence, beginning to slow and take on the tiniest bit of wobble, indistinguishable to anyone but me. It was time.

I opened the vault door in the concrete floor and lowered myself into the coffin-shaped space there, then stripped off my coat and tie and set them carefully into a cedar box resting at my feet before taking off my shirt as well. Then I lay back until I felt the gears in the bottom of the mechanism engage smoothly with the flywheel in my back. Once in contact, the gears began their slow, delicate winding motion. A few months would have all my springs back to proper tension again, and then I would lie waiting, sleepless but not awake, until the time came again for me to rise and do what Noah Lyman built me to do.

The lid slowly closed above me, leaving me alone in darkness with the sound of my own slow workings. I had done my job to the best of my abilities, but I would have time now to consider what I could have done better—what I *would* do better next time, because I knew that no matter what happened in the milder Midsummers to come, I would be awakened when the thirty-nine year cycle came around again. There would likely be an entirely new generation of Lymans to protect by then, and perhaps more. It was not such a long time to wait in the quiet dark, not for something like me.

I was content.

RED DREAMS

JONATHAN MABERRY

Wyoming Territory, 1875

McCall saw the star fall.

Like a match struck against the hard dome of the sky and then dropped, trailing sparks, burning out.

It fell slowly, though. Not like other falling stars that were there and gone, mostly caught out of the corner of the eye. This one wanted to be seen.

For a moment McCall thought it was an angel, but then he blinked his eyes clear and shook cobwebs from his head.

An angel, maybe, he thought bitterly, *but if so, then it's sure damn coming for me with a flaming sword.*

He wanted to tell himself that he didn't deserve fiery justice or burning retribution, but McCall wasn't much good at lying to himself. Besides, the light from the falling star was dropping toward the east— the way he'd come—and by its bright light it wouldn't require divine perception to see the truth.

So many bodies. Animal and man. Red and white.

The stink of gunpowder still burned in McCall's nose. That smell and the death smells. The copper of blood, the outhouse odor of shit and piss. And, just as the sun set an hour ago, the first sick-sweet stink of rot. Bodies out here in the Wyoming heat didn't wait long before they turned foul.

So many dead.

And at the end of that crooked trail, one last survivor. A guilty man and his blood-streaked horse, both of them alive by chance or miracle. Alive when they should have been as dead as everyone else. The last survivors of a massacre, now required to sit and witness the death of this piece of cosmic rock.

The comet moved slowly across the sky, so big and so bright. Going down in a blaze of glory, firing its last as it died, declaring itself bold and powerful even while the world was poised to snuff its fire out.

"Now ain't that a sight?" McCall asked his horse, a big paint named Bob.

His voice sounded thin even to his own ears. It sounded sick and old.

Old before my time, he mused, but that wasn't true, either. A preacher once told him that a man aged according to what he did, not by how many years he lived. A good man lived forever.

A bad man?

McCall was a short footstep over forty years and felt like he was ninety. Before the fight—before the *massacre*—he'd felt younger, but that was a relative thing. He couldn't remember ever feeling *young*. Maybe back in Philadelphia when he was a boy. Before he signed on to guard wagons heading west. Before he went to work killing red men. Before he began chipping days or maybe weeks off of his life every time he pulled a trigger.

Weeks or maybe years.

Far above, pieces began breaking off of the comet. Like people jumping out of a burning building. McCall had seen that once. Way back in Philadelphia when a hotel burned right down to the ground. People from the top floors jumped out of the windows. They weren't trying to escape the flames. Not really. Most of them were already on fire. They just wanted it to end. They wanted the hard pavement below to punch the suffering out of them, to get it all over fast so they didn't have to live through their own deaths. That was how McCall saw it. People who didn't have the guts to go all the way down to the end.

McCall couldn't understand that. He could never have jumped out of that building. Death wasn't a destination he wanted to get to a second or a step sooner than he had to. No, sir. When his time came to go into the big dark, then he was going to fight every step of the way. It wouldn't be cowardly kicking and screaming, either. Jonah McCall was going to make death come for him. He'd make death work for it, earn it, sweat over it.

More and more debris fell from the comet, but the heart of it was still intact when it suddenly vanished behind the eastern wall of red rock mountains. There was a huge flash of white and green, and for a moment

McCall fancied that he could see the bodies sprawled on the plain. The Cheyenne dog soldiers with their breech clouts and war bonnets, the rest of McCall's team of riders, and the horses from both sides, all torn and broken and splashed with light. But that was crazy. The battlefield was miles to the west and all that light really showed was the lumpy terrain.

McCall waited for the sound of the impact to come rolling across the hardpan toward him. He'd seen a lot of stars fall; you couldn't help see them out here. Only twice had they been this big, though, and each time they hit hard and hit loud.

He waited, his tin coffee cup an inch from his mouth, holding still to keep his own sounds from hiding any that were trying to find him.

Nothing.

He cocked his head and listened harder.

Nothing at all.

"Must have burned itself all up," he told Bob.

McCall felt vaguely disappointed. He was kind of looking forward to that sound, to the rolling echo of it. It would have been like hearing thunder. It'd been a long time since he'd heard thunder. It had been a long, hot summer, fraught with drought and dust storms. Even on days when the clouds stacked up all the way to God's front porch and they turned black as shoe polish, it never rained. The hot wind always pushed those storm clouds into someone else's sky. They went west, like fleets of ships, but none of them landed on the shores of the Wyoming desert. McCall and his boys had been riding this land for sixteen weeks and hadn't felt a drop of rain on their faces. Not one.

He was a thin man. The last time he'd looked at himself in a mirror he saw a scarecrow wearing his old cavalry trousers and a Pinkerton duster he'd bought secondhand after its owner had been killed. The woman at the general store mended the bullet holes in the back, but even with the fine stitching the fingers of the wind wriggled through each hole.

He sipped his coffee and cradled the cup in his palms, taking its warmth.

Movement in the corner of his eye made him turn, but it was only the wind pushing a piece of bloodstained rag along the ground. A sleeve, thought McCall. Torn, frayed, slick with wetness that was as black as blood in this light. Most of the cloth was dry and that part whipped and popped in the breeze; but the wet parts were heavier and they kept slapping the ground. In the variable wind, the effect was like some grotesque inchworm lumbering awkwardly across the landscape. *Whip, pop, slap.* Over and over again as it crawled toward the shadows and out of his line of sight.

"Damn," he said, and the sound fled away to chase the tattered sleeve into forever.

McCall shivered.

The open range was always so damn cold at night. Hotter than Satan's balls during the day, though.

Something scuttled past him in the dark, a quick scratchety-scratch sound. Probably a lizard chasing down a bug, or running from something bigger. Night was a lie out here. During the day, under all that heat, it was easy to think about dying because everything you saw looked like it was dying. Plants and trees dried to brown sticks; bones bleaching themselves white. And all those endless miles of empty nothing. Under the sun's brutal gaze you expect things to die.

He thought of the fallen star as he sipped his coffee.

Out there behind the hills it had died. Died in its own way.

Died, as sixteen of his men had died.

Died, as thirty-four of the Cheyenne had died.

As this star now died.

McCall poured some hot into his cup and tried to chastise himself for that fanciful notion, but it was hard to hang scorn on yourself for any strange thought when you're in the vast, cold night all alone. And it was easy to think of things dying, even chunks of rock from outer space. Who knows how long it had been out there, flying free in the big empty of the endless black. Then it took a wrong turn and came to the desert sky, and that desert sky killed it as sure as McCall had killed Walking Bear, the war chief of the Cheyenne dog soldiers.

It had come down to the two of them. Walking Bear on a chestnut gelding, a Winchester '73 in his hands; McCall on his paint with a Colt he'd just reloaded.

McCall suddenly shivered.

It was so abrupt and so deep that it rattled his teeth and caused some coffee to slop onto the ground. His whole body shuddered worse than when he'd had the ague down in Louisiana after the war. The shiver was so violent that it felt like cold hands had grabbed him and were actually shaking him back and forth.

Then just as suddenly it was gone. McCall stared at the night as if there should be something at hand to explain what just happened.

"The hell was that?"

But his voice came out all wrong. It startled him because…

He listened to the night.

And heard absolutely nothing.

No insect sounds.

No scuttle of animals or lizards across the ground.

Not a single cry from a night bird.

There was nothing.

Nothing.

And there was never nothing.

McCall shifted the coffee cup to one hand and with the other he touched the handle of his Colt. He could actually hear the rasp of his callused palm against the hardwood grips. Like sandpaper.

He closed his hand around the gun, as much to stop the sound as to seek comfort from the weapon's deadly potential. That gun had killed at least nine of the Indians today. Nine, including that big son of a bitch Walking Bear. It had taken five rounds to put the Indian down, and the bastard fought all the way, working the lever of his Winchester. The rifle rounds burned the air around McCall, and one hit the big steel buckle of his belt and knocked him right out of the saddle. McCall had landed hard and for a wild few moments the world spun around him in a kaleidoscope of red and black. Then the world went away.

It was Bob who woke him up. The big paint stood over him, legs trembling, sides splashed with blood, licking the beard stubble on McCall's face.

The pain in his belly was white hot, and when McCall examined the buckle he saw that it had been folded nearly in half by the impact. He rolled over and slowly, painfully climbed to his feet.

Everything and everyone was still and silent. Walking Bear lay there, five red holes in his chest, eyes wide, mouth open. The big Cheyenne did not move. Could not move. The Indian was dead and so was everyone else. McCall's men and the dog soldiers and all of their horses.

Only McCall and Bob were left.

That moment had been as still and silent as the darkened desert was now, hours later, with the night holding its breath all around him. His stomach still hurt from where the bullet had struck the belt buckle. The skin felt pulped and there was a burning feeling deep inside, like maybe the impact had busted something. Sitting there, listening to the silence, he felt that bruise throb and throb.

McCall snugged his hand down around the handle of the Colt, but the gun withheld its comfort. Even so, McCall clutched at it and tried not to be afraid of the dark even though he knew for certain that there was no living soul anywhere around here.

Gradually, gradually… the night sounds returned.

The tension in McCall's body faded into occasional shivers that were inspired by nothing more sinister than the chilly wind.

McCall sipped his coffee and thought about Walking Bear. He was a strange man. A full-blood Cheyenne who'd been taught his letters by Quaker missionaries. The Indian could read and write better than half the white men McCall knew, and that book-learning had helped him rise to power within the Cheyenne community. Walking Bear had even once gone all the way to Washington D.C., along with a dozen other chiefs, to talk to President Grant. Not that it did much good, because treaties weren't worth the paper they were printed on and everybody knew it. A treaty was another tactic. Not of war, but of business. A treaty was honored only as long—and until—the land the Indians lived on was needed by someone with white skin. Ranch land, gold mines, whatever. Protected Indian land was as much a myth as a man telling a woman that he won't never go no farther than touching her knee. It all amounted to the same.

McCall figured that Walking Bear knew all this, and he had to give the big Indian credit for trying to make the white man stick to his word. Then Walking Bear had apparently decided that guns and scalping knives were more useful than writs and lawsuits.

The territorial governor put a bounty on Walking Bear's head, and a coalition of cattle barons had quadrupled it. Two hundred dollars for Walking Bear and fifty for any dog soldier who rode with him. The most McCall ever made in a single year was one-fifty, and most years it was closer to one hundred dollars. Two hundred for a single bullet was a king's fortune to a man who lived in the saddle.

So, McCall hunted Walking Bear and his party for months, occasionally catching up long enough for someone or another on either side to take a bullet or get his throat cut. Early on the Cheyenne, along with some rogue Arapaho, held the upper hand with more men, more horses and a better knowledge of the terrain here in Wyoming and down in Colorado. But the Indians had only one rifle for every two of them, and the men in McCall's party each had a hand gun and a long gun. And all of them hungered for that bounty, which was paid out in gold coins. The tide turned slowly, but it turned.

The funny thing was that McCall rather liked Walking Bear. The big

Indian had been the last surviving son of Chief Lean Bear, who had been shot by soldiers under the command of Colonel John M. Chivington, the same maniac who attacked a Cheyenne village at Sand Creek in the Colorado Territory. That had been a bad business. Most of the village's fighters had been out hunting during the attack, but Chivington ordered his men to kill everyone in the camp. Every elder, every woman, every child. Even little babies. Seven hundred riders of the Colorado Territory Militia had gone thundering in and hacked the Indians to red ruin and pissed on the bodies as they lay spoiling under the stark November sun. Seven hundred armed soldiers against a couple of hundred Cheyenne. Maybe twenty of the Indians had been fighters. A few people escaped. One hundred and sixty-three Indians died.

McCall had been one of the colonel's men. He'd been right there when Colonel Chivington had made the statement that defined his view of the "Indian problem" as people called it. Chivington had said, "Damn any man who sympathizes with Indians. I have come to kill Indians, and believe it is right and honorable to use any means under God's heaven to kill Indians."

Chivington was one of those men who glowed with holy purpose. Blue light seemed to shine from his eyes. And McCall, so much younger then, had yelled as loud as anyone as Chivington's speeches whipped them into a frenzy. By the time the colonel aimed his militia at the Cheyenne he didn't have to use much energy to pull the trigger.

A lot of what happened there at Sand Creek seemed to take place inside a dream. It never felt real to McCall. Maybe not to most of the men. The colors were too bright. The blood was the color of circus flags. The white of bone was like snow. The screams rose like the cries of birds. And the things they all did…

Did men ever do that kind of stuff except in dreams?

McCall could not actually remember what he did that day. He couldn't remember what his guns did, or his skinning knife, or his hands. None of it. As soon as it happened it all started to fade into pieces of memory, like the way you remembered a play after it was over. You knew the story, but you can't remember every scene, every line. Why? Because it wasn't real.

It was just a dream. Chivington's dream, in fact. McCall and everyone else was an actor, a supporting character, in the colonel's fantasy.

That was back in 1864. Nearly a dozen years ago.

A lot had happened since then.

Cattlemen from Colorado had gone crazy cutting Wyoming up into private plots that were bigger than some countries in Europe. They moved herds up into the grasslands and let them breed like there was no tomorrow.

Of course… that was true enough for the Cheyenne. There was no tomorrow.

Chivington was court-martialed and left for Nebraska in disgrace—but without remorse. His men were scattered to other jobs. McCall went north into Wyoming to work security for the cattle barons and eventually put together his own team. They were not as bad a lot as Chivington's militia—they didn't take scalps or ears or fetuses as trophies, and they didn't make tobacco pouches out of scrotums. But they were all killers, McCall could not say otherwise. The barons wanted the Indian problem solved, and McCall was one of a dozen such men who formed teams to solve it.

Today wasn't the only day that ended in slaughter.

Not the second, not even the tenth.

He stared down into his cup, but it was a black well that looked too far down into the truth. So he leaned back and studied the night sky. The stars were all nailed to the ceiling of the world. Nothing else fell.

McCall got up, wincing at the pain in his gut, and collected some fresh wood for his meager fire. He built it up so that its glow drew his focus, tricking his eye and his mind away from the night and all that it held.

And that was good. That worked.

Until the screaming started.

McCall jerked upright, yanked out of a doze by the terrible sound that tore through the darkness.

He fell forward onto his knees, pivoted, drew his gun, thumbed the hammer back, brought it up, one hand clutched around the grips and the other closed like a talon around the gun hand, head and barrel turning as one. All of that done in a heartbeat, done without thought. His horse cried in fear and reared, hurling its weight against the line that was made fast to a bristlecone tree.

The echo of the scream rolled past him and was torn to pieces by the desert wind.

McCall could feel his heart pounding. He could *hear* the thunder of it in his ears.

His breath came in short gasps.

Silence fell like snow. Soft and slow, covering everything.

"A cat," he said, and his voice was as thin as the lie he told himself. "Mountain cat."

After a long time he lowered his gun and exhaled heavily. Behind him his horse blew and nickered uneasily, shifting from foot to foot, tail switching in agitation.

"Just a damn mountain cat, Bob," said McCall. "That's all it is, don't you worry."

Bob blew and stamped.

The echoes faded until they were nothing.

"Y'see, Bob? You dumb son of a mule? Stop being such a—"

The second scream tore the night apart.

It was huge and massive and so loud that it punched into McCall's head. He screamed, too, and threw himself to one side, spinning on his hip to bring the pistol up again, aiming behind where he'd been facing.

The scream rose and rose.

And even as McCall screamed back at it he knew that this was no cat. No mountain cat and no jungle tiger like the one in the traveling circus. The sound was too loud, too prolonged, too shrill.

It was more like…

Like what?

If there was an answer to that question then McCall's mind did not want to give it. His brain refused to put a name to it.

The shriek went on and on, louder and louder and louder.

The gun fell from McCall's hand as he clamped both palms over his ears. He screamed as loud as he could, trying to push the sound back with his own scream.

Still it went on and on and on and…

Nothing.

Gone.

Stopped.

There was absolute silence. Immediate and total.

Only when McCall stopped screaming could he hear the echo of the screech rolling away from him. He lay there, gasping like a trout on a riverbank. His horse stood trembling, coat flecked with nervous sweat, foam dripping from the bit.

"Steady on, Bob," gasped McCall. "Steady on. It's just a..."

His words trailed off into nothing. McCall didn't try to lie to the horse. Or to himself. This was no cat or anything else whose cry he'd ever heard. This was a banshee wail, like in the stories his grandmother used to tell him. Wailing spirits that warned of death trying to sneak into the house.

But there was no house out here. McCall was sprawled on the sand in the dark wind, and the sky was empty of everything but dying echoes.

And then there was movement out there.

McCall lunged for his fallen gun, clawed the ground for it, scrabbled it into his fist, raised it toward the shape in the darkness.

"No," said the shape.

"Step into the damn light or I'll blow your head off," snarled McCall.

The figure moved closer. It was a man. Tall and broad-shouldered, McCall could see that much; but he stood just beyond the reach of the small campfire's glow.

"No," the man said again. "No reason to fire."

McCall did not fire, but he did not lower the gun.

"No," the man said a third time as he stepped forward into the light. The glow illuminated a face that was hard and angular and streaked with blood. Firelight glimmered in the slanting dark eyes and glistened on the edges of five ragged bullet holes in the broad, flat chest. "No need to shoot. You've already killed me."

McCall stared up at Walking Bear.

And he screamed.

Then he fired.

One, two, three...

Six shots that burst in the air with hot yellow flame and sharp cracks. The bullets punched into Walking Bear, striking him in the chest, in the stomach, in the thigh, the arm, the throat, the face.

Every bullet hit a target.

Cloth and flesh puffed up from each impact. Blood and bone flew.

The hammer clicked down against a spent shell.

Click.

Click.

Click.

McCall's finger jerked the trigger over and over. The cylinder turned with impotent desperation. The clicks chased the gunshot echoes into the darkness.

Walking Bear stood there.

He did not fall.

The new wounds did not bleed.

His face was unsmiling.

"No," he said again.

McCall cried out. A small, mewling sound. Once more the pistol fell from his fingers and thudded into the dirt.

Walking Bear stepped closer. A single step, but it sent McCall scrabbling backward onto his buttocks, then into a skittering crab-like scuttle on hands and heels until he was almost in the coals of the fire. He recoiled from the flames and fell onto his side, panting, sweating, tears boiling from his eyes.

"Oh god," he whispered. "Oh god..."

Walking Bear sighed and stepped forward again, but not toward McCall. There was a large stone near the fire and he lowered himself onto it.

McCall goggled at him. He could feel the skin of his face contract, could feel his lips curled back in terror and disgust from the thing that sat on the rock. When he could force the words out, his voice was a strangled whisper.

"What *are* you?"

The Indian snorted. A soft sound, with only a splinter of amusement gouged into it.

"I'm dead," said Walking Bear. "What the hell do you think I am?"

"I killed you."

"Yes, you did. Twice, though I'm not sure the second time counts."

Walking Bear's voice was so normal that it made McCall want to scream again. It had the casual tone and cadence of a city man, a gift from the Quakers who'd taught him English. But the accent was Indian. There was no mistaking that odd lift at the end of each sentence. Not like someone asking a question. Indians just had a little hook at the end of everything they said that lifted their tone and then went dead flat.

"How are you... I mean... how...?" McCall couldn't patch together a sentence that made any sense.

Walking Bear shrugged. He bent down and picked up a handful of small stones, considered them, and dropped them one at a time. No pattern to it, no haste.

McCall sat up with a jerk. With one hand he fumbled for his fallen pistol and with the other he began pushing cartridges out of his belt. He managed to open the cylinder and drop the spent shells, dropped most of the fresh ones, clumsied a few into place, slapped the cylinder shut and held the gun out in two trembling hands.

The Cheyenne looked faintly amused. "Damn, white man, how many times do you want to kill me?"

McCall licked his lips nervously. "Until it takes, damn you."

Walking Bear dropped the rest of the pebbles and placed his fingers over the holes in his chest, then showed those fingers to McCall. They were smeared with blood.

"It took the first time out."

The gun barrel shuddered like a reed in a windstorm.

"I…"

"You're going to try and make sense of it," said Walking Bear. He shook his head. "But it doesn't make sense. Not the way you think."

Before McCall could organize a reply to that, there was more movement out in the darkness. He flinched and swung the barrel around.

But it was a horse.

A big roan with a blanket instead of a saddle. It walked slowly past the camp, cutting a single glance at the two men without pausing. It gave Bob a soft whinny, but didn't stop there, either. McCall stared at it. There were three bullet holes in its stomach and one in its chest.

"That's not… that's not…"

"Possible?" finished Walking Bear. He shrugged and they watched the horse walk away and vanish into the darkness. There was a long time of silence as they both looked at the shadows. Then another horse came walking by. Its stomach was torn open, entrails dragging in the dirt as the animal followed the hoof prints of the roan.

"Jesus Christ the savior!" cried McCall. "That thing's *dead*."

Walking Bear gave him a pitying look. "I thought we covered that."

"But *how?*"

"Why are you asking me?"

"Because… because you're dead, too."

"Sure."

"Then how are you here? How can you be sitting there? How can you be talking to me, god damn it?"

But Walking Bear shook his head. "I don't know, white man. I woke up dead. You shot me full of holes and I fell down. Then I woke up."

"Are you… a ghost?" demanded McCall. "Tell me if you are."

"I don't know. I'm dead."

"How can you not know?" McCall lowered his pistol, laying it on his lap. "You're a ghost. You have to be."

"Then I'm a ghost." Walking Bear seemed to think about it. He scratched at the bullet hole in his face. "What's a ghost, though?" he asked. "I mean, to you whites?"

McCall didn't answer.

"Sure," said Walking Bear, as if answering his own question, "I read the Bible with the Quakers. There was a lot in there about ghosts and spirits. Jesus was a ghost, I suppose. He came back from the dead."

"He was a spirit," said McCall, calling on what little he remembered of proper Sunday school. "The Holy Spirit."

"Okay, sure," agreed Walking Bear. "But I remember reading that he was flesh, too. At least when he first came back. He met with his disciples and even ate with them. Fish, I think. And one of them touched his wounds to prove that he was really there."

"Thomas," said McCall softly. His mouth was as dry as paste.

"Thomas, right. So, I guess that's what happens."

"I've seen a lot of dead people, damn it," growled McCall, "and none of them ever came back."

Walking Bear turned and looked at him, his dark eyes as cold and hard as chips of coal. "How would you know that?"

There was a sound behind them and they both turned to see four men milling at the edge of the clearing. Not Cheyenne. These were white men in jeans and canvas coats, with gun belts and Stetson hats. McCall knew them, every one. Lucas Polk and his brother, Isaac. Dandy McIsle. And Little Joe Smalls.

All of them were on McCall's payroll. They'd been at the battle. They'd each killed one or more of the Cheyenne.

All of them were dead.

Bob whinnied in fright and tugged at the rope that held him.

The four men stood together, speaking to one another in low whispers. McCall couldn't make out the words. They cut quick looks at him, and Dandy McIsle gave a single shake of his head. When they began walking, they edged around the camp, staying at the very edge of the spill of orange firelight.

"Hey!" cried McCall. "Lucas... Joe..."

But the men ignored him and hurried away. They headed in the same direction as the two horses.

"Where are you going?" McCall yelled.

There was no answer. McCall wheeled on Walking Bear.

"What's happening?"

The Indian seemed to think about it. "I guess they're going home."

"Home where? Little Joe's from Arkansas. Dandy got off the boat from Ireland two years ago. He's been with me ever since. He doesn't have a home."

"I guess he sees things another way now," said Walking Bear. "I guess they all do."

"What in tarnation are you talking about?" McCall wanted to laugh. He wanted to slap himself across the face and wake up from what was obviously a dream. But he sat there, clutching the gun that lay in his lap, talking nonsense with a dead Indian. "Come on," he snapped, "tell me what you're talking about. Tell me how this makes sense."

More men walked past. Indians and his own men. Some of them walked together, heads bent in conversation so private that McCall couldn't catch a single word. Others walked alone. The expressions on their faces were mixed. There was fear on some faces, and even terror on a few. Some looked profoundly confused, and these men stumbled along in the wake of those whose countenances showed determination. But whether that determination was bred from actual understanding or if it was in the nature of those men to believe they understood what was happening at all times, McCall couldn't tell. One man staggered past, arms wrapped tightly around his chest, eyes screwed shut as he wept with deep, broken sobs. And one man went by, singing a slow, sad Presbyterian hymn. Every man was pocked with bullet holes, pierced with arrows, or opened by blades. Every single one. And yet they walked without evident pain, even those who limped on shattered legs. One man waddled past on the stumps of legs that had been hacked off below the knee. Josiah Fenton, one of the youngest of his riders.

McCall watched them go.

All of them.

Every man who had ridden with him, and every Cheyenne they'd died to kill. He even saw two men—an Indian and one of his own men, Doc Hogarth, walking together as if it was something they'd always done. As if it was something normal to do. Even Walking Bear seemed surprised to see that.

"Hunh?" grunted the big Cheyenne.

Doc Hogarth had an arrow all the way through his head. The barbed tip stood out ten inches from the back of Doc's split skull, and the fletched end stood out four inches from the shattered lens of the right side of his glasses. In a dime-novel drawing it might have been bizarre enough to be funny, but McCall gagged when he saw it.

Doc heard the sound of him retching and turned to him, a flicker of sympathy and perhaps disapproval in his remaining eye.

The men passed, some coming so close that firelight danced on their faces and in their eyes, others staying well away so that they were vague shapes in the darkness. It seemed to take a long, long time for them to pass. Too long.

Then McCall cried out as he realized why it was taking this long.

There were strangers mixed in among the known dead.

Other Indians. Too many of them. Some white men, too, but not as many as the Cheyenne.

"Who are they?" he barked, pointing to the Indians.

Walking Bear shook his head. "I don't know them."

Somehow, McCall felt that this was a lie. Or, at least, not a whole truth. The tone of his voice suggested that he knew, or guessed, something.

"What is it?" hissed McCall. "*Do* you know them?"

Walking Bear only shook his head.

The line of straggling dead swelled and soon there were hundreds of bodies moving past. Not just Cheyenne, but Arapaho and Crow, too. And Shoshone and Utes. Even Comanches.

Every one of them was marked with violence. The first few hundred had clearly been shot or cut with sharp blades. McCall knew those kinds of wounds. Cavalry swords. But eventually these thinned out and the ones who followed were marked by other kinds of violence. The duller but still deadly wounds of sharpened stone axes. Cruder arrows. Rounded red craters from hurled rocks.

All dead, all carrying with them the proof of their own deaths.

No, McCall thought, correcting his own error in perception. *The proof of their own murders.*

And that's what this was. A procession of the murdered. The slain. None of them looked withered from disease or starvation. Every single man here had been clubbed or stabbed or shot.

Even this perception had to be corrected, and McCall closed his eyes for a moment to summon the will to see what was there.

He opened his eyes as a woman walked past. Her clothes were torn to reveal bruised breasts and bloody thighs, and she carried the broken remains of her child in her arms. The child wriggled against her breast, seeking milk that had gone cold and sour in the grave.

There were other women.

Other children.

Many of them.

Too many of them.

Were these the children of Sand Creek? If he looked too closely would he see faces that had looked up at him as his blade had plunged down? Would he see accusation in eyes that had watched him take aim with pistol and rifle?

"You don't have to look," said Walking Bear.

"I..."

The Cheyenne pointed. A white woman staggered past, her clothes as completely torn as the Indian woman's had been. Her eyes as haunted, her skin bled as pale. Three children followed her, their bodies crisscrossed with cuts. Hundreds of cuts.

They hurried to catch up with the Indian woman, and as McCall watched, the women fell into step with one another.

Tears burned their way down McCall's cheeks.

He said nothing as the legions of the murdered passed by. Walking Bear put his face in his hands and wept silently. They stayed where they were, one sitting on a rock, the other sitting on the dirt, both of them witnessing the procession.

Soon there was another change. The white corpses thinned and eventually there were no more of them. But the Indians changed, too. Their clothing and jewelry was different. Elaborate beadwork gave way to dyed leather, and then to plain leather. And finally to rough hides of buffalo and other animals.

These Indians had different faces. More like Chinamen, but coarse and blunt, with broader noses.

Yet each of these, even the most savage-looking among them, bore the mark of a stone knife, a heavy club, or the splayed bruising of choking hands.

"All of them?"

The words startled McCall and he turned to see that Walking Bear, his face scarred by tears, was staring at the dead. He shook his head slowly back and forth in a denial so deep that it made his whole body tremble.

"What?" asked McCall.

"Look at them," said Walking Bear. "Every single one of them."

McCall didn't need to ask what Walking Bear meant. He knew. He saw.

He understood.

Eventually the last of the Indians walked past, and it was only then that McCall realized that there had been many animals walking with them. All along, starting with the horses.

Dogs, wolves, antelope, elk.

Every kind of bird.

Rabbits and squirrels.

Their fur or feathers slick with blood that had leaked from the wounds that had killed them.

"Every one of them," echoed McCall.

"Every one," agreed Walking Bear.

Now it was only animals. And some were strange. Some were like things McCall only ever saw in circuses or in books. Big elephants, but they looked bigger and they were covered in long, shaggy hair. Bears that towered taller than the greatest grizzly. Monstrous wolves. And beasts unlike anything McCall had imagined in his drunkest nights or in his worst nightmares. Things like reptiles that were so massive that their footfalls shook the world. Bob screamed as they passed. Some lumbered along on four titanic legs; creatures whose heads rose on necks that arched up as long and slender as tree trunks. Others stalked forward on two immensely powerful legs, while absurdly small forelegs clutched at the night air.

Even here, even as these giants from nightmare or from Hell itself thundered past, McCall could see that their bodies were worn by tooth and claw.

"Every god damn one of them," he said.

They sat there and watched and watched as the wheel of night turned and the dead paraded by. Finally, Bob tore free of his tether and he ran off into the night. McCall expected him to run away from the grisly procession, but the damned crazy horse galloped at full speed in the same direction.

Eventually...

Eventually.

Silence settled over the camp. The last rumbled footsteps of the giants faded. With slow hesitation the night sounds returned. A cricket. An owl. The crackle of the logs turning in the fire.

McCall looked at Walking Bear. Both men had long ago stopped crying. Their tears had dried to dust on their faces.

"Every single one," said McCall once more, and the Cheyenne nodded.

With a long, deep sigh, Walking Bear got heavily to his feet.

"Guess I should go, too."

"Go?" asked McCall. "Go where?"

"Wherever they're going."

"And where's that?" McCall's voice was sharp and cold. "Are they going to Heaven? To Hell?"

Walking Bear shook his head. "I'm not a shaman, white man. I'm a warrior. It's not for someone like me to understand the mysteries."

"Isn't it?" demanded McCall.

The big Indian gave him a small, slow smile. "Are you coming?"

McCall tried to laugh, but the effort hurt his stomach.

He got to his feet, though. "Go where?" he asked again.

Walking Bear said nothing.

"I *can't* go where you're going," insisted McCall. "You're dead."

"You should know."

"I *do* know. Like you said, I killed you twice."

"Once was probably enough," said Walking Bear.

For some reason that McCall could not understand, they smiled at each other. Then they laughed out loud.

"I guess I'm sorry for shooting you," said McCall after their laughter bubbled down and died out.

"No," said Walking Bear. "You're not. If you could, you'd do it again. I think you got the habit now. I mean… twice."

They laughed again.

"So," said McCall awkwardly, "what now? Is this some kind of lesson? Am I supposed to ask for you to forgive me?"

"I wouldn't," said Walking Bear. "I know I was educated by the Quakers, but I'm pretty sure I don't forgive you. At least not yet. I've only been dead for a little bit. Maybe I'll come round to it."

"Yeah," said McCall. "Maybe. But where does that leave me? Are you going to just walk off? How am I supposed to deal with this? How am I supposed to live with this kind of thing in my head? Is this some kind of spiritual lesson? Am I supposed to go back to town and devote my life to good works? Is that how it ends?"

Walking Bear looked at him for a long time. Half a minute, maybe more.

"No, white man, I don't think that's how it ends. And I'm pretty sure you know it."

McCall tried to look at him, to see the meaning in Walking Bear's eyes, but he couldn't do it. He turned away.

"Don't," he said. "I know what you're going to say, but don't say it."

Walking Bear was silent.

"I'm *not* dead, god damn it."

Walking Bear said nothing.

"I'm not."

"Okay," said the Cheyenne.

"Okay," said McCall.

His stomach hurt. He touched the bent belt buckle. Felt where the rifle bullet had struck. Traced the outline of the curved metal.

Felt the hole.

Slipped a finger inside. It was cold in there.

He turned and looked at Bob. Saw the big ragged exit wound where a bullet had punched its way out of him.

Closed his eyes.

A last tear broke from the corner of his eye.

"Shit," he said.

"Yeah," agreed Walking Bear. "But… you knew it already. Didn't you?"

McCall tried to hold in a sob, but it snuck past his clenched teeth.

The night wind whistled through the branches of the bristlecone tree.

"It…" began McCall, but his voice broke. "It doesn't make any sense."

"No."

"If we're dead, then where are we?"

"I don't know."

"Is this heaven?"

"It's not any heaven I heard of," said Walking Bear. "It's not the Quaker heaven and it's not Cheyenne heaven."

"Then what? Are we in Hell?"

"Does it feel like Hell?"

McCall thought about it. "No."

"Then I guess it's not Hell. Half the people we saw weren't killers. Not the women or the children. Why would they go to Hell just because they were murdered?"

"Then if it's not Hell, *what* is it?" growled McCall.

"I don't know," repeated Walking Bear, leaning on each separate syllable.

They stood in the dark, in the wind, in the night.

"I'm going to go," said Walking Bear.

This time McCall said nothing.

"Are you coming?" asked the Cheyenne.

"You don't know what's out there," said McCall softly, nodding toward the east, where everyone and everything else had gone.

"No," agreed Walking Bear. He touched the bullet holes on his chest. "I only know what's here."

With that he gave McCall a single nod, turned, and walked slowly toward the eastern darkness.

Jonah McCall stood there, watching him go. The pistol was a cold, heavy weight in his hand. He raised the gun and held it out. Starlight gleamed along its length. He uncurled his fingers one at a time and then pulled back his thumb.

The gun toppled to the ground for the third time.

For the last time.

"I'm sorry," he said. But he didn't say it loud enough for anyone to hear but himself.

He brushed the tear from his cheek, took a long breath, let it out very slowly, and began walking. Maybe he'd catch up with Walking Bear. Maybe not.

He thought about the comet that had burned its way across the sky and wondered if it had been an omen.

Probably.

But of what?

He didn't know the answer to that question, either. Maybe there would be answers out there in the darkness.

Maybe not.

He kept walking.

The night, very gently but very firmly, closed its fist around him.

BAMBOOZLED

KELLEY ARMSTRONG

Dakota Territory, 1877

"Are you sure she can do it?" the boy asked Nate as he watered their trio of horses.

Lily was standing right beside him and had both a name and ears. But she knew the boy—Will—wasn't trying to be rude; he was simply like most of the young men they recruited: rarely set foot off his family homestead, rarely seen womenfolk other than his momma and sisters. And frontier mommas and sisters did not look like Lily.

Even now, as Will talked about her, he couldn't look her way—as if merely to glimpse her might damn his mortal soul. Lily could point out that his soul ought to be a lot more worried about the thieving that was coming, but to a boy like Will, that was part of life. Pretty girls with painted faces were not.

Lily's face was, of course, not painted right now. She was dressed in breeches, boots, and an overcoat, with her hair pushed up under her hat. It didn't matter. Will still wouldn't look.

"Can she do it?" he asked again. "I mean no offense—"

"Then stop giving it," Nate growled.

Lily noticed a cloud of dust cresting the rise. "I do believe my wardrobe has arrived."

Emmett and Levi rode up, their horses run hard, flanks heaving. They had arranged to meet at midday and the sun had passed its zenith a while back.

"Had some difficulties," Emmett said as he nudged his horse to water.

"That it?" Nate pointed at the wrapped parcel behind Levi's saddle. When Levi nodded, Nate took it and said to Lily, "Come on."

* * *

Lily let Nate lead her behind an outcropping of rock. Emmett and Levi knew better than to sneak a look while she was dressing, and Lily was quite certain Will wouldn't dare, but Nate believed in coppering his bets. Otherwise, things would get messy. Nate didn't take kindly to trespass of any sort.

"We cutting the boy loose after the job?" he asked as they walked.

She nodded. "That's best. It's not working out. You promised Wilcox you'd try him. You did."

Nate grunted and handed her the parcel. As she untied it, she snuck a peek at him. Six feet tall. Well built. Rough featured, but not in a way that was displeasing, at least not to her. What she noticed most, though, was what she'd noticed about Nate from the start: the uncanny way he carried himself. When he moved, he was like a catamount on the prowl. Yet most of the time he wasn't moving at all, standing so still he seemed a statue, only his eyes moving, his gaze scanning the landscape.

It wasn't natural, that complete stillness, that constant alertness. She wondered why others never thought it peculiar. She had, right from that first time, seeing him across the saloon. He'd noticed her, too, but not in the way men usually did. He'd only stared, no expression, no reaction. Yet his gaze hadn't left her as she'd taken a table with the rest of her acting troupe.

The trouble had begun later that evening, when a gambler made the mistake of equating actresses with whores. It was a common misconception. Lily couldn't even properly blame the man, considering that her two companions had already accepted paid invitations. The acting life required a second income; Lily made hers with light fingers.

She'd told the gambler she wasn't for sale, but he'd thought she was only haggling. That was when Nate had come over. He'd asked the gambler to let Lily be. When the man laughed, Nate fixed him with a stare as cold as a Nebraska winter. It hadn't taken long for the gambler's nerve to crack. He'd gone for his Colt; Nate broke his arm. Just like that. Lily saw the gambler reach for his piece and then he was screaming like a banshee, his arm snapped, bone sticking out, blood gushing. That's when she realized Nate wasn't quite human.

Now Nate turned his gaze on Lily as she undressed. Lily was used to men staring at her. They'd been doing it since she was fourteen, which was when she discovered it was so much easier to pick a man's pocket if he was gaping at her bosom. Nate wasn't like that. He gazed at her with what seemed like his usual expressionless stare, but Lily had learned to read deeper, and what she saw there now was hunger. He didn't move, though, not until she adjusted the dress and twirled around.

"How do I look?" she asked.

Nate growled an answer and, before she could blink, he was on her, one hand behind her head, the other at her rear as he pulled her into a deep kiss.

"I really ought not to have bothered putting on the dress," she said as she broke for air.

Nate chuckled and hoisted her onto the nearby rocks.

They rode into town after sundown. That was best. There were many variations on their game, but in each they'd learned the value of a late approach. By morning, the town would be buzzing with rumors of the party that arrived under the cover of night. A slip of a girl, bundled in an overcoat but riding a fine horse and wearing a fine dress. A proper young lady, escorted by a surly uncle and three young gunmen.

As the day passed, the story grew. The girl's uncle kept her under close watch at the inn, but they'd had to venture out, as she was in need of a new dress. And what a pretty thing she was, with yellow hair, green eyes, and the sweetest French accent.

The girl was shy, the uncle taciturn, and no one in town learned much from either, but the young fellows with them were far more talkative, especially after a drink or two. They said the girl came from New Orleans. Her parents were in California, expanding their empire. Shipping or railroad, no one was quite sure which, but they were powerfully flush. A suitor waited in California, too. A rich man. Very old, nearing sixty. The uncle was taking the girl to her parents and her fiancé and her new life. They'd been diverted here by news of Indian trouble and were waiting until the army had it in hand. Until then, the party would pass the time in their little town.

Lily's mark came at dinner. It was earlier than they'd expected—most men didn't like to seem eager. But it was said that John Anderson was keen to wed. Or wed again, having recently lost his young wife in a tragic accident. It was also said that "accident" might not have been quite the proper word to use. Anderson hadn't been as pleased with his bride as he'd hoped. Her daguerreotype had sorely misrepresented her and she had not cared for ranch life. She'd also objected to her husband's ongoing association with the town's whores and his penchant for bringing them home. Women could be quite unreasonable about such things. So Mrs. Anderson had perished and her grieving husband was impatient for a new bride.

Lily and Nate were dining at the inn. They'd barely taken their seats when Nate made a noise deep in his throat, too low for others to hear. He kept his attention on the wall-posted menu while Lily glanced over to watch their mark stroll through the door. They said John Anderson was a handsome man, but she couldn't see it. Or perhaps it was simply everything she'd heard about him that tarnished her opinion. She did, however, watch him until he looked squarely in her direction. Then her gaze darted away as she clutched her napkin and cast nervous glances at her "uncle."

Anderson stopped at their table, took off his hat with a flourish and introduced himself. Gaze lowered, Lily waited for Nate to reciprocate. He didn't.

"I see that you have not yet begun to dine," Anderson said after an awkward silence. "May I invite you both to join me at my table?"

"No," Nate said.

"Does that mean I may not ask or you will not join me?"

Anderson's lips curved in the kind of smile that would warn another man off. Nate only stared at him.

"No."

"All right then. May I ask—?"

"No."

Lily simpered and shot looks at Anderson, her eyes pleading with him to excuse her uncle's behavior.

"I see," Anderson said. "Well, then, perhaps I'll have the pleasure of seeing you both around town."

Nate's answering snort said, "The hell you will." Anderson nodded stiffly and retreated to his table.

They had been in town for nearly a fortnight. During the course of it, Lily found increasingly more opportunities to see John Anderson. It was a difficult wooing with her "uncle" seemingly so determined to keep the rancher away, but they met in furtive assignations that grew ever more daring until Anderson finally extended the required invitation to visit him at home. Not that he was quite so forward. He simply said he had a hound dog with pups that would surely delight Lily and he wished for her to see them. Naturally, it would have to be at night—*late* at night, after her uncle was abed. But Anderson would send his foreman to accompany her so she would be safe. At least until she arrived.

And so the foreman—a man named Stewart—arrived at the appointed hour of midnight. Lily informed him that her uncle was deeply asleep, having been aided by a draught of laudanum. They set off into the night.

Nate and the boys followed.

Lily slowed outside the big ranch house and looked about nervously.

"It is dreadfully dark, monsieur," she said.

"Mr. Anderson is right there, miss." Stewart pointed at the lit front window. "Waiting in the parlor."

She gave a sheepish smile. "I am sorry to be such a child. I have not visited a man's home without an escort." She dipped her gaze. "And I have *never* visited at night."

"There's nothing to worry about, miss. Mr. Anderson is a proper gentleman. You have my word on that."

Lily continued to stall. Nate insisted on scouting before she ventured inside. Finally, she caught sight of Nate's distant figure, poised in the side yard, gazing about, face lifting slightly to sniff the breeze. He motioned to say that he'd circled the homestead and all was well.

"I am ready to go in, monsieur," she murmured to Stewart, and he took her up to the front door.

An hour later, Anderson lay passed out on the parlor settee. He looked very peaceful, Lily thought, as she knelt beside him. He would not be nearly so happy when he woke, but even without his odious reputation, Lily would not have regretted bamboozling him. Men like Anderson were no better than bunko artists themselves—seducing young women in the expectation the ruined girl would be rejected by her suitor and then she, and her inheritance, would be handed to him by parents hoping to make the best of a bad situation. It proved such men were not as worldly as they believed or they would know it was a ruse unlikely to succeed. This was not English society where one eager bride could easily be exchanged for another. Out on the frontier, a good woman was like a fine horse or pair of boots: you hoped they'd be pleasing and well-formed, but you expected they'd been used a time or two. That was fine—it saved the fuss of breaking them in.

Anderson hadn't even won a flash of bared ankle. Lily was adept at the art of the tease, a skill she'd learned as an actress. In cities, she was expected to perform in actual plays, but that was not required in the Territories. Out here, men came to see pretty girls in pretty dresses teasing and dancing and warbling on stage.

Other women who worked this game would be required to lie with the mark, even if she had a beau in the gang. Out here, a girl was lucky if her lover didn't toss her garter onto the poker table and give her away for a night when his luck soured. With Nate, Lily didn't need to worry about that.

Once she'd confirmed that Anderson was out cold, she dashed through the house to be sure it was empty. When she'd arrived, she had Anderson take her on a tour of his "lovely home." He'd dismissed the help, as men usually did. She still checked, in case a maid or hired hand had snuck in the back. The house was clear.

Lily brought Nate and the boys in and gave them quick instructions on where to find the best goods. Emmett and Levi needed little guidance and Will would simply follow them. The five worked together on the parlor and adjoining rooms. Then Nate told the boys he was taking Lily outside to "scout for trouble." Will looked confused. Levi smiled and shook his head. Emmett winked and told Nate to have fun. Nate grabbed a parcel he'd left by the door and off they went.

Naturally, Nate and Lily were not heading outside to scout. This, too, was part of the routine, and Emmett and Levi seemed to think it was quite reasonable that the boss would whisk his girl off mid-job for a roll in the hay barn. After all, they'd been forced to sleep apart for a fortnight now. Could anyone blame him? Well, yes, they could, but the boys never seemed to realize it was the least peculiar. With Nate, they were accustomed to peculiar.

"Did it go all right?" he asked as they slipped around the house.

Obviously it had, if Anderson was asleep and the boys were emptying the home, but Lily knew that wasn't what Nate meant. "He didn't lay a finger on me."

"Good."

As Lily walked, she unfastened her dress, keeping to the shadows of the house. That took a while, and she didn't stop moving until she had to wriggle out of it. She glanced over to see Nate watching her.

"No," she said, waggling her finger.

He growled deep in his throat. She laughed and took the parcel from his arm.

"Don't grumble," she said. "You know it's better if we wait."

Another soft growl, this one less complaint than agreement. She laughed again and tugged on her breeches, shirt, and boots. Her pistol was there, too—a little derringer that tucked neatly under a shirt or a dress.

"Did you find him?" she asked when she'd finished.

"Out back. Farthest building from the house."

She smiled. "That ought to make it easy."

Lily peered through the open window. Stewart was at his kitchen table, playing solitaire while drinking whiskey straight from the bottle.

Growing up in New Orleans, Lily had been subjected to more church-going than any child ought to be, which had much to do with her running off at fourteen. Too many gospel mill lessons pounded in with a strap. From what she'd learned there, the nature of demons was quite clear. They were hideous beasts with wings and scales and horns. They did not, in short, look like Theodore Stewart. But as she'd come to understand, most church lessons were less than useful in the real world.

Stewart was a demon. Or a half-demon, fathered by one of those unholy beasts whom, Lily was quite sure, hadn't borne scales and horns when he seduced Stewart's momma. Stewart had, however, inherited his father's predilection for hell-raising, which was why they were there.

While their thieving provided a handsome income, it was merely a front. The real prize sat at that table, drinking himself to sleep. This was the world Nate had introduced her to, one filled with creatures that the church deemed "monstrous aberrations." Half-demons, witches, sorcerers, vampires, werewolves, and others. Monsters? Perhaps. Monstrous? She glanced at Nate, peering through the window, sharp gaze assessing his prey. No, not always. But they did cause trouble with somewhat more regularity than average folk, which meant there were plenty with a price on their heads, like Stewart.

Nate leaned over and whispered into her ear, so Stewart couldn't hear through the open window.

"I'll go in here. Can you take the front?"

She nodded.

"Be careful," he murmured.

She nodded again, but there was rarely any need for her to be overly cautious. While she had starred in the opening acts of this performance, Nate took that part now. Like the understudy for an actor who never took sick, Lily's new role was rather dull. In all their jobs together, only once had a mark even noticed Nate, and that was only due to an unfortunately placed looking glass. Even then, Nate had taken their mark down before he reached the door.

Lily still undertook her role with caution, derringer in hand as she crept around the tiny house to the front door. There she found a suitably shadowy place to wait.

When she heard a faint noise to her left, she wheeled and swung her pistol up, her eyes narrowing as she strained to see—

Cold metal touched the back of her neck. "Don't move."

She calmly assessed the voice. Did it sound firm? Confident? Or did it waver slightly, suggesting a man uncomfortable with pointing a gun at a girl of twenty? And perhaps even less comfortable with the prospect of pulling the trigger.

"Lower the gun," he said.

That voice. She recognized it, though the tone was not one she'd ever heard him use. She cursed herself—and Nate—under her breath.

"Will?" she said.

"I told you to lower—"

"Please don't hurt me, Will." She raised her voice a little, knowing Nate's ace hearing would pick it up. "If you want a bigger share, I'm sure we can manage it. P-please don't—"

He kicked her legs out from under her. She tried to twist as she fell, but he'd caught her by surprise. Will grabbed her gun arm. Before she could throw him off, his fingers burned so hot she gasped as agony ripped through her forearm and Will plucked the derringer from her grasp.

Obviously Will was a fire demon, like Stewart. They'd been euchred.

"William!" a voice called from the cabin. "Bring her in."

The boy grabbed Lily by the hair and dragged her to the cabin door. He pulled it open and shoved her through, his gun at her neck.

Nate and Stewart faced off inside. Nate glanced at Lily. Then he looked away.

"Seems we have your girl," Stewart said.

Nate grunted.

"William here tells me you're fond of her," Stewart continued. "That you would, I presume, not wish to see any harm befall her."

Another grunt.

"I'll take that as a yes. Now, as I'm sure you know, there's many a man who'd pay handsomely to mount Nathaniel Cooper's head on his wall. But I have a buyer who'd prefer you alive. He's quite interested in your special skills. There aren't nearly enough of your kind out here. So here's what I'll do. You come with me and we'll take the girl, too. None of my men will harm her. And, yes, I have men. Or half-men, half-demons, rather." Stewart raised his voice. "Bob? Jesse?"

Two answering shouts came from outside. Nate took advantage of the pause to glance at Lily again. She held his gaze before he turned away.

Stewart continued, "As you see, there is little sense in running, although I'm quite certain you won't attempt it, so long as we have your pretty mate—"

Nate spun and fired… right at Lily's chest. She managed only a strangled gasp of shock before slumping to the floor.

Theodore Stewart stared down at the girl's body, her shirt bloody, limbs akimbo, sightless eyes staring up.

In the world of supernaturals, it was generally accepted that Nathaniel Cooper was a bastard. That was true of most of his breed—violent, unsociable loners. But even among them, Cooper was renowned as a heartless son of a whore. Still, William had said he was fond of the girl. *Very* fond of her.

Apparently, William had been mistaken.

Stewart crouched to close the girl's eyes. He ought to have foreseen this. William was but a boy and didn't understand the ways of men. And yet Stewart had still been caught unaware by Cooper's move, which was exactly what the bastard intended. He'd killed the girl and then fired off a second round at Stewart as he bolted out the door.

As Stewart rose, the door banged open and William strode in.

"You get him?" Stewart asked.

"Not yet. Jesse and Bob are tracking him. I reckoned I ought to make sure he didn't circle back and try to collect on his bounty." William walked to the girl. "Damnation. She was a pretty painted cat. I was really hoping to get a poke." He nudged the girl's arm with his boot. Then he bent and touched it. "She's still warm." His gaze traveled over the body. "You think it'd be all right if I—"

"No. Get outside and scout."

Stewart waited until William left. Then he looked down at the girl. The boy was right. She was finer than anything he'd seen in a while.

He fingered the bottom of her shirt. He wouldn't do *that*, of course. That was disgusting. But there was nothing wrong with taking a look.

Stewart unfastened her bottom button and then the next one, slowly peeling back her shirt. Out of the corner of his eyes, he caught a movement, but before he could lift his head, a hand grabbed him by the throat and threw him across the room.

Lily reflected that this was perhaps not the most opportune moment to end her performance. Yet she wasn't about to play dead while he disrobed her.

Her side blazed as she sprang to her feet. Bullets hurt, no matter how good a shot Nate was and how careful he'd been to shoot her where there was little risk of serious injury. Her eyes stung, too, from staring at the ceiling until Stewart had done the Christian thing and closed her eyelids. She supposed she ought to have shut them herself, but she knew that open eyes would be the most damning proof of her death, and she was a fine enough actress to manage it.

Stewart was still lying on the floor, dazed, trying to figure out how he'd arrived there, clear across the room. When he saw Lily coming at him, he only gaped.

Lily yanked Stewart's gun from his holster and tossed it aside. Only then did Stewart snap out of it. He caught her by the arm, his fingers flaring red-hot, fresh pain scorching through her already-burned arm. She ignored it and grabbed him by the neck. His eyes bulged as she squeezed. They bulged even more as her hand began to change, palm roughening, nails turning into thick claws.

"You didn't expect this?" she said as she lifted him from the floor. "You *did* call me his mate."

"No. You can't be—"

"Do you smell that?" Lily turned her face, nose lifting. "I do believe we're about to have company."

The door flew open and Will stumbled in.

"Cooper," he said, panting. "It's Cooper. He's…"

He saw them, her hand around Stewart's throat. His mouth worked. He had one hand still on the door. Then it crashed open, sending Will scrambling out of the way as a massive wolf charged in. The beast's nostrils flared. Its gaze swung to Lily. Then, with a grunt, the beast tore after Will as he dashed for Stewart's gun, his own obviously lost.

Will made it halfway across the room before the wolf leaped on him. He hit the floor and rolled onto his back. His hands shot up, fingers blazing. The wolf's jaws swung down and ripped out his throat.

"*No*," Stewart whispered as Will's life's blood spurted onto the floorboards. His gaze shifted to Lily. "I have money."

"And so will we, when we collect the bounty on you."

"Whatever they said I did, it isn't true. I have enemies. Lying sons of whores—"

"A Kansas wagon train two years back," she said. "A train full of settlers massacred and left for the buzzards, after your gang had some sport with the womenfolk."

"I… Wagon train? No. That wasn't…" He trailed off. "I have money. More than any bounty—"

"I'll take the bounty," she said and snapped his neck.

"Stop grumbling," Lily said as Nate daubed her bullet wound with a wet cloth. "I told you to shoot me."

Which she had, mouthing it when he'd glanced at her during the standoff. That did not, she understood, make him feel any better about the situation.

"It passed clean through," she said. "We heal quickly. I won't want to shift for a few days, but I'll be fine otherwise."

He still grumbled. She leaned forward and brushed her lips across his forehead.

"I need to be more careful," he said.

"We both will be."

"That boy…" A growl as he glanced at Will's body. "I ought not to have been duped."

"We both were. We'll have a talk with Wilcox about this. He was the one who asked us to take the boy. And he was the one who set us on Stewart."

Another growl.

"We'll have satisfaction," Lily murmured. "In the meantime, presuming those half-demons were from Stewart's old gang, we ought to be able to collect bounties on them, too."

Nate grunted. The prospect, she knew, did not cheer him immediately, but it would, after she'd recovered and he'd finished chastising himself for letting them be bamboozled.

"You did well," he said as he dressed her wound.

"I've not forgotten how to act," she said with a smile. "And you gave me all the other skills I required."

It had taken work to convince him to share his curse with her. Eventually, he'd come to realize that the only way a werewolf's mate could be safe was if she was truly his mate. The process, as he'd warned, had not been easy. The life, too, was not easy. But she would never regret it. Lily knew what she wanted—the man, the life, the person she wanted to be. And she had it. All of it.

"We ought to hurry," she said. "The boys will be waiting back at the inn by now." She paused. "Do you think they heard anything before they left?"

Nate snorted.

Lily laughed. "Yes, they're not the cleverest of lads. Which is the way we like them." She got to her feet. "Let me find a clean shirt."

She looked at him, still naked after shifting back from wolf form. "And we'd best find your clothing. Although…" Her gaze traveled down his body. "The boys *are* very patient. I suppose they wouldn't mind waiting a mite longer."

SUNDOWN

TOBIAS S. BUCKELL

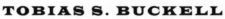

State of Colorado, 1877

Willie Kennard rode into the town of Duffy dangerously late, looking back over his shoulder at the height of the sun and squinting. He dropped down from the old mare he'd borrowed off Wilson Hayes and hitched her to a post.

Every step shifted two days' dust and grit off his long coat, and his thighs ached so bad it felt like he'd been punched in the groin.

"You're a fool to walk into Duffy," the old Pawnee man Willie had hired as tracker muttered when they'd split up outside of town on the bluff. "Once night comes, you won't need to be worrying about your quarry. It's the town that'll get you. They'll string you up. Whether or not you're wearing a silver badge."

Judging by the stares the white folk sitting outside the hotel gave him, Willie knew it was truth.

"Help you?" an older man with a long beard asked in a hard voice.

"Looking for the sheriff," Willie said. "I need his help finding a man that might be hiding somewhere around these parts."

"What kind of man?" the old timer asked. It was a pointed question.

"The murdering kind," Willie said.

"Sheriff's at the Longfellow Ranch," said a dapper man crossing the wooden slatted walkway. He looked to be a store owner of some kind, in his carefully pressed suit.

"Now why'd you go tell him that?" spat the old man.

"Cuz he's a Marshal, Pat. You see his star?" the shopkeeper said. "And cuz it's getting late."

They glared at each other, and then the old man pointed a wizened, crooked finger down the other side of town. "Ranch is down that way."

Willie looked down the dusty road, sunk deep with wheel tracks and horse shit. Then he looked back over his shoulder at the sun, moving toward the horizon.

Best to get on with it. He sighed.

He tapped a finger to his hat at the younger gentleman and made his way back to the horse.

As he rode past, he asked, "What's the sheriff doing at the ranch?"

"Indians mutilated the cattle," spat the old man. "Damned heathens."

Willie spurred the horse into an awkward gallop, the best it could manage, leaving a plume of dust in the air that set the old man coughing.

Willie rode up onto the ranch hard. The damned horse was heaving and bitching about the work, but he didn't pay it much mind. Dropped out of the saddle while the mare still trotted down to a slower pace, left it with a muzzle flecked with foam and turning circles in the dirt.

His boots scuffed up dust as he ran for the door, glancing around.

"Hello Longfellow Ranch!" he shouted, right hand dropped low to brush aside his coat. He put a palm to the Colt's grip.

The faded gray wood of the door creaked as it opened slightly. "Who's that?"

"I'm looking for the Sheriff of Duffy," Willie said. "I'm Marshal Willie Kennard."

"Marshal?" A ruddy face frowned from the gap in the door, looking out at Willie. "Never seen a negro Marshal before."

"Don't imagine there're many of us," Willie said. He tapped the silver star. "But here I am, nonetheless."

The dark green eyes flicked down, noted his draw stance through the crack in the doorway. "You seem agitated, Marshal Kennard. Mind if I ask why?"

"Been tracking a murderer through the scrub a couple days," Willie said. "Tracked him to Duffy. Hoping I could rely on your help."

With a horrible creaking sound, the door opened the rest of the way. "I'm Sheriff Bostick Keen. Come on in, I'm talking to Dr. Longfellow here about what happened to his cattle recently."

Willie'd seen them on the way in. The cattle ripped open, ribs exposed and drying in the sun, tongues lolling.

"Dr. Longfellow is getting us a drink of water," the sheriff said.

Sheriff Keen had a puffy, round face but was a stick of a man, really. Wind-swept lean. Meant he didn't hide in his office, but walked out in the windy grit. Did his job.

Willie respected that.

Dr. Longfellow came back into the room with a tray of glasses and a pitcher filled with water fresh from the well. Beads of sweat rolled down the rounded belly of the pitcher.

The ranch owner bent forward to pick up a glass and fill it.

Willie stared at the man's neck.

Before the sheriff could move, Willie drew. As Dr. Longfellow straightened, he looked at the barrel of the Colt, as if for a second fascinated by it.

The gunshot filled the room with its violent crack, and Dr. Longfellow's brains splattered out across the wall behind him. Only, the brain tissue was all wrong. Black goo, filled with insect-like fragments that dripped down toward the ground. No blood. What looked like a wasp's stinger the size of a thumb was stuck fast in the plaster.

Sheriff Keen screamed like a child, raising his hands in front of him, then recovering and reaching for his gun. "What the hell..." he started to say, then stopped and looked at the oversized stinger. It twitched and wriggled slowly. Not a slow man, he realized something wasn't right. "What was that in his head? What was that?"

Willie pulled his left piece out and aimed it at him. "Turn around," he ordered.

The sheriff took a deep breath, his eyes wild and wide. "No."

Willie cocked his head. "No?"

"If you gonna kill me, do it right to my face."

"Most likely, I won't kill you," Willie said. "But I do want to see the back of your neck. If you don't show it to me, chances are you do end up dying. I gotta make sure you're not like him. You understand?"

Keen's face scrunched up in defiance and anger. Finally, after several short breaths, he screwed up his face in disgust and turned around.

He trembled a bit, expecting the shot.

But Willie nodded. "You're all right." He slid the two Colts back into their holsters. "I apologize for drawing on you."

Keen yanked his own, overly large revolver out, but Willie ignored him. He moved around the house, kicking open doors and looking into rooms as the sheriff followed him, gun aimed. Willie paused in front of a store room in the back. Looked at the bodies on the ground.

"See that?" he asked Keen.

The sheriff's green eyes took it all in. Shattered human ribs poking through broken skin. Glazed eyes staring at the ceiling. The wife, the two children lying in her arms. "Like the cattle," he said.

"Like the cattle."

"How'd you know?" Keen asked.

"Seen it before. Some men attacked a camp I was providing protection for. Wasn't pretty." Willie remembered muzzle flashes and glazed eyes, men with broken legs dragging themselves toward him.

"Would he have gone for me?"

"Guessing so."

"Then I owe you my life," he said. "But I still gotta take you in."

Keen waved the gun at Willie, pointed outside. There was a horse and wagon waiting.

Willie looked at the old mare. "Sheriff, I got the impression I wouldn't be welcome in Duffy after sunset. That was the word. You telling me I got that wrong?"

The sheriff shook his head. "Putting you in the jail. For protection."

Willie raised an eyebrow incredulously. "Protection?"

"The cattle. It isn't just Longfellow's farm. They're all over the place," he said. "All around town."

All around town.

"There's a Pawnee tracker I hired to help me get here. He's just outside the other side of Duffy," Willie said. "If you don't mind, I'd like to pick him up or let him know to run like hell. If that's all right with you."

Sheriff Keen nodded. "After what I just saw, I'd say that's fair. But my shotgun'll be resting here on my lap, and you're still coming with me."

Willie nodded. He had time to think about what to do next on the ride out. Time to decide whether it was better to lay in with the people of Duffy or leg it out into the dark wilds knowing there were strange things out there.

He got up in the back of the wagon, looking around the farm.

The sheriff urged his horse forward, and they rumbled out over the dirt road in the dim light of a nearly setting sun.

"Damn."

Willie stood on the edge of the wagon and looked down at the tortured body of the Pawnee man who'd led him here. They were well into dusk, the last sliver of sun slipping down under the trees. Residual orange light dappled the scrub.

"Never even got his name," Willie said, a bit of anger touching his voice. "What a thing."

The sheriff looked over at the horizon. "Figure we got time to bury him?"

"No difference to him now, and I doubt that's a good idea, tarrying here. I think it's time we got moving along," Willie said.

"What are they?" the sheriff asked. "I know I saw what I saw. Enough to turn my wits shaky."

Willie nodded. "You saw what you saw. And I don't know what they are either. I just know they overran us. We set up camp for a night, on the way to the goldstrike outside your hills. They killed the men I was being paid to shotgun for. Murdered them before I understood what was going on."

"But why? What did they want? What demonic thing is happening out here?"

"Never really had a chance to ask," Willie said. "Been moving behind them and trying to get my revenge since they hit."

He'd been turning over the idea of overpowering the sheriff and walking out into the desert. But to do that he'd have to steal the man's horse and leave him without a gun here.

Not a fair thing to do to a man in these circumstances. Not with what might be out in the dark. And Willie was a man of the law. Sure, most hated him. But there was a respect he'd come to expect, and that had been earned by being a stickler for rule of law. Drilled into him even earlier by the army and his years in uniform.

Sheriff Keen was a fellow officer; leaving him out here alone was not a brotherly thing.

And the murderer who'd escaped Willie's camp was somewhere around Duffy. Willie had sworn he'd bring justice.

Willie sat down on the bench in the back of the wagon and tugged his hat down lower. "Sheriff, what kind of trouble are your townsfolk going to make for me?" he asked.

Keen shifted uncomfortably in his seat. "Well…" he said. "I've been thinking on that. I can pass you off as someone I caught and lock you up, keep you under watch. But that could end up going the wrong way. I'd rather explain to the mayor what's happening. Because if those things are all around Duffy now, what happens when they start coming in? Either way, I'm getting you to safety and standing outside with a shotgun."

Willie thought about the shambling forms ripping through the darkness of the camp toward him. It might be dangerous back in the cell. But certainly not as dangerous as it certainly was out here. In the dark.

"Promise me something, Sheriff," he said.

"What?"

"Put a key to the cell in one of my boots, and my guns in a box under the bed. No one has to see them, but I want them there. In case."

Sheriff Keen thought about it for a long moment.

Then he nodded.

The mayor glared belligerently at Willie through the bars of the cell. He didn't say anything. Quirked the edges of his mouth, then stalked back to Keen's desk. They started arguing.

Willie sat on the wooden bench and leaned back, sighing.

He could see where this was going.

The mayor wasn't about to let some "darky" tell them all how some possessed people were out there lurking in the dark. That maybe they'd come attack townsfolk.

Didn't make no sense, the mayor insisted.

"I don't care how deputized you are," the well-dressed mayor hissed. "You don't come into my town spouting half-crazed bullshit like that and expect any of us to believe you. You killed Longfellow. You may well have killed his family, too. And that Indian the sheriff saw. I think we'll keep you locked up in here and locked up good."

Willie didn't say anything. That was always the better course in these situations.

He just eyed the man levelly until he swore and walked out.

The sheriff checked his shotgun, then sat at his desk. "You think, whatever those things are, they're going to come for the town?"

Willie leaned back against the wall, relaxing a bit. "Hope they don't," he said.

"That all you got? Hope?"

"All any of us ever had, Sheriff," Willie said as he lay down on the bench and pulled his hat down over his head.

He woke at night to the sound of the sheriff cursing.

First he stretched, worked out the kinks in his arms and back, and then splashed water on his face from a small jug Keen had put inside the cell with him.

"They are gathering outside." Keen drew the rough burlap curtains closed against the flicker of torchlight. "And I cannot see their necks," he said, clearly exasperated.

"So we don't know whether they are here to lynch me for being in Duffy after dark, or to kill us and fill our heads with insect parts," Willie observed.

Keen looked back at him, horrified.

"I'm just saying, either reason is a messy one," Willie said.

"You're right. We need to get out of here," Keen said. "If they're here for a lynching they're likely to come after me for trying to help you."

Willie was already pulling the box out from under his bench. He holstered up and took a step toward the metal bars, and right as he did so the front doors busted open. Three townsmen stumbled in, and Sheriff Keen wracked a round into his shotgun. "Now there!" he shouted. "You stay back or I'll shoot."

"Sheriff," Willie muttered through the jail bars, key in hand as he tried to unlock the door. "I'd get in here with me quick…"

They didn't look like the hanging type, the three that stepped forward. They looked drunk. Vacant eyed. Although once they saw Willie, their heads tracked him.

Sheriff Keen stepped forward. "Get outta here," he growled.

"We want the nigger," they growled right back. Willie stiffened. Lowered his hands to his belt.

Keen aimed the shotgun at them. "I'll shoot," he said. "Jamie, Nicodemus, Alex, you know I mean it."

They swung their heads to regard Keen. Willie scuttled over to the edge of the cell. "Sheriff, I—"

Keen fired. Buckshot ripped through all three men, and both Keen and Willie swore to see the black ichor and chitinous pieces mixed with skull slap against the wooden doors. Jamie and Alex slumped dead to the ground, but the one Keen had called Nicodemus jerked forward like a sped up marionette.

Willie fired from between the bars of the cell, got him twice in the chest, but the man kept on. It took a third shot to get him in the head, and by then the rest of the mob was kicking through the door.

"Keen!"

The sheriff never even backed toward the cell. Stood and reloaded his shotgun, fired, moved to reload again, then pulled a pistol. He threw his keys with his spare hand back toward the cell without a word.

He went down, covered by townsfolk ripping him apart, limb from limb, with one last muffled shot.

And then when they were done, they stood up and looked at Willie.

There were more of those possessed townspeople out there than he had bullets for. And he could hear more of them shuffling around in the dirt outside. They pawed around the sheriff's remains, looking for the keys to the cell with those vacant eyes as Willie watched them.

He figured he'd shoot as many as he could as they came in, once they figured out how to break through the cell.

Willie dragged the bench out to the middle of the cell, pulled the blanket off it, and set his spare bullets down on the hard top. Checked his two Colts.

Twelve in. Ten loose on the bench.

Thirty townsfolk.

"Marshal, sheriff, you still in there?" shouted someone in the street on the other side of the mob. "Lie down flat! I am opening fire!"

Many other men would have paused or asked a question back.

Willie did no such thing. He dropped and kissed the dirty floor without a second thought, and as he did so the *chack chack chack* sound of a multi-barreled Gatling gun ripped through Duffy's main street. The windows exploded, wood cracked, splinters flew around the room. Black ichor stained the bars, Willie's hat, coat, the floor.

The barrels wound down.

Wounded townsfolk scrabbled around the floor.

"I'm standing up!" Willie shouted. He shook black goop from himself, and then shot the nearest man still stirring. He let himself out of the cell, dispatching anyone that even groaned, and stepped through the door warily.

There was a wagon parked in the middle of the street with a Gatling gun mounted to the back. A grandfatherly black man in a duster with a marshal's star on his lapel stood behind the still smoking and crackling barrels, reloading the ammunition belt by himself. When he saw Willie, he swung the gun at him. "Show me your neck," he said.

Willie leaned forward and exposed it.

"Good enough," the stranger said. He had a shock of white hair that he'd left long. It framed his lined and strong face, off which a strong snowy white beard hung. The eyes glinted in the firelight of the street's torches.

"Sheriff's dead," Willie reported. "My name's Willie Kennard. Who're you?"

The man looked around the town warily. "I'm Frederick Douglass," he said.

"The abolitionist?"

"Yes."

"Thank you for the assistance," Willie said, surprised. What was Douglass doing out west? And at this particular moment? "Do you know what in hell is going on?"

Douglass looked down the street. Now Willie heard a faint buzzing in the dark distance of the night lurking around the edges of the town. Like a hive of bees, but lower pitched.

A beam of light lanced out of the sky and illuminated the scrub. Strange, haunting shadows danced and moved across the horizon.

"We'd better get up into the crags and hills," Douglass said, pointing Willie toward the rider's bench and the reins. "They'll have a harder time catching up to us amongst the rock. I'll tell you what I know as we ride."

The team of horses ran like the devil and dragged the wagon along over the rough dirt road leading out of Duffy. Willie could hardly hear Douglass over the racket of hooves, the creaking wagon, and the bouncing of his chair. Douglass was cleaning the mounted gun and arranging belts of ammunition, grunting with the effort.

"I've been appointed a marshal of the District of Columbia, by President Rutherford B. Hayes," Douglass shouted. "Ostensibly it is so I can bring more of our folk into civil service. And with those strong jobs previously denied to them, we might rise in our stations. I'm the first negro man in this position. We have had many firsts since President Lincoln—God rest his soul—passed emancipation. I see you, and I see a marshal. All over this land, even despite the fact that President Hayes agreed to end Reconstruction in the South, we are making great strides, Mr. Kennard. Great strides."

That flying beam of light stabbed out and lit up the world like a second sun.

"I know. I served with the Seventh Illinois Rifles," Willie said, urging the horses on faster. The droning sound, a hellish one if he'd ever heard it, had grown louder. It was associated with that infernal light in the sky. "What is that in the sky?"

Douglass shielded his eyes and looked up. "They've spotted us." He swung the Gatling gun up and squinted through the sights.

The howl of the machine behind Willie deafened him. Shells bounced around the wagon's floor, smoldering as they struck wood.

The droning sound lessened, and the light dimmed.

"The marshals report directly to the president," Douglass said, clearing the gun and awkwardly loading a new belt of ammunition. "Sometimes they're used as instruments of executive policy. In this case, I was asked to find the lost crew of an airship. And the airship, too, if possible. The president chose me because most cattle hands or cowboys in these western territories are either black or Mexican, and he felt I might better navigate these parts with my team."

Willie blinked. "An airship?"

"You've heard of hot air balloons? Lighter than air travel?" Douglass asked.

"I saw one once. In the war. Used to spot troop movements." The great globule had hung impossibly in the air, tethered to a pine tree by a rope over a bloody meadow growing a black gunsmoke cloud that soon obscured the machine.

"Our army built a rather advanced version of a balloon, one capable of moving under its own power. Like a steamship of the air. A wealthy count from Prussia who observed balloons here during the war and was quite taken with the concept of using lighter than air machines for military purposes worked with the army to help build an experimental hydrogen airship. Perfect for avoiding the treacherous and snowy grounds of the territory of Alaska."

"Alaska?" Willie glanced back at Douglass. "The territories we purchased from the Russians after the war?"

"Yes. President Hayes demanded a modern day Lewis and Clarke expedition. We hardly know what, if any, resources lie in the territory, after all."

Willie looked up into the sky at the pursuing beam of light. It must be like a lighthouse signal, focused to become a spotting light. And behind it, a floating machine.

"The army is chasing us?" Willie asked.

"No, Mr. Kennard. It looks like they lost control of their machine when they were overrun, just like this town was." He looked up into the sky and pulled the Gatling gun into position. "I need to fire off another belt to keep them farther back from us again, I'm afraid. They're trying to get close again."

An ember landed in the road ahead.

Willie squinted. Then slewed the horses off the road as hard as he could. He reached back with a hand to steady Mr. Douglass, who pitched to the side. The whole wagon tilted onto two wheels and the horses screamed.

And then the world exploded in a rush of dirt and violence that blew Willie off the wagon.

"Can you hear me, Mr. Kennard?"

Willie looked off into the night and blinked. Shook his head.

"Are you well?" Douglass asked. The old man was holding him up, helping him stumble through the stunted, scraggly trees and toward a cut in the foothills. Blood ran from one of Douglass's nostrils.

Willie looked down and saw the front of his shirt stained with dark blood. "Am I hurt?"

"Was the horse," Douglass said.

"I don't remember any of it," Willie said.

"We took a violent tumble thanks to that damn dynamite they were tossing from the airship," Douglass said. As if to underscore his point, a nearby explosion filled the air with a cloud of sharp-smelling dust. "Fortunately they've lost sight of us again, and are randomly tossing the stuff out in hopes of hitting us."

They hobbled together, helping each other over rocks and up scree toward the cut. The beam of light had died out—maybe they'd run out of fuel for its light. Willie could discern a large, cigar-shaped shadow gliding between the stars and him. Which meant that at any moment a lit stick of dynamite could land near them.

"The last thing I remember is you telling me that airship thing was made by the army," he said.

Douglass grunted. "One of the last reports before the machine went missing was that they'd found a crater. With a large metal object buried in the center of it. One of the officers sent back a simple sketch via carrier pigeon."

Both men winced as another stick of dynamite exploded. But this one was farther away than the last, and Willie breathed a sigh of relief. That old instinct to shelter he'd learned from being shelled by artillery hadn't gone away, but there was no betraying whistle of an incoming shell to help him here.

"There's a book by a gentleman by the name of Jules Verne called *From the Earth to the Moon*," Frederick Douglass said, "where some men from Baltimore build a gun large enough to shoot a sort of bullet with men inside of it to the moon."

"I have not heard of it," Willie allowed.

"Well, the illustration the officer sent to us could have been taken right from its pages. It was a scarred and burnt tip of a bullet, nestled in the center of a crater it caused. I believe, from what I've pieced together since arriving here, that the creatures that infected the crew of the airship above us, and the townspeople of Duffy, are creatures from another world that arrived on it. That arrived via some kind of machine, like Verne described."

"These are moon people?" Willie asked incredulously.

"I do not know whether they are from the moon, or from Mars. There is an astronomer, Giovanni Schiaparelli, who said just this year that he has seen canals on the face of Mars. Maybe these things come from there. Maybe from farther away. I do not know. They do not parlay; I lost the men I traveled here with when I tried that futile initial gesture. The creatures are violently hostile."

Willie nodded as they struggled up loose rock and into the safety of the narrow crevices of a valley made by carved cliffs. He found himself a bit relieved they were not facing demons, but creatures. Even if otherworldly ones. Creatures could be shot. And hunted. "But why are they here?"

"Our world? I don't know."

"No, I mean, why Duffy?" Willie asked. "Why did they take the airship? Why did they fly all the way down here?"

"That I can't tell you," Douglass said wearily. "Come, there is an abandoned mine just ahead of us. It is stocked with supplies and weapons, and should be easy to defend from the entrance."

They passed a trio of fresh graves just inside the mouth of the mine, which was located in a natural cave entrance at a high point in the rocky canyon-like area of the foothill. A very defensible spot, Willie noted with pleasure before he walked deeper inside. Willie had been around a few gold strikes before. Enough to tell that the timbers looked thick and recently placed. This one had been dug in quick for exploration, then abandoned.

Several crates were stacked deeper inside.

Not surprising to find a mine here, he thought. Just ten miles away was a bustling hill full of prospectors who all used Duffy as their nearest town. The camp he'd been hired to protect had been planning to try their luck there.

"Only one way out," Douglass said. "But it means we can stop them from coming in if they find us."

"For a while," Willie observed. "But we'll be the rats. And they have dynamite. Better for us to get our ammunition and stay out front to hold them off than try to hide. How did those men out near the front die?"

"I brought them here. Three other marshals I took with me for this mission. They may have become those… things. But the men I'd traveled with deserved a Christian burial," Douglass said. "Listen, we just need to last until tomorrow afternoon. Can we defend this mine that long, do you think?"

"In a pinch," Willie agreed. "But what happens then?"

"Cavalry stationed at a fort forty miles away. I sent for them via pigeon." Douglass levered open a box full of rifles and ammunition. Willie looked in with approval. He picked up a small pistol that he didn't recognize.

"What's this?"

"A Very pistol. It's a Navy signal device they just designed. It shoots a burning flare into the sky. I'll be using it to signal the cavalry where we are."

"And what do you think the cavalry will be able to do against that airship?" Willie asked.

Douglass looked at him with troubled eyes. "Shoot it down with the rockets I ordered them to bring."

"Rockets?"

Douglass sang, "'And the rockets' red glare, the bombs bursting in air?' They'll get high enough."

It sounded possible. If the airship was still around.

But a stick of dynamite boomed somewhere in the distance. The possessed crew of the airship seemed obsessed with finding and destroying the two lawmen.

Willie had a feeling they would still be out there.

They broke open a case of canned food and levered it open by candlelight, risking the flicker since they were deep in the mine for now, and ate cold canned beans with wooden spoons that Willie quickly whittled out of a piece of the crate's top.

"How'd you end up deputized to be a marshal?" Douglass asked.

Willie tapped a piece of hardtack against the side of the can of beans, an old habit. The long-lasting, brick-like biscuit was fresh though, as nothing wriggled out. "After the war I came out west. Did this and that for some years. Four or so years ago I fetched up near the town of Yankee Hill. They needed themselves a new marshal."

Douglass raised an eyebrow. "What happened to the old one?"

"Up and died," Willie said, picking at the hardtack. "Lost two marshals to a gunslinger by the name of Barney Casewit. They tried to bring him in for the rape of a girl of fifteen years' age. And killing her father when he struck out for vengeance. As well as other murderings. I figured, with the war over, our folk voting and getting jobs, that I would ask for the job. Particularly as they were a town of very scared white folk desperate for a solution, I allowed myself to think that maybe they'd overlook the color of my skin in their desperation for a marshal."

Douglass laughed. "This man, Casewit, though?"

Willie didn't laugh. "As hard a man as they come. But then, he'd never been on the other side of a Confederate line of soldiers facing a company of fellow negro riflemen, knowing that they'd never give you surrender."

Douglass's smile faded.

Willie continued, "The town's councilmen asked me to arrest Casewit right there that minute. I don't know if they were looking for entertainment, or desperate to end that despot's reign. But I agreed. Took the star, pinned it, and made my way across the street to where Casewit was playing poker with two of his hands, where I then told him he was under arrest."

"Just like that?" Douglass asked. They both stopped, though, and cocked an ear. No more dynamite had exploded since Willie started his recollections.

The airship was backing off from the hills. Maybe finding somewhere to drop down its crew. Douglass blew out the candle. They'd need to move out front to defend their spot soon.

Willie grimaced and continued. "Just like that. Casewit's sitting there and he asks if he's just supposed to follow me. I told him it was his choice: jail or hell. So he stood and reached for a pair of Colt .44s. I shot them both in the holster."

"What? Why?" Douglass was engaged, but didn't take his eyes off the entrance to the mine. With his night sight coming back, Willie could see where starlight seeped down to faintly illuminate the wooden frame.

"The councilmen told me to arrest him, not kill him. I was trying my best to do it," Willie said. "Casewit's two partners drew, and since no one told me nothing about whether they were to live or die, I shot them both between the eyes. Casewit put his hands up and surrendered. I hanged him the next morning after the trial for raping that girl and his murderings. Bastard kept trying to shimmy back up the pine tree I hung him from, but after twenty minutes or so he finally gave up and hung."

Douglass nodded. "And then you became their marshal, just like that?"

"Some didn't much like me as marshal," Willie said. "Some tried dueling me to get rid of me."

"Yeah? What happened?" Douglass asked.

"They're not here to talk about it, are they?" Willie said, leaning back against a crate. If that airship had dropped off more attackers, he needed a rest to get ready for them. "Think I'll take advantage of your hospitality, old timer, and take the first sleep while you cover the entrance."

Willie settled down with one of his Colts on his chest and closed his eyes.

The sound of a Winchester firing and the lever-action reload snapped Willie awake with his Colt coming up in the direction of the shot. He ran up from the depths of the mine in time to see movement down the hill in the scrub. After fetching a Winchester of his own, he joined Douglass and leaned against a large slab of rock.

"You let me sleep all night down there?" he asked Douglass. "Or did you fall asleep on watch?"

"I wanted the gunslinger you told me about last night to be as fresh as possible for the morning," Douglass said with a tired smile.

Willie sighted down the scree and rock. "Miners," he said.

"What?"

"You're holding off a band of miners. That one's got a pickaxe." He looked up at the morning sky and squinted with a sour expression. "Means that airship's gonna be floating around too any moment."

One of the miners made a stumbling run up at them. Willie's Winchester cracked, and the man stumbled and dropped. He began to pull himself along with his hands, fingers digging into the hard soil to drag the rest of him toward the two marshals.

Willie snapped the lever down, back in, shot again, and the body fell still.

There were more coming up from the scrubland. How many miners had been out at the strike outside Duffy? He couldn't remember.

A bullet whined and struck the ground to the left of the mine opening. Willie moved in toward the rock for better cover.

Douglass reached inside his jacket and checked a pocketwatch on a long chain. "Six or seven hours to go, Mr. Kennard," he said, patting the signal gun in his waistband.

The droning sound Willie'd heard last night returned. The cigar-shaped airship passed overhead and floated over the canyon. Steam and black smoke poured from slanted, sideways stacks in a metal basket underneath the massive gas bag.

Willie stared, the miners momentarily forgotten. The thing was the size of a large city building, floating lightly through the air.

"What a thing," he said to Douglass.

But Douglass was more focused on the crowd lurking behind cover, trying to advance on them. His rifle cracked out, dirt puffed, and the possessed miners hung back.

For now.

"I count a hundred figures," Douglass said, his dust-flecked face lined with exhaustion. Red eyes betrayed the man's lack of sleep. "I was not expecting so many, so quick."

And despite a full night's worth himself, Willie was already tired of shooting at shadows.

"They're massing for a charge. They'll be easy to shoot when they come over that open ground, but they're just too many," Willie said. "And without a Gatling gun or something as serious, I don't see how we kill them fast enough."

"I just had the one," Douglass said. "I was tracking the airship after I sent the pigeon for the cavalry. When I saw the mob, I thought I'd lend a hand."

"Was the gun damaged? I can't remember after the dynamite," Willie said.

"Dirty, on the ground. And not here," Douglass said.

The murmuring of the crowd shuffling about the loose rock downhill had been growing.

"If we climb up over the rock, the airship will see us in the daylight and shoot at us or drop dynamite. And if we go down there we'll face these miners," Willie said. "If we stay here, we will be overrun before noon."

"It is a despicable position we are in," Douglass agreed. "I can bring more rifles and ammunition up for our last stand. But I'll understand if you want to make a run for it. I, however, will make a stand and fire off the flares before I fall. I cannot imagine what these things would do if they were to get into a city. Think of New York or Philadelphia falling to them. It makes me shudder."

Willie leaned against the rock and thought of that for a moment, and then decided it was best to focus his imaginations on the present.

"Mr. Douglass, we should take our chances heading over the hills and staying alive," Willie said. "If we do that, we can alert the cavalry."

"The airship…"

"It'll be dangerous, but I think it best we engage with it if we have to," Willie said levelly. "I will smite these god-damned possessed men out of the sky if I must. But hopefully we can keep running long enough for the cavalry to save us."

They crawled out of the canyon with difficulty, hauling rucksacks with ammunition and several rifles with them.

And the signal guns.

Willie stopped twice to fire back at the horde behind them. Any of them able to climb with any precision dropped off the high hill face.

The horde waited patiently for them to make their climb.

Sweat drenched their dusty, tattered clothes by the time Willie and Douglass topped the hill and began to leg down into the next canyon. For another hour they hiked it, stopped to drink water, and then climbed up the other side.

It felt pointless skirting the foothills of the mountain, but once they had a canyon between them and the horde, they sprinted downhill, back toward Duffy.

"This way," Willie muttered after a half hour of fast walking.

Douglass said nothing. He looked focused on his breathing, and Willie eventually offered to take the man's rucksack. Douglass refused with a snarl.

And that snarl turned into a chuckle when the older marshal suddenly realized where they were. "Hell, Mr. Kennard. You wanted an old friend back, didn't you?"

Horse flesh littered the ground and draped off scrub. Flies buzzed. Pieces of the wagon were scattered around, and the Gatling gun was buried upside down in the dirt.

"We don't have much time," Willie said. "Help me drag it into the clear area."

That horde of mining men would not be too far behind.

The gun was mounted in such a way it wouldn't tilt up to aim into the sky. Why would it? No one had designed it with airships in mind.

But the Gatling would let Douglass hold his own.

They could hear the trampling march of feet in the distance. See some heads wavering over the low-lying scrub. The dust and desert made it easy to spot the first elements of the charge.

Willie grabbed the rucksacks and opened them up, pulling apart a knot and unrolling them. Set on the rock, their small arsenal was at the ready.

He picked up a pair of the signal guns.

Douglass glanced at his pocketwatch. "It is eleven. We still have an hour with even the most optimism."

Willie paid the time no attention. "I'm not thinking about your cavalry," he said.

"Then what…"

The airship swooped in from the hills with a buzz and swoosh of steam and smoke.

"Shoot at it with your rifle," Willie said. "Let them know we're down here."

Douglass looked reluctant to let go of the Gatling. He picked up a Winchester and fired off at the airship. It adjusted course, bearing down on them.

It vented something from the gasbag and lowered. Willie eyed it as being some five hundred feet off the ground.

"Come lower," he said sweetly.

And it did, responding to the crack of Douglass's Winchester.

It passed over the masses of miners advancing on them, some of them shooting wildly in their direction. A brown whale, shifting slightly as the wind bumped at it.

"Mr. Kennard?" Douglass asked. "What do you plan to do?"

"It's easier to shoot if you wait until you can't miss," Willie said, and fired the Very pistol. The flare sparked and fizzed as it arced out toward the airship.

Willie picked up the next pistol and fired. Same arc, slight adjustment based on the course of the last shot.

The first shot still hadn't hit as he picked up and fired the third.

And then one, two, three flaming orbs of light struck the gasbag.

The first one hit the nose and bounced off. People in the metal understructure were running back and forth, and already the airship was beginning to change course. Lift.

The second ball of light hit a piece of rigging. And stuck. It began to burn merrily.

Willie sighed and picked up the fourth Very pistol. The last one. He looked at the three rifles waiting beside them. The backups for the last stand.

The third flame, the last adjustment, arced over the nose of the airship and toward the area he'd seen the venting. There was enough left over gas in the air still.

It caught.

A wild, dancing flame ran along the top of the airship, and then like a devil it lanced downward. The entire envelope began to glow like hell itself, and then flames burst out from every corner and seam.

The cigar-shaped inferno staggered out of the sky and dropped to the desert floor before them.

When the hesitant crowds of miners walked around the remains of the airship, Frederick Douglass and the Gatling gun raked them with a withering volley of gunfire, while Willie stood on a tall rock and sighted with a Winchester, picking them off one by one with shots direct to the head.

Willie walked from body to body, examining them. Douglass followed him.

The cavalry had arrived, following the smoke. They'd help flush the town out. Drag the dead bodies to the street. They'd done the same to the mining camp.

Now Willie could look for the murderer that he'd tracked here. Make sure his job was done.

"I wonder," Willie mused as he walked down the line of carnage. "Why here?"

"What do you mean?" Douglass asked.

"Why Duffy? Why did creatures from some other world fly their airship all the way from the Alaska territories to Duffy? It was the mine, wasn't it? Just like everyone else coming here?"

Douglass thought for a moment. "If their machine was damaged, they could have been looking for metals."

Willie nodded. "That was what I wondered." He stopped. And squatted. Looked into a familiar face.

Well that was that, then: He'd found the man that had come into their camp. Killed his employer. Killed the other men.

Willie stood up. "Thank you, Mr. Douglass. I'll be on then."

"I have a counter-proposal," Douglass said abruptly. He waved his hand around at the uniformed cavalry stacking dead bodies. "There are still possibly other infected out there, in the countryside. You are a steady man with a gun, and with flint in his heart. We could use you, out here. And elsewhere. With… other things that pose a threat to the nation out here in this country."

Willie nodded. "I understand. But I was headed east, hoping to find myself a good woman."

Douglass leaned forward. "Now, I don't take you as the settling down sort. I asked around about you via telegraph yesterday," Douglass said. "Learned about you and Billy McGeorge. How'd you bring him in?"

Willie scratched his chin. "Offered a reward. Met him in town when he rode up to discuss the matter with me."

"He came to you?"

"Well, he wasn't too happy about the reward," Willie explained. "Everyone else was offering north of $300. I figured $50 was good enough for him. He figured that was insulting."

"Insulting?" That smile had come back to Douglass's lips again.

"Yep. Met his whole gang when they rode into town right in the middle of the street with my shotgun. Ended up shooting one of his men when they drew on me. Led the rest of them off to jail. Hung McGeorge from the same pine I hung Casewit on."

"Just like that?" Douglass asked.

"Just like that."

Douglass looked easterly, down the main street. "No room for a man like you back east, Kennard," he said softly. He gave him a business card. "If you don't find that woman you call on me."

Willie nodded.

They'd gifted him a swift horse on Douglass's orders, though they grumbled about it. Willie left, riding east, leaving Duffy as the sun began to sink toward the horizon in the west.

LA MADRE DEL ORO

JEFFREY FORD

New Mexico Territory, 1856

I was adrift in Las Cruces with no dime in my pocket and an empty stomach. I'd started west from Pennsylvania at age sixteen, four years earlier, working a little and then traveling till my money ran out and then working some more, in hopes of reaching the gold fields of California and making a killing. My Ma and Pa told me I was foolish to leave the East, and they were right, God bless them.

In any event, there I was on a July morning, having just arrived, standing by the stagecoach post in the bright sun under a clear blue sky. I squinted into the distance, trying desperately to figure how I could get a meal. Hungry and half in a daze, I looked around at *The Town of Crosses*, as it was called.

There was a short main street of adobe buildings, a few ranchero-style places, mostly wood, but one of stone and mortar. It looked as if the natives had built some huts out at the edge of town. I saw a tin lean-to or three out there as well. There was a hot breeze, and I could taste the dirt in the air, smell the horse shit. Flies all over. People were jawing about a killing that took place in town the night previous to my arrival. I cocked my head and heard a terrible story. Some fellow they called Bastard George had supposedly killed and ate a young woman name of Pearl Gates. The old man standing nearest me repeated, "Ate 'er like a rump roast."

I moved away from the stage post and stumbled through town, searching as I do when I land in a new place for any signs of opportunity. I approached a few friendly-looking men and women, told them I was new in town and inquired if they had knowledge of any gainful employment to be had. Folks talked to me, me being so young-looking, and I do believe my freckles, which I always hated as a kid, made me seem like a vision of innocence they'd not seen in those parts.

The fact is I was far from innocent. In the four years I'd been traveling, I'd laid with whores, stole food and money, and carried in my satchel a brand new LeMat Revolver I swiped from a drunken soldier in an alleyway in Cleveland, Ohio. I practiced with that pistol when I could afford the bullets and got pretty good with it. It had two bores, and one of the tricky things about it was that, in addition to its six bullets, it fired a barrel of grapeshot too if you flipped a little lever. Like a shotgun in one hand. I'd learned to always keep it loaded, either stuck in my belt under my cold weather coat or handy in my bag. That gun got me out of a lot of scrapes but my sweet face got me out of more.

I was drenched with sweat, and it finally dawned on me how hot it was. Must have been a hundred degrees, no lie. That and my hunger were doing a wicked job on me. And the bustle in the street was dizzying. For a place in the middle of drop-dead nowhere, there were a fair amount of people in that town. There was a saloon big enough for a second floor of rooms. I thought I'd go in there and see if I could beg a drink, but just when I was stepping up out of the street onto the walk in front of the place, I heard a commotion off to my left. I stopped and looked, and there was a man in the street and there were a bunch of folks crowding around him. All I had to hear was that he was looking to hire some gents to do a job.

I quick made my way over there to catch the drift of what he was saying. Moving through that crowd sideways and abouts, I eventually slipped up to the front. First thing I saw was the fellow's badge. He was a deputy sheriff, and wore two six guns in holsters. His flat-top, wide brim hat was the same black as the bandana round his neck. He looked about as old as my Pa would have been, and had his same expression between a sigh and a strain. Just when I got there, it seemed folks started drifting away. The deputy said, "Where are the courageous citizens of Las Cruces?" I heard laughter, drifting away. "Wait now," he said, "I already said four dollars a day."

A minute later, there was only me and another character present, waiting on the deputy to say something else. He looked us over and shook his head. "You gentlemen are signing up?"

"Yes," said the other, and so I said, "Yes."

"Follow me," said the deputy. He started walking, and then he stopped, turned to me, and said, "How old are you, boy?"

"Twenty," I told him.

"You got a gun?"

"Yeah," I said. "A LeMat."

"I ain't gonna ask you where you got that from," he said with a smile. "Can you ride?"

I told him I'd spent a year working on a farm in western Indiana and learned to ride passing fair. It was true.

"Good enough," he said.

He went on, and we followed him to the saloon where he took us into a back room. The owner of the place, a small man with a missing left ear and long hair in the back but none on top, came in and asked the deputy what he wanted.

"Fetch me a bottle and three glasses, Billy," he said, "and bring each of these gentlemen a plate of that fine horse turd stew you're famous for." The deputy laughed.

"Fuck you," said Billy and laughed as well. He left and the deputy took to rolling a cigarette, which gave me time to look across the table at my new colleague.

"Name's Franklin," I said to the heavyset man. He wore a blue and white checkered suit of clothes, white shirt and spatz, a bowler that sat on his big ol' head like a pill box on a melon. He wore a pair of wire rim specs, pushed low down the bridge of his nose. "Fat Bob," he said. We looked to the deputy, who by then had his cigarette going and through a cloud a smoke he told us he was Deputy Stephen S. Gordon.

"I been instructed by the honorable Sheriff Fountain to deputize you gentlemen for a government posse with the mission of apprehending George Slatten, a.k.a. Bastard George, in connection with the commission of murder in the first degree and the heinous act of cannibalism. You will be given four dollars a day, to be paid in full upon the capture of the guilty party. If we return without him, you will be paid two dollars a day. Anyone who shoots him dead will receive a bonus from me personally of an extra dollar. Gentlemen, I'll make it clear now, I aim to kill the Bastard. We're gonna gun this dog down and get back here as soon as possible with the body. You with me?"

We nodded.

"Good, then meet me at the stable at dusk and we'll saddle up and head out. Be prepared to be gone for about four days, I figure. Any supplies you might need, ammunition, a blanket, whatever, head on over to Malprop's store across the street. The governor of the Territory, Mr.

David Meriwether, personally wants this dog done away with, and he's willing to pay the bill. He's got some relation to Miss Gates, I believe I've heard. So stock up, within reason. We'll travel tonight into the Jornada. I hope you like the heat."

That said, the door opened and a fetching young woman, wearing a loose shirt and a pair of britches, no less, carried in plates of grub and a bottle of whiskey. We ate while the deputy drank. The plate of stew saved my life, but it very well could've been horse shit. When we were done chomping and slurping, the deputy poured us each a shot of whiskey and we drank to the death of Bastard George.

That afternoon, at the general store, I put a new pair of boots and socks on the governor's tab. I didn't need ammunition. I'd saved up enough over the past two years to kill Bastard George about twenty times over. Luckily, I'd never had to actually shoot at anyone, but I waved the thing around a lot like I might. The old fella behind the counter, Mr. Malprop, asked me if I was part of the posse that was going after Bastard George. I nodded.

"You best get a bigger hat, wide brim to cover more of your face."

I owned only the sailor's cap I presently wore on my head.

"You're going out into the Jornada," he said, squinted, and laughed.

"What is that?" I asked.

"Jornada Del Muerto," he said. "The Trail of Death. A hundred miles of brimstone up the Camino Real."

"It gets hotter than this?" I asked.

"Lordy, boy. After the devil's been out there, he goes to Hell to cool off. Might be a hundred and thirty up there today. And that ain't even mentioning the Mescaleros."

"Mescaleros? You mean Apache?" I said.

"They'll kill ya, if the summer sun don't fry you first."

"I heard they take scalps."

"The Apache?" he said. "No. The Mexicans were taking Indian scalps to collect the bounty for a while. Not sure that's still going on."

So a wider-brimmed hat it was, white, as not to take in the sunlight. I stowed my cap in my bag, and, now fed and gainfully employed, I strolled over to the stable where they found me a spot to lay down on the hay in the barn till Deputy Gordon came at sunset to lead us out.

I tossed and turned and sweated through the noon-day heat so that when I was finally nudged awake by a boot, the straw was soaked. I came up out of a dream of being run down by Apache in the burning desert and thanked the deputy for saving me. He grunted. Along beside him was another man.

Gordon said, "This is Sandro. He's our tracker."

I nodded to the new man, but he gave no sign of recognition. He was thin and wiry and very still, but I got the sense he could be fast as a snake if he wanted to be. The instant I thought that, he smiled as if he knew I had. Trimmed mustache and a prodigious head of black hair. Dark eyes. I'd never met one, but I figured Sandro must be a Mexican. His guns had ivory handles.

While I was sleeping, the deputy had a horse chosen and outfitted for me. It was a mustang, brown and white, with a white mane. Tied on was a bedroll and a string of eight canteens. "Climb aboard, Franklin," said Gordon. I removed the LeMat from my satchel and stowed it in the waist of my drawers. Stepping up into the stirrup, I lifted myself onto the saddle. The deputy got on his horse, a sleek Arabian that was loaded up with supplies. Sandro also rode a mustang, gray, smaller than mine.

We passed through the stable doors as the sun was setting. There in the yard outside sat Fat Bob on an American Saddlebred. Something didn't seem right about a man in a checkered suit on a horse, but it was clear he'd ridden before. He held the reins in front of him like an old woman clutching a purse closed, and he sat straight-backed as he could.

Once our mounts all stood in close together, the deputy said, "No one drinks water unless I tell them to. Understand? If anything happens to me out on the trail, Sandro is in charge." We nodded. "Let's move out," said Gordon. The Mexican gave his horse a verbal command and the creature took off down the dirt byway that was the main street. I followed him. Fat Bob was behind me and Gordon brought up the rear. Folks who saw us making our way out of town pointed and laughed as we went by.

Las Cruces faded behind us into twilight. There was a line of orange behind the distant mountain range, and the fresh night was becoming considerably cooler, offering relief. Before the night finally settled itself upon the land, I looked out into the distance and saw nothing but dry flatness—creosote bushes here and there, some pepper grass.

We rode for a couple of hours, nobody speaking, the horses remaining an equal distance apart. I was beginning to get a little sore as I'd not rode a horse in some time. Most I rode was the stage from St. Louis. So when Gordon raced past me and told me to hold up, I was thankful for the chance to get down for a spell. He allowed us to drink from one of the eight canteens we each carried. "Two shots is it," he said. Turning to Sandro, who'd just ridden up and slipped sideways off his horse, the deputy asked, "You got a bead on him?"

The Mexican nodded.

"How do you see anything in the dark?" I asked.

"The moon will soon be in the sky," he said.

Before getting back on his horse, Fat Bob pulled a pint bottle from his pocket, uncorked it and took a swig. "Any of you gentlemen care to join me?" he asked.

I reached for the bottle, but Gordon held my arm. "That'll dry you out quick," he said to me. He looked up at Bob and said, "You're gonna turn into a little ball of dust, Fat Man, if you keep drinking that whiskey."

"I need to lose a few pounds, Deputy. You keep an eye on the boy. I've been on these jaunts before, don't you know."

Gordon shrugged, mounted his horse, and we began again.

Slowly the moon came up, creamy white and big as a platter. It cast a glow across the landscape. Bits of mineral in the busted rock strewn along the ground sparkled with its light. The weather dropped cooler still, and I had a slight shiver, but not enough to fetch my coat. We rode on through the night. There was a point where I suddenly woke up and caught myself from tipping off the horse. I immediately peered ahead to make sure that Sandro was still in front of me. He was, the clouds of dust from his horse's hooves visible in the moonlight. We rode through dawn and kept going until the sun was well up in the sky.

The Mexican led us to a large outcropping of rock about twice the size of the saloon in town. It had an overhanging ledge. He dismounted, took his horse by the reins and guided it into the shadows under the rock face. I did as he did. The heat of the day had already become nearly unbearable, but under that ledge it was still cool from the night. We sat down with our backs against the rock and waited for Fat Bob and the deputy. They came along soon enough, and we were all together like insects under a rock.

The sun showed its power and you could smell the landscape roasting. Waves of heat rose rippling in the distance. I'd heard about mirages. Gordon gave us all the order to drink and we did. We had to give the horses some of our supply. "Tonight, we'll reach the Pool of the Little Dog and we can water them for a few minutes there, but we'll have to start out late afternoon, so rest up." He unpacked some dried beef and biscuit for us. The deputy gave the order to drink our fill, within

LA MADRE DEL ORO

reason. We did. And then we just settled back, kept as still as could be, and sweated. The coolness I'd noticed under the rock overhang was gone within an hour of our arrival.

The deputy rolled a cigarette; Sandro closed his eyes and went to sleep; and Fat Bob, who never removed that little hat, took a small book out of his inner jacket pocket, pushed the specs an inch up the bridge of his nose, and commenced reading, moving his lips and whispering. I was curious to find out what book it was, but I kept quiet. I don't really know how much time passed, but somewhere in there, Gordon piped up and said to Bob, "You're a hired gun, ain't you? I heard of you before. You killed every member of the Falan gang."

Fat Bob never took his eyes off the page. A small smile formed amidst his jowls, which were bunched up atop his tight collar. "That would be a fact, Deputy," he said.

"Did somebody hire you to hunt down Bastard George?"

"That's right," said Bob, and turned the page.

"Who?" asked the deputy.

"You."

"You ain't here at the behest of no one else?"

"I'm a free agent. My best days are behind me. I'm just a fat man trying to scrape by."

"How many did you kill?" I asked.

"Mind your manners, sonny," said Fat Bob.

"Franklin," said the deputy, "if you want a long life, I'd suggest you not ask a gunman how many people he killed."

I thought Sandro was sleeping, but with eyes still closed, he laughed.

"My apologies," I said to Fat Bob. He reached up and touched the tip of his hat, and we went back to quietly baking.

We rode out in the late afternoon. The sun was unforgiving, and those few hours before dusk lasted forever. When night finally came and with it the cool breeze, I realized just how jumbled my thoughts had been. When the moon came up, it seemed to ease my confusion and leave me with a clear head. About an hour after dark, we came to the Pool of the Little Dog and let the horses have their fill. We didn't light a fire so as not to be spotted by Mescaleros. Gordon rolled me a cigarette, and I smoked with him and Sandro.

"I thought he'd head north into the white sands," said the Mexican, "but he's changed direction and is running east to the San Andres."

"He might have a hideout in the foothills, but shit, I don't want to be chasing the wretch that far. We gotta catch him and kill him in the next couple days," said Gordon.

The shadow of Fat Bob moved among our circle. He was puffing on a pipe, sending smoke rings out into the moonlight. "What do you know about George Slatten?" he asked.

"Not much," said Gordon. "He shows up in town every couple months. Usually starts some kind of trouble. We've had him in the lockup a few times—mostly raging drunk or fighting. He bit Bill's ear off in a brawl. I had a feeling I'd have to kill him sooner or later."

"And you are saying he ate this young woman, Miss Gates?"

The deputy nodded. "It was a sight chilled me straight through."

"What do you mean when you say he 'ate' her? I need particulars. Did he cook her?"

The deputy said, "Nope. He just ate right into her with his teeth. The Doc said she was still alive when he started. Went for the soft parts—stomach, cheeks, rear end, you get my drift. He probably whacked her on the head with something and just started chewing."

"*Hijo de perra*," said Sandro and tossed the butt of his cigarette. "I heard he crawled out of an abandoned mine when he was a baby. A gold mine out here dug by the Conquistadores."

"Who put him in there?" I asked.

Sandro shrugged. "When he crawled out, that's the first time he was ever seen. Like he was born way back in the mine somewhere."

"Did they find the mother?" asked Gordon.

"She was down there fucking *El Diablo*," said Sandro. There was a moment of silence in which I got a chill, and then the Mexican burst out laughing. "*Gringos*." He shook his head as he walked toward his horse.

"Deranged," said Fat Bob.

There were a few more moments of silence, and the deputy said to Bob, "Don't that suit itch the hell out of you?"

We rode hard for a few more hours, and I dozed. Luckily, I woke just in time to pull my horse up sharp next to Sandro's riderless mount. I looked around and saw the tracker's shadow a few feet away, crouched near the ground. I got off my horse and went over to him. He looked at me as I approached.

"The rider let his horse go here and went on by foot," he said.

Fat Bob and Gordon rode up on us. The deputy asked Sandro to fill him in.

"So, he should be right out here somewhere," said Gordon.

Sandro stood and pointed away into the night. "He left the horse maybe an hour, maybe two hours ago."

"We can catch him tonight?"

"I think so."

We saddled up fast and struck out. Gordon had us ride four abreast now, some distance between our mounts. He wanted to make sure we kept up the pace and swept like a net across the desert. We rode hard for an hour straight, and at one point my horse leaped over a tall line of creosote bush to keep its place in the formation. I was delirious with lack of sleep, caught up in the whirling bright stars of the night sky, speeding headlong in pursuit of Bastard George.

As we rode on, the hard-baked dirt of the desert floor gave way to white sand, and soon enough we were traveling over tall dunes. That's when I realized the wind was beginning to pick up. I looked at the moon and saw dark clouds approaching. Then I felt the sand against my face and knuckles. I affixed the chin strap of my new hat so as not to lose it. The rhythm of the horses' hooves had slowed as the wind grew more powerful. It soon became necessary to squint in order to see any distance.

Sandro cried out, "There he is, ahead." We halted and Gordon pulled out a spyglass.

I looked up into the blowing desert and thought I saw a shadow twitch at the very edge of night. It could have been the Bastard. Gordon nodded, as if he also saw the fugitive. He reached back on his horse and grabbed a Sharps rifle from its saddle holster. He took aim and fired.

"He's still running," said Sandro.

The deputy handed over the rifle to the Mexican, who barely took any time to aim, but fired off a shot. With the sound of the report still in our ears, we were hit by a blast of wind that pushed even the horses backward. The sand followed in a rush, stinging face and neck and hands. The wind was suddenly screeching. Last thing I saw was Sandro hand the rifle back to Gordon, and then I could no longer open my eyes. My horse was turning in circles. I was numb with fear.

Who knows how many times we went round before I felt the presence of another horse next to mine and realized I'd stopped circling. I heard Sandro's voice, weak beneath the scream of the wind. "I know a place to hide," he said. Then we were off through the storm. Somehow the Mexican had tethered my horse to his, so I gave myself up to huddling in my saddle with my arms over my face.

Eventually, we passed behind something that blocked the wind, and I looked up. Without the moon and stars and with all the debris in the air it was difficult to see anything. I stared for a long while until my eyes finally adjusted to the sight of a huge outcropping of rock. It was bigger than any we'd sought refuge from the sun beneath. This one, as well as being wide, went straight up a good ways and appeared to turn into a spire.

Sandro was on his horse next to mine. I could see him in the dark; he didn't look the least frightened, as I certainly was. Instead, he seemed to be listening intently. How he could hear anything was beyond me. I got off my horse and moved next to the rock wall. Sandro followed me. He sat down and took out his tobacco pouch and papers. Before he lit that cigarette, Fat Bob came riding in out of the storm.

"You see Gordon?" Sandro yelled to him.

Fat Bob took his specs out of his jacket pocket and put them on. He got down off his horse, and I thought I heard the beast sigh with relief. Taking a seat next to us, he heaved to catch his breath. Finally, he said, "No. I think he was behind me for a while, but then not."

"That's not good," said Sandro.

"It's a bitch out there," said Bob, and then leaned back against the wall.

I was so tired I fell asleep even amid the roar of the storm.

Later, when I woke to the whispered sound of my name, the world was calm. I opened my eyes and there was light on the horizon. The air was still cool. Fat Bob was standing over me. When he saw I'd awakened, he motioned with his arm for me to get ready. Sandro was already on his horse. He waited patiently for me and the gunslinger to mount up. Once we did, he said, in a low voice, "Keep the guns handy." Then he turned and we started out, riding away from the rock wall. At a distance I glanced back, and in the weird morning light it looked like a small cathedral.

We found Deputy Gordon before the sun was halfway to noon. He lay in the white sand. Half his face was eaten and his bowels had been chewed out. There was blood and a prodigious number of flies. The air buzzed with them like the remains of Gordon's last scream. The horses were spooked by the stench of the carnage and did an erratic dance. None of us dismounted to inspect closer.

"I'm impressed by the Bastard's appetite," said Fat Bob.

I started shaking, and Sandro gave me a quick, sharp look. It prevented me from getting hysterical, and I managed to eventually calm down.

"Do we go on?" he asked.

Fat Bob said, "I don't know about you two, but I need the money. I'll be bringing back Bastard George by myself if I have to."

"And what about you, 'dog of the little pool'?" said Sandro. "Do you need the money?"

I did.

"Watch for vultures," he said, and we rode.

It was full daylight and we moved along at a slow clip, it being already too hot to run the horses. As it was, we'd given them a good portion of our water. It was clear Sandro was going to have to find another pool before tomorrow.

As we lurched along, Fat Bob rode up next to me. "If I were you, sonny, I'd not take Gordon's demise too hard. He was a fine enough fellow, but, let's face it, he didn't know what he was doing."

"What makes you say that?" I asked.

Fat Bob gave a quiet bark of a laugh. "Well, he was eaten to death by the very man he'd been sent to apprehend. That's not what I would call a man who knows his craft. But take this fellow, here, Sandro." He pointed at the Mexican, who rode about thirty yards ahead of us. "He knows what he's doing. He'll find George Slatten. And when he does, I'll kill the Bastard, because that's what I do. And I know what I'm doing. Do you understand?"

I nodded.

"Well, what is it *you're* doing?" he asked.

I didn't even try to think, but said, "I don't know."

"Exactly," he said, and rode on ahead to join Sandro.

I don't know how much time passed then under the beating sun. We seemed lost in an ocean of white dunes, up and over. I grilled in the saddle, delirious, for miles it seemed, before Sandro stopped to point at something. There were birds circling over the next dune.

I came more awake and drew my gun. We didn't advance any more quickly. We couldn't—the horses needed water as it was. As we crested the dune, I noticed the sun was finally going down. The next thing I noticed was the body, lying in the sand a few yards down the descent from us. Sandro got off his horse and walked to it. He waved his arms and made noise to shoo off a big vulture.

Fat Bob and I dismounted and went over to stand with Sandro. This poor fellow had also been face chewed, gut chomped, and his ass was all but missing. The only thing left of his face was the part that held his beard. I turned away and vomited from the sight and smell of it.

"Is it him?" asked Fat Bob.

Sandro nodded. "Bastard George."

I was confused.

"I don't suppose he ate himself," said the gunman.

Sandro crouched down. "The ground shows there was someone else. Very strange foot mark, though. Not an animal. On two feet."

"Maybe the wind changed the prints. I've seen that," said Bob.

Sandro nodded and stood.

"Apache?" I asked.

"Never," he said.

"Maybe Bastard George has a bastard kid out here," said the gunman.

Fat Bob was the lookout while Sandro and I bagged what was left of Bastard George in a tarpaulin the Mexican carried. We bound that package with ropes and tied it onto the back of my horse. The smell was wretched, and the thought of riding in the heat with it made me dizzy, but I knew I dare not complain. We were all jumpy, looking over each shoulder and then again. Fat Bob said he didn't like it at all and stood with his pair of Colt Dragoons drawn.

"Are we going to hunt down the killer?" I asked as we finished up the job.

Sandro laughed.

"You should tell jokes for drinks at a saloon, sonny," said Bob.

We mounted up and headed back toward town, each riding with a gun drawn. Dusk was coming on, and since we'd ridden through the day, there was no way the horses would make it without rest and water. I knew this meant that we'd have to put up at one of Sandro's rock formations just off the white sands. The prospect of spending a night in the desert, sitting still while whoever ate Bastard George was roaming around in the dark, twisted my outlook.

Just before twilight, near the edge of the sands, the scrub desert in view, we passed a huge dune with a hole in it. Looked like a giant mouse hole at first.

"Never heard of a cave in a dune before," said Fat Bob.

"That wasn't there before," said Sandro. "The wind must have shifted the sand and uncovered it."

"Maybe a good place to set up for the night if it stays calm," said the gunman. "Easy to defend."

"Easy to be trapped," said Sandro. Still, he moved his horse in its direction.

Guns drawn, we stepped into the shadow of the mouse hole. I don't know what stopped me from just pulling the trigger of the LeMat. I wanted to kill the darkness. I was too exhausted to be as scared as I should have been. Sandro struck a match with his thumbnail. It flared suddenly, and then its glow dimly illuminated the cave.

At first, I felt like I was in church—the dark and the candles—but the rotten meat smell of the place put me off that notion pretty quick. My traveling companions' faces in the candlelight were cut by deep ravines of shadow and made sinister. The match blew out and the dark clapped down. I almost fired my pistol. It took me a moment to catch my breath. Another match was ignited and held up toward the ceiling. The flame burned for a half minute. Enough time to judge from the beams and supports, the remains of a wooden walkway leading back into the rock that ran beneath the sands. It was some kind of old mine.

"La Madre Del Oro," said Sandro. The light went out. I made to bolt, but Fat Bob put his hand on my shoulder and we stood there in the dark.

"A gold mine?" asked the gunman.

"The Conquistadores took a lot of gold out of this land."

"Is it worth a look?" asked Bob.

"People have found gold nuggets in buckets in these mines," Sandro said. "It was like the old Spanish soldiers left the area all at once in the middle of their work."

"I have a little lantern strapped on my horse. Go get it, sonny."

I was afraid to be in the mine, but I was more afraid to go outside by myself. I inched my way out into the last light of day, gun hand trembling. It took me twice as long as it should have to fetch the lantern. I kept looking over my shoulder and spinning full around in the process. Making my way back to the mine entrance, I noticed a cool breeze coming and knew we'd still be in the mine when night fell.

Sandro lit a match and Fat Bob held the lantern. A better light now filled the mine head. My compatriots moved over to where the shaft led down into the rock.

"These Conquistadores were rather small fellows," said Bob, judging the opening.

"You'll go first," said Sandro.

"Franklin," said Fat Bob. "You stay here and anybody comes in behind us, shoot them."

"At least give me one match," I said.

Sandro reached into his shirt pocket and retrieved one of the wooden strikers. I walked over and took it.

"A whole new vision of hell," said Fat Bob. He ducked and held the lantern out in front of him. The light was slowly swallowed by the mineshaft, and I was left shivering in the dark. Eventually, my vision adjusted, and I could make out the entrance. When I sat down, gun in hand, facing it, I could see a star up in the sky. At every moment, I expected a sudden shadow to block it from view.

My mind reeled with possible ways to get out of there. For a moment I thought I'd just leave, get on my horse and light out away from all of it. After that, though, I had a better idea. I thought that if I fired the gun, they'd come running. I could tell them I saw someone lurking outside and took a shot at him. They might doubt me, I knew, but it would put a caution in them as well I suspected. And we'd leave. I lifted my gun, but before I could pull the trigger, I heard a shot.

It echoed up the mineshaft. That one report was followed by a whole volley of shots from at least two different types of guns. My first thought was they were shooting each other. There was silence for a brief time, in which—if I could have worked my legs—I would have run. Two more gun blasts came up from below followed by a terrible scream of agony. From deep down in the ground I heard the sound of scuffling. Then two more gun shots.

A moment later, I saw the light coming up the shaft. Dim at first but coming fast. It was Fat Bob. First thing I could make out was his hat had been knocked off. It became clear he had no gun in his hand, but held the lantern in one and clutched his throat with the other. He staggered forward as if he might fall. The lantern finally showed me his blood-drenched suit and shirt. He moved his hand, and I saw his throat had been torn away, a huge bloody gash. "Run, sonny," he said in bloody bubbles, and then went over on top of the lantern, breaking it and smothering its flame.

I didn't need any further orders. I was out of the cave. In a split second, I decided to take the Arabian—it had the rifle, was bred for the desert, and had no stinking weight of Bastard George tied on back. I jumped up into the saddle. Before giving the horse my heels, I turned to the mine entrance to see if Sandro might emerge. Instead of the Mexican, two other figures came out of the mouse hole. They were tall and thin with long heads. One got down on the sand and sprang toward me like a human rabbit. It bounded twice, and I was in shock, watching it. Then it snarled and leaped high in the air. I saw it flying toward me, watched for only a heartbeat its deformed face and sharp teeth, before I lifted the LeMat, flipped the little lever, and shredded that face with a barrel of grapeshot. The creature made a high pitched whimper that set my horse to running. I tried to look back and see if the monster's companion was coming after me, but by then the mine opening was lost in the dark, and I was flying across the desert on the Arabian.

I don't know what direction I rode in. I may have gone in circles for a day or two. At one point I woke and found the horse gone. I staggered along, cradling the Sharps in my arms like a lover. After that, I remember falling into the sand. There was a dream of being run down by Apache. A woman's voice in an odd language. Water.

I woke in the Apache village. They'd found me unconscious in the desert and, since I was alone, they decided to rescue me. I spoke to them through an Indian fellow, Goyathlay, who knew English very well. When I was finally well enough to speak to the elders, I was brought before them and asked to tell about what happened to my friends.

They saved my life, so I couldn't lie to them, although I wanted to. I told them everything that happened.

Goyathlay told me they wanted me to describe the thing from the mine. Through him I told them, "I only saw it for a second. Around its eyes and down across its nose and lips it had the beaded skin of a viper. Its eyes, just black buttons." I made a circle with my fingers. "Skin looked pale and leathery, and it had a kind of fish fin at the back of the neck. Webbed fingers, I think. Other than that, and the fact its teeth were all sharpened, it could have been a man. Oh yeah, and it leaped like a rabbit."

When I was done, the chief looked around at his council and shook his head. Looking over to me, he spoke, and it was translated. "The white man is not good for much he said, but they do have fierce demons."

"Do you know it?" I asked.

The chief listened to the question and said, "No. It must have come with the Spanish. Slaves for their gold digging."

A few days later, I was better. They took the Sharps and told me if I ever came back they would kill me. The chief wanted to know what I was going to do. I knew I couldn't return to Las Cruces what with the deputy and the whole posse dead and no Bastard George. They'd think I did something wrong. I told the old Mescalero that I was going to California and make a killing on gold.

He spoke a few words and laughed raucously.

I asked Goyathlay what the chief had said, and he told me, "He says you're stupid."

I relayed to him that my parents had told me the same thing.

When I left the village, the chief handed me a roll of folded American money and patted me on the shoulder. I inquired where they came across the cash and was told, "Dead white men are generous." They also gave me back the LeMat but caught and kept the Arabian. Two men and Goyathlay took me a three-day journey on horseback to a spot where I could cross the Colorado River on the rope ferry by Fra Cristobal.

I made it to California and took to prospecting near John Fremont's gold fields in Mariposa. After spending two years at it (I won't say how much gold I dug or didn't), I heard a story from a fellow prospector about a situation at one of Fremont's mines where an entire crew of Mexican workers he'd brought in were slaughtered and eaten by something that came up from deep in the Earth. No one else believed the tale, but it was enough for me to pack up and head back East. All the way across the country those creatures pursued me in my dreams, and even now, safe at my dead ma and pa's homestead, Deputy Gordon, Sandro, Fat Bob or the monsters themselves sometimes emerge from the darkness of my mind.

WHAT I ASSUME YOU SHALL ASSUME

KEN LIU

Idaho Territory, Circa 1890

AMOS

The ray of light came over the eastern horizon like a sunrise, like the door to a dank jail cell cracking open, like the sweeping fiery sword before an angel of judgment. It elongated into a thin, bright, yellow wedge that washed out the stars and revealed the shining parallel tracks before it, dividing the vast, dark continent into halves, leaving behind the endless vegetal sea of the Great Plains and plunging heedlessly toward the craggy, ancient, impassive peaks of the Rockies.

Only then did the piercing cry of the steam whistle finally reach Amos Turner on the hill a half-mile away. His mass of untrimmed white beard and shaggy hair was momentarily illuminated, making his face—full of deep lines carved by the winds of many winters and summers spent in a saddle in the open—seem like a snow-capped mountain in the wilderness.

"Whoa," Amos said, and patted Mustard's neck as the mare snorted and skittered back a few steps. The ground trembled as the locomotive rushed by, pulling behind it cars laden with the goods and people of the East, contentedly dreaming of free land and fresh starts.

But to Amos, the train seemed a malignant serpent, a belching, unfeeling monster, a long and heavy chain that ended in shackles.

"Time to go on."

Gently, he turned Mustard west and began the long journey into the unknown. Soon, the sound and light of the locomotive faded away, and he was again alone with his thoughts under a sky studded with brilliant stars, the way he preferred.

* * *

The ponderosa pines and Douglas firs grew denser as the days passed. This used to be gold-mining country, and from time to time the horse and rider came upon abandoned mining camps next to streams, now full of the late spring meltwater. Some nights, Amos chose to camp in one of them, sitting alone amidst the abandoned shacks while he fed Mustard a handful of oats; chewed a rabbit leg or sipped venison stew; and puffed on his pipe long into the night as he sat by his lone fire, the light dancing against the shadowy cliffs of his face, the crackling of logs the only sound in the darkness.

This particular morning, the fog had rolled in, and Amos felt as though he and Mustard were floating in a sea. The deer trail that they had been following also seemed to dip and twist more than usual. Since he had no particular destination in mind, he allowed Mustard to go wherever she pleased.

"Slow down, girl," Amos advised. "Don't rush and hurt yourself." He felt uneasy, being unable to see more than a few yards into the fog.

But Mustard liked the taste of the grasses and shoots along the trail, many of which were new to her, and she picked her way slowly through the mist and carefully sniffed each plant to be sure it wasn't poisonous.

"Smart," Amos said, leaning forward and lightly scratching her withers.

He looked up at the sky, trying to see the sun, but the fog refracted the light so that it came from every direction at once, and he could not tell east from west.

A passing breeze momentarily revealed a ghostly figure in the mist, like a fish seen through murky water.

"Who goes there?"

There was no response. Amos straightened in the saddle and reached for his Winchester. *Is it a mule deer, a bear, or a Shoshoni hunter?*

A stronger breeze tore away more of the mist, and a man appeared, standing between two trees. He was tall and lean, and there was a long white scar dividing his face diagonally. He politely tipped his hat to Amos, but Amos noted the gleaming handles of the pistols at his belt, ready to be drawn.

Amos drew back on Mustard's reins, signaling her to back up. He kept the rifle pointed at the sky.

"Just passing through," Amos said. "Fog here always this thick?"

The man between the trees chuckled. "It's especially bad today." But his voice held no mirth. "Not the best day for hunting," he muttered in a lower voice.

The man's tense posture hinted at something darker. Amos didn't want to linger. "I'll be on my way then. Anyone else down the trail I should know of? Don't want to be shooting at shadows in the fog."

"There are a few more of us if you go down that way," the man said. "We're hunting vermin. You don't want to be hurt accidentally. Best you go back the way you came."

Amos sat still on his saddle. "I reckon it's best I keep going where I'm headed. You see, I've already been where I came from."

"Suit yourself," the man said. "But don't get involved in business which ain't yours."

As Amos went on, the trees grew denser, the trail turned more twisty and the fog thicker. Mustard moved forward gingerly.

He noticed bits of paper fluttering in the branches lining the trail. Reaching out, he took hold of a few. They were full of dense, tiny print, and appeared to be pages from law pamphlets of some kind.

> Whereas, in the opinion of the Government of the United States the coming of Chinese laborers to this country endangers the good order of certain localities within the territory thereof...

> ...the coming of Chinese laborers to the United States be, and the same is hereby, suspended; and during such suspension it shall not be lawful for any Chinese laborer to come, or, having so come after the expiration of said ninety days, to remain within the United States...

Like most matters pertaining to the law, the crooked, impenetrable sentences seemed to Amos to pile one upon another, twisting and turning, writhy and snakish, growing foggier and foggier the more he read. He threw the papers away.

Mustard splashed across a small stream. Amos gazed at the water, looking for fish. Maybe this would be a good place to camp for the evening. It was getting late, and Idaho spring nights were chilly.

A clump of bushes rustled somewhere up the hill.

Amos was just about to shout out a warning not to shoot, that he was no vermin, when the bushes parted, and a human figure stumbled out and rushed at him.

He almost shot at the figure before realizing that it was a woman, who wasn't dressed like the Indians and not like the settlers either. She had on a loose, gray dress, cut in a manner Amos had never seen, long strips of cloth that wrapped around her legs like large bandages, and black cloth shoes.

A few steps from him, she collapsed to the ground, and a knife fell from her hand.

The woman thrashed and struggled to sit up.

They stared into each other's eyes.

Amos saw that she was probably in her fifties, short and lean. Her clothes were drenched in mud and her left shoulder was a bloody mess.

Some kind of Oriental, Amos thought.

"Damn it," the woman croaked. "Thought the words would hold you longer." Then she collapsed and stopped moving.

YUN

Yun dreamed.

In her dream she was again fifteen, a Hakka girl lying—dying really—under the hot sun.

But she did not sweat. The field she was in was as dry as her body. It hadn't rained for three years, but the governor still refused to release the grain from the Imperial warehouses.

All around her, the lifeless land was stripped bare, as though a swarm of locusts had passed over it. Every shred of tree bark, every blade of grass had been eaten, and the bodies of men and women were strewn about, their bellies filled with dirt, the last meal of desperation to assuage the demons of hunger.

Could it be? A line of ants appeared in the distance. She licked her lips, her tongue dry and heavy as a stone. She would wait until the ants got closer, and then she would eat them.

The ants came closer, grew, and became a line of marching men, their banners flapping and shimmering in the heat. She watched them approach, thinking they were like soldiers descended from heaven, like wandering *hsiake* that the traveling storytellers always spoke of, who toured the land to right wrongs.

"Drink, Sister," one of the men said, and held a cup to her lips.

She drank and tasted rice, as cool and nourishing as *ganlu* dripped by Guanyin, the Goddess of Mercy. She felt every pore in her body scream with the almost-forgotten pleasure of food and water.

"We're soldiers of the Heavenly State of Taiping," the man said. "We worship the Heavenly Father and Jesus, His Son. *Tienwang*, Jesus's Brother, has been sent to deliver us from the Manchus."

Yun remembered the tax collectors who had come the fall before, warning the villagers about the Taiping Rebels and their dangerous leader Hung Hsiu-ch'üan, who called himself *Tienwang*, the Heavenly King. Anyone who dared to oppose the Manchu Emperor and support the rebels—really just brazen bandits—would be put to death by being sliced a thousand times by a knife. And oh, of course the Emperor's taxes still had to be paid, even if it meant taking away the last cup of rice left in the family's grain jar.

"Thank you, Master," she tried to imitate the unfamiliar words of the man. "If you give me another drink, I will join the Heavenly State of Taiping and become your servant forever."

The man laughed. "Call me Brother, and you shall be my Sister. In the Heavenly State of Taiping, there are no masters and servants. All of us are equal before the Heavenly Father."

"All of us?" This made no sense to her. The world was made up of chains, hierarchies, rules that ranked superiors and inferiors. At the top was the Emperor, his Throne held up by the noble Manchus; below them came the servile Han Chinese, with the Hakka lowest of all among them, their lot to till the rockiest fields. And a Hakka woman? She was like a worm, a nothing, barely worth the air she breathed.

"All of us," the man affirmed. "Men and women, Han and Chuang, Cantonese and Hakka, we're all equals. *Tienwang* even has armies made up of women soldiers, who can rise to become generals and dukes just like men. Now drink to your heart's fill, and let us pray of toppling the Manchu Emperor and opening his storehouses so that all of us can eat white rice!"

And she drank, and drank, and the cold rice porridge tasted like heaven.

Still drinking from the cup held to her lips, Yun opened her eyes.

A face, framed by unkempt hair and a bushy beard, hovered a foot or so from hers. In the flickering firelight, it looked like the face of one of the men who had attacked the camp, killed Ah San and Gan and the others, and then chased her all the way here.

She shuddered and tried to push herself away, but she was too weak and only managed to spill the water all over herself.

"Easy now," the man said. "I won't hurt you."

It was his voice, more than the words, that calmed her. She could hear in it a gentle weariness, like an old mountain that had been worn down by eons of ice and water. She saw now that, though the man was white, he was much older than the five who had come to her camp.

"You a lawyer?" Yun asked.

"No," he said, and chuckled. "Though I tried studying to be one, a long time ago."

"Then how did you get through my maze so quickly?" she asked, gesturing at the dark, dense woods, the twisty trails, the thick mist that made the fire crackle and turned the sparks into glowing fireflies. She spoke slowly, so that he could understand her accent.

He looked around at the foggy forest again, like a man who suddenly found himself in an unfamiliar place. "This fog, the trees, the trails—*you* did all this?"

She nodded.

"How?"

"With these," she said, and reached inside a fold in her dress to pull out a few sheets of paper, full of tiny, dense print.

Of course the man wouldn't understand.

She sighed. So much had happened. So much to explain. Words, she needed words to help her, words in this beautiful, foreign tongue that she loved but would always wield like an unfamiliar sword.

"Excuse me," she said, and struggled to sit up straight. Slowly, carefully, she bowed to Amos. She tried to put grace and deliberateness into her movements, as though she were sitting at a formal banquet, dressed in ceremonial armor draped with silk. "We haven't met properly. I am Liew Yun, formerly a general of the Heavenly State of Taiping, and now placer gold miner of Idaho."

The five men had come to her camp in the evening.

Hey, Chinamen, said the one with the scar across his face. His name was Pike, and he had been threatening the Chinese miners in the valley all spring. *Didn't we tell you to get out of here last week? This is my mine.*

The mine's ours, Ah San explained. *I told you, you can go to the courthouse and check our claim.*

Well lookee here! We got ourselves a law-abiding Chinaman! Pike exclaimed. *You want to talk about the law? The law?*

Then Pike explained to the Chinese miners that Congress had already decided that all Chinamen needed to be gone from these mountains and go back to where they came from. Indeed, all law-abiding citizens had a right and duty to *deport*—he savored the word—the Chinamen into the sea.

One of Pike's men took out a sheaf of papers and shook them in the miners' faces. *These are laws,* he said. *Some old, some new. You Chinamen are scared of laws, aren't you? Then you better pack and run.*

Yun grabbed the sheaf of papers out of his hand and started to read from them aloud:

...and may be arrested, by any United States customs official, collector of internal revenue or his deputies, United States marshal or his deputies, and taken before a United States judge, whose duty it shall be to order that he be deported from the United States as hereinbefore provided...

I don't understand, she said. *I can't make any sense of these words. Do any of you really understand them?*

Pike's gang gaped at her, amazed that she could read.

One of the men recovered. *The law says that you have to pick up and leave before we make you.*

Before we shoot you like vermin, Pike added.

Gan was the first to take a swing at him, and the first to be shot. Then chaos was all around Yun as deafening gunshots and flowing blood seemed to put her in another time, another place.

Run! Ah San screamed, and pushed her.

She saw Ah San's head explode into a bloody flower before her eyes as she turned to run into the woods. Something hit her left shoulder hard and made her stumble, and she knew that she had been shot. But she kept on running along the deer trail, as fast as she could.

She heard more shots fired after her, more cries that suddenly became silent, and then, the sounds of pursuit.

She said a prayer to God and Guanyin each. *I'm hurt. But I can't die. Not yet. I still have a mission.*

And she saw that she still clutched the pamphlets that the men had brought to the camp with them, pamphlets full of words that none of them could understand, words that made up laws they claimed said she was unwelcome in this land.

They were her last chance.

She ripped the papers into strips and scattered them behind her. As she passed, trees gathered behind her, the mist rose, and the path bent, forked, and curled around itself.

The sounds of pursuit scattered and grew fainter.

AMOS

"You can do magic with words?" Amos asked.

"Words hold magic for the desperate and the hopeful," Yun said.

Amos looked at her, certain that the woman was mad. *A general of the Heavenly State of Taiping.* He shook his head.

When she had been asleep, her face had been relaxed and peaceful, almost smiling. He had thought she looked a bit like one of the taciturn but friendly Shoshoni women on the plains of Wyoming sitting around the fire on those cold nights he had sought shelter with them.

But now her eyes, feverish, intense, bore into his face like a pair of locomotive headlights.

A wolf howled in the distance, soon echoed by others.

Then followed the sound of a gunshot, and the howling ceased.

"They're getting close," Yun said, gazing into the dark mist. "It's this fire. You've led them straight to me."

Amos picked up the kettle and poured water on the hissing fire to put it out. Soon they were wrapped in darkness, lit only by the light of the moon through the fog.

"I can carry you on Mustard," Amos said.

Yun shook her head. "I'm not leaving."

"Why?"

Yun's glance flickered to a small mound some distance away. Amos squinted and made out a conical shelter made out of chopped tree branches leaning against each other.

"It's the gold, isn't it?" Amos asked. "That's why you ran here."

After a second, Yun nodded. "We moved it out here when Pike's gang started to harass us this spring. All the gold we've mined and saved for two years is here."

Amos's heart grew heavy. "You can always get more gold."

She shook her head.

"This is not my fight," Amos said.

"Then leave."

Amos felt a wave of disappointment that turned into anger. He strode over to Mustard and mounted. Gently, he nudged the mare with his calves and rode away from the hill, away from the howling wolves and the pursuing men.

Amos held Mustard's reins loosely, lost in his thoughts.

She can't let go of that gold, he thought. *A fool*. He had seen far too many die from greed out here.

In the years he had been wandering, he had grown more and more mistrustful of the hearts of women and men. Having more than a few of them together always seemed to lead to schemes, plots, robbery disguised as something more respectable. He would sometimes go warily to the towns to trade for goods that he could not do without, but he far preferred to be alone under an open sky, accompanied only by the howls of coyotes and wolves, dangers that he understood better and feared less than the dangers hidden behind the smiling faces of settled men.

In Kansas, he had seen the light of hope go out in the eyes of black families as they realized that they were free in name only. In New Mexico, he had seen the sorrow on the faces of the Indians forced to swallow their pride and anger as they learned of yet another betrayal. And now, it was the Chinamen's turn.

He tried to push Yun out of his thoughts, but the grief and terror of her tale refused to let go. He shook his head angrily.

Every year, as the railroads expanded and ramified like the roots of some tenacious weed, they brought along with them the homesteaders, and farms turned into villages turned into towns turned into cities.

In his mind, Amos saw the railroads as chains yoking the land around him to an East that was full of noise and stale air and invisible bonds that weighed down a man's spirit until nothing was left of it except the capacity for brutality in masses. Even the Chinamen were once welcomed out here, when the land was open and empty. But now that it was filling up and fewer mines were panning out, they became vermin.

Was it really greed? he thought. The look on her face when she had refused to leave wasn't one of lust for the luster and weight of gold, but one of determination to live like a free woman, not hounded prey.

A Chinaman's chance was bad enough. But a lone, crazy China woman?

An image from long ago came unbidden to his mind. *Help me,* a young man's voice croaked. Amos closed his eyes, trying to make the voice go away. Then he shuddered as he heard the gunshot again.

He opened his eyes. Somehow Mustard, who knew him better than he knew himself, had already turned around and was heading back the way they came.

Amos dismounted, grabbed his rifle from the saddlebag, and walked over to Yun. The woman sat serenely and followed him with her eyes, not having moved since he left her.

"I knew you'd be back," she said.

"Why?"

"You're like a *hsiake* from back home in China."

"What's that?"

"A hero."

Amos laughed bitterly. "I'm no hero."

AMOS (1864)

The generals and politicians would eventually call it the Battle of Olustee, but for Amos Turner, it had been hell.

A young clerk struggling to learn the law in Boston, he had volunteered out of a sense of duty, a desire to end the sin that was slavery, the stain upon the honor of the Republic that the abolitionists denounced in the streets.

But in those Florida pine woods on that day, there were no beautiful ideals, no duty and honor, no God and country, only confusion and slaughter. Too frightened to even think, he charged mindlessly into hailstorms of bullets and screaming artillery even as his companions disintegrated on each side of him.

"Leave them!" He looked over and saw a white Union commander shouting at the remnants of some colored troops, who had barely been trained before entering the battle. The black men were reluctant to leave their wounded comrades behind, but the officer wanted them to haul away the artillery instead, in the hasty retreat.

Then the ground exploded near him, and Amos was thrown into oblivion.

When he awoke, it was evening. All around him, he could hear the intermittent cries of the wounded. Union or Rebel, they sounded equally pitiful. After a while, he realized that he was crying out, too, whether for rescue or the quick relief of a bullet to the head he knew not.

Then he saw the Rebels. In small groups, they scoured the field, methodically picking rings, watches, money from the wounded and stripping the clothes from the dead.

He saw some of the Rebels raise their bayonets and thrust down, and a cry would be silenced. The Rebels moved efficiently and mechanically, like marionettes.

They were murdering the wounded, Amos realized.

Desperately, he tried to crawl away, but his legs and elbows slipped in the mud.

"Help me," a soldier nearby said, his voice rasping.

He saw that the soldier—one of the black men the Union commander had ordered abandoned—was very young, barely more than a boy.

"Quiet," Amos whispered to him harshly. "You'll draw them."

The soldier turned his head and focused his eyes on Amos. "Help me," he begged, louder.

A few Rebels turned in their direction.

Amos pushed the soldier down and crawled away as quickly as he could. He shifted a few corpses around and buried himself under them, praying that the ruse would work.

And then he forced himself to remain still as the men came closer. One of the Rebel officers stepped over the pile of bodies that Amos hid under and squatted next to the dying soldier.

"Help me," the soldier said. "Please."

"You dumb thing," the officer said. "The devil has you now." Amos willed himself to get up and say something, to stop what was happening, but his body refused to obey.

He heard the sound of a gunshot. And it echoed in his head for a long time.

Though many Union men were taken as prisoners on that day, very few were black.

Amos crawled away from the field in the night. He did not know for how many days he lay in a feverish dream, licking the water from the leaves that draped about him and sometimes chewing the leaves for sustenance.

When he was coherent again, he was consumed with shame at his cowardice. He was no better than the commander who had given the order to abandon the wounded black soldiers.

There was also rage, and fear. He could not understand how men who joked and drank and collapsed into fits of laughter over some bawdy tale could suddenly become automata, like interchangeable gears in a machine that they did not comprehend, and become as will-less as the guns in their hands. When the right orders were given, all men could murder in cold blood like devils.

Amos got up and walked west, hiding from anything that looked like an army patrol, until he had left behind the world of cities and laws and the men who crafted them and submitted to their power.

Was it not the world of strictly construed laws and glittering money and elegant clothes and refined speeches that had decided one man could be the property of another? Amos remembered. *And it was that same world that had declared ritualized, anonymous slaughter sweet and fitting. It was that same world that would abandon the wounded, knowing what fate awaited them. What was the use of talk of freedom and ideals? Civilization was a lie, through and through.*

And so he moved ever westward, searching for and escaping into the trail-less, wordless wilderness beyond the frontier line.

"I don't care what you did or didn't do," Yun said. "What matters is you're here now."

An owl hooted not too far away, startled from its perch.

"They're coming," Amos said. "We better get ready."

He had already decided that the best spot for defense was between two fallen trees near the top of the hill. It would give them some cover and allow them to see the men approach.

"Get me there first," Yun said, pointing to the conical shelter made out of sticks.

"It's not gold you need right now."

"It's not gold I'm after," Yun said impatiently. "It's words. Magic."

Amos had no choice but to help her over. Her legs were unsteady and her breathing was labored as they walked. She leaned into him, as light as a foal.

"Open it up," she said. There was a natural authority to the way she spoke, as though she really was used to giving commands and having them obeyed.

Amos peeled back the branches to reveal a few wooden boxes underneath, on top of which lay a few bundles wrapped in oilcloth. Yun pointed at those. Amos handed them to her.

She unwrapped the bundles. They were filled with all kinds of printed material: pages torn from books, sheets of newsprint, picture cards with words on their backs.

Though worried about the approaching pursuers, Amos was intrigued. "What are they?"

She stroked the papers lovingly. "Another kind of treasure. Probably the better kind. Words I've read and liked."

She picked up a page from the top and handed it to him. "I'm tired. Read it to me."

By the faint light of the moon, Amos read:

The mass of men lead lives of quiet desperation. What is called resignation is confirmed desperation. From the desperate city you go into the desperate country, and have to console yourself with the bravery of minks and muskrats.

"Wise words," she said.

"Wise words are not enough," he said, thinking of all the ugliness in the world.

"Are they not?" And before he could stop her, she snatched the page out of his hand, tore it into tiny pieces, and began to eat some of them.

"What are you doing?" He stared at her, dumbfounded.

"I am in *desperate country*," she said, after swallowing, "and I need all the *bravery* I can get. But I will have nothing of *resignation*." She spat out a wad of wet pulp.

And he saw a hardened set to her jaw that was new, and heard a strength in her voice that had been absent before. She seemed literally to have grown bolder.

"You read but do not believe," she said.

"You do not know what I have seen," he said. He thought of that young man long ago who had believed himself to be brave and noble until the truth was revealed to him.

She laughed. "I have seen words free the minds of men who thought they were slaves."

* * *

YUN (1885)

The men who had rescued her brought her back to Tienching, the Heavenly City, capital of the Heavenly State, where she became a soldier just like all the other Taiping women. She was bright and worked hard, and soon she was selected to study how to read and write.

Her teacher, Sister Wen, was a former prostitute who had learned to read and write from her clients in Canton. She freely admitted that she did not know how to write like the scholars, only like a child. "But the magic of writing is strongest in the least skilled," she said, "just as in the Bible it is the last that shall be first, and the first last."

Sister Wen wrote the characters for the Heavenly State of Taiping on a slate.

"This is the character *tien*, which means 'heaven,'" she said, pointing to the third character. "It is like a man standing with a beam over his head, which he must keep balanced over him."

This made sense to Yun. It was her old life. A man was weighed down by the world of his superiors, and a woman's burden was even heavier. Looking at the character, she could almost see the person's back bend with the weight.

"It has been written this way for thousands of years, but no more." Sister Wen erased the line at the top and redrew it, so that it tilted like the man was throwing off his weight.

"*Tienwang* decided that we can write 'heaven' like this, and already you can hear the Emperor in Peking quaking with fear."

Yun looked at the character on the slate and felt her heart beat faster. But still, she doubted.

"How can we just change it?" she asked. "Hadn't our ancestors always written *tien* the old way?"

"Our ancestors are dead," Sister Wen said. "But we are alive. If we want something, then we must take it and make it true. Have you ever known poor women like you and me to read and write, to fight with swords and arrows next to their brothers and fathers? Yet here we are."

Yun could almost see the invisible strands of power rise from the slate into the hearts of all the men and women around her.

"If we wish to express that which has never been thought, we must create new characters. There will be no more concubines, no more bound feet, no more rich and poor, and no more shaved foreheads and queues to show our submission to the Manchu Emperor. We will be free."

And Yun felt the ground tremble under her, and she was sure that the tremors could be felt in far away Peking.

No way of thinking or doing, however ancient, can be trusted without proof.

She chewed on the words and swallowed them.

"I saw a single character shake the foundation of an Empire," she said to Amos. "And you dare tell me that words are mere words. Now, eat."

She handed him a slip of paper.

What a man thinks of himself, that it is which determines, or rather indicates, his fate.

He ate it, masticating the bitter pulp slowly.

She looked at him. "You could have left me to those men. Yet you stayed. Doesn't matter if you want to be. You *are* a *hsiake*."

A wave of heat rose from his stomach and suffused his body, gradually seeping even into his limbs and extremities. He felt as though he had the strength of many men flowing through him.

"Now, you see," she said, her voice strong as a Douglas fir.

AMOS

As the shadowy figures crossed the stream, Amos fired his first shot. It hit the water near the leader and made a big splash, the water glinting white in the moonlight.

"Go back!" Amos shouted.

The man in the lead—Pike—swore. "I told you to mind your own business, stranger!"

"There's been enough killing," Amos said.

"It's her hoard, isn't it? What did she promise you? Don't be foolish. We can take it all, together, and pay you your share."

The stream, reflecting the moon, gave him light to aim by. Amos shot again, closer to Pike's feet. The men scrambled back onto the bank of the stream, fell back among the trees, and returned fire. In the darkness, their shots thudded into the fallen trees Amos and Yun hid behind, and bits of bark and dirt rained down around them.

"Foolish," Yun said. "They're wasting bullets."

"They're wiser than you think," Amos said. He showed her a handful of brass cartridges. "These are all I've left. If they keep on drawing my fire, I'll run out before they do."

Yun shuffled through the papers in her bundles. "Here, I knew this would come in handy."

Amos saw that she was holding a small poster showing a colored drawing of a Fourth of July celebration. Someone was making a speech. In the background, fireworks filled the night sky.

Yun flipped the poster over: the words to the *Star Spangled Banner*.

She tore the paper into strips, wet the strips with her mouth, and wrapped a few of the words around the cartridges: *red glare, bombs, rocket*.

Silently, Amos loaded the cartridges. The added bulk of the paper seemed to not hinder the smooth slide of metal on metal, but he was afraid that the doctored cartridges would misfire.

Muttering a prayer, he aimed and fired.

The first shot exploded into a bright ball of red fire in the woods on the other side of the stream. Pike's men yelped and rolled on the ground to put out the flames on their clothes.

The next shot turned into a series of explosions that was so loud and bright that Amos was temporarily blind and deaf.

The return fire from the woods ceased.

"They're not dead," Yun said. "But this will stun them and make them think twice about shooting. Maybe they'll be more reasonable in the morning."

"I suppose we're safe for the time being," said Amos, still not quite believing what he had seen.

Satisfied, she sang in a low voice:

"Then conquer we must, when our cause it is just,
And this be our motto: 'In God is our trust.'"

Amos settled in for the standoff.

"Tell me," he said, "what happened to *your* rebellion?"

YUN (1860)

The Taiping armies were invincible. Wherever they went, the Emperor's forces fell back like sheep before wolves. Half of China now belonged to the rebels. *Tienwang* spoke of sending emissaries to France and Britain, fellow Christian nations that would come to the Heavenly State's aid.

But, gradually, rumors began to spread of how the commanders and generals had taken concubines and hoarded treasure for their own use, even *Tienwang* himself. While food was still plentiful in the capital, stories described men and women starving in far away provinces, just like they had under the Manchu Emperor. There was even talk of how the other Christian nations said *Tienwang* was a heretic, and they would support the heathen Manchus, who were amenable to European demands for concessions, and not the Taiping.

The Taiping armies began to lose battles.

Now a general herself, Yun steadfastly refused to believe those stories. She was always the first to lead a charge and the last to retreat. She kept none of the conquered goods but shared them all with her sisters and brothers. She prayed and preached, and taught everyone in her army how to write *tien* with a tilted roof.

Still, the convoys of supply wagons from the Heavenly City dwindled, and streams of refugees stole away from the Taiping territories at night like rats leaving a burning building. Yun noticed that the banners of the other commanders were becoming tattered, their character for 'heaven' drooping, falling back into the old ways.

One night, Sister Wen came to her tent in the middle of the night and woke Yun.

It had been a few years since Yun had last seen her teacher, who had stayed behind in the capital. She was startled to see how white the older woman's temples had grown and how stooped her once-straight back had become.

Sister Wen wore a thick coat meant for a long journey. Yun's heart sank. "You're leaving?" Yun could not keep the anger out of her voice. "You would abandon the Heavenly State in its hour of need?"

Instead of turning her face away in shame, Sister Wen looked at her calmly. "You visited the capital a year ago. Could you tell *Tienwang's* palace apart from the Forbidden City in Peking?"

Yun had no answer to that.

"It's not too late to leave," Sister Wen said. "You can still escape to the remote mountains and hide in the bamboo groves, where the Manchus will never find you and you can leave this world to its own ugliness."

Instead of answering, Yun took her sword and wrote the character *tien* on the ground, the bar at the top tilted like a ladder to the sky.

Sister Wen stared at the character. She was weary. "When the heart no longer believes, the magic of words is useless."

And that was the last time Yun saw her.

"When Tienching fell a few months later, the Manchu slaughter turned the streets into rivers of blood: men, women, children, the elderly, the wounded, none were spared.

"I and a few others escaped to islands scattered in the East Sea, and made our way to the Philippines. From there we got on a ship and came to America."

"So the magic of words failed," Amos said. He was disappointed. The story had seemed like a fairytale, one that he wanted to believe in.

"No," Yun said. "We just picked the wrong words."

Yun and her companions had never seen so much empty land.

The wilderness of Idaho was pristine, absolute. In China, every *mu* of land had been worked on and shaped by the plow for generations, but here, there were no marks but those of God. It was an empty page waiting for old ideas to be thrown away and new ones to be written.

(Later, she would learn about the Indians who had once been here. Every story was more complicated than it appeared at first, yet hope sprang eternal.)

Refugees from every land, following every creed, had come with the dream of striking gold. In this place with no rules, they became violent, soulful, self-reliant. They fought with the land, with the Indians, with each other, and yet they also discarded old animosities, welcomed strangers, gave the newcomers aid and succor when they needed them.

Yun and the other Taiping survivors worked hard to carve a fresh life in their new home, and in the evenings, she studied the language of this new land, as hardy as her mountains, as pungent as her forests, as varied as her population, as rich as her mines.

Along with gold, she discovered words, bountiful and beauteous words that sang of a love of freedom that beat in sympathy with her rebellious heart. Nowhere else were men so ready to embrace new words—*pogonip*, *pai gow*, *cowboy*—immigrating from other tongues, arising from inventive minds, becoming respectable despite origins in error. Like fresh trails crossing virgin territory, new words allowed thoughts to travel to glimpse new vistas.

Yun read and savored and built up a treasure trove of words that struck her. She saw that no people believed more in equality, in the power of ideas, in the right to take up arms against tyranny, than the people of America.

And she saw where the Taiping had erred.

With a stick, she began to write on the ground.

"There are countless ways to write the last character in the name of the Taiping, *kuo*, which means 'state.' *Tienwang* could have chosen to write it like this—

"—composed of the character *min*—that means 'the people'—inside the four borders. But instead he chose to write it like this—

"—composed of the character *wang*—that means 'the king'—inside the four borders."

"So he created the Heavenly Kingdom instead of the Heavenly Republic," Amos said. It was an old story, and a familiar one. Those who sought freedom were tempted by power instead, and became indistinguishable from those they sought to overthrow.

"For years, decades now, we've mined gold and sent it back into

China, where the money has kept the fire of rebellion alive. Right now, there's a young man back there, Sun Yat-sen, the greatest magician with words I've ever seen. His pamphlets have given the people faith again, and struck terror into the heart of the Emperor. The gold in those boxes isn't for me, but for him and his revolution."

"What if he fails? What if this rebellion, like yours, also turns dark? You said that the magic of words is fragile, subject to the corrupt hearts of mortal men. What good is a lovely name if you can't live up to it?"

"Then we'll just try again, and if that fails, yet another time. It's not so easy to shake off heavy chains. The Taiping Rebellion failed the same year that a war ended slavery here. Yet this country still feels the shadow of those shackles. China may not be free from the phantom of the Manchu yoke for a hundred years. But my time here has shown me what is possible when men believe."

"How can you say that?" Amos wanted to grab her and shake her. "Have you not seen how Congress has decided that you're to be deported, like rats for Pike and his men to slaughter?"

Yun looked him straight in the eye. "And yet here you are, defending a crazy Chinawoman against the likes of them."

"I am just one man," Amos said.

"Everything starts with one person, a man or a woman." She paused, chose her words carefully, and went on. "You doubt because you see only the ugly words, the words of hypocrisy and fear. Dark laws grow out of confused hearts that have lost faith, and I hope one day to see Congress change its mind. But the words I love I found not in the smoky halls of power in great cities, but in the wilderness out here, among lonesome rebels, refugees, men with nothing to their names but hope."

Amos closed his eyes. She seemed to say aloud what he had only thought. *The Western frontier, like a kite high in the sky, is where the ideals of the Republic take flight and soar, with the stagnant East pulled behind it like a reluctant boy.*

She caressed the papers in her lap lovingly. "Words do matter. Their magic comes from one mind reaching another across miles and years, and what one assumes the other shall also assume, what one believes the other shall also believe. Words take root and grow in the hearts of men, and from there faith springs eternal."

He looked at the pages, at the woman, and at the land bathed in starlight around him. And he seemed to see the land itself as a laid-open book, a record of the long and winding struggle toward freedom by one people—out of many, one.

Yes, it was true. Words did matter. A piece of paper from a court, a little novel, a proclamation, a few amendments to an old parchment—had these not torn a Republic apart and then sewn it back together?

AMOS

For a while, there were occasional shots from the woods across the stream, as though Pike's men were trying to keep them awake. But even that had stopped an hour ago.

The eastern sky was growing brighter.

"I think they're gone," Amos said.

Yun let out a deep breath and almost fell over. Amos was quick with his arm and held her up.

"It's been a long night," Yun said. She sounded exhausted. "Well, if you think we're safe, maybe you can patch me up." She winced as she tried to move her left arm.

"I'm no doctor."

"Not that way," Yun said. She picked up another sheet of paper from her bundle, turned it over so that the blank side faced up, and handed it to him along with a pencil she found in the folds of her dress. "Write down how you want me to feel."

Amos stared at the paper, surprised and confused. "I don't know how. Why can't you just do the magic yourself?"

"It doesn't work that way. The magic of words comes from two people: one writes, one reads. I can't just write whatever I want and make it come true—that's just wishful thinking. I can pull out the magic of words others print in books, and it works just as well if they write it by hand. But the writer has to believe what he writes, which is why I had to wait till now with you."

Amos took the pencil and wrote:

ALRIGHT

"Sorry." He paused. "I always write it as one word though it's supposed to be two. Let me try again."

"Write it the way you like," Yun said. "Dictionaries and schoolmarms care only for binding words down with rules, fitting them into neat little grids where they can't move. If they had their way, there'd be no new words and no new magic. Who knows, maybe your shorter word will heal me quicker."

Amos laughed. And he wrote some more.

O.K.

"Now that's an American word, a real word of power."

She took the paper from him, chewed it, and swallowed. Amos was pleased to see she had that contented, happy look again. A healthy glow returned to her face, and when she moved her arm again, there was no wince.

"See if you're recovered enough to get on Mustard. When the sun's up, we can get out of here."

While Yun shortened the stirrups and talked to Mustard to get acquainted, Amos sat by the fallen trees and flipped through the other papers in Yun's bundle.

> *The runaway slave came to my house and stopt outside,*
> *I heard his motions crackling the twigs of the woodpile,*
> *Through the swung half-door of the kitchen I saw him limpsy and weak,*
> *And went where he sat on a log and led him in and assured him...*

Limpsy, he thought. *Yun is right. This is a land of new words and new ideas, always renewed by the endless wilderness in which man can find solitude and faith in himself—*

A loud shot shattered the peaceful air like thunder. Mustard whinnied and reared up on her hind legs. Yun barely hung on.

Amos looked down and saw the wound in his stomach, from which blood flowed freely, then the pain doubled him over and he dropped his rifle.

Pike and his men stood in a semi-circle about twenty feet away.

"You didn't think we'd try crossing the stream upriver and come up behind you?" he sneered.

"You're right," Amos said. He felt waves of dizziness and struggled to stay sitting up. "You got us."

"Now you can die with your Chinawoman."

From the ground, Amos looked over at Yun, still sitting on Mustard. She made no attempt to get away. Indeed, he could tell that she was thinking of coming over to his aid, even if they would both die.

He locked eyes with her, and then quickly glanced over at the boxes of gold, making sure she remembered.

He dragged his left arm listlessly on the ground, through the leaves, the bits of bark, and the dark soil, as though he was in too much pain to control himself. As Yun stared at him, her eyes full of fire, he traced out the strokes of the character *tien*: one, two, three, and then the last stroke, a defiant diagonal, like a ladder to the sky, like lifting off the weight from a limpsy heart.

Her eyes grew wet. But she nodded, almost imperceptibly.

What I assume you shall assume.

"Now, run!" Amos shouted.

Yun dug her heels into Mustard's sides, and the mare leaped down from the hill, galloping away toward the woods.

Pike's men scrambled to aim their guns at her fleeing figure. No one was paying any attention to the dying old man.

With every bit of his remaining strength, Amos snatched up his rifle.

Yun had wrapped three cartridges in the words of the *Star Spangled Banner*: *red glare*, *bombs*, and *rocket*.

He had shot two, and now the last one was levered into place.

He pulled the trigger, and Pike and his gang—along with the smiling Amos—disappeared in a great ball of fire.

YUN

When Yun came back, she saw a little charred crater where the fallen trees had been.

She jumped off Mustard, who sniffed the ground, whinnied, and then kept her head low. Yun knelt next to the crater and bowed her head to the ground three times.

"Today, I have seen a true *hsiake*," she whispered.

The wind carried a few pieces of paper, their edges burnt, to her feet. She picked one up:

They are alive and well somewhere,
The smallest sprout shows there is really no death.

* * *

Author's Note: The Heavenly Kingdom of Great Peace (1850–64), or Taiping Tianguo, did indeed modify the way the character *tien* is written in its name; however, the particular modification presented in this story was used only on coins minted in a particular province for a brief period.

In general, Wade-Giles is used instead of pinyin to romanize Chinese names in this story for historical reasons.]

THE DEVIL'S JACK
A STORY OF THE DEVIL'S WEST

LAURA ANNE GILMAN

The Territory, Three Days' Ride Northeast of the Canyon, July 1801

The horse was an old one, and piebald to boot, warning he'd go lame sooner rather than not, but Jack would be damned if he'd give up and walk.

The fact that his stubbornness came too late for his soul didn't make him any more willing to relent.

"Whoa now, hoss," he said, reining back gently with his left hand, shifting his weight to ease the ache in his buttocks, and squinting at the horizon. The smudge in the distance might be an outcropping of stone… or it might be yet another hallucination brought on by exhaustion and hope.

Only way to find out was to ride on.

The sun had shifted to the western half of the sky, casting his shadow odd-angled in front of them, a beast with four legs and two heads and a sway to its movement that looked more like a shambles-beast than anything living.

There were days Jack wondered himself if they'd already died and been too stubborn to fall.

But if he'd have died, the devil would have called his name for sure.

"We're still here, hoss," he told the piebald. "For all the good it does us."

The horse had no opinion. It lifted one foot in front of the other with weary determination, moving forward across the broken plain because going back was not an option, and they neither of them were fool enough to stop.

Hooves hitting stone woke Jack from his riding doze, the change from the softer clodding of dirt and dust jarring his senses into full alertness as much as the singing of an arrow or the smell of black powder.

He'd been right: rock, an entire massive ridge cresting out of the hill, solid and deep. Deep enough down to touch the core of the world. Deep enough down to be protection, for a little while. Jack let out a sigh and the piebald's sides heaved in echo, its head drooping down to its knees.

"Yeah, you're a good hoss," he said, patting the withers with almost-affection. "Time for a rest."

Jack swung out of the saddle before he could talk himself out of it. His thighs protested the move, and his feet ached with the weight of his body, but the press of his boot-soles against rock was a sweet pain.

He paused, almost unwilling to breathe, but the rock remained steady underfoot, and his thoughts stayed his own.

Deep enough, for a while.

Unhooking the canteen from his saddle, Jack took a long swig, wiped his mouth with the back of his hand, and considered pouring the rest over his head to wash the dust and grime from his skin.

"No, hoss. Can't do that," he said. "No telling how long we might be here."

Not that long, never that long; soon enough he would have to move on, driven to another town, or farmstead, or fugitive's trail.

He looped the rawhide reins loosely around the horn so they wouldn't drag, and then stepped forward, trusting the piebald to follow behind.

The ridge was lumped like the bare bones of a skeleton, dusty-dry and rust red. Not even moss grew on them, here under the blazing sun.

Hard rock was good. Hard rock was safe.

For now, experience told him. *Don't you dare relax.*

There were strips of jerky in his saddlebag, and another canteen of water, half-full and stale, but drinkable. The piebald could graze and drink when they came to pastures, but Jack had not sat to a meal without worry since longer than he could easily remember.

"No," he said, thinking back. "Two weeks past? The riverboat, coming up past Louistown."

Water was safe, too. Water and stone.

Stone was better, though. The devil couldn't reach through that much stone.

"You played. You lost."

The gambler had had a jovial look that Jack had distrusted at once. But only a fool trusted the man who held the deck, and Jack prided himself on being no fool. Young, yes, and green, he owned to that, but never foolish. He sat warily and played carefully and never bet more than he could afford to lose. That was how you got to be old, in the Devil's West.

"I played and I lost and you've taken your winnings," Jack said. "And now I'll be stepping away from the table, like a sober man."

More sober now than he'd been an hour before: the dealer had a run of luck that could only be cursed, and every card that turned called out for mortals to beware, until the river turned and drowned him, once and for all.

And the other men at the table had breathed a sigh of relief that it had been Jack, and not them.

"Leaving, broke and sober. 'Tis often the fate of mortal man," the dealer agreed, and his jovial expression was only kind. Jack's left hand flexed, feeling for the gun that did not hang by his side.

You removed your weapons before you sat at the table. The saloon girl with the saucy eye held them for him, his gun and his hat, and no way to reach either before he was dead. The fact that every soul in the saloon was in the same boat did not warm Jack, not with the way the dealer watched his face, and not his hands. This dealer feared no powder and shot, nor an arrow from ambush, nor a knife in the dark.

Jack had known who he played with, when he slid his coin across the felt. That had been the point. That was why men came here, to test their luck. He swallowed, the sick feeling he had at the loss—everything he had, from cash to horse—eclipsed by a worse sensation in his gut. Not two years on his own, and he had failed, utterly. The devil cherished the prideful, his mentor had warned him, the better to break them of it.

"One more hand, to win it all," the dealer said, and his hands moved over the cards, shuffling them without sound. "One more hand to win it all, and more."

It was a devil's bargain, in the heart of the Devil's West, and only a green-sapped fool would have taken it.

But Jack-as-was had not been as wise as he thought.

The rock eased his pain, and Jack slept soundly within its hard embrace, no darkly sounding whisper searching for him, poisoning his rest. That knowledge had been hard-won and cherished, that through the solid rock and shifting water, the bones and blood of the Earth, the devil could not call.

Before the sun rose, he woke, curled under a rough blanket, still fully dressed save his boots, those tied to the piebald's saddle to keep scorpions or worse from making them a home.

He had played that final hand and lost. The fruit of his bargain, the payment of his debt: seven years and seven and seven again, he was bound. The devil's dog, the devil's boy. But there was a loophole: if he did not hear the call, he could not be summoned. If he could not be summoned, he could not do the devil's work.

It must amuse his master to play this game, to let Jack play at it, the days and weeks he could avoid the call, only for the devil to yank him back the moment he came within reach. Seven years and seven and seven again to pay, and nearly sixteen of them gone now, along with even the memory of the things he had hoped to regain. Sixteen was eight twice: numbers of protection for normal men, but there was no protection for Jack, save water and stone, the blood and bones of the earth, and that lasted only so long. If he died while bound, he was the devil's forevermore.

Jack had long ago lost the taste for living, but he had no intention of dying any time soon. He rose and stretched, saluting the morning sun rising clear across the face of the outcrop, the sky still clouded and dim behind him.

"Human."

Jack turned and spun, reaching not for the pistol that once pressed against his thigh but the packet of herbs he now carried in the holster, the dried bits catching in the wind as he scattered them, a free-moving arc of glittering brown-green.

"That's hardly polite," another voice said, this time behind him, and it sounded both amused and hurt. Two? More? Or one demon, inhumanly fast?

Magicians roamed these lands, and demons, and the devil. Jack feared none of them, anymore, but lack of fear did not mean lack of caution.

"You came to us and slept in our home. We came merely to say good morn, and you react... thus?"

Two... no, four, or five, from the shadows that crept around him. Slender and dark-skinned like savages, bare in their skins, dark hair long and wild, braided with feathers of impossibly bright colors, like a fancy-girl's beads. Like humans, until you saw them move, joints turning too smoothly, eyes glittering too bright. Until you saw the shimmer like heatstroke under their skin.

The herbs had pushed them back, but they had not fled. The horse, dumb beast that it was, shifted its weight from leg to leg, but did not otherwise react. It had seen far worse, in its time under Jack's leg.

"We don't scare you?"

"Only a damned man isn't cautious around demons," Jack replied. He couldn't tell which one spoke, they moved so restlessly, and he didn't want to watch their mouths, not so close to those glittering eyes. "Never heard of your kind taking to hard rock, before." It wasn't a question— even a damned man did not ask a demon questions it might answer.

"You know many demon, then, human? To carry bane, and not a pistol, to wear the sigil instead of a cross?"

He'd never worn a cross, not even back then. The sigil on a thong around his neck wasn't much more use—but it showed a certain amount of respect. Demons and magicians knew the Hanging Man, who had been here long before the bleeding god.

"I'm the devil's Jack," he said, having no desire to play their game. "You may have heard of me."

They hissed, but did not back away. The devil had no claim on them, as soulless as the piebald. But they would—most like—not interfere with his dog, either.

"We grant you the use of our rock," one of them said. "You may remain as long as you like." Mocking: they knew he could not remain, dared not stay too long.

"I may leave freely, then." Again, not a question, but merely to confirm: to make them agree, and not slide a card out from their sleeve.

"Yes. Yes, blasted human, you may."

They could not. Their words, the tone of their words, gave them away. They had been bound to this hard ridge—some magician exercising his power, for some reason only magicians understood.

A wise man—and a damned man both—avoided thinking too much why a magician did anything.

"You could stay, and amuse us," another one said. "We are so terribly bored."

That was why they had come to him, then. Something new, on this barren ridge, to distract them. He felt no pity: they were demon. And yet, to be trapped on this ridge, for however long, was not a fate he would wish on any creature.

He had spoken truth, earlier: demon did not take to hard stone. They lingered on river banks and in shadowed caves, not here under the hot dry sun. "No doubt some terrible act angered the magician, that he bound you here, with no release."

"Not so terrible. Not so anger-making. He was far more terrible than we, and woe to the human who bore him. His magic would have ripped him from her womb and burnt her to ashes from the hot malice in his bones."

Magicians were made, not born. But there was something in the demon's tone that made the story ring true.

Not that Jack would ever know, one way or another. Yet, demon had no reason to lie for sheer meanness; they were no more evil than a tornado, merely set on having their way no matter what a human might wish or do.

Much like humans, he knew. It was a rare soul who came at you with unselfish good. It simply wasn't the way the world had been made.

This ridge offered safety, but a lack of evil did not mean a lack of harm, from tornado or demon, and a wise man got out of their way.

"I'll water and feed my hoss, and be gone," he said. "No need to fret yourselves on my account."

They stared at him, like wolves in winter stare at elk, and he lowered his head and set his shoulders, same as the elk might do. *Do not mess with me*, his posture warned. *You might win, but you would not like the cost.*

They stared, and then scattered, gone as swift as they'd come, and the piebald and he were alone on the rocky ridge.

The ridge ran some distance toward the north, and Jack walked it through the morning, not pausing when the sun reached devil's peak and bore down on him, rivulets of grimy sweat sticking his shirt and pants' legs to his skin. The piebald's girth was loose, its step slow and steady, and every now and again it reached over to nip at Jack's hair in a gesture of what he thought might well be affection. Or hunger.

"Grazing for you, soon enough," he promised it. "Just a bit longer." The ability to stretch his legs without worry was sweeter than fresh water. He would have to leave this haven before long and be on his way, but not just yet.

He thought, safe on rock, of his mother and his sister. His teachers, back East. His first riding companion, near twenty years back, who had taken the green youth under his arm and taught him how to survive.

Old Matthew, who'd died north of Smithtown when the savages

overran their camp. Died by his own hand, rather than be taken captive. "Never let them take you," Matty had said. "Never do anything other than by your own free will. Promise yourself now, to never give up that will."

He had been, in the end, no better a student to Matty than he had been at reading the law.

Those memories were only safe on rock, and they never did him any good. Jack forced his mind to consider each step, the colors and striations of the rock, the crunch of his boot heel on timeworn rubble, and the sough of the wind against his ears, until his brain went numb once more.

Finally, the day came to a close, and while the ridge ran on a while more, there was the blur of blue shadow in the distance that told Jack there was a town off to the south.

People—settlers and traders, common folk—were wary of him, knowing without being told there was something gone wrong with him, but he missed hearing them speak, even when they did not speak to him. To sit, briefly, at a table, and pretend he could stay... it broke him, every time, and yet still he could not resist.

If he was fortunate, his master would have no summons for him.

Briar, the signs at the boundary line named the town, and it seemed well-called: sparse and spare, the color of deadwood and sand. But the buildings were sturdy, and the children clean and strong-limbed, and the sound of their play was the first thing he heard when he rode into town.

"Trust in God but Watch the Border" was inscribed at the archway of the church, a lookout on its spire, and Jack stared at the arch a while before riding on.

The saloon looked clean and orderly, and Jack barely hesitated before swinging down off the piebald's back, wincing as his soles touched dirt.

Silence. Silence in his head, silence in his bones.

Looping the piebald's reins around the post, he gave it a pat and a cube of close-hoarded sugar, and went through the sand-brown doors of the Briar's Last Hope.

As usual, the folk gave him a wary circle: other strangers might be pestered for news or begged for a story, but they left him to his table and his whiskey, the girl serving him a plate of something that looked well-marbled but tasted of gristle and bone. He ate it, and the dry potatoes, and drank his whiskey, and let the noise wash over him, better than any bath he'd ever had.

And then it came.

No words: there were never words, only the command. The game was over, for the nonce: he had all-unwitting come where his master wanted him, where men waited, dreading, unknowing, for his hand on their necks.

Ten men of Briar, sold of their own free will to the devil, waiting only to be claimed.

"All right," he said, as though he had a choice. His meal done, he would rise up—no more avoiding the dirt that clung to him, now that the deed was done—and walk through the town, and find who had taken his master's coin.

Whatever border they sought to guard, whatever god they trusted, it had not been enough.

They were waiting for him when he came: nine of them, on the church steps.

"Avram ran," the oldest of them said, when Jack put one foot on the faded wooden steps and looked up at them, his hat angled back so they could see most of his face in the light coming from the open door behind them. "He broke and ran when we knew you were coming."

Word had spread: like the demons, the townsfolk of Briar had heard of the devil's Jack.

"But you waited."

"We did what we had to do. Our children are safe. That is all that matters."

Their calm was almost disturbing. The damned bargained. The damned wept. The damned offered you everything they no longer possessed. They did not stand like god-fearing men.

"The border. What is it?" You could ask humans questions you did not ask of demons. They would lie just as easily—but they did not always, and there was no risk in listening.

They looked at each other, the nine men of Briar, and if they wondered at his question, they did not show it. Finally one, neither oldest nor youngest, spoke. "A magician lived here, back before there was a town. Bitter and sour, and not able to stop fiddling with things that would not be under his control. And in his fiddling, in his disregard for what was natural, he called up the briar-rock from the breast of the Earth and let loose abominations on the land. The founders of this town, they contained it, somehow. But they left no instructions, no grimoire we could follow, and when the ground rumbled underfoot last year, the first abomination returned."

It had the sound of a story long-told, worn with the repetition. "You've no magicians, none to hire or lure, to strengthen the barrier?" Better to bargain with a magician and risk his whim than sell your soul outright.

Another man, a freeman from his skin, as upright as the others, spoke then: "There was no time. The devil was there."

"Yes. He often is." Jack's words were dry, but the townsmen took them as solemn gospel.

"And now you will take us." The freeman again, resigned.

He was the devil's dog. "Yes."

"Does it hurt?"

He could not tell who had asked that question, a voice within the group. "Yes." Now, and forever. That was what it meant, to give over to the devil. Not a great pain, not always, but a never-ending one. The sour bile of regrets; the loss of hope; the abandonment of fleeting, innocent joy for the more grim knowledge of sorrow. He felt them all, scraping at his insides.

They would exist within that pain, their souls' protection forfeit, for the rest of eternity.

Sixteen years of taking the devil's price had hardened Jack to regret. But these were good men. Honest men, who had waited for their fate. Looking at them, something inside Jack rebelled.

"Go make your peace with your families," he said. "No memories will save you now, but there is no reason to leave them with pain."

Lie to them, he meant. *Give them a pretty story to believe. They won't, but they will remember that you tried.*

"I'll be back come dawn. Don't make me have to find you."

He had some hard riding to do, before then.

The moon rose low and cold in the sky, and the devil pinpricked him the whole ride back to the rock ridge, but Jack gritted his teeth and clenched his jaw and did not relent, even when the pricks became jabs, and the jabs drew blood from his skin.

The devil was *always* there; but he could not be everywhere at once. So long as he did not turn his full attention here, Jack had a chance.

No. Jack had no chance. He let the thought go, became empty and bare as the grasslands around him, all life hiding away the closer he came to the demons' rock.

They met him on the lowest ridge, five sleek shadows glowing and shifting under the moonlight. This was their time, their place, and he was no longer a stranger to them, that they would hide their true form.

He had never thought to gamble again. Never thought to bargain, or hide a card in his sleeve.

He stopped, the horse's hooves barely settled on the rocky spine, and called to them. "What would you risk, to be entertained?"

"What would we not, to no longer be bored," came back the answer. "Have you come to be our fool, human?"

"I am already my own fool," he said. "But if you can manage it, you will have entertainment—and strike a blow against the memory of the magician who bound you here."

That had their attention, he could tell by the way they paused in their restless, graceful swirl.

"Tell us more." A swirling demand, five voices as one.

"Those who stood against the magician, those years ago. The humans. Their descendants sought to continue their work—and sold themselves to my master, to do it."

The swirl picked up again, disdainful. "That is your business, not ours."

The fabric of his shirt stuck to his skin, pasted by sweat even in the cool night air. "Ten men, my master claims." Nine who waited, and one who ran. "What would you do for an entire town? Yours to observe, to entertain you, without any cost to yourself."

"Ours? No cost?"

"My master cannot touch you, not here, not bound as you are."

That was not the same as no cost, but he was playing on their boredom, and their greed, to blind them. "An entire town, brought here, for the length of the lives of those who swore their oath," Jack said. "The natural life, and no more. When that last man dies, the town goes free."

Dying, bound to the rock... Jack did not know what would happen to their souls. But they would be unclaimed, and therefore not belong to the devil. Perhaps their god would intervene.

The swirling slowed, paused. He had their interest, now.

"Can you do this? Can you hold them to you, secure within the stone?"

He had his cards; he did not know what they held.

"If willing, we can."

That was enough. They haggled over terms for the rest of the night, Jack making them each one agree to every term. And when the moon set but before the sun returned, they had a bargain.

"They will agree? They will be bound?"

Jack shifted in his saddle, feeling his bones ache, exhaustion gnawing a hole in his skull. "They will have no choice."

The men were waiting, as he knew they would be, on the steps of the church. No children played on the planed sidewalks this time, no women gossiped in the stores, no youths recited lessons, or brought in the cows.

Briar waited.

"Is it time?" a voice asked.

Time, and past. He stared at them from the back of the piebald. "What would you give, to stay with your family?"

"You make a joke of our fate?" The youngest spoke, his face pale and tight with grief, while the others stirred uneasily around him.

"I'm asking you a question." Jack's temper, unused to dealing with people this long, frayed thin. "Answer it, or be damned. Would you break oath, give yourself—and your families—over to a lesser evil, to keep your souls and save them from heartbreak?"

It was too late to save them, too late the moment they made their deal. But there were different levels of damnation.

"Yes." Not the oldest nor the youngest, nor the speaker from the day before, but a slight, slender man with the look of a storekeeper about him, narrow-faced with sideburns too large for his chin, and spectacles perched on his nose. "Whatever price, it cannot be worse than what we have already pledged."

"Nathan, be quiet," another man said. "There is always something worse."

A town of foolish men, but not fools, it seemed.

Jack, bluntly, told them what they faced.

"Decide now," he said, cutting off any discussion. "You who made the bargain must seal this the same way, else it cannot work. Ten souls bound, either way you go."

"We are only nine," Nathan said.

The oldest man, their leader, looked to Jack. "The devil's dog will deliver the last. Will you not?"

Jack did not answer the obvious, but merely waited for them to decide.

As he had told the demons, they had no choice.

Nine men and their families, and the family of the tenth man, and the ties they had made—it was nearly two hundred souls and their households Jack led to their fate. Briar was left near-empty behind them, but it was a sturdy town; it would survive. And this time, Jack thought, they would know to lure a magician and heed their town's warning.

Nearly two hundred souls, all of them willing, he led to the rock's spine, and delivered them from the devil.

The hollow of the stone was barely a dozen feet long and half that across. But it was large enough to contain them, and give them the illusion of land stretching beyond. A man's lifetime was only so long, even the youngest of them, and once the nine died, their children and children's children would be released, unstained by their fathers' folly. The demon gathered above the hollow, stretched on their flat stomachs, watching the town rebuild itself the way humans watched a game of dice.

Jack, forgotten, gathered the reins and swung up into the saddle. Digging his heels gently into the piebald's sides, the pair moved down off the rock and onto the endless plains. The devil did not hold a grudge. This one time, Jack had outplayed his hand and taken the pot. But one game changed nothing: he had a missing man to chase down and deliver unto the devil.

Obedience kept him alive. If he lived long enough, he could outride his own damnation.

In the Devil's West, only a fool asked for more.

THE GOLDEN AGE

WALTER JON WILLIAMS

Alta California, Spring 1852

So here we are, sitting in ambush on the Sacramento River down below Sutter's Mill, and I still don't know what it's about. Of course I'm not a complete raving imbecile, I know the *ambush* is about the *gold* that's coming down the river. What I don't understand is why I'm dressed like Admiral bloody Nelson, and talking like a toffee-nose imbecile, and waiting for a man dressed like a carrion-eating bird to swoop down on us.

I want the gold, but more than that, I want answers.

When I first arrived in Alta California, I found myself a lucky man. I served as a topman on one of the first merchant ships to sail through the Golden Gate after Commodore Stockton secured the place, and therefore I was one of the first to hear of the strike on the American River, where gold nuggets were said to be just lying on the ground. I promptly deserted my ship—along with the other sailors, and all the officers, too.

I got to the gold fields ahead of the rush. I wasn't a forty-niner, I was a forty-*eighter*. And by Jove, I found those nuggets just lying there, and more than a few of them.

But it wasn't long before you had to do more than stroll along the riverbank to find gold. You panned up and down the stream, hoping to find enough ore to justify building a rocker box or a sluice box. You could stand or squat in freezing water for hours, and often enough you found nothing at all. Tens of thousands of people were flooding into the territory—not just Americans, but Mexicans, Chinese, Mormons, Australians, and even a gang of Kanakas from Hawaii. Turn your back for an instant and your claim was gone, and maybe your gold with it.

It was impossible to carry on alone, so I recruited a gang of fellow gold-seekers—we called ourselves the "Gentlemen of Leisure," though we were anything but. I tried to get as many sailors as I could, because sailors know how to *do* things—build structures, haul ropes, stow supplies, handle the canvas we used for our tents. About half were English, like me, and the rest came everywhere from Tipperary to Timbucktoo. Soon they were calling me "Commodore"—as a joke, like.

There was absolutely no law. No constables, no judges, no sheriff, and no military because all the soldiers had deserted and run to the gold fields. If you had a dispute, you settled it yourself.

Settling one of those disputes was what brought me up against the Condor.

The winter of '49 had settled in, and most of our party decided to take the *Sitka* steamboat down the Sacramento for a little vacation in San Francisco. We'd staked ourselves a decent claim on the Middle Fork that was bringing in a steady amount of income, nothing spectacular but regular. Some of the more ambitious of us argued for striking off to other parts in hopes of finding better paydirt, but we decided to postpone that decision till the spring.

There were a couple lads who offered to stay on the claim over the winter, which should have made me suspicious. But I was eager to spend the gold I felt burning in my pockets, and if I felt any doubts, I brushed them aside.

When I had first landed in San Francisco, it was a little mission station called Yerba Buena, but the place had the new name now, and it was a fine time we had there. The growing town was a perpetual buzz of activity, because it was in the act of transforming itself from a tiny settlement of a few hundred people to the city it is now. We paid nothing for lodging, because we moved into one of the scores of abandoned ships in the harbor. That allowed the Gentlemen of Leisure to spend our money on the things a sailor enjoys: drink and ladies. Though it has to be said that both were expensive.

Still, I managed to save enough of our funds to buy supplies for the return trip and the mules to carry them. So it was that we rollicked into our camp on the Middle Fork one fine April day, only to find a bunch of Australians working our claim. Working with our flume, which we'd built, and our sluice box, which we'd left in place back in December.

If I'd had an idea that any of this was going on, my approach would have been more cautious, but instead I just strolled right into the camp leading one of our mules and blinked in surprise at all the activity going on around me. And before I could think, I opened my mouth and shouted out.

"What in blazes is going on here?"

One of the Australians waded out of the shallows and confronted me. He was a well set-up cove, over six feet tall, with tattoos sprawling all over his powerful arms. He wore a Bowie knife in a scabbard at his waist. He loomed over me like a big redwood, and I didn't like the look of him at all.

"We're workin' our diggins, mate," he says. "You have any objections?"

I recognized those flattened Australian vowels and was reminded that most of the inhabitants of that country were convicts—and that the British didn't transport prisoners thousands of miles for *little* offenses. This might be a criminal gang, for all I knew.

Still, I brazened it out.

"This is our claim," says I, "so you lads will just have to hook it."

"You wasn't here when we arrived," says the digger. "All we found was an abandoned cabin and some moldy old tents. So this claim is ours now, I reckon."

It wasn't till later that I figured out what happened. The two chaps we'd left at our claim were among those who had argued for striking off to find better diggings, and that was just what they'd done: they'd taken our remaining supplies and equipment and gone upriver, and either they'd planned to be back in time to meet us or they hadn't. I wouldn't know, as I never saw either of them again.

"I con it thisaway," says I. "You lot just move on now. Keep the gold you've taken—you've worked for it. But this claim is ours. You can ask anyone up the Middle Fork or down."

I was bolder now, because the Gentlemen of Leisure had come up behind me, all nine of them, and I knew I wasn't alone. By now we were an experienced, well-equipped party, and each of us had a Colt Dragoon pistol, and as well we carried some old Hall carbines and brand-new Sharps rifles for hunting. I had a double-barreled shotgun strapped to the pack saddle of my mule, and a big knife at my side.

If the Australian saw any of this, he decided to disregard it. I could see color rising into his face like a red tide.

"You abandoned your claim, and now it belongs to the Sydney Ducks!" he says, gesturing at his mob. "You clear out, or you'll get thumped!"

Instead, it was me that thumped *him*. Remember that I was a sailor, and had been at sea since I was a boy. I'd been hauling rope and rigging all that time, and the sort of labor I'd found in the gold fields wasn't the sort to soften me. My hands were covered in callus as thick as my little finger, and as hard as horn.

So what I did was slap the Duck across the side of the head with one of my hard, hard hands, and he was knocked silly. He sprawled unconscious to the ground, after which I turned back to the mule to unstrap the shotgun.

My own lads were quick to brandish their pistols and rifles, but the Sydney Ducks weren't so slow, either, and came roaring at us with shovels and picks and knives and pistols of their own. Bullets whirred through the air. I yanked the shotgun from the lines holding it in place, drew the hammers back, and fired the first barrel at one of the Australians that was coming at me with a shovel. I'd been hoping to kill a grouse for dinner, so the gun was loaded only with birdshot, but it struck him in the face, and he reeled back howling.

That was when I heard the cry of the Condor for the first time, a high-pitched *Ky-yeee* that echoed from the granite walls of the Sierra Nevada, and then there was a great thumping crash between my shoulder blades, and I went down face-first in the gravel. While I lay stunned, trying to decide whether or not I'd been shot, I heard a wild volley of pistol fire, and a series of meaty thwacks followed by the sounds of bodies falling. My head awhirl, I staggered to my feet, and I turned around to see the most preposterous sight I'd ever seen in my life.

This was a man dressed in a feathered costume, with a large red hood pulled up over his head and down over his face, with only his piercing blue eyes peering out. Add to that a hooked beak made of boiled leather that hung over his mouth and a kind of contraption mounted on his shoulders beneath a streaming cloak.

That and the fact that he was fighting like an absolute demon. He was fighting *everybody*, my own party as well as the Sydney Ducks. He was punching, kicking, clawing—and sometimes he'd pick someone up and simply hurl him into one of the Jeffrey pines that surrounded the camp.

The stranger was so outlandishly dressed that I thought the camp was being attacked by Red Indians, and I reached down for my shotgun. And that only attracted his attention, for he leaped down the bank at me, snatched the gun from my hands, and flung it into the American River.

"No guns!" he shouted. "Everyone throw down your firearms!"

I watched in surprise as my shotgun disappeared in a great splash. Then rage filled me, and I swung back to the stranger.

"Damn you!" I said. "That shotgun cost me six dollars!" And I swung one of my hard hands at his head.

He slipped the strike easily and landed two blows on my ribs. Which only made me the more furious, so I lashed out again.

I should point out that I'm good with my fists, and though I'm no true prizefighter I've been up to scratch any number of times, defending the honor of my ship in ports all over the world. I had every expectation of giving the stranger a good hiding, especially as he was cumbered with that heavy cape and the bits of gear that I could see hanging from the thick belt he wore around his waist.

But the stranger turned out to be a regular Tom Cribb. I never touched him. He cut me to pieces in just a few seconds, and then I felt like a top-maul had just smashed me in the jaw, and I fell into darkness.

I woke some hours later, bound hand and foot and strapped to one of my own mules, my head hanging down one flank, my feet the other. Pain was driving spikes into my skull and my beard was soaked with half-dried blood. I gave a snort and jerked my head up, and to my amazement I saw four of the Gentlemen of Leisure stumbling alongside the mule, their arms expertly tied behind their backs, their faces covered with bruises. A long rope linked them together by the neck, and they looked nothing so much as a coffle of slaves, shuffling off to market.

"Oi!" I called to the nearest. "What's going on?"

"No talking!" came a stern voice. I looked up again and saw the stranger in his feathered costume striding toward me. I tried to ignore the pain that was stabbing my brain.

"Who in blazes are *you*?" asks I. "Spring-heeled bloody Jack?"

Because in the costume he looked like that celebrated Londoner, at least as pictured in the penny press.

"I'm the Condor," says the stranger.

Now, I had never heard the word *condor* before. It's Spanish I suppose, and I don't speak that lingo beyond a few words. Naturally we'd seen condors flying overhead, lots of them, but we just called them vultures or buzzards.

There's a theory that on account of his Spanish name, the Condor is a Mexican. I don't believe he is, for he speaks American English—a sort of generalized American, without a hint of the regional dialects common in the country. Other people have heard him speak Spanish, but none said he spoke it like a native.

"What the hell's a condor?" asks I.

"*Gymnogyps californianus*," says he, with perfect seriousness.

I should point out that the Condor, as long as I've known him, has never demonstrated the slightest inkling of humor.

"You won't get any ransom," says I. "We spent all our money before coming back to the Middle Fork."

He glared at me with his blue eyes. "It's not ransom I'm after," says he. "What I'm after is Justice." You could just hear the capital J in his tone.

"Justice?" I was bewildered. I looked at him more carefully, just in case he was someone out of my past, someone to whom I'd done a bad turn. I couldn't think who that would be, but then I'm not always sober, and I might have injured someone and forgot.

"You shot a man," says the Condor sternly. "And your gang tried to steal that other party's claim."

"*Other party's claim?*" I demanded. "They jumped *our* claim!"

"I've been patrolling the Middle Fork for weeks," says the Condor. "And I've never seen you there."

He *patrols*? I thought.

"We left two men behind when we went for supplies in the autumn," says I. A dark inspiration struck. "Those Australians probably murdered them."

"You'll have a chance to defend yourself," says the Condor, "at your trial."

"*Trial?*" cries I. "There are *trials* now?" There was barely any law in San Francisco, let alone in the Sierra Nevada.

"There will be, in time," says the Condor.

"And what are you going to do with me in the meantime?" says I. "Keep me tied up till someone gets around to appointing a judge and constables?"

"I'm taking you to the jail."

The only jails I knew of were in the various military posts, and I supposed that was what he meant. But in fact there *was* a brand-new civilian jail, in the brand-new town of Sacramento City, which had been established near Sutter's Fort under the sponsorship of John Sutter, Junior. Sutter the Younger was tired of the loiterers, drunkards, and thieves hanging around his father's compound, stealing and drinking, breaking fences and stealing his father's cattle, and he was determined to bring law and order to the area. But he had no actual authority to do so, and so his arrangements were entirely improvised.

It took two and a half days to get to Sacramento City, during which time I and the Gentlemen of Leisure stayed bound and secured. The Condor lived up to his name and kept a careful watch on us, just as a buzzard keeps an eye out for carrion. After I'd recovered sufficiently from the clouting the Condor had given me, I was made to walk, tied into the slave-coffle with my mates.

When we shuffled into Sacramento City, I didn't like the look of the loiterers hanging around the jail, the usual tobacco-chewing, jug-swigging riff-raff you see in all western American towns—"border trash," as I have heard them called. If *they* were my jury, I thought, they would see me hanged just for the pleasure of seeing me twitch.

The jail was a plain log building sitting on what was probably meant to be a grand city square some day, but which was now nothing more than a muddy pit. The fellows in charge seemed to have met the Condor before. We were bundled into cells, four or five of us to a room, our weapons and gear were locked in a storeroom, and our animals were turned into a paddock. I told them the arrest was illegal and refused to give my name, so I was put down as "the Commodore," which was what my mates called me.

We were given a dinner of beans with a little bacon, and then locked in. The jailkeepers kept no watch in the nighttime, but went home. I reckon that Sutter Junior wasn't paying them much.

Other fellows in the jail enlightened us about the Condor. He'd first appeared just after the New Year, when he'd begun breaking up fights and apprehending rustlers. No one knew his true identity or where he was from. One man swore that he could fly with that cape apparatus of his. I told him I wasn't drunk enough to believe that, and then set about escaping.

It wasn't hard. I don't think anyone in Sacramento City had ever built a jail before, and they'd put it right on the ground, as if it were a backwoods cabin. We were able to break up our beds to make digging tools, and use our slop buckets as well. (As I say, sailors know how to *do* things.) Before midnight, we were all free. Some of the others in the jail dug out alongside us, but I wouldn't let them join our group. If they lacked the enterprise to dig themselves out of the jail after all the time they'd spent in it, we didn't want them in our party.

We broke into the storeroom and found our weapons and supplies. Then we freed our mules from the paddock, along with some other animals, and took them all. We broke into Brannan's mercantile store for more weapons, powder, and food, and then we legged it into the Sierras.

It was only a few minutes before we ran into friends—the five missing members of the Gentlemen of Leisure, who had been beaten by the Condor in the fight, but had run off before they could be captured. They had followed our party cautiously down to Sacramento City, and had been hoping to rescue us. I'm glad we escaped on our own, because though I appreciated my comrades' pluck, they weren't the brightest sparks among us, and if we'd waited for them, it might have been the next century before they'd managed to organize themselves for the job.

We laid down false trails and crossed and re-crossed the American River several times, but I always knew where we were headed—back to the Middle Fork, where I planned to meet up with our old friends the Sydney Ducks. We found our old camp before any trouble caught up with us, and we properly sneaked up on the Australians—when we came out of ambush with our guns trained on them, they knew better than to do anything but surrender.

We took their gold and their supplies, smashed the placer, and gave them all a thorough hiding for good measure. I told them that if we saw their ugly faces in the Sierras ever again, we'd kill them.

Oddly enough, they took me at my word and cleared out. The Sydney Ducks later became a criminal gang in San Francisco, at least until the Committee of Vigilance hanged most of them.

Better them than me, I've always thought.

Now that we were no longer accidental criminals but proper road agents, I reckoned we might as well be hanged for a sheep as a lamb. We moved up the Middle Fork and robbed and plundered more or less at random. I'd like to be able to claim that we robbed only bad people, but in fact we preyed on whoever seemed prosperous and careless about keeping a proper watch.

One of the groups we robbed was, I swear to God, a band of Freemasons from Nova Scotia, Traveling Lodge Number Something-or-Other. They'd not just carried mining equipment into the Sierras, but all their masonic regalia as well, aprons and chains and such. They must have had cozy little lodge meetings beneath the Ponderosas, chanting all their nonsense and building Solomon's Temple out of the stars in the sky.

One of these anointed turned out to be no less than a Past Grand Commander of the Knights Templar, which entitled him to a military-style uniform, complete with sword, bullion epaulets, and a cocked hat with an ostrich plume. One of the lads put the cocked hat on my head, saying "Here you are, Commodore Sir," and we all had a laugh. But the hat fit, and so did the uniform coat, and the sword was impressive in its way, so when we left the scene, I was dressed up as the Commodore in truth. If the world was going to assign me a role, I thought, I'd play it.

That was the moment when the madness really began to take hold.

I may always have had it in mind that I'd meet the Condor again. I knew he'd be after us, so I always tried to camp in a place that was defensible, and we were careful to build our fire in a hollow where it couldn't be seen. We couldn't do much about the smoke, I suppose, but then the trees were thick and screened us pretty well. We kept lookouts.

Of course it didn't help. Of course he found us in an unguarded moment. We had just forded the river and decided to take a breather and a bit of dinner on the bank. I'd just fetched a cup of coffee from the fire and was walking along the pebbly alluvial strand, thinking that if we were ever to take up mining again, this would be a good place to set up the sluice box. Then came that *Ky-yeeee* cry from the trees, and I looked up in great surprise to see the Condor soaring toward me on kite-like wings.

The idiot in the Sacramento City jail had been right after all. The Condor *could* fly, or at any rate glide, and he'd launched himself from one of the Douglas firs that stood like great masts around us and aimed himself right at me.

I was so startled by the sight that my boot slipped out from under me, and I sprawled on the strand—which was what saved me, because he was aiming to kick me in the chest with both feet, which would have collapsed me like a piece of torn canvas. He whirred right over my head, and I felt the breeze from his cape on my face. I jumped to my feet and drew my sword.

I had a pistol hanging from my belt. Yet I drew the sword. That's because the lunacy had me by then.

The other members of my gang were more practical. They produced their weapons and opened fire, but they were standing all around us and they fired away in a panic. Bullets hummed all around my head, and I shouted at everyone to stop shooting—which they did, as soon as they emptied their Colts.

The Condor had recovered from his swoop and turned to face me.

The scent of gunpowder swirled over the scene. The wild firing seemed to have done him no harm.

"So, Commodore," says he, with what seemed grudging respect, "you want to face me in single combat?"

He thought I was challenging him, calling for the shooting to stop and standing there with the sword in my hand. That wasn't my intention at all—what I really wanted was to not get shot. But if he was willing to credit me with a noble motive, I was willing to take that credit.

"I've always considered myself a fair gent," says I.

"But you have a sword, and I do not," says he. "Is that a fair combat?"

"It was hardly fair to swoop on me from ambush," says I. "So I'll hang onto my advantage for the present, I reckon."

And then he charged, swirling his cape at me to dazzle my senses. I managed to make a cut with the sword anyway, and to my surprise I struck sparks—this is when I discovered that the long gauntlets that covered his forearms were sewn with steel splints to parry weapons. He lodged a couple punches to my floating ribs, and then I slapped at him with my free hand—my hard, horny hand, which knocked him back.

And then it was back and forth across the strand, my sword striking sparks, his fists flashing out. One of his kicks caught me in the thigh, and then I knew to watch out for his feet as well as his hands.

I thrust with the sword, and he parried it very low, to drive my guard down, so I reckoned a high attack was about to follow. I ducked, and he leaped clean over me with a flying kick. His cloak flapped in my face, and I grabbed a fistful of the fabric and lunged forward, taking the cloak with me. The Condor was yanked right off his feet, landing hard on his back, and I stepped on the cloak to keep him from rising again. I looked down at him as, half-strangled, he struggled to release the cape—after which I knelt, grabbed a rock off the strand, and bashed the Condor right between his blue eyes.

Those were our humble beginnings, right there. The first fights between the Condor and the Commodore were these little scrimmages by the Middle Fork, nothing like the titanic battles we fought later.

But on that afternoon I had no idea of what was to follow, so I gazed down at the unconscious Condor while the Gentlemen of Leisure ran up to congratulate me. Some of them were all for shooting the Condor then and there, but I stopped them.

I did not have it in me, then or now, to shoot a helpless man. And while I was happy to play the robber, and fight in self-defense if I had to,

I felt that deliberate murder was a line I was not prepared to cross. Killing the Condor, I thought, would have bad consequences somewhere down the trail, consequences possibly involving a mob, a rope, and a tall tree.

So we settled for stripping him naked, beating him silly, and tying him to a tree. Once we had his hood off, I looked carefully at the face to see if I recognized it, but I didn't. It meant nothing to me. And even if I had known him, he was so covered with bruises and gore that I might not have recognized him anyway.

We examined his equipment. Not only did he have his gliding rig, but he carried other gear on his belt that made him a regular Vidocq—spikes for climbing trees, a small spyglass, a magnifying lens, measuring tape, a small supply of plaster of Paris, a notebook and pencil, and a phrenological chart. He used all this scientific apparatus in the pursuit of criminals, not that I knew what to make of it at the time.

One of my lads tried to fly with the cape apparatus and promptly broke an arm. We laughed, and I ordered the gear destroyed.

That night, the Condor managed to escape his bonds and flee into the darkness. I was more relieved than anything. Without clothing and his equipment, I knew it would be some time before he'd be on our trail again.

Once the Condor was gone, I began to try to think of a way out of our dilemma. And dilemma it was, for all that most of my crew hadn't realized it.

Our pillaging had been successful. We had more gold than we would have got by working a full year, but in this remote area there was nowhere to spend it. The thought of returning to civilization with our gains was tempting, but I'd be recognized if I ever returned to Sacramento City, and thrown back in their ridiculous jail.

There was no choice but to keep doing what we were doing. But I decided against continuing along the Middle Fork, where the miners knew to look out for us, and instead led the lads over the Sierras on a trek to the South Fork. It was only ten miles as the condor flies, but it took us five days, creeping along under Lookout Mountain and Big Hill Ridge and a lot of mountains and ridges that hadn't been named yet, at least by white men. We encountered nothing but a few Indian camps, and as we saw no women in these, there was no reason to be friendly, so we left them alone.

The South Fork runs through somewhat more open country, and once we arrived we could make better time heading downstream. The miners had no warning of us, and we plundered the more prosperous-looking of them.

Eventually, we reached Sutter's Mill, where the Gold Rush had begun, and where John Sutter, Senior, hired folks to mine for him. They were robbing him blind, of course, so we robbed *them* and headed downriver for the junction of the American and Sacramento rivers.

There we avoided Sutter's Fort and Sacramento City, and headed downriver partway to the Delta, where we flagged a steamboat.

It wasn't hard. When the Gold Rush started, there'd been only a single steamboat on the Sacramento, the *Sitka*, but now there were over a score, as well as dozens of sailing craft. The steamboats had all been built in New York and Boston and had floundered their way clean around the tip of South America, their decks stacked with all the fuel they could carry.

Of the steamboats that chugged by that day, I chose mine carefully—I wanted a fast, rugged craft, a sidewheeler able to spin on the water like a crab, with a flat bottom drawing only a couple feet of water, and I found one in the *Chrysopolis*. So we stood on the bank and waved a flag—actually a looted Masonic apron lashed to a stick—and *Chrysopolis* obligingly came near the bank to pick up passengers. That was how things were done in America—you stood on the riverbank and waved, and the boats were happy to take your money and let you and your animals on board.

As soon as we got on the steamboat, we produced our weapons and robbed all the passengers. They were heading from San Francisco to Sutter's Fort, so they'd spent the money on good times or on mining equipment and didn't have much cash on them. We set the passengers and crew ashore, then took our new prize upriver. It took us a few days to learn her ways—I knew nothing of steam engines, but some of my crew did—and then we began our career of piracy.

I'd reckoned that there was no point in robbing individual mining claims when we could simply take our pick of everything traveling along the river—gold, steamboats, fancy clothing, furniture, and all. We'd come charging out from a half-hidden slough, or from behind an island, and swoop down on a boat coming down from the diggings, our rail crowded with men waving weapons, while I stood by the wheelhouse in my uniform and commanded our victims to surrender through a brass speaking trumpet.

There was a lot of gold coming down that river. Some of it in strongboxes, some in the miners' pockets or their dunnage. They'd try to hide it, of course, but we got more than our share. And then we'd let our victims go, along with their boat, to go upriver and dig more gold for us.

By this point I was quite the swell. I'd got myself more bits of uniform from the captains and officers of the steamboats, and I had a couple pistols in my belt and my fancy Masonic sword. I shaved my beard except for a proper set of whiskers; very dashing, I thought. I started dipping into looted gold snuffboxes instead of chewing tobacco, and using words I'd heard from educated people. I stopped dropping my aitches. I wore lace and knee breeches and silk stockings, and I had a bullion epaulet on each shoulder.

I was completely ridiculous. The madness had me completely in its grip.

I was uneasy about the Condor. When we moored the boat for the night, I tried to keep it away from tall trees. A few weeks went by without my hearing that *Ky-yeee* ringing in the air, but I was no easier. *He's up to something*, I thought.

What I didn't know was that the Condor was busy dealing with a couple other filibusters, the Haunt and the Highwayman, each of whom was robbing in the vicinity of Sutter's Fort. It was only when he'd had them locked up in the jail that he came looking for me.

And he didn't come gliding down from the trees. He crept up on the moored *Chrysopolis* on a tiny raft made up of inflated seal skins, a hand crank, and a screw propeller.

He knocked out a pair of sentries and set a fire in the steamboat's grand salon. Then he climbed to the Texas deck with a grapnel and a line, entered the captain's cabin where I was sleeping, and knocked me unconscious before I even came awake. When I woke, I was back in the Sacramento City jail, my boat had burned to the waterline, my fortune had for the most part been lost, and my crew were stranded on Sutter's Island.

The Haunt, I discovered, had already escaped—being a conquistador who had been dead for a hundred years or more, he could supposedly walk through walls. (At least at night: he's more vulnerable in the daytime.) There was still no law—no judges, no juries, no sheriffs or deputies, which had not stopped the Condor from filling the jail with a host of other offenders, most of whom professed themselves willing to join my crew, and the Cavalier—a Frenchman who was dressed in the black leather outfit of the French king's musketeers of the seventeenth century—offered his aid, though he was not willing to join our gang.

The jail had been improved, so it took us all of three days to break out. We went straight to the wharfs and aboard the *New World*, which had just arrived from New York. It was a floating palace, with red plush benches, marble tables, and crystal chandeliers, and the fastest boat on the river besides. It was easy enough to overpower the crew and set forth. We dropped off the Cavalier below Sacramento, then headed for Sutter's Island, where I found my old crew staring at the snag-filled waters of Steamboat Slough and waiting for rescue.

Those were the glory days. Every day brought adventure: a whiff of powder or a clash of blades or the clinking of glasses. Either we were plundering the gold traffic moving to and from the Sierras, or we were enjoying ourselves at our secret forts in the Sacramento Delta. The delta featured hundreds of miles of waterway and dozens of islands. And, because we had gold, we suddenly had friends. People would bring barges of fine things up from San Francisco, and we'd pay them well.

We had champagne and brandy. Linen. Fine weapons. Women.

In Alta California, the men still outnumbered the women five or six to one, but many of the ladies had come entirely for the gold. Gold we had aplenty, and the ladies found both the gold and us. It was a splendid time we had together. We had to be the envy of all those poor, frozen miners on the American River, who could go a whole year without seeing a female.

I even had a sort of wife for a while, Pirate Sally, who wore a kerchief over her red-gold hair and wielded matching cutlasses. We plundered together till I caught her one night sneaking off with my personal stash of gold. Turns out she'd fallen for the Cavalier, that frog bastard, so I heaved her into the river and let her swim for it. For revenge the vindictive bitch led the Condor to us, and I got to spend another few days in the Sacramento City jail before escaping.

By then a regular circus parade of colorful madmen had come to the diggings for their piece of the proceeds. Quiet, black-clad Doctor Tolliver, with his bottles of explosives. The Mad Emperor, who set up his kingdom by Lake Tahoe and demanded we worship him. Captain Hypnos, with his legion of mesmerized followers. The Bowery B'hoy, a New Yorker with a red shirt, plug hat, lead-weighted cane, and soap-locks like a Jew.

Nor were they all robbers or poachers. Aero Lad raced through the skies on his Mechanical Dragonfly. San Francisco produced the Regulator and the Hangman, both of whom pretended to uphold the law as they went about bashing people and stringing them up. They were no more law-abiding than I was, though for some reason they were thought to be great heroes and I was not.

Every race or nation had its own champion. The Indians of this area had never organized above the village level, and they never had a Sagamore till the Sagamore showed up to lead them in trying to drive the white men from the diggings. The Masked Hidalgo fought for the Mexicans. And then there was Shanghai Susie, who defended the Chinese miners with some kind of strange fighting magic called "cong foo." I *hated* her, for she attacked with a host of strange weapons and was better with a sword than me.

It was hard to say just what side these last were on. They fought to defend their own people, but they also fought each other, and they fought to defend law-breakers against the Condor or anyone set to catch them. I fought all of them at one time or another, and fought alongside them as well.

Those of us on the far side of the law didn't just fight the law-men, we fought each other. With both the Condor and the likes of the Mad Emperor likely to turn up at any time, slavering for my freedom or my gold, you can bet I took care for my safety. Our forts in the Delta were defended by cannons, sentries, and elaborate pits and traps that would drop the unwary into nests of snakes or incinerate them in a flaming blast of coal oil. (That's how the Hangman went, and good riddance to him.) And I wasn't about to have another boat burned out from under me— we covered the *New World* in nets, set cannons to cover every approach, and set even more elaborate traps. (We failed to catch Aero Lad in one, but we did get his Dragonfly, which kept him off our necks till he built a new one.)

Still, it was the Condor who was my truest companion. We battled almost continually, with the honors about even. He dragged me to the hoosegow more than once, and I captured him as well. I was still reluctant to kill him directly, so I'd suspend him over a pit of sharpened stakes or send him down the river tied on a flaming raft, or throw him into a cage with a captured mountain lion. Damned if he didn't make his escape every time.

Once, when he'd captured me and was marching me to jail trussed up like a turkey-bird, he prosed on the way he did when he had a captive audience, and he told me that he found me "worthy of his steel." Not that he *had* any steel—he always fought with his fists—but I have to admit that a part of me was pleased to have earned his respect.

I told him that I'd never have become a pirate if he hadn't clouted me that first time on the Middle Fork when I was trying to defend my claim against poachers.

"You follow your nature," says he, "and your nature was bound to lead you to folly sooner or later."

"Folly, perhaps," says I. "But where was it written that I was destined to become a river pirate until you made me one?"

"Do not attempt to shift the blame for your actions to me," says he. "Your very anatomy proclaims your depravity." He prodded me on the back of the head in an unpleasant, over-familiar way. "Your skull shows that your adhesiveness is deficient, whereas your destructiveness and combativeness are overdeveloped. Science itself condemns you."

I was annoyed at being poked in this phrenological manner and shook the hand off. "And what about *your* nature?" says I. "Is it the bumps on your head that led you to become the Condor? Why do you swoop down from the trees to whip offenders off the trail?"

He gave no answer, simply shoved me along ahead of him.

"Whatever happened must have been a great blow," says I, "to force you to do something as barmy as this."

By this time, there were all sorts of stories about the Condor and who might be behind the mask. It was claimed that he was a belted earl from England, or the son of a New York shipping nabob—someone rich, anyway, who had pelf enough to indulge himself in the eccentric hobby of floating from tree to tree and thrashing the wicked. There was another story that he was a Mexican caballero whose activities were supported by a secret gold mine (and I believe the Mad Emperor spent a lot of time searching for that mine). I heard yet another story that the Condor was an army officer whose wife had been murdered by bandits, and who had sworn vengeance on the whole criminal tribe.

All the stories were ridiculous, of course. Yet none were more absurd than the Condor himself, who marched behind me on yet another trek to the jail in Sacramento City.

As we walked along, I probed further still. "What compels you to dress up as a great carrion bird?" says I. "Attack perfect strangers and haul them to the calabozo? How does this benefit you in any way?"

"I benefit as any citizen benefits," says he, "when order is maintained in society."

I lost my patience. "Tell that to Mrs. Siddons!" says I scornfully. "You're not in this for some abstract pleasure in establishing order." I glared at him. "You're cracked! You're completely cracked! What I can't work out is what cracked you!"

He gave me a steely look from either side of his ridiculous costume beak. "Could a madman do what I do?" he asked. "Could a madman fight so well or so long?"

It occurred to me afterwards that there was a bit of pleading in his voice. That he was hoping for understanding, that I would somehow comprehend the necessity and rightness and perfect sanity of his mission. But I'd lost my temper, and I was having none of it.

"Damn you," says I, "you *started* this! If it weren't for you, I'd never have become the Commodore! Doctor Tolliver would be selling quack medicines in Pittsburgh, and Captain Hypnos would be performing in a music hall! We're all inmates of your private madhouse—none of this would exist without you! This is all part of your demented fantasy, you glibbering moon-calf!"

Whereupon his blue eyes flashed, and he landed a right hook to my jaw that laid me out on the trail.

He apologized afterward for losing his temper. But by that point I wasn't interested in his explanations, and as soon as I could manage it, I lurched to my feet and stalked off in the direction of Sacramento City and its jail. Nor could I resist the Parthian shot that I hurled over my shoulder.

"And that war cry of yours?" says I. "That *ky-yeeee*! That's a hawk, you know, not a condor! Condors only *grumble*, as if they're mouthing some ridiculous, impotent complaint against the state of the universe."

If he had any reply to this, he had no chance to utter it, because at that point the Gentlemen of Leisure sprang their ambush, firing their muskets and pistols. I threw myself headlong on the ground, as I knew from long experience that the fire of my crew was marked both by its enthusiasm and its general lack of accuracy. By the time the fire ended and I rose again to my feet, the Condor had fled, and I was surrounded by my jubilant crew of freebooters.

After my capture, you see, the Gentlemen had taken the *New World* upriver by way of obscure sloughs and passages, and sent a party ashore to hide in the trees and bushes and wait for the Condor to march me into their ambush. Once they'd liberated me, we paraded in triumph to our steamboat, where we raised bumpers of champagne as we made our way back to one of our hidden forts.

Little did I know it, but that was the last of the carefree time, the joyful cut-and-thrust of the freebooting life. It was less than a week later that I heard a strange throbbing in the air, and looked up from the pilothouse of the *New World* to see Professor Mitternacht's great black airship as it floated over the Sacramento Delta, the sinister outline of a cruising shark black against the sun, the great fore-and-aft screw propellers whirling. I felt a shiver run up my spine as I saw the machine, and I began to feel a suspicion that for the first time my steamboat had been thoroughly outclassed.

Mitternacht and his *Schrecken* had crossed half the world and the entirety of the United States, and he was on his way to San Francisco, where he opened his campaign by dropping fluorine bombs of poison gas that killed a third of the population—after which the *Schrecken* came to a landing, discharged troops, seized the town, and raised the black-and-gold flag of the Austrian Empire.

The airship was large, but it couldn't hold a vast number of soldiers, only half a battalion or so of Croatian Grenzers. But it was still half a battalion more than anyone else had in Alta California, and Mitternacht made up for his lack of numbers by ruling through terror: there were executions and violations, and the survivors were enslaved and put to work building camps, fortifications, and a landing field for the airship.

Mitternacht and his fluorine bombs came as a literal bolt from the blue. While I had been in Alta California, prospecting and breaking out of jails and fighting back and forth with the Condor and the Bowery B'hoy and Shanghai Susie and so on, there had been revolutions all over Europe. Hungary had tried to break free of the Austrians and been defeated; and their hero, Kossuth, had come to the United States in order to raise funds for another rebellion.

Professor Mitternacht was outraged that Uncle Sam was sheltering the rebel instead of hanging him outright; and so he flew from his secret base in the Tyrol all the way across the ocean to punish the United States and annex Alta California to the empire of the Habsburgs.

The Austrian government, when they heard about all this months later, denied they'd had any part in it; but for all those of us on the Sacramento knew, young Franz-Joseph had actually declared war. Swarms of refugees fled San Francisco on every boat and raft they could find, and they spread stories that were even more fantastic than the reality.

It was then that I realized that the game had changed. Instead of carefree freebooters trying to outwit each other in plundering the wealth of the diggings, there was a homicidal madman in the sky raining death on helpless civilians.

Nor was there any more plunder to be had. No miner had any reason to carry his gold to San Francisco when Professor Mitternacht would only confiscate the gold and enslave the miner. Perhaps worse, the flow of supplies coming up the river from the city was interrupted. Not only were there no more immigrants, no picks and shovels, no mules or canvas or line, no wine or whiskey or champagne, there was no *food*. No flour, no bacon, no corn meal. Some victuals were trekked in from Monterrey, but not nearly enough. The miners at the diggings were all in danger of starvation unless they somehow turned themselves into farmers overnight—and with autumn coming on, there was no time to get a crop in the ground.

Professor Mitternacht offered to feed anyone willing to become one of his slave laborers. I believe that a few desperate people accepted that offer.

My own folk were all right. We had food and drink in plenty, and—with no piracy to contemplate—little to do but enjoy ourselves. Though I tried to savor our celebrations, I wasn't really inclined to pleasure. Instead, I worried that our hidden bases and forts were all visible from the air, and I occupied myself with schemes to hide ourselves from the *Schrecken*, and ways to bring the craft down. I experimented with cannon rigged to fire on a great incline, like a mortar, but the tests were not a great success.

There seemed to be a truce among the various forces in California while we worked out what to do about the invader. The Condor was active in trying to liberate Mitternacht's slaves. The Bowery B'hoy made a raid on San Francisco just for the devilment of it and rescued a young woman who became his Bowery G'hal. Aero Lad tried to board the *Schrecken* from his Mechanical Dragonfly, but was captured and thrown overboard to a long fall and death. The Regulator was captured, broken on the wheel, and killed.

Aye, Professor Mitternacht was a glorious bundle of fun, all right.

That was where things stood when the Mad Emperor, from his castle fortress on Lake Tahoe, declared war on the Austrian—and sent a courier to deliver a message calling Mitternacht a slimy, jumped-up, demented foreigner. The message was so successful, in fact, that Professor Mitternacht lopped the head off the courier and took the *Schrecken* up the Sacramento to bomb the Mad Emperor's fortress.

Which was the end for the Emperor. Not that I missed him—he had a certain style, but in the end, the essential monotony of your self-promoting conqueror is difficult to ignore.

It was while Mitternacht was about this errand that I had a visit from the Condor. He came in a small steamboat, his cape streaming out behind him as he waved a white flag. Which, as a gentleman pirate, I was compelled to honor.

The Condor came aboard the *New World* and got straight to the point, as was his practice.

"The *Schrecken* is on the far side of the Sierras," says he. "If things go on as they are, we'll all starve to death by spring. But we've got a Miners' Militia now, well-armed, and if we can get our troops across the Bay we can recapture the city. There aren't many of those Grenzers, you know."

I knew perfectly well where this was headed. "You don't need the *New World*," says I. "There are plenty of steamboats on the river."

"It's not the boat we need." He gave a look at one of the cannons I had mounted on the foredeck. "We could use your guns," says he. "We need something that will intimidate the Grenzers in their forts."

I give him a narrow-eyed look. "And after the battle?" asks I. "How do I know you won't bang me on the head and drag me up in front of some vigilance committee?"

He drew himself up and looked at me solemnly. "I give you my word of honor," says he. "You and your crew will have a fair opportunity to withdraw once the city is ours."

Well, I couldn't do better than that. And truth to tell, I was fretting in any case, knowing it was only a matter of time before the *Schrecken* appeared overhead to pacify the Delta by dropping poisonous fluorine on me and all my men. The airship's absence seemed by far the best chance to give the flying madman a knock. Best, I reckoned, to strike while the striking was good.

So it was, barely two nights later, that I found myself conning the *New World* down the river and across the Bay. The city—renamed Sankt Ruprecht after the patron saint of Salzburg, of all places—was guarded by three masonry forts, charmingly named Angst, Tod, and Panik. Angst and Panik had been built by slaves, and covered the western and eastern approaches; Fort Tod was the old Spanish Presidio on the Golden Gate. Fortunately Mitternacht was forced to defend so much of the peninsula that the forts didn't support one another. We made Fort Panik, on the east side of the city, our first target.

I had two companies of militia on board, partially protected by log ramparts, and I was trying to peer around the wood cladding of the pilothouse when I saw, walking along the Texas deck, a tall, cadaverous cove, dressed in a long black cloak and a stovepipe hat. He carried a strange pipe-like weapon that was attached to a canister he wore on his back. I stuck my head out of the wheelhouse, then gestured for him to join me.

The weapon, I discovered, made strange muttering sounds, like a coal fire in a boiler with all the dampers shut.

"That gun of yours ain't going to set my boat on fire, is it?" asks I.

"I hope it will set *everything* on fire." He spoke with a ponderous Russian accent. He gave a formal bow. "I am the Nihilist," says he. "It is my mission to destroy all forms of oppression, starting with the champion of Habsburg reaction across the Bay."

I regarded him. "When you say *everything...*" says I.

"I mean everything," says he flatly. "In order for humanity to be liberated, it must be returned to a complete state of nature."

"Well," says I, "it's hard to find a less civilized place than the gold fields."

"Yes," says he, "but the miners still pursue *gold*, the single vital element of our oppressive economic system. This greed must be..." He searched for the word. "*Cured*," he decided.

I gave him a hopeful grin. "I trust you will avoid curing us until Professor Mitternacht is dealt with."

"I am a reasoning man," says he. "I am capable of making tactical alliances."

Another solemn madman, thinks I. He wants to liberate San Francisco only to burn the place down.

The Nihilist, I reckoned, was another of a new breed of cranks and enthusiasts on their way to California, and who were already well on their way to spoiling the place. The only difference between him and Professor Mitternacht was that Mitternacht had a more efficient way of killing people.

I determined in the upcoming battle to send the Nihilist straight at the enemy, and to let fortune determine the rest. He could destroy civilization, I decided, or die trying. Preferably the latter.

I returned my attention to guiding the *New World* to its destination, and to worrying that I would get a roundshot through my tripes before I ever saw an enemy.

It is impossible to make a surprise attack with steamboats—they make a lot of noise, from the clanking of the engine to the thrashing of the paddles to the great throat-clearing howl of the relief valves—and my heart was in my throat for much of the crossing as I imagined myself in the sights of some diabolical German engine from Professor Mitternacht's laboratory.

There were twelve steamboats in our fleet, and most of them towed sailing craft or barges crammed with men. The militia were half-crazed with drink before we even set out, and their shouting and singing and accidental discharge of firearms were hardly the thing to boost my confidence.

Yet we were within a couple thousand yards of Fort Panik before star shells went up and the first cannon flashed in the fort's embrasures.

I had timed things pretty well. A golden dawn was just creeping down Blue Mountain to the west, but the Bay was still in darkness, and from the ramparts our boats were just shadows on the deep black water. As cannon shot came skipping over the waves, I rang to the engine room for more speed.

I think the Condor had it in mind that I would keep *New World* offshore and engage the fort in a gun duel. This was the best recipe for suicide that I could think of, and so I ran in as quickly as possible. I threw out a kedge anchor so that I could pull the boat off the mud flats if I needed to, then ran her in till she just touched ground, after which I lowered the gangways and watched the drunken militia charge forward, sloshing through water and muck and wrack and flotsam to dry land. I thought I saw the Nihilist's stovepipe hat in the throng.

I looked up at the fort, which was still booming away, and decided that I would be safer on land than sitting atop a boiler filled with steam and subjected to plunging shot from above. So I ordered the cannons fired, then drew my sword, waved my hat, and led my crew in a charge.

Nor was I alone. The rest of our fleet had come to shore and unleashed their passengers. I saw the plug hat of the Bowery B'hoy amid the throng, and his lead-weighted cane waving in the air; there were the long ringlets and the broad plumed hat of the Cavalier next to the scarlet kerchief of my traitorous bitch of an ex-wife. The Masked Hidalgo swooped along in his cloak, his rapier flashing; and one mob advanced in complete silence, the mesmerized followers of Captain Hypnos. Shanghai Susie ran nimbly along with a party of Chinese, their pigtails flying. And Doctor Tolliver walked ashore absolutely alone, because no one wanted to be anywhere near his box of explosives.

My heart gave a great lift at the scene, at all the great champions united against a single enemy, and I gave a halloo and ran like a madman for the fort.

As I sloshed through the muck, I happened to look to my left, and to my great surprise I saw the Condor being hurled into the sky like a rocket. He'd had a catapult constructed on his boat to fling him aloft so that he could spread his wings and sail down into the fort.

A great mob had surrounded the fort by this point, firing like mad into the embrasures and trying to scale the masonry walls. The scent of gunpowder filled the air. The Condor disappeared into the fort, and I suppose there was the usual thwacking and thumping that followed one of his descents. Doctor Tolliver began hurling glass bombs into the fort, not particularly caring if he injured the Condor as long as he killed Grenzers; and then the Nihilist stuck his pipe-weapon into one of the embrasures and let loose with a great jet of fire; and there was screaming and shrieking and the sound of cartridges detonating, and that was the end of the Battle of Fort Panik.

Truth to tell, without the *Schrecken*, the Grenzers were doomed. There weren't many of them; they were scattered in small detachments trying to hold too much ground; and they were infantry, not trained artillerists—none of their shot had come close to our little flotilla. And they had damned few cannon to fire—the rusting old Spanish guns at the Presidio hadn't kept Commodore Stockton out in '46, and they weren't keeping us out this time. Fort Panik had only a few ill-assorted pieces scavenged from ships that happened to be in the Bay when Mitternacht turned up, and very little powder and shot.

As soon as dawn gave us a clear view of the proceedings, we organized and marched inland. South of the city, we overran the landing field that Mitternacht had built for his airship, and the factory that he had created to build new fluorine bombs. We freed the slave workers there, then crested the city's hills and marched in a great surging mob down to Fort Angst, which we stormed in about three minutes. I found myself fighting alongside the Condor, slashing with my sword as he pounded Grenzers with his fists, and I had a chance to observe the flush of battle on his cheeks, and blue glow of combat in his eyes. *He* lives *for this!* thinks I, and then some giant Croat lunged at me with a sword-bayonet as long as my leg, and I had to look to my own safety.

Angst fell, and that left only the Presidio. Which, if inadequately armed and garrisoned, was at least a proper fort; and it might have given us trouble if I hadn't remembered those fluorine bombs sitting in their racks at the factory. So I had the Condor's catapult fetched from his steamer, fixed one of Mitternacht's own projectiles in it, and ordered it hurled toward the fort.

It took a while to get the fort's range, and we came damn near to gassing ourselves; but once a few gas bombs had dropped behind the walls, the surviving Grenzers came staggering out waving the white flag. The black-and-gold of Austria came down the flagstaff and the American gridiron flag went up, and Sankt Ruprecht was San Francisco again.

The enslaved citizens of San Francisco poured out to welcome us, at least once we unlocked their barracks, and there was a massive day-long party.

The Gentlemen and I were extremely popular. For one thing, I was the only person wearing anything resembling a uniform, so it was widely believed that I had generaled the city's rescue. I was cheered wherever I went. I believe I could have run successfully for mayor.

Since people were inclined to obey my orders, I had the remaining fluorine bombs carried to one of the abandoned hulks in the Bay, which was then towed out to sea and sunk. And we made plans to ambush and capture the *Schrecken* once it returned to its base. Enough of the slaves had watched the airship's landing to know the procedures followed by the ground crews, and these volunteered to dress up in Grenzer uniforms and lure the *Schrecken* to the ground, where it could be stormed by our army.

I also made a few little plans of my own. Some machinery was quietly slipped from the factories and carried down to where the *New World* waited on the mud flats. A few Austrian engineers were likewise carried to my pirate craft, rolled in carpets so they wouldn't be lynched. If anyone noticed, they probably thought I was just looting.

The Austrian flags went up again, as decoys, and plans were laid— and just in time, for no sooner had we got over our hangovers than the thrumming of the great vessel's propellers was heard overhead, and the ominous black shadow began to circle the landing field. Our false Grenzers trotted out to take hold of the cables and guide the airship to its mooring… but then it all went wrong.

Half our army was still drunk as lords, and as soon as the *Schrecken* was within range, a great many of the fools opened fire. Once the musketry started popping, Professor Mitternacht knew that something was up. The gun smoke gave away the positions of those who had fired, and he maneuvered the warship to drop fluorine bombs on the reckless marksmen.

Only a few of the more inebriated died, as the bombs were easy enough to avoid if you knew to flee the area beneath the airship—and in addition there was a brisk wind that whipped the gas away. I was in no danger myself, for I'd managed for once to keep my crew in hand, and none of us had fired. But it was clear that the ambush had failed, and I moved my men to a safer place while the *Schrecken* circled the city and dropped bombs on anyone it could see.

Though luckily enough there were few bombs to drop. Mitternacht had used up most of his ordnance exterminating the Mad Emperor and his legions, and he was unable to land and load more bombs from his factory. So here he was far away from home, with only a small crew, and without any weapons more useful than a carbine.

He circled the city for two more days, doubtless trying to puzzle out a plan that would bring San Francisco back under his control—and then *Schrecken* turned its great nose eastward and began the long journey back to Austria.

No doubt the city will hear the roar of those propellers again. Possibly next time there will be more than the single airship. I can't imagine Professor Mitternacht taking defeat in his stride.

After Mitternacht's departure, there was another great party that lasted the better part of two days, and right into the middle of it wandered a deputation from Monterrey that included the famous scout, Christopher Carson.

Carson—a tiny, unassuming little cove, by the way—had led a small party over Donner Pass in the middle of winter—a remarkable feat in its own right—and brought the message that an American relief force was under way.

We leaders met in the City Hall to listen to Carson's message, beneath a portrait of George Washington that had been found in the cellar and placed over the gilt double-headed Austrian eagle that Mitternacht, that pretentious ass, had mounted on the wall.

It had taken nearly three months for news of Mitternacht's arrival to reach the government in Washington. The relief force, two brigades under General Winfield Scott and a naval force commanded by Commodore Matthew Perry, would take months more to arrive. Experimental weapons to be used against the airship were being constructed by the Swedish engineer Ericsson.

Carson's own journey west had taken months, and it was likely that the armada had already begun its long voyage around South America.

An odd sidelight to this affair was that in addition to commanding the army, General Scott was running for the highest office in the land. If he won, Alta California would be a military zone commanded directly by the President of the United States.

I was far from delighted by this news—I rather suspected that the two Mexican War heroes would disapprove of a pirate presence within their area of operations. Assuming that I could keep Commodore Perry from hanging me out of hand, I doubted that it would be as easy to escape from military prisons as it had been from Sutter the Younger's jail in Sacramento City.

What surprised me was the reaction of the Condor. I marked an expression of fierce grief in his eyes as he heard the news, and I realized that Scott's arrival would mark the end of his adventure, as well. With law established in California, the Condor would be superfluous.

Afterwards, there was another celebration in honor of Carson, Scott, Perry, and that guiding genius of the nation, Mr. Fillmore. The party was held in one of the great rooms of City Hall, and there were rivers of liquor and a band playing jigs and polkas: "Arthur McBride" and "Old Dan Tucker," and that great anthem of the Gold Rush, "Oh! Susanna."

I accepted a cigar from a well-wisher and went into one of the galleries to smoke it. I looked into the ballroom and saw the colorful throng at their sport, the last great rollicking occasion we were all together: me, the Condor, the Masked Hidalgo, the Highwayman, Shanghai Susie, and all the rest, in a great surging, dancing, laughing mob. All rivalry forgotten, all animosity put aside.

Soon the army would come, I thought, and put an end to all this.

I saw the Condor standing aside, and I guessed his thoughts were very like mine. I approached him. "I don't suppose that General Scott will be needing any masked vigilantes in his district," says I.

"Well," says he. "There is much of the West that is still without law."

"You could go to Utah and thump the Mormons," says I hopefully. I was hoping to direct his activities in any direction other than my own.

He offered a thin little smile. "The Mormons are law-abiding, or so I understand."

"Aside from being in rebellion against the United States—and then of course they have a habit of polygamy."

"The rebellion is more in General Scott's line," says he. "And how would I foil a polygamist, exactly? Kidnap his wives? I'd end up with a bigger harem than Brigham Young."

I looked at him in surprise, for this was the first touch of humor I'd heard from him. Yet there was no smile, no amusement gleaming from the blue eyes. Maybe he was completely serious.

"Well," offers I, "there's New Mexico."

His eyes glittered with interest. "What are your plans?" asks he.

"I expect I'll be leaving the city in two or three days," says I. "Beyond that, I have no idea."

Which was not strictly true. I knew law would come to Alta California sooner or later, and I had considered shifting my base to another part of the world, anywhere from the Russian colonies in Alaska to Taheetee, Hawaii to South America. I could keep much of the gold for myself, distribute the rest among my men, then try to disappear into the local population.

The problem, of course, was that gold fever is not confined to pirates. All it would take was for one of the crew to get drunk and speak a few indiscreet words, and whole armies would come after us—either the authorities with charges of theft and piracy, or a mob of greedy robbers ready to cut our throats.

I had not made up my mind whence I would flee. I was leaning toward Australia—there had been a gold strike there, and a swarm of strangers with gold in their pockets might not seem too out of place. And of course the whole continent was a prison, so even if they caught us, what could they do? Send us to England?

Still, I did not want to share even these half-formed plans with the Condor.

"You'll be returning to your old habits, then?" says he.

"Aye," says I. "It's the river for us."

There was a glint in his eye. "I will see you there, no doubt," says he.

"Sir," says I, "I would expect nothing less."

He bowed, and so did I. And so, between us, the silent promise was made—we would have our final battle somewhere on the Sacramento some time before General Scott arrived, and it would settle matters between us once and for all.

"You know," begins I, "if you hadn't joined the wrong side, that time on the American River—"

But that was as far as I got, because at that moment a man ran into the room shouting "Fire! Fire!" and that was the end of the party.

San Francisco had been set alight. We were up the next day and a half fighting the flames, and despite our efforts half of the city burned.

The Nihilist was suspected, though it had to be admitted that the city had already burned two or three times without his efforts. Judging by what had happened in the past, it would all be rebuilt quickly.

Once the flames were extinguished, I returned with my crew to the *New World* and pulled the boat off the mud. The miners returned to their diggings. And I advanced my plans.

I would swoop back to San Francisco one night, I thought. We'd swarm aboard an ocean-going ship, then tow her out to sea and set sail. I hated the thought of abandoning the *New World*, so we'd tow her as we sailed away.

For Hawaii first, I thought. Hawaii was a sovereign kingdom and might not honor a foreign arrest warrant.

And if they did, I would escape. I had grown very good at escaping.

But first, I wanted to keep my promise to the Condor, and I found that a perfect opportunity beckoned. The miners had been hoarding their gold in the Sierras while Professor Mitternacht was ruling his little kingdom of Tyrolia-on-the-Bay, and now that supplies were coming into the port again, they were eager to go to what remained of San Francisco and help themselves to its comforts.

It was announced that commercial steamboat service would be resumed with *Great Columbia*, the first grand boat to leave Sacramento City for San Francisco carrying passengers. There would be fireworks, speeches, and a band.

Of course it's an ambush. They *want* me to attack; they wave the gold beneath my nose to make sure I take the bait. The boat will be packed with militia.

I will intercept *Great Columbia*, of course. And the Condor will defend it. And so we will meet, perhaps for the last time.

So here I am, now, standing on the bridge, the *New World* lurking on the sweet gold-bearing waters of Steamboat Slough with steam up and weapons ready, waiting for our sentries on shore to signal *Great Columbia*'s arrival. I'm prepared to hear *Ky-yeee* as the Condor arrows out of the sky to engage me in final battle for plunder and freedom. And maybe, when I finally beat him and have him at my mercy, I'll finally have answers to some of my questions.

What are you? I'll ask. A crusader for justice? A madman in a cloak?— but not simply a madman, but rather a madman who has so infected Alta California with his own brand of lunacy that an entire host of strangers are now donning masks and swirling capes and brawling over the flood of gold coming down from the Sierras? Fellow lunatics who, like me, would have simply gone about our lives if we hadn't somehow been chosen to share the Condor's dream?

Without the Condor, the Nihilist wouldn't have burned the city, and Professor Mitternacht wouldn't have choked all those people with his gas. I would be a miner up to my knees in cold muck, thinking simple thoughts of a warm fire, a bottle of whiskey, and maybe a girl.

Who are you? I will demand. It's time I knew. Southern planter or Mexican caballero or fiend from Hell, I will know his name. I will know his station. I will know what drove him to this.

He will not want to tell me these things. But I will make him.

I will not kill him. I am not fated to be the one who ends the tale of the Condor.

But I am game for other methods. If I must, I will hang him upside-down over a burning pit, and that may loosen his tongue.

For he has assigned me this part, and I will play it till it breaks me. Or him.

I see the flag signal now, my lookout waving frantically. *Great Columbia* is on its way.

I call out orders. *Up the anchor! Fill the boilers with fuel! Full speed! Stand by the guns!*

And then I smile. *Cast off the airship!*

For I have not been idle since I made off with some of Professor Mitternacht's gear—and the Austrian engineers I'd abducted were very happy to cooperate with my plans once I'd explained that the alternative was to be strung up by their former slaves. The result is that I now have a modest airship of my own, powered by what my engineers are pleased to call a *Lichtätherkompressor*, the Aetheric Concentrator, which I gather works by compressing an invisible fluid alleged to fill the universe. Which may sound like airy German metaphysics to you and me, but it seems to lift my little aerial barge with fair efficiency for all that.

The *Commodore's Fancy* isn't as massive or magnificent as the *Schrecken*—it's only a platform fifty feet long—but it's still one of two flying machines in all the world, and my heart gives a great surge as we lift off *New World's* Texas deck, and suddenly we see the great winding watercourse of the Sacramento below us, the ash and willow and cottonwood, and the beautiful picture below us.

See how the smoke boils from the stacks of the *New World*, the fine white foam flies from the paddle wheels! Hear the whirr of the airship's great propeller! Ahead, see the white gingerbread lace of the *Great Columbia*, the decks packed with miners bringing their gold to the markets! See the sun glinting from the muskets and weapons of the militia, who think to ambush me even as I ambush them! See their confusion as the *Commodore's Fancy* darts toward them! No doubt they think of Mitternacht's fluorine bombs and tremble.

I would never carry such a filthy weapon, but I hardly mind if my enemies think I do. And the Condor can't drop on me now, not when I'm flying well above the tallest trees. I laugh as the wind tugs at my whiskers. If the Condor is on that boat, I have him trapped.

I'll have him soon, and then I'll have my answers. I signal to the gunner on the airship's bow, to fire the traditional warning shot across the target's bows.

Then there's a sudden burst of flame on the *Great Columbia*, and suddenly I see a figure arrowing for the sky on a tail of fire, cloak rippling as he rises.

It's the Condor, and he's somehow rigged himself out with a skyrocket, shooting himself into the atmosphere to gain altitude so that he can drop on me. I snarl as I curse the ingenuity of the man, and then I laugh.

I am the Commodore! What does it matter who or what made me—? I am myself, here in my cocked hat and epaulets, brandishing my sword on the swaying bridge of my glorious airship. It's far too late to quibble over origins, over who struck who on the Middle Fork... What matters is the battle to come, the final confrontation between the titan of order and the grand nabob of piracy. The last great fight of the Golden Age.

Can you see him? There—a swift shadow against the sun?

Can you hear it? Above the sound of the hissing steam, the thrashing paddles, the scream of the whistles? The sound that brings a snarl to my lips, that causes me to brandish my sword in defiance at the diving bogy in the sky...

Ky-yeeeee.

NEVERSLEEPS

FRED VAN LENTE

Monument Valley, Near Navajo Territory, Northbound on the Northwest Pacific Express, 120 years after the Awakening

There were three Pinkertons. There were always three. One was a white man, one was black, and the other was a Celestial. They may have been something else before, but now they were Pinkertons. Same brownish-grey tweed suits, same bowler hats, same obese-caterpillar mustaches lurking below their noses.

Simon Leslie was playing hold-'em in the parlor car when the train slowed between two mesas in Monument Valley with a puff of steam and a sigh. Through the window he saw the Pinkertons get off and march in a flawless triangular phalanx up the nearest brick-red ridge. From the looks of it, they emerged from the express car in the center of the train; maybe the railroad kept them stacked in crates with the sacks of parcels and the safe where they laid, stiff-necked, their tattooed eyes open and unblinking, waiting to be needed. They were nicknamed "Neversleeps" for a reason. Simon Leslie knew. It had not been so long since he was one of them.

"Your bet, Si. Come on! You're growing cobwebs." The futures trader who got on with Leslie in New Orleans wasn't nearly as funny as he thought he was. Leslie reflexively looked at his hand: it was still the Ten and Page of Pentacles. The turn had just been set down, so the Eight of Wands, the Tower, the Empress and now the Queen of Cups showed on the table. He had a modest gut-shot straight draw going, so he bet half the pot.

"Christ on a Crutch, will you look at that," said another player, a fat lawyer taking his pretty young third wife to the West Coast for their honeymoon.

Everyone looked out the window: an array of Navajo warriors lined the ridge astride soot-colored ponies, the feathers tied to their spears a-flutter in the breeze. They looked like they had materialized out of thin air, but Simon spotted the shaman among them, an emaciated crone wearing nothing but a cloak of raven feathers, shaking a gnarled rattle of bone. No doubt they had been standing there the whole time, cloaked in spirit, awaiting the train and the Pinkertons.

"They're—they're not going to attack, are they?" asked the lawyer's wife, a short, befreckled redhead who had been giving Leslie smiles he probably should have been ignoring the whole game. He'd given her smiles in return he definitely should not have. He didn't have time for it. Not this trip.

"They wouldn't dare," the futures man said. "There's been peace with the Four Corners tribes for a generation."

There was a time, not so far distant, at the beginning of the Awakening, that the Navajo and the Ute and the Zuni and the Hopi would have hungered for war, along with all the indigenous and oppressed peoples of five continents. The ancestor-worshippers and dream-walkers and totem-bearers thought they could feel the yoke and heel of the European easing from their collective necks, once all the spirits and spells from the days before the Age of Reason returned in a joyous shriek to the world. The native had been in touch with Supernature far longer than the colonizer, their touch with the Invisible had not atrophied from millennia of smelting and steam engines and monotheism. The Awakening, to them, was the first day of their inevitable return to power.

How wrong they were.

They forgot how adept those who seize power are at retaining it, no matter how *outré* the circumstances. Within a few years the enchantments and sorceries long-suppressed by European churches thrust back into prominence and were ruthlessly employed by those already in charge. There would always be those maddening fools who love the bosses, who love a firm, guiding hand on their nape and revel in the harsh disciplining of those who try and buck it. The Neversleeps were among the most feared of these servants. Though outnumbered by stony-faced braves twelve to one, the trio marched unafraid up the ridge to the lead Navajo warrior, resplendent in buffalo horns, to receive what they believed, without any hesitancy or doubt, was always rightfully theirs.

Simon Leslie said, "What they're doing now is *avoiding* a war."

The poker players watched as the braves parted so two squaws could deliver to the Pinkertons a handcuffed, hooded figure and accompanying baggage.

"Is that…" The redheaded newlywed squinted at the captive. "Is that a woman?"

"Not just any woman," Leslie said. "That's Nicola Tesla."

His fellow players turned and gaped at him. "Not the atomist? The descendant of… of you know? *Him?*"

Simon Leslie nodded.

"The savages were harboring her laboratory on their reservation? That's where she was hiding out?" Since the raid on her experimental cyclotron in Colorado Springs, Nicola Tesla had been the West's most wanted Science Criminal, with a million-dollar bounty on her head. The Four Corners chieftains no doubt delighted in frustrating the will of the Bureau of Animist Affairs by hiding her. Finally, though, a headman competing for tribal supremacy had ratted her out, able to sow enough uneasiness with the elder matriarchs about the risk of death raining down on them from Washington for the sake of some white woman practicing electrical heresy that was as taboo to their faith as it was to that of the hated Federals.

Fortunately for her, someone in the Bureau had, in turn, leaked news of her capture and details of the prisoner exchange to Simon Leslie's comrades in the White City.

"Poor girl," the fat lawyer tutted as the Pinkertons enveloped their prisoner in the center of their phalanx and returned to the train. "They're taking her to San Francisco, no doubt, to be burned at the stake."

"Or shipped to the prison mines of Alaska Territory," Simon Leslie said.

"Ain't you just a font of useful information," the futures trader said. "I don't rightly recall what you said you did for a living."

"No?" As he said it the trader slapped down the river card: the Nine of Swords. He had made his straight.

"I'm a gambler."

The men at the table blanched. The redhead grinned.

"All-in," Simon Leslie grinned back.

Once the Neversleeps were safely on board, the twisting, cord-like dragon towing the train spread its wings with a snort and a roar and launched itself back into the shimmering ley line coursing across the horizon and beat its leather wings toward California.

* * *

The redheaded bride's name was Marion and she had spent her whole life until her wedding day in Lafayette, Louisiana. She told Simon her new husband made love to her like it was a necessity he tried to get over with as soon as possible, for she stood between him and sleep.

When she stole into Leslie's private sleeper berth he pulled her nightgown over her head and left it there as he kissed every inch of her freckled skin and once she was covered in goose bumps he picked her up by her bare thighs and lay her on the tiny bed and made sure that she knew she was a rare delicacy to be savored and adored and pleasured. She was not a means. She was an End. And she bit her long red hair to keep from crying out.

After, he thought maybe he should wake her and send her back to her snoring husband for her own safety, but she looked so peaceful lying in his bed he couldn't bear to. Instead he opened his trunk and popped open the false bottom to reveal The Clockwork Chrysalis. He had waited long enough. They would be nearing the point in the Sierra Madre—according to his guidebook and compass—where the Donner Party made a miserable repast of itself all those years ago. He had chosen this as his disembarkation point for a reason.

The Chrysalis creaked like an old battleship when he peeled it over his naked body, most of it thick rawhide that somehow felt no heavier than a thin layer of oil on his skin. The boots slipped silently over his feet and he pulled the hood down over his head. He flipped through lenses of the brass goggles over his eyes and set them to the widest aperture; within moments the great proboscis of the filter over his mouth began straining his breath, bringing only the purest air into his lungs, free of the stink of Enchantment.

The atomists of the White City originally designed the Chrysalis to prevent any skin scales or stray hairs from leaving agents' bodies while conducting anti-sorcery operations, to say nothing of blood or saliva. Everything the body shed or excreted could be turned against it by the enemy; scryers could find you anywhere in the world; diviners could predict your next move with unerring accuracy; necromancers could cast sudden death on you from hundreds of miles away.

But soon the White City realized that the suit could be so much more.

Leslie snapped the gun braces over his arms and strapped the brass duck's-foot pistols onto them, combustion-based projectile technology, simple possession of which had been a capital crime for nearly one hundred years. He stepped gingerly over the naked woman in his bed to the sill, slid the glass open and pulled himself onto the roof of the train car, closing the window with his heel before the whistle of wind could rouse Marion from her slumber.

The train cleaved through snowcapped peaks and rolling carpets of pine with nary a sound, except the occasional sheet-on-a-clothesline flap of the Li Ying Lung dragon's wings. The night air lashed at him but even though he felt as naked and vulnerable as a newborn he did not feel any cold. The paucity of oxygen at this altitude made his lungs clench but after a few seconds of crouching atop the sleeper car, carefully listening to his heartbeat, he brought the rhythm of his breath under control. The brass electrodes studding the inside of the Chrysalis helped greatly with that. They captured his bioelectric field and redistributed it inside the suit, where it could not be hijacked by mediums or magic-users.

Such a manipulation of the psychic lacuna led to depression and erratic behavior in all but the most mentally disciplined operatives; Simon Leslie had had to spend a year mastering meditation techniques all but unheard of in the West to endure the sense of insignificance and hopelessness that enveloped him once he cloaked himself in the Chrysalis's self-contained, absolute reality. He was cut off from self-deception, unmoored from myth, the caul of perception was ripped away, leaving nothing but what truly is, independent of him, in its stead. Unless his mind correlated most or all of its contents, the experience could crush his soul, by convincing him in an instant that he did not have one.

On the plus side, the Chrysalis also rendered him completely immune to magic.

He bounded from car to car. Innumerable (highly illegal) micro-filament wires crisscrossing the Chrysalis turned his second skin into a giant eardrum; vibrating through his soles he could hear snoring widows, the squeak of hip flasks being unscrewed, the tinkle of lantern glass: a parlor car. Then, the clatter of plates, the laughter of dishwashers trying to out-mock each other: the dining car.

Then, he bounded to the next: he heard silence beneath his feet. This would be the express car he had seen the Pinkertons return to when the train stopped in Navajo country.

He flexed the tendons in his wrist, rotating the guns that crowned them until, with a pneumatic hiss from a catch pressed in his palm, a tiny projectile sprang out of the multi-barreled pistol and stuck in the car roof. He hopped back to the car edge as the clockwork timer on the top whirred to detonation.

The split-second, right before: his breath catching, pulse racing like a thoroughbred, thrilling to the randomness of life without thaumaturgy, the keenness of a skate down the razor's edge, without horoscopes that definitively told him what the next day would bring, without love enchantments to spark others' desire, without the certainty magery's manipulation of reality brought. The joys of not-knowing: this was why he risked his life and the eternal servitude of his immortal spirit to serve the White City.

He hadn't really lied to his fellow poker players when he told them he was a gambler.

He just didn't name the game he played.

The (*obscenely* illegal) plastic explosives inside the bolt blew a hole in the roof of the express car three feet in diameter; Leslie leapt through boots-first with the last cascade of wood and shingle.

Inside, the Pinkertons were ready for him; their heads had transformed beneath their bowler hats into blazing phosphorus eyeballs—a metaphor-made-flesh, embodying the advertisements of their detective agency prior to the Awakening: *We Never Sleep.* They blasted him as one with a ghostly fire that would have ignited anyone else into a screaming bonfire of agony. But he wore the Chrysalis, with the shaded lenses snapped over his goggles, so he didn't even get spots in his eyes.

He leapt toward the nearest Eye and flicked his wrists a different direction and twin Tamil katar blades shot out of the brass braces. With the left dagger he sliced through a retina the width of his face and was already moving away as gelatinous white burst out of it, turning and spinning and burying the right dagger up to its hilt in the chest of the second Eye next to him.

The third Eye, intuiting further attacks against the Chrysalis would be useless, turned the stream of his spirit-fire onto the floor of the car, blowing a hole in it nearly as big as the one Leslie's explosives had blown in the roof. Though the Chrysalis rendered him immune to magic, those people and things outside it were still very much *mune.* But Leslie pinwheeled sideways away from the eruption and unloaded the explosive rounds from the fan-like pistols into the Eye's midriff. He was dead before the blowback smashed him against the wall.

Nicola Tesla sat on the railroad company safe, amidst bags of mail inside the express car cage, handcuffed to the bars, hood still over her head. Leslie dug the keys out of the jacket of the Pinkerton slumped against the wall and opened the door.

When he pulled the bag off her head she sneered at him. "Edison stooge." Slight Serbian accent, darkly beautiful, same knowing baleful gaze as her famed ancestor. She spat on the floor at his feet.

Leslie groaned through the small speaker set in the front of his mask. "Ms. Tesla, I am nobody's stooge."

"*Doctor* Tesla."

"Mr. Thomas Edison may have founded the White City, but we operate solely on the universal principle of returning science to the world. We should be allies."

"Your Edison publicly recanted science to save his neck. My great grand-uncle did not and he burned. Your secret society was founded by a thief and a coward and nothing good will come of it."

He jangled the keys in front of her. "I take it then I am too morally compromised for you to accept my help?"

She pouted. She was beautiful. "Go ahead," she said, turning her face away.

She sprung to her feet as soon as he unlocked the cuffs and opened a medium-sized steamer trunk in the corner of the cage. Leslie recognized it as one of the pieces of baggage the Navajo had turned over with her. "I'm afraid we need to leave your things behind," Leslie said.

"Not this." She removed a long mahogany rifle with a steel sphere at the end of a filigreed brass barrel.

"What do you have there?"

"An apparatus for generating, intensifying, and amplifying electrical force in free air."

"Ah."

"A lightning gun," Dr. Tesla said slowly.

"Yes, thank you, I know what a lightning gun is."

"How should I know? I am sure you have received all sorts of erroneous notions from the followers of that degenerate Edison."

"Ma'am. The War of the Currents ended over a century ago. This is no time to declare that hostilities between your family and the Edisons have resumed. We have mutual enemies to unite against."

She sniffed. "It would appear I have no choice but to accept the aid of my inferiors. Very well, then; take me to your White City. I have no doubt your clock-punchers and patent lawyers will benefit greatly from someone with genuine scientific knowledge."

"No doubt," Leslie said dryly.

He helped her through the hole in the roof then hoisted himself up. As soon as the mountain air hit him he was brought up short by the crackling of the wireless in his ear. The White City always maintained radio silence during delicate operations such as this.

"Si. Si, can you hear me? Our three on the train went blind, so you must be there. Say hello to your old friend." Morgan Ash's deep mahogany laugh froze Leslie's blood. Ash was the First Ward Boss in Manhattan. His former employer.

"Possession of wireless radio technology is a Class A felony which carries a sentence of up to twenty years in prison," Simon Leslie said. Tesla looked quizzically at him, but he held up a finger for the explanation to wait. "Ah, but that's right—the rules don't apply to you, do they?"

He could almost hear Ash ensconced in his suite in the Dakota Hotel overlooking Central Park, a cigar in whichever hand wasn't holding the receiver. "For your information, Si, I am not violating our sacred ether with electromagnetic radiation in order to transmit sound, but rather a spell cooked up by the boys in Applied Thaumaturgy that resonates with your transceiver in much the same way."

All this talk of "ether" was, of course, pseudoscientific nonsense. But with magic the bosses had the power to force their pseudoscience on the world and make it true. "I'm afraid I'm not at liberty to chat, Morgan. Kind of in the middle of something."

"So you are. But I don't believe you're quite aware of what that something is." The chuckle again. "The leak inside the Bureau of Animist Affairs, that told the White City where the handoff for Dr. Tesla would be, and which train? The source of that leak would have been me."

Simon Leslie stood up straight as a roar echoed from the rear of the train. He looked down to the caboose and saw a second dragon, a Ying Lung Wang, an enormous purple blue creature with a long funnel-like snout, as it oared its sea-turtle flippers through the borealis of the ley line. Pinkertons covered its leather-plated shell, enormous head-eyes glowing beneath bowler hats.

The sky above them rippled and flashed and an airship descended from the clouds—a gondola swarming with Pinkertons hanging from a sinewy P'an Yin Lung, fur-like licks of white fire straggling from its jaw.

Dr. Tesla grunted, and Leslie looked at her, and was surprised to find her smiling.

"You have fallen for a trap, Edison man," she said. "I was just bait. They want your Chrysalis."

* * *

The Neversleeps poured over the turtle dragon and dropped from the sky, spitting gouts of white flame and whirling sigils of burning gold. They were mostly humans, but he saw *Sidhe* and dwarves mixed among them too, and that made Simon Leslie think of the Homestead Strike, in which Morgan Ash had ordered him, as leader of the local Neversleeps, to summon the dwarves' ancestral enemies from their former home in the Nine Worlds: the monstrous two-headed Ettin. The giants had scooped up diminutive miners six at a time and popped them into razor-lined mouths and crunched down on them like popcorn. After that day of horror Simon Leslie resolved to find a better way to live, or die trying. Fortunately the White City found him.

But now it seemed like he would die anyway.

"I would *strongly* advise giving yourself up, Si," Morgan Ash purred in his ear. "Ain't no shame in it. We sent numbers enough to crush the Four Corners, much less one traitor and one extremely misguided Slav bitch."

Tesla yanked back the lever on her lightning gun and cried out a curse in Serbo-Croatian ("*Nabijem te na kurac!*" he thought he heard) as blue tines crackled out of the metal sphere, zigzagging through the night and finding the Pinkertons wherever they were with the unerringness of falcons and stiffening them with electric fire.

"Seeing as how we have history, you and I," Ash rambled on, "I promise you, once you get to The Tombs, the inquisitors won't torture you too much. Sure, the judge'll order a requisite number of Hexes of Excruciating Pain, but beyond that the severity of the interrogation is largely up to the discretion of the presiding officer. Which, just so you know," his voice dropped to a whisper, "will be *me*, regardless of what copper's name is actually on the register.

"I'll only ask you to name a few names," Ash continued. "Five? The main atomist leaders. Where the White City is. How you've managed to keep an entire hive of damn heathens invisible from our scrying mirrors.

"And, of course, our experimental thaumaturgians will be going to town on your leather jumpsuit. They'll crack it. Trust me, they're smarter than a barrel full of Teslas. If they can't find a spell to get past the Chrysalis's defenses, shit, they'll write one. Don't think they won't."

"*Down!*" Leslie cried, and Tesla ducked dutifully, allowing him to blow the Pinkerton who had landed behind her off the train with a booming round to the chest. The cloud dragon overhead had managed to overtake the dragon pulling the train and was dropping off Neversleeps to outflank them. They could not survive a two-front war. Leslie leapt forward, grabbed a protesting Tesla and bounded back to the express car, dropping through the hole he'd made so they could regroup behind the imposing iron safe.

"This doesn't look promising," Leslie said in an off-handed way. He could barely hear himself over the throbbing pulse in his neck. He nodded at Tesla's silently steaming lightning gun. "Busted?"

"Bite your tongue. Overheated. Give it ten seconds of cool-down."

The roof erupted in a roar of unearthly flame that blackened and ripped whole chunks off in plumes of embers. Within seconds it would be gone, and they would be fully exposed.

The man and the woman looked at each other. Their short destinies were written plain on each other's faces.

Then, the woman had a spark.

"Your Chrysalis, it self-generates a localized bioelectric field, yes?" She feverishly snapped open compartments and undid screws on the lightning gun.

"*I'm* generating the field, the suit just keeps it in continuous circulation in a closed system... Hey, don't break that down, we can still use it—"

"No, no we can't. We need to eliminate more of our enemies at once." She removed a small metal box from the side of the gun. "We'll use the cavity resonator. It can expand the Chrysalis's bioelectric field."

"But the field is self-contained. How can you attach your resonator to it?"

"We need to breach the—"

"No!"

"Listen to me—"

"The first rule of the White City is *you never breach the Chrysalis*—"

She slapped him. He barely felt it inside his leather mask, but she kept talking. "That's Edison talking! Use your imagination, man!"

Before he could respond, the flaming roof of the express car collapsed and the room filled with Neversleeps. He grabbed her by the wrist and pulled her through the far door into the adjoining car. Passengers already awakened by the sounds of chaotic battle all around them began screaming once they saw the mosquito-like proboscis of the Chrysalis. They rushed to fill the aisle to get away from them; the fugitives managed to hop and weave around the masses but the column of Pinkertons slammed into them, forestalling pursuit.

Morgan Ash radioed, "Hellfire and damnation, boy, don't you know when your bell's been rung? I promised my kids I'd read 'em a bedtime story before their nanny puts 'em to sleep."

Through two more sleeper cars and a combine they ran, to burst through into the first and final car, little more than an open platform in the center of which the driver sat in the Lotus position. He was a Celestial, of course, communing with the dragon in a single conjoined mind to keep its simple lizard's brain calm and pliant. The Celestial sprang to his feet when the intruders burst through the door and launched into a high-pitched call in Cantonese for Fire, the Element of Greater Yang, but Simon Leslie scissor-kicked him sideways off the train before the third syllable. The Chinese hit a fir tree by the side of the ley line and dropped like a stone to the ground.

Nicola Tesla crouched by his waist with a utility knife, pressing down on the Chrysalis, probing for a good place to make the incision. "We are doing this, yes?"

He was taken back when she looked up at him for his response. It was the first time she had solicited permission from him; perhaps it was the first time in her life.

"What about the other passengers?" he asked.

"What about them?"

Simon Leslie shook his head. It was insane. The whole thing was insane.

"Go ahead," he said.

He groaned as if it was his own flesh cut when Tesla made an incision in the Chrysalis just above his pelvic bone to remove an electrode from its underside. This she inserted in the box-shaped resonator, which she then hooked to his belt. From inside the second skin he could feel the nature of himself alter; the breath caught in his throat. Though the bioelectric field was invisible, as he pulled Nicola Tesla closer to him he could feel it envelop her; her cheeks suddenly flushed looking at him, and he knew she felt the same way too. A sudden conjoined intimacy, not borne of word, deed, or desire, but real all the same, and it moved both of them deeply.

A small ladder led to the ceiling hatch of the "engine," and from there they hopped onto the muscular ripple of the dragon's back; its scales were cold and shiny and impossibly smooth; he lost his footing several times until he started to grab onto the ridges of the lizard's vertebrae and use them as handholds to pull himself along its back. A Li Ying Lung was mostly a serpent, with two vestigial limbs dangling on either side of its undulating expanse. Uncoupled from the mind of its human handler, the dragon huffed and roared with irritation at the two pests skittering across its skin, amber eyes roiling with confusion, but the leather harness attaching it to the great bulk of the train prevented it from flexing its back and hurling the interlopers off.

Leslie reached the base of the lizard's head and peered over its snout at the ley line coursing beneath it. A gently spinning cylinder of infinitesimally narrow beams of blue, gold, and green light coursed from horizon to horizon. Below he could see they were just now crossing a massive ravine through which coursed the Humboldt River.

"This is where I was going to have us jump off anyway," he yelled over the thunderous whomp of the dragon's wings. "Are you ready?"

"*Of course not,*" Nicola yelled back. She wrapped her arms around his neck, nearly choking him. "*Do it anyway!*"

A Pinkerton's ocular blast shot past him. Already the Neversleeps had reached the driver's car; already they were climbing across the lizard's back in pursuit.

"Fuck it," he said to no one in particular.

He planted his foot on the skull ridge between the dragon's hate-filled eyes and leapt over its snorting nostrils. The expanded field of magic-annihilation from the Chrysalis met the psychic resonance of the ley line, and confronted it with its own impossibility.

And in that instant, it ceased to exist.

The enormous dragon did not need the ley line in order to fly, of course; it had wings for that. But the enchantments cast on the ten train cars it towed required interactions with the line to stay aloft. And when the ley that cut through the Sierra Madre abruptly winked out of existence, the train plunged like a ponderous chain into the canyon below, dragging the screaming, spouting dragon down with it.

Leslie hit the water first, dislodging Tesla from his neck. Even the breathing apparatus built into the Chrysalis could not keep the wind from getting knocked out of his chest. Gasping, the first thing he did was unhook Tesla's resonator from his waist for he could feel it overheating, trying to burn a hole in his side as he fell.

As he pushed it away from him he saw out of the corner of his eye, in what little light could be stolen from the murky brown by his goggles' enhancements, Tesla's curls trailing behind her as she sank unconscious into blackness.

At the same time out of the corner of his other eye the shadows of the dropping train cars blotted out the surface of the river above him.

Then a great invisible hand swatted him out of the way just as the train crashed into the water in the exact spot where he had been; the river vomited him upward onto a stony heap of slate in a shallow narrow.

He watched the Li Ying Lung dragon crashing down atop the heap of compartments jutting from the water. The wyrm wriggled and ripped his way free of the damaged harness, then sprang into the sky with a breathless shriek of terror; it disappeared with frantic flaps over the nearest peak, the two dragons that had brought the army of Pinkertons instinctively chasing after it.

Leslie spotted Tesla lying facedown in the water near the edge of the shale bar, sputtering and coughing. He raced to her and picked her up from behind, gripping her abdomen and forcing her to cough up as much water as he could. He saw bits and pieces of the resonator floating past on the current and he realized what had happened: the device overheated and exploded, creating a shockwave that hurled its creator and him to safety.

"We've made 'atomist' synonymous with murderer and anarchist in the headlines," Morgan Ash chuckled in his ear. "Thank you so much for providing the newspapers pictures to match."

The bodies of Pinkertons floated everywhere around him as glass-ravaged passengers splashed out of the train through shattered windows and took turns in desperate dives below the surface to rescue those trapped in the two or three fully submerged cars. He burned with regret and nearly dropped Tesla to dash and help them.

But descending all around him were Neversleeps and All-Seeing Eyes. Their stunt had killed many, even most, but not all. Not enough. And when Simon Leslie had torn off the resonator he'd exposed the breach in the Chrysalis to the outside air; he might as well have torn it to shreds for all the protection it provided him now. The Pinkertons knew it, too; they were just waiting for Ash's orders to boil his blood, to turn his skin inside out and dump his organs out onto the river rocks like wet sacks of garbage.

"For what it's worth... I'm sorry it had to end like this, Si," Ash said. "As I'm sure you are too."

The Eyes closed in a tight circle around Leslie and Tesla. "Don't tell me what to think, you preening ass. This is exactly how I wanted it to end."

Ash's mahogany chuckle. "Si, Si. Cocky little shit to the last, huh?"

"Oh, no. I'm serious. Don't you read the guidebooks?"

A gust of wind howled through the canyon. The Neversleeps hesitated, spinning their great ocular globes an extra few revolutions.

"You ever hear about the Donner Party, Ash?"

"*Wendigos!*" somebody cried. But it was too late.

The Cannibal Spirits dropped from the edges of the ravine, their spindly arms spread out to envelop the Pinkertons like a net. Jaws retracted to head-width and sank themselves into the meat and bone of the Pinkertons, ignoring the ectoplasmic eyes. One Neversleep was able to blast back a Wendigo with a manna missile but he was immediately dropped with a claw swipe from behind.

Leslie could feel Tesla tense beneath his arms and he pulled her close to him, hoping he could seal off the breach in the Chrysalis with her body—not enough to fool the sophisticated spells of the Neversleeps, but to confuse the primitive senses of the Wendigos. One came near Nicola trailing long, straggling corpse-hair and sniffed her cheek with his noseless skull, but Leslie put a gloved hand over her face, hoping that would make her partially invisible to the Cannibal Spirit.

With a snort and a dissatisfied shake of the head, the Wendigo turned, spotted a Pinkerton with his left leg ripped off below the knee trying to crawl across the crimson-choked river to safety. The spirit gave up on Tesla and launched itself atop the fugitive and commenced to feast.

"Better luck next time, Morgan," Leslie said, but silence was his only reply. He ripped the receiver out of his hood in case the bosses figured out how to track that, too, and, keeping Tesla close to his body, fled up the ridge through the pines to safety.

At dawn they stumbled across a ghost town on the side of the mountain: pale gray timber shells like giant wasps' nests. It had been settled since its abandonment, as one might expect, by ghosts, mindless revenants acting out the routines of life: children chasing hoops, women hanging invisible clothing on non-existent lines, men fighting in the streets over long-dead causes.

Inside the largest intact structure, half-burned and festooned with meadow heath, Simon Leslie ripped off the Chrysalis in a stream of muttered self-denunciations.

Tesla watched him with a furrowed brow. "Whatever is the matter?"

"What...?" He looked at her, astounded and naked, sweat slick on muscles still taut for battle. "Did you not see what just happened? How many innocent people did we kill with that stunt?"

Tesla shrugged. "The train couldn't have been traveling more than forty-five, perhaps forty-eight kilometers an hour. I'm sure there were far fewer fatalities than you think."

"*One* is unacceptable. You hear me? One innocent life is far too many."

She laughed at him. "You are trying to remake the world, Edison man. How did you hope to accomplish that without blood and thunder? You think our enemies give one thought to these 'innocents' of yours, whoever they are?"

"We're supposed to be better than they are. We have to be. Otherwise, what's the point of any of it?"

An exasperated sigh exploded out of her. "My great-grand-uncle had a laboratory in Colorado Springs, just after the Awakening. You heard of it?"

"Yes. He was conducting wireless telegraph experiments. Before magic rendered them obsolete, of course—"

"No. No, no, no. That's just what the Inquisition wanted everyone to believe, after they arrested him, and he burned. He was working on the wireless transmission of *energy*. My uncle wanted to generate free power for all, everywhere around the world. That's what scared them. Not the science. Not the difference of philosophies, whether faith or facts is the superior basis for living. The people who run the world have no use for such trivia. All they want is *control*.

"That is why you are better than your enemies, Edison man. Not because of your body count. Because you are fighting for what is real and true and natural. The world behind their veil of lies and superstition... The common man, the worker, the peasant, does not need oracles and magicians to get ahead in that world. All she needs is what she was born with. That is what makes us different, Edison man. That is what makes us different." She jabbed a finger into his bare sternum. "And that is why we will win."

Simon Leslie couldn't stop grinning. "I think I love you, Nicola Tesla."

"I would not be surprised if you did. I am quite attractive by conventional standards."

She turned away from him, and began to remove her still-soaking blouse and her dress to ring them out. Soon they would both be naked inside the burnt empty building, chests heaving, breath not yet caught.

He heard a sound, and looked to the corner of the room. They must have been in a former saloon, for the ghost of a guitar player sat on an invisible crate and stared at nothing and moaned out a song:

I'm, I'm coming home
'Cause I feel so alone
I'm coming back home
And meet my dear old mother
'Cause that's where I belong

Soon, however, the sun had risen all the way, and the light crept in through the open doorway. The phantom faded with all the others, burned away with the morning fog.

DEAD MAN'S HAND

CHRISTIE YANT

Deadwood, Dakota Territory, 1876

The whisper of the cards as they're shuffled is a deception, a ritual enacted to make you believe that your hand will be fairly dealt.

The fly that lands on the whiskey glass by the dealer's hand means that the deck is cut three cards deeper than it would have been. The hand you're dealt is not the one that would have been dealt a moment before.

Your cards are dealt anew every moment of every day. So are the cards of the other players.

A ♦ A ♣ 8 ♠ 8 ♣

Black Hills Weekly Pioneer
A.W. Merrick
Deadwood, Dakota Territory
August 2, 1876

J.B. "Wild Bill" Hickok Shot Dead at the No. 10 Saloon

A somber mood has gripped the town of Deadwood tonight, with the news that notable gunman and showman "Wild Bill" Hickok has been shot and killed. A shot was heard throughout the bustling community at 4:15 this afternoon, drawing a crowd of the concerned and curious to the door of the Number 10 Saloon owned by Mssrs. Nuttal and Mann. The body of James Butler Hickok was discovered therein, dead of a gunshot to the head.

Local miner Jack "Broken Nose" McCall approached Hickok from behind, drew his pistol, and fired the bullet that instantly took Hickok's life. McCall has claimed the act was a matter of blood debt, Hickok having killed his own brother in Kansas.

Hickok was well known amongst frequenters of the No. 10 to always sit with his back to the wall and facing the door, lest enemies made during a notable life on the plains exploit a lack of vigilance. On this day it is said that the only seat available at the table faced away from the door, and it was thus that McCall was able to enact his craven deed.

The scene of the murder was one of solemn reflection and practical determination, as the saloon proprietors and townspeople of Deadwood sought to put the shooting behind them. After Hickok's remains had been cleared away, there remained only a grim still life to mark the event: on the floor beside the seat lately occupied by Wild Bill lay the dead man's hand—two pair, aces and eights—a good hand, this reporter is told, but one which brought him no luck at all.

J♠ J♥ J♦ 7♣ 7♦

Black Hills Pioneer Gazette
Albert Merrick
Deadwood Gulch, D.T.
March 1, 1877

"Wild Bill" (James) Hickok Hanged for Murder

After a decade of outwitting the law, no amount of ill-gotten gold could tip the Scales of Justice in favor of the legendary outlaw and gunman James Butler Hickok, best known by the infamous moniker "Wild Bill." His last ride has ended in Yankton, Dakota Territory, at the end of a rope.

On August 1, 1876, the Bella Union Saloon was the scene of violence as a man was callously murdered over a debt in the amount of two dollars and fifty cents. The night had proceeded in the usual fashion, until it was learned that local miner Jack McCall, sometimes known as Sutherland, was unable to cover a hand lost to Hickok. Despite a promise to pay the following day, Hickok reportedly grew incensed, and bellowed, "A man ought never overbet his hand. That's no way to play cards!"

Captain William Massey, who had also been at the table, attempted to intervene, despite warnings from bystanders. "I told him not to get in

Bill's way when he gets like that," Mr. Tom Miller, proprietor, recalled. "But he wouldn't listen. He'd been an officer in the Union Army once, and I think that stayed with him."

Hickok drew his gun and aimed it at McCall's heart. Once a sharpshooter of world renown, Hickok's sight had reportedly been failing in recent years, driving him off the trail and into the saloons to make a meager living as a card player. His first shot missed McCall entirely, and the bullet instead struck Captain Massey, who Dr. McKinney says will carry it 'til his dying day.

Wild Bill's second shot aimed true, however, and McCall was killed instantly.

Hickok affected an escape by way of a rear door to the property and the theft of a horse. It was thought that with no sheriff yet elected in Deadwood the notorious outlaw had once again escaped justice, but he was apprehended a week later in the city of Laramie, Wyoming by one Deputy Marshal Balcombe.

On the night of the murder this reporter made a survey of the scene and there discovered the very cards that had cost an honest man his life. McCall's losing hand had been scattered across the table amid the other discarded hands, but in the place where Hickok had been seated, five cards remained fanned out in a characteristic display of arrogance. Not being well versed in the complexities of games of chance, this reporter consulted Mr. Mann on the likelihood of Hickok's cards winning the game.

"It's a good hand, and hard to beat," Mann said. "But I hope I don't see those cards come my way any time soon." With a shudder he added, "That's a dead man's hand."

J ♠ J ♣ 10 ♠ 10 ♦

Deadwood Weekly Pioneer
Albert M. Werrick
Deadwood Pines
August 5, 1876

Heroism in the Black Hills

It was civilian justice in the form of local businessman Bill Sutherland, who with a single bullet put an end to the threat of violence that

Deadwood has lived under since infamous outlaw J.B. "Wild Bill" Hickok arrived in town.

Uncowed by Hickok's brazen demeanor and deadly reputation, Mr. Sutherland strode into the Progressive Hall Saloon at 4:15 p.m. on Wednesday past and took vengeance for the death of his brother, one Jack Sutherland, also known as McCall. Witnesses claim that Mr. Sutherland drew his gun and said only, "Damn you, take that!" before the report from the gun echoed through the town. Mr. Sutherland immediately turned his weapon over to Ed Durham, proprietor, and waited peacefully while a miners' jury was assembled, Deadwood as yet still being without an elected sheriff.

Mr. Durham, responsible for restoring the scene to order, has told this reporter that in the aftermath he gathered the cards from the table, with the intention of presenting them to Mr. Sutherland upon his inevitable acquittal, in token for his heroism. When asked what the dead man had been holding, he told this reporter that he would only reveal the content of the dead man's hand to Mr. Sutherland, the hero of the Black Hills.

Hickok's remains will be returned to his widow in Cheyenne. No services are to be held in Deadwood. May God have mercy on his soul.

A♠ A♣ 8♥ 8♣

Black Hills Chronicle Weekly
A. William Merwick
Deadwood, Dakota Territory
August 5, 1876

Local Miner Dead in Shoot-out at No. 10 Saloon

On the afternoon of August 2, the fragile peace of Deadwood Gulch was broken by gun fire, and afterward a man lay dead.

Drawn to the scene by the sound of a gunshot, this reporter was approached by Captain James "Will" Massey who emerged from the saloon in some distress, cradling his bloody hand.

"Wild Bill shot me!" he exclaimed. The accusation was happily learned to be unfounded, though he can be forgiven for his confusion in the face of pain and violence.

Inside the saloon the scene was a gruesome one. Witnesses say that a game of poker was underway when local miner Jack "Crooked Nose" McCall suddenly rose from his seat. McCall, under the heavy influence of drink, was heard to say "Damn you, take that!" as he aimed his pistol at renowned lawman and gunslinger James "Wild Bill" Hickok. Before McCall could pull the trigger, Hickok—with reflexes honed on the prairie as a scout for the Union Army—drew his own weapon, and with the marksmanship that is his claim to fame, put a single shot through McCall's crossed eye.

McCall's gun discharged as he fell to the floor. This led Charles Rich, also seated at the table, to draw in self-defense, and in the confusion fired his own weapon, resulting in the injury sustained by Captain Massey.

"It was over in no more than the blink of an eye," said Carl Mann, one of the saloon's proprietors.

Hickok, in full view of this reporter, stood and swept up the cards he had held moments before, along with the unturned hole card, and tucked them inside his vest pocket.

"A souvenir to send to my wife," he explained, referring to his wife of seven months, Agnes Lake Hickok, lately of Cheyenne. He paused, and turned over the cards that lay at McCall's place at the table: two pair, aces and eights. "That right there is a hand you don't want," he said. "A dead man's hand."

* * *

Author's Note: The "Dead Man's Hand" as it is known today is comprised of "aces and eights," but there have been as many hands by that name as the coward Jack McCall had alibis and aliases. The earliest reference to aces and eights—rather than a full house of jacks and tens, or jacks and sevens—appeared in 1900, and the phrase wasn't connected to Hickok until the 1920s, nearly fifty years after his death.

ACKNOWLEDGMENTS

Many thanks to the following:

My Publisher/Editor: Steve Saffel, for acquiring and editing the book, and to the rest of the team at Titan Books.

My Agent: Seth Fishman, who I think of as "the Best American Literary Agent," and my former agent Joe Monti (now a book editor), who was there when this idea coalesced and the one who helped me bring it to fruition.

My Mentor: Gordon Van Gelder, for being a mentor and a friend.

My Colleague: Ellen Datlow for revealing the mysteries of anthologizing.

My Family: my amazing wife, Christie; my mom, Marianne, and my sister, Becky, for all their love and support.

Author/Contract Wranglers: Deborah Beale, Sarah Nagel, Kathleen Bellamy, Kristine Card, Josette Sanchez-Reynolds, and Vaughne Lee Hansen.

My Fact-checking Brigade: Ben Blattberg, Elias F. Combarro (*¡en Español!*), Kate Galey, Jude Griffin, Andrew Liptak, Stephanie Loree, Robyn Lupo, Kevin McNeil, Shannon Rampe, Earnie Sotirokos, Patrick Stephens, and Stephanie Sursi.

My Interns: Lisa Andrews, Britt Gettys, Amber Barkley, and Bradley Englert.

My Writers: everyone who wrote stories for this anthology, and any of my other projects.

My Readers (last but not least): everyone who bought this book, or any of my other anthologies, and who make possible doing books like this.

ABOUT THE CONTRIBUTORS

KELLEY ARMSTRONG

Kelley Armstrong is the author of the *Women of the Otherworld* paranormal suspense series, the Darkest Powers young adult urban fantasy trilogy, and the Nadia Stafford crime series. She grew up in Ontario, Canada, where she still lives with her family. A former computer programmer, she's now escaped her corporate cubicle and hopes never to return.

ELIZABETH BEAR

Elizabeth Bear was born on the same day as Frodo and Bilbo Baggins, but in a different year. When coupled with a tendency to read the dictionary for fun as a child, this led her inevitably to penury, intransigence, and the writing of speculative fiction. She is the Hugo, Sturgeon, and Campbell Award-winning author of almost a hundred short stories and twenty-five novels, the most recent of which is *Shattered Pillars*, from Tor Books. Her dog lives in Massachusetts; her partner, writer Scott Lynch, lives in Wisconsin. She spends a lot of time on planes.

TOBIAS S. BUCKELL

Tobias S. Buckell is a Caribbean-born speculative fiction writer who grew up in Grenada, the British Virgin Islands, and the U.S. Virgin Islands. He has written several novels, including the *New York Times* bestseller *Halo: The Cole Protocol*, the Xenowealth series, and *Arctic Rising*. His short fiction has appeared in magazines such as *Lightspeed*, *Analog*, *Clarkesworld*, and *Subterranean*, and in anthologies such as *Armored*, *All-Star Zeppelin Adventure Stories*, and *Under the Moons of Mars*. He currently lives in Ohio with a pair of dogs, a pair of cats, twin daughters, and his wife.

ORSON SCOTT CARD

Orson Scott Card is the best-selling author of more than forty novels, including *Ender's Game*, which was a winner of both the Hugo and Nebula Awards. The sequel, *Speaker for the Dead*, also won both awards, making Card the only author to have captured science fiction's two most coveted prizes in consecutive years. Recent books include *The Lost Gates*, *Ruins*, *Earth Aware*, and *Shadows in Flight*. He is also the author of the acclaimed historical fantasy series The Tales of Alvin Maker.

DAVID FARLAND

David Farland is the author of the best-selling Runelords series, which began with *The Sum of All Men*; the latest volume, *A Tale of Tales*, came out in 2012. Farland, whose real name is Dave Wolverton, has also written several novels using his real name as his byline, such as *On My Way to Paradise*, and a number of *Star Wars* novels such as *The Courtship of Princess Leia* and *The Rising Force*. His short fiction has appeared in *Peter S. Beagle's Immortal Unicorn*, *David Copperfield's Tales of the Impossible*, *Asimov's Science Fiction*, *Intergalactic Medicine Show*, *War of the Worlds: Global Dispatches*, and in John Joseph Adams's anthologies *The Way of the Wizard*, *Oz Reimagined*, and *The Mad Scientist's Guide to World Domination*. He is a Writers of the Future winner and a finalist for the Nebula Award and Philip K. Dick Award.

JEFFREY FORD

Jeffrey Ford is the author of the novels, *The Physiognomy*, *Memoranda*, *The Beyond*, *The Portrait of Mrs. Charbuque*, *The Girl in the Glass*, *The Cosmology of the Wider World*, and *The Shadow Year*. His story collections are, *The Fantasy Writer's Assistant*, *The Empire of Ice Cream*, and *The Drowned Life*. *Crackpot Palace*, a new collection of twenty stories, was recently published by Morrow/HarperCollins. Ford writes somewhere in Ohio.

ALAN DEAN FOSTER

Alan Dean Foster is the bestselling author of more than a hundred and twenty novels, and is perhaps most famous for his Commonwealth series, which began in 1971 with the novel *The Tar-Aiym Krang*. His most recent series is transhumanism trilogy *The Tipping Point*. Foster's work has been translated into more than fifty languages and has won awards in Spain and Russia in addition to the U.S. He is also well-known for his film novelizations, the most recent of which is *Star Trek Into Darkness*. He is currently at work on several new novels and film projects.

LAURA ANNE GILMAN

Best known as the author of the popular "Cosa Nostradamus" novels, and the award-nominated "Vineart War" trilogy, Laura Anne recently sold three "Devil's West" novels (set in the same universe as her story for this anthology) to Saga/Simon & Schuster. The first title, *Silver on the Road*, is scheduled for 2015. She has also dipped her pen into the mystery field, writing as L.A. Kornetsky (the "Gin and Tonic" series), while continuing to write and sell short fiction in a variety of genres. She is a member of the writers publishing cooperative, Book View Cafe.

HUGH HOWEY

Hugh Howey is the author of the acclaimed post-apocalyptic novel *Wool*, which became a sudden success in 2011. Originally self-published as a series of novelettes (including the one you'll find in this anthology), the *Wool* omnibus is frequently the #1 bestselling book on Amazon.com and is a *New York Times* and *USA TODAY* bestseller. The book was also optioned for film by Ridley Scott, and is now available in print from major publishers all over the world. The story of *Wool*'s meteoric success has been reported in major media outlets such as *Entertainment Weekly*, *Variety*, the *Washington Post*, the *Wall Street Journal*, *Deadline Hollywood*, and elsewhere. Howey lives in Jupiter, Florida with his wife Amber and his dog Bella.

RAJAN KHANNA

Rajan Khanna is a writer, musician, and sometime bon vivant. A graduate of the 2008 Clarion West Writers Workshop and a member of the NY-based writing group, Altered Fluid, his fiction has appeared in or is forthcoming from *Shimmer Magazine, Zombies: Shambling Through the Ages, Diverse Energies, Beneath Ceaseless Skies, Escape Pod*, and *The Way of the Wizard* (among others) and has received Honorable Mention in the *Year's Best Fantasy & Horror* and the *Year's Best Science Fiction*. He sometimes writes articles for Tor.com and occasionally narrates podcasts for sites like *Podcastle, Lightspeed*, and *Pseudopod*. Rajan also writes about wine, beer, and spirits at FermentedAdventures.com.

JOE R. LANSDALE

Joe R. Lansdale is the author of over thirty novels and numerous short stories. His work has appeared in national anthologies, magazines, and collections, as well as numerous foreign publications. He has written for comics, television, film, newspapers, and Internet sites. His work has been collected in eighteen short-story collections, and he has edited or co-edited over a dozen anthologies. He has received the Edgar Award, eight Bram Stoker Awards, the Horror Writers Association Lifetime Achievement Award, the British Fantasy Award, the Grinzani Cavour Prize for Literature, the Herodotus Historical Fiction Award, the Inkpot Award for Contributions to Science Fiction and Fantasy, and many others. He is Writer In Residence at Stephen F. Austin State University. He lives in Nacogdoches, Texas with his wife, dog, and two cats.

KEN LIU

Ken Liu (http://kenliu.name) is an author and translator of speculative fiction, as well as a lawyer and programmer. His fiction has appeared in *The Magazine of Fantasy & Science Fiction*, *Asimov's*, *Analog*, *Clarkesworld*, *Lightspeed*, and *Strange Horizons*, among other places. He has won a Nebula, two Hugos, a World Fantasy Award, and a Science Fiction & Fantasy Translation Award, and been nominated for the Sturgeon and the Locus Awards. He lives with his family near Boston, Massachusetts. Ken's debut novel, *The Grace of Kings*, the first in a fantasy series, will be published by Simon & Schuster's new genre fiction imprint in 2015, along with a collection of short stories.

JONATHAN MABERRY

Jonathan Maberry is a *New York Times* bestselling author, multiple Bram Stoker Award winner, and Marvel Comics writer. He's the author of many novels including *Assassin's Code, Flesh & Bone Dead of Night, Patient Zero* and *Rot & Ruin*; and the editor of *V-Wars: A Chronicle of the Vampire Wars*. His nonfiction books are on topics ranging from martial arts to zombie pop-culture. Since 1978 he has sold more than 1200 magazine feature articles, 3000 columns, two plays, greeting cards, song lyrics, poetry, and textbooks. Jonathan continues to teach the celebrated Experimental Writing for Teens class, which he created. He founded the Writers Coffeehouse and co-founded The Liars Club; and is a frequent speaker at schools and libraries, as well as a keynote speaker and guest of honor at major writers and genre conferences.

SEANAN MCGUIRE

Seanan McGuire is the author of two ongoing urban fantasy series (the October Daye books, starting with *Rosemary and Rue*, and InCryptid, starting with *Discount Armageddon*), both published by DAW Books, as well as many works of short fiction. Under the name "Mira Grant" she writes science fiction thrillers full of viruses and zombies. Between her two identities, she is a ten-time finalist for the Hugo Award, and was the winner of the 2010 John W. Campbell Award for Best New Writer. She has released five CDs of original music, and is a founding member of the Hugo Award-winning *SF Squeecast*. She currently resides on the West Coast, where she shares her home with three enormous blue cats, a great many books, and the occasional wayward rattlesnake. Seanan regularly claims to be the advance scout of a race of alien plant people. We have no good reason to doubt her.

MIKE RESNICK

Mike Resnick is, according to *Locus Magazine*, the all-time award winner, living or dead, for short fiction. He has won five Hugos (from a record thirty-six nominations), a Nebula, and other major awards in the USA, France, Japan, Croatia, Poland, and Spain. He is the author of seventy-one novels, more than two hundred and fifty stories, three screenplays, and the editor of more than forty anthologies. His work has been translated into twenty-six languages, and he was the Guest of Honor at the 2012 World Science Fiction Convention.

BETH REVIS

Beth Revis is the *New York Times* bestselling author of the young adult science fiction series, Across the Universe. The third and final book, *Shades of Earth*, came out in 2013, and she's currently working on a new SF series. Beth lives in North Carolina with her husband and dog.

ALASTAIR REYNOLDS

Alastair Reynolds is the author of the Revelation Space series, which includes the novels *Revelation Space*, *Chasm City*, *Redemption Ark*, *Absolution Gap*, and *The Prefect*. Other novels include *Century Rain*, *Terminal World*, *Pushing Ice*, and *House of Suns*. His latest novels are *Blue Remembered Earth*, the first in the Poseidon's Children trilogy, and *Dr. Who: Harvest of Time*.

FRED VAN LENTE

Fred Van Lente is the #1 *New York Times* bestselling author of *Marvel Zombies, Incredible Hercules* (with Greg Pak), *Odd Is On Our Side* (with Dean R. Koontz), as well as the American Library Association award-winning *Action Philosophers*. His original graphic novel *Cowboys & Aliens* (co-written with Andrew Foley) is the basis for the major motion picture starring Daniel Craig and Harrison Ford. Van Lente's other comics include *The Comic Book History of Comics, Taskmaster, Archer & Armstrong, Amazing Spider-Man* and *Hulk: Season One*.

TAD WILLIAMS

Former singer, shoe-seller, radio show host, and inventor of interactive sci-fi television, Tad Williams established himself as an international bestselling author with his *The Dragonbone Chair* epic fantasy series. The books that followed, the Otherland series, are now a multi-million-dollar MMO from dtp/realU/Gamigo. Tad is also the author of the Shadowmarch books; the stand-alone Faerie epic, *The War of the Flowers*; two collections of short stories (*Rite* and *A Stark and Wormy Knight*), the Shakespearian fantasy *Caliban's Hour*, and, with his partner and collaborator Deborah Beale, the childrens'/all-ages fantasy series, the Ordinary Farm novels. Recently, with *The Dirty Streets of Heaven*, Tad has begun publishing the Bobby Dollar novels, noir fantasy thrillers set against the backdrop of the monstrously ancient cold war between Heaven and Hell and following the adventures of a certain maverick angel. Tad is also the author of *Tailchaser's Song*, which is in production as an animated film.

WALTER JON WILLIAMS

Walter Jon Williams is an award-winning, best-selling science fiction author. His first novel to attract serious public attention was *Hardwired*, described by Roger Zelazny as "a tough, sleek juggernaut of a story, punctuated by strobe-light movements, coursing to the wail of jets and the twang of steel guitars." In 2001 he won a Nebula Award for his novelette, "Daddy's World," and in 2005 another Nebula for "The Green Leopard Plague." The fantasy *Metropolitan*, which was nominated for a Nebula Award, begins a sequence continued in a Nebula- and Hugo-nominated second novel, *City on Fire*. His latest work is *The Fourth Wall*, the third book in his series of near-future thrillers featuring game designer Dagmar Shaw.

BEN H. WINTERS

Ben H. Winters is the winner of the Edgar Award for his novel *The Last Policeman*, which was also an Amazon.com Best Book of 2012. Other works of fiction include the middle-grade novel *The Secret Life of Ms. Finkleman*, an Edgar Award nominee; its sequel, *The Mystery of the Missing Everything*; the psychological thriller *Bedbugs;* and two parody novels, *Sense and Sensibility and Sea Monsters* (a *New York Times* best-seller), and *Android Karenina*. Ben has also written extensively for the stage and is a past fellow of the Dramatists Guild. His journalism has appeared in *Slate*, *The Nation*, *The Chicago Reader*, and many other publications. He lives in Indianapolis, Indiana, and at BenHWinters.com.

CHRISTIE YANT

Christie Yant is a science fiction and fantasy writer, and Assistant Editor for *Lightspeed* Magazine. Her fiction has been featured on *Wired.com* and *io9*, in the magazines *Analog Science Fiction & Fact*, *Fireside*, *Beneath Ceaseless Skies*, *Shimmer*, and *Daily Science Fiction*, and in the anthologies *The Way of the Wizard*, *Year's Best Science Fiction & Fantasy 2011*, *Other Worlds Than These*, and *Armored*. She lives on the central coast of California with two writers, an editor, and assorted four-legged nuisances. Follow her on Twitter @christieyant.

CHARLES YU

Charles Yu is the author of *How to Live Safely in a Science Fictional Universe*, which was a *New York Times* Notable Book and named one of the best books of the year by *Time* magazine. He received the National Book Foundation's 5 Under 35 Award for his story collection *Third Class Superhero*, and was a finalist for the PEN Center USA Literary Award. His work has been published in the *New York Times*, *Playboy*, and *Slate*, among other periodicals. His latest book, *Sorry Please Thank You*, was named one of the best science fiction/fantasy books of the year by the *San Francisco Chronicle*. Yu lives in Santa Monica, California, with his wife, Michelle, and their two children.

ABOUT THE EDITOR

JOHN JOSEPH ADAMS is the series editor of *Best American Science Fiction & Fantasy* published by Houghton Mifflin Harcourt. He is also the bestselling editor of many other anthologies, such as *The Mad Scientist's Guide to World Domination, Armored, Brave New Worlds, Wastelands, The Living Dead, HELP FUND MY ROBOT ARMY!!! & Other Improbable Crowdfunding Projects*, and The Apocalypse Triptych consisting of *The End is Nigh, The End is Now*, and *The End Has Come*. He has been nominated for six Hugo Awards and five World Fantasy Awards, and he has been called "the reigning king of the anthology world" by Barnes & Noble. John is also the editor and publisher of the digital magazines *Lightspeed* and *Nightmare*, and is a producer for Wired.com's *The Geek's Guide to the Galaxy* podcast. Find him on Twitter @johnjosephadams. Visit the official website for *Dead Man's Hand* at johnjosephadams.com/dead-mans-hand.

For more fantastic fiction, author events, exclusive excerpts,
competitions, limited editions and more

VISIT OUR WEBSITE
titanbooks.com

LIKE US ON FACEBOOK
facebook.com/titanbooks

FOLLOW US ON TWITTER
@TitanBooks

EMAIL US
readerfeedback@titanemail.com